Praise for the novels of Angelina M. Lopez

"Romance often gets belittled for its escapism,
but what Lopez offers is almost a publishing magic trick in itself.
She delivers that escapist fantasy in spades... But then she digs
into the wounds and hard work underneath that fantasy,
exposing the truth that a happily ever after in the context
of reality is all the more rewarding."

—*Entertainment Weekly* on *Lush Money*

"Lopez successfully flips the gender switch on the
wealthy CEO trope while at the same time incorporating
a generous dash of fairy-tale glitz and glam into the
captivating storyline of her marvelous debut... Everything fans
of sexy contemporary romances could ever crave."

—*Booklist*, starred review, on *Lush Money*

"Angelina M. Lopez is a master at writing both sex
between people who are angry with each other
and sensual lovemaking... This classic enemies-to-lovers
story will leave you sweating."

—*Self* on *Hate Crush*

"This is a sexy, steamy novel full of twists, turns and surprises
on the way to success—and happy ever after."

—NPR on *Hate Crush*

"[A]ngsty, delightful and sexy all at once."

—*Blood & Milk* on *Hate Crush*

"As always, Lopez's work is one dash Jackie Collins,
two dashes something wholly her own."

—*All About Romance* on *Serving Sin*

AFTER HOURS ON MILAGRO STREET

Angelina M. Lopez

carina
press

carina
press®

Recycling programs
for this product may
not exist in your area.

ISBN-13: 978-1-335-63992-9

After Hours on Milagro Street

Copyright © 2022 by Angelina M. Lopez

For questions and comments about the quality of this book, please contact us at CustomerService@Harlequin.com.

Carina Press
22 Adelaide St. West, 41st Floor
Toronto, Ontario M5H 4E3, Canada
www.CarinaPress.com

Printed in U.S.A.

To Mary and Mario. I miss you every day.
I wish you were here to read this.

AFTER HOURS ON MILAGRO STREET

Chapter One

Weighed down with everything she owned, Alex Torres slammed her bare shoulder into the door of her grandmother's bar. The cold, cloying drizzle that had started just as she drove into town and the streetlamp that popped right when she staggered into the alcove had made it a bitch to get the key in the lock. Now the worn-out building was gritting its teeth to keep her out. But Alex hadn't quit her job, packed up her life, and driven ten hours from Chicago to let a stubborn dick of a door make her sleep in her car. She again slammed her strong, cocktail-shaker-built shoulder against the peeling wood, causing the glass in the frame—only the *L* and *tt* in *Loretta's* were even legible—to rattle angrily.

With an outraged resistant squeal, the door gave way.

"That's right, asshole," Alex muttered triumphantly as she struggled inside with all her bags and backpacks. She slapped through the useless saloon doors and winced against the raucous ringing of the cowbell that had been welcoming people to Loretta's since her grandparents opened the bar forty years ago.

That fucking cowbell was the first thing that was going to go.

She staggered blindly into the heart of the dark bar and vengefully flung all her worldly possessions onto the old boards. They gave a satisfying groan of dismay before Alex had to wrap her arms around her collarless New Order T-shirt as a cold spot settled over her.

It was exactly the kind of welcome home she expected.

Loretta's, in the old Hugh Building on the corner of Milagro Street in the tiny town of Freedom, Kansas, had been the home-a-block-from-home for every member of her large, multigenerational Mexican-American family for four decades. Of course, it would be cold, dark, and forbidding when Alex returned to whip it into shape.

On her drive back to Freedom, Alex had called her sisters to tell them that it was time to stop talking about purchasing Loretta's and make their grandmother an offer.

It was only time, her big sister Gillian had said, because Alex had prematurely quit her job and now needed them to save her ass.

But Gillian and her kids, who'd flown in from DC, and Sissy, who'd driven down from Kansas City, were already in town visiting their grandmother.

They'd all meet at the bar in the morning.

Their grandmother had decreed when they were girls that they were going to inherit Loretta's and no one in the family argued with Loretta Torres, least of all the three Armstead sisters. The inevitability of inheriting the bar's unpaid tabs, bad food, and deteriorating building had once felt like a genetic disease they were dreading. But after their Granmo's terrifying fall three weeks ago, one of them had brought up buying the bar and building *now*, taking Loretta's over to give their grandmother the retirement she couldn't afford and the financial support she wouldn't accept any other way.

Alex couldn't remember who'd suggested it, but the idea had caught momentum fast. She'd talked more to her sisters in the last three weeks than she had in thirteen years.

What she hadn't told them in the flood of early-morning

texts and late-night phone calls—and what was pretty fucking urgent after last night's showdown—was that the best bitch in bartending was going to dismantle and rebuild Loretta's to show the world just how good she was.

Esquire had coined Alex "The Best Bitch in Bartending," two years ago, after a reporter had shown up at the Fantasy Box, the most exclusive speakeasy in Chicago, for an article on the best and worst bartenders in the US. She'd heard Alex Torres was both. But the quality of Alex's drinks, the fact that she led the movement connecting Midwesterners with mezcal, the carefully curated abuse she heaped on patrons and her rabid social media followers, and her innate bad-girl aesthetic—spiky black hair, the tattooed right-arm-sleeve of vibrant flowers, the tight jeans she wore over her full sweetheart of an ass—led the reporter to devote a multi-page spread to her.

Her bosses had hung the article above the bar. They would have had it tattooed on her forehead if they could have.

But the article hadn't prevented them from promoting that asshole Randy over her. Randy, who'd only bartended the Sunday-Wednesday shifts, lorded his restaurant management degree over everybody, had gone and done what the entire staff had worried about when he'd become manager and created a drink menu that was too long, with too many specialty ingredients, that took too much fucking time to make at the height of the rush.

Alex had swallowed her rage until last night. Last night, she'd had it.

If the number of notifications on her social media feeds were any indication, people's phones had caught her clapping back.

There was shit even the best bitch in bartending couldn't get away with.

Now she was exiled to the void of southeast Kansas, in a town she never wanted to spend more than an occasional weekend or holiday in, betting it all on a bar that hadn't been profitable since flip phones, knowing she'd have to make her sisters and mother and grandmother get out of her way if they didn't fall in line.

Alex rubbed the shorn black hair at the back of her head. She needed a drink.

Thunder rumbled as she took one step in the dark bar and heard a creak behind her.

Every hair on her body stood up.

But she'd spent too much time in Chicago kicking the ass of regular ol' scary things to stop her instinctive response now: she whipped around, grabbed the hand shining a weak flashlight into her face, yanked it toward her as she straight-armed a throat—a man's throat—and used the momentum and her stuck-out leg to whip the body—a man's tall, big body—to the floor.

The flashlight and something else clattered to the ground. The light rolled and directed the weak beam on his face. Floppy brown hair, wide-set eyes, a deadly ski jump of a nose, thin lips open in shock. He was a big, noticeable stranger in a town where, even after thirteen years of only occasional visits, she still knew everybody. He was propped up haphazardly on her bags; the warmth of his body was like a heater. She kept her grip on his throat, kept his hand pulled away from his body so he had one less weapon.

"Who are you?" she barked. You handle encounters with muggers and bears the same way—growl louder.

He gaped at her. "You're…you're not a ghost."

She didn't give him an inch, even though she'd had the same thought. She'd been thrilled when she'd seen a flashlight, felt warm, firm flesh when she'd grabbed him. Of course, the old boards of this creaky building had stayed quiet until he was right on top of her.

"Who are you?" she demanded again.

"I'm Jeremiah Post. I'm a…" He stiffened and scowled. "Who are you?" His voice was low and deep. Precise. Definitely not a local. He looked her over, glared suspiciously at the arm of tattoos that led to his throat. "Does Loretta know you're here?"

He was a big guy. Alex was actually getting tired of holding his heavy arm up. But he hadn't once tried to pull away, and he was protective of her grandmother.

She let him go and stood, weaved around a table stacked with chairs to reach the bar, and pulled the chain on one of the knockoff Tiffany lamps that defined the place as much as the cheap beer, crappy food, and the many Hernandezes, Leons, Martinezes, and Torreses that flowed in and out.

She turned around and put her hands on her ample hips, resisted rubbing them over her arms as she looked down at him in the mellow light of the lamp. It was chilly away from his nuke reactor of a body.

"She doesn't know I'm here but I gotta key that says I can come in whenever I want." No matter how much the old Hugh Building might resist. "Now your turn."

He was a splat of heavy limbs over her bags. He tilted back his head to look around. "I need…" he said, trying to right himself. "Do you see my glasses?"

She did now, round tortoiseshell glasses that had skittered under a table, and she went to pick them up.

When she turned around, he was standing up. And up and up and up.

He wasn't big. He was huge. Broad shoulders, long arms, platter-sized hands. He had to be six feet two or three, towered a good foot over her. His fancy gray flannel pajama top with white piping showed strong shoulders and a good chest. Matching PJ pants covered long, long legs and expensive leather slippers covered big feet.

You know what they say about big feet. She snapped her mouth closed.

"You're a tenant," she said, noticing the vintage Rolex watch on his wrist as she handed him his glasses. Her grandmother rented out the two rooms across from the office on the second floor. With nothing to offer but hotplates and a shared bathroom, Alex was shocked anyone still rented them. Especially someone who screamed money like this guy did.

She'd planned on sleeping in one of the rooms tonight since her sisters, niece, and nephew had claimed all the available space at her mom's house.

"That's right," he said as he put on his glasses then looked at her through their round lenses. He studied her.

Then his whole face crinkled up into a smile. Lines sprang out from his eyes, eyes that were a mix of green and gold and brown. He had two deep dimples in his late-night scruff, high and defined cheekbones, and a cleft in his chin. Even his hair looked friendly, thick and deep brown and eager to flop onto his broad, strong forehead.

He brushed his hair back before he put out his hand. "You're part of her family! Why haven't we met before? I'm Jeremiah Post, an assistant professor from the college. I've been renting here for a year."

He was huge. And he was hot. Like stop-her-breath-in-her-throat hot.

Now she *really* needed a drink.

The patter of rain began to pick up against the window and thunder boomed closer.

She ignored his hand and walked to the bar, hopped up

onto the squeaky brass foot railing to lean over the counter, and grabbed two jelly jar glasses.

"Vodka or whisky?" she asked, feeling for the well bottles in the rack.

When he didn't answer, she glanced over her shoulder at him.

His eyes quickly jumped from her heart-shaped ass to her face.

She smirked. Damn right he gave it a look. It was worth looking at. "Vodka or whisky?"

Holy shit, he was blushing. She'd guess he was a little older than her, maybe in his early thirties. There was a blush climbing up his strong, pale neck. "Um…whisky?"

She poured them both healthy slugs, turned around with the glasses and the bottle, and walked back to shove a jelly jar into his hand.

"Alex Torres, Loretta's granddaughter, nice to meet you." She tapped her glass against his. "Why'd you think I was a ghost?"

She knocked back her shot then watched him expectantly. He looked at her, then at his glass, then sighed. She imagined Mr. Fancy Pants usually drank the high-end stuff. The well whisky her grandmother bought could strip paint.

He tossed it back, closed his eyes but didn't cough, and his hot got scorching.

Alex needed another drink. A good fuck wouldn't hurt either.

"Alex?" he said, looking down at her intently through his glasses. "I don't recognize… You have a big family."

Alex snorted to cover up the fact that he apparently knew a lot of her family but had never heard her name.

Saying she had a big family was the understatement of the century.

Freedom, Kansas had been the home of her sprawling Mexican-American family for five generations, starting with her great-great León grandparents who'd arrived near the beginning of the 1900s. It was a story she'd gotten tired of explaining to people. No one expected a woman that looked like her—brown skin, ball of a nose with a wide bridge, black hair, and deep brown eyes—to be from the heartland.

No one anticipated that her family sometimes had deeper and longer roots in the country than their white families had.

Few León descendants had left this little speck in the corner of southeast Kansas. But Alex had. She'd never once in a million years considered moving back.

Was it really a wonder that this guy had never heard her name?

Rain began to knuckle the front windows.

She poured them both another shot. "So you were worried I was a ghost?"

He looked chagrined down into his glass. "This building creaks a lot."

"Old buildings do."

"Yes, but…there are unexpected cold spots. Weird shadows. Light bulbs blow all the time." His voice went quieter as her smile grew bigger. "I heard the entrance bell ringing and thought…"

"You thought ghosts before meth heads?"

"Meth heads?" he objected. He took a sip of his whisky, then made a face, as if he'd forgotten what was in his glass. "I hear people jiggling the lock every now and then. But things in Freedom haven't gotten *that* bad."

Alex gave him a look, then tossed back her shot. There was a reason she hadn't left her stuff in the car. As soon as she got rid of that fucking cowbell, she was investing in a security system.

Milagro Street, on the east side of town and about half a mile from Main Street, had been thriving when her grand-parents and great-grandparents were young—some of her grandmother's favorite stories were about running in and out of the Mexican tienda, bakery, bank, and community center that met the needs of a vibrant east side and its many Mexican Americans. There'd even been a small hotel at the other end of Milagro Street's two blocks that served travelers coming out of the long-defunct train station across the street.

But Milagro Street started dying before Alex was born, dying right along with the whole, dwindling town, and the only draw now to this street of mostly shuttered businesses was the cheap beer and rambunctious family found at Loretta's, in the old Hugh Building.

The high-and-mighty Hughs, who loved clinging to the family name and their reputation as town founders, seldom made it to this side of town. Neither did their country-club friends or this big guy's coworkers from Dupen College.

Alex was going to rewrite that script.

"What's a professor doing living here? Don't you know it's a rule that college and townies don't mix?"

Dupen College, the tiny but elite private university ten minutes outside of town, had always been in a bubble, as if by providing its own residences, restaurants, and shopping for their students and faculty, they could ignore the fact that they were stuck on the flat plains of Kansas.

He shrugged his thick shoulders as he looked at her and the way he did it made him look like a giant overgrown puppy. "I like town. Don't you?"

She wondered if this puppy liked to tussle.

"Not particularly," she said, taking hold of his big hand, pulling the glass out of it, finishing off the whisky, then putting it down on a nearby table. "That doesn't mean we can't get to know each other better."

He looked delightfully confused—great big puppy—as she ran her palm over the back of his ring-free left hand and stepped closer to him. "I'm a little keyed up after a long drive," she murmured, having to crane back her head to look him in the eyes. "Want to help me blow off some steam?"

Now he looked shell-shocked. "I…"

When he didn't complete the thought, she put his hands on the hips of her oversized and ripped-up jeans, turned them both a little, aimed, and shoved.

He *oophed* down onto a sturdy armless chair that hadn't been put up for mopping.

Perfect landing. She climbed into his lap, straddling him.

His eyes were gigantic behind his glasses. They were a pretty mix of swirly colors, with the gold in them shining like a bulb in one of the knockoff lamps. "C'mon," she purred, rubbing her hands down his thick biceps. "Who else is going to keep you safe from the ghost?"

She kissed his delicate pink bottom lip. Softly rubbed her lips across it. His eyes closed as his big hands slowly curled around her waist and his mouth opened hesitantly. She smiled against his open mouth and licked inside. He tasted like toothpaste and high-octane liquor.

He was adorable.

"Is this okay?" she asked between kisses. He nodded without opening his eyes.

Fucking adorable.

"Do you have a condom?"

His hands squeezed her waist as he startled back from her.

"Why would I have a condom?"

Guys she hooked up with in Chicago never went anywhere without a condom.

"That's fine," she said, getting off his lap then scanning her bags on the floor.

There. She unzipped the side pocket, pulled a condom out of a box, then turned back to him and began undoing her Urge Overkill buckle.

Luckily, her jeans were wide enough to come off right over her Chucks.

When she looked at him again, his eyes were wide on her bare thighs and bright red panties.

"Maybe we should slow down," he said.

What he was packing beneath his fancy flannel jimjams didn't look like it wanted to slow down. "You wanna do this?"

He swallowed. Even his Adam's apple was big. The dude was proportional everywhere. "Yes," he said.

She climbed back on his lap and dipped her hand under his waistband. He jerked like he was ticklish before she pulled him out. Mr. College might not carry condoms in his PJs, but he went commando in them. Nice.

She ripped open the condom package with her teeth and saw him squeeze his eyes closed behind his glasses.

"You good?" she asked as she stroked the latex down his long, thick length. The Hugh Building had been a dick about letting her in, but it sure was giving up gifts now.

"Yes," he grunted without opening his eyes. "It's…been a while. And…when the condom comes out…it…it really turns me on."

"Professor," she laughed, delighted, as she raised herself up, pulled aside her underwear, and positioned him. "That's so naughty."

"Don't," he moaned, low and breathy, but his fingers were digging into her ass cheeks as she rotated her hips and lowered down to sink him inside. Somebody had a hot-for-teacher kink.

It was her. Definitely her.

She ran her hands up his muscular chest, hung on to his shoulders, and began to rock, not moving up or down, but just rocking her clit against his pelvis and squeezing him with her muscles.

"God, god," he panted, eyes closed tight behind his glasses. She leaned down to lick his Adam's apple. "Oh that... Oh god, you feel good."

Yes, she did. She began to move her ass in his lap.

"Oh God." He grabbed her hip with a surprisingly strong grip and his face clenched. "Jesus, wait, wait..."

He bared perfect sparkling teeth. And then he groaned. She felt it, the kick of his big penis inside of her. The warmth of him flooding the condom.

"Jesus." He opened his eyes and stared at her, mortification in his wide eyes and a scarlet flush working up his neck. There was sweat at his hairline. "I'm so sorry. It's been a while."

She gave him a kiss on the blade of his nose and straightened his knock-skewed glasses. He was hot as fuck and cute as a bug. "It's fine, big guy." He was still thick. And warm. He was like an electric blanket with a dildo attachment. "I got it."

She pulled her panties aside with her middle finger and began to rub her clit.

When he slid his hand from her hip to her thigh and said, "Here, let me..." she put her free hand over his mouth.

"Shhh..." she said, her eyes closed. "Let the adults work."

In thirty seconds, he groaned again and lurched as her panting orgasm squeezed him inside of her. A bright blast of lightning flared through the windows.

Only the storm leveling the bar so she could start from

scratch would make this a more perfect welcome home. Alex regained her breath and wiped her fingers on her thigh.

Rain began to pummel the building.

She clambered off of him and started gathering her bags.

"Uh…here…let me get rid of this condom and then I can help you…"

It was a recordable moment to watch him look befuddled down at his condom-covered penis, then around the bar for a trash can, and then at her for salvation. She hoped he was a good professor 'cause he sucked at being a sex god.

She chuckled as she slung a bag over her shoulder. "No worries. I got it."

"Just…" He was pulling the condom off and tying it. "Can I get your number? Take you out for coffee?"

"Awww." She fake smiled. "You're sweet, Josh."

His face fell. "It's Jeremiah."

"Sorry," she fake apologized.

"I told you that twice."

All of her bags hung off her as she grabbed her jeans. "I'm gonna be real busy while I'm here. But I'm sure we'll run into each other."

She gave him her don't-call-me-I'll-call-you smile and headed for the stairs as the March thunderstorm let loose on the old Hugh Building.

She'd close herself up in the vacant room next to his, hopefully wouldn't see him in the morning, then move into her old bedroom at her mom's house tomorrow. But she would be running into him: one of her first moves—after the cowbell and before the security system—was going to be kicking him out. The tenant rooms her grandmother prized as a haven for those were who lost and lonely were just an invitation for any asshole to wander around the bar in the middle of the night.

If he ever stopped deluding himself, he'd thank her for throwing him out.

Alex was going to be trapped at Loretta's until she made a name for herself big enough to erase the disaster of Chicago and earn her a position—director of a beverage program in Vegas or Toronto or Atlanta would be nice—that let her escape. But Alex was a big girl and could take it.

Poor Professor Josh had been hiding his sweet, academic eyes behind his pretty manicured hands and ignoring what everyone in her family already knew.

Ghosts were real.

And the old Hugh Building, home of Loretta's for forty years, was totally haunted.

Chapter Two

With the early-spring rainstorm beating against the roof the next morning, Alex stubbornly resisted any impulse to rush as she closed the door of the tenant room where she'd changed. She even took a couple of seconds to look at the *milagro* hanging from a frayed red ribbon on the door—it was an inch-long leg made of pressed tin.

A prayer for travelers? Because they…had legs?

Her grandmother had hung a different *milagro* on every door in the second-floor hallway—the back fire-escape exit, a narrow storage closet, the two tenant rooms, the bathroom that lodgers had to share, the office, and the larger storage room. Alex guessed it'd be overkill if she took some time right now to switch a few of them out for little tin houses with sturdy roofs.

She'd had to catch so many leaks up here, she'd run out of buckets.

Where are you???????? her big sister Gillian had texted while Alex had been ass-up in the storage closet looking for more containers. You better not have bailed already. This was ur idea!!!!!

Alex hadn't meant to be late to this morning's meeting. But, as she started slowly down the stairs with the last gleam of her good mood from last night's refreshing fuck sputtering out, she made sure to live up to her family's expectations to disappoint.

She paused on the landing and took a video of a single rivulet of water running from the ancient stained-glass window and down the warped wallboard. She applied a filter, uploaded the video to her social media feeds, and captioned it, "Washing away the old and stupid and starting fresh."

As her first response since Saturday night's incident, it was snarly enough to appease her fans and cryptic enough to keep them coming back for more. She never read her notifications and seldom engaged with her multitudes of social media followers other than the occasional, "Go fuck yourself."

But she needed them coming back for more. The follower numbers that continued ticking up since Saturday night were the only thing that made her betting it all on a falling-apart bar in southeast Kansas even viable.

Continuing down the stairs, she clocked more she needed to add to her already gargantuan list of building repairs: Replace the roof. Fix the window. Manage the mold. Refinish the worn wooden steps and fit with treads. And, since this was the stairwell where her grandmother had slipped, broken her hip, and gotten a concussion, install a goddamn handrail.

As she'd scrubbed pen ink off her face this morning, got her battle gear on, and distributed buckets, she hadn't missed the number of duct-taped repairs—if there'd been any repair at all—on Loretta's second floor. She dreaded to see the condition of the first.

How had the family let things get so bad?

Nostalgia hit her like a plank as she stepped out of the stairwell and into the bar's mopped-floor smell of rosemary, lemon, and vinegar. The four women of her family glaring at her was familiar, too.

"Thanks for *finally* joining us," Gillian said, the sleeves of her cashmere sweater coat pushed up her crossed arms as her leopard-print flat tapped annoyingly. Alex's big sister had really been working those highlights in her shoulder-length wavy brown hair. "The kids and I have a plane to catch and they don't run on your schedule."

"We'll make sure you're there on time," Sissy soothed from where she sat next to their grandmother. She gave Alex a look that mixed pity with empathy. From the baby sister Alex had always protected, that look stung. "But Mom wanted to run back to the house to say goodbye to the kids before opening the bar…"

Alex swallowed her frustration and gave a smile she knew would irritate. "I'm one of the top bartenders in Chicago," she reminded them as she walked toward her grandmother. "I think I can handle opening Loretta's." She'd opened the bar a million times alongside her grandmother before she'd moved.

Apparently, she and her sisters could only get along long-distance. That didn't change what she was here to do. She would double Gillian's investment and make sure Sissy's recipes shined on the menu.

They didn't have to like her. They just had to stay out of her way.

Her mother smiled with that long-suffering patience that drove Alex up a wall.

"You don't have to go to any trouble, mija," her mother said. Mary wouldn't accept a Band-Aid if her head was chopped off. "I'll just stay here instead of saying goodbye and…"

"It's not any trouble—"

"You *were* one of the top bartenders—"

"Why don't we all just—"

"Niñas," her grandmother said, commanding instant silence. She crossed one dark hand over the other. "What are we doing here?"

If this bar was the heart of their ginormous, multigenerational Mexican-American family, then Alex's seventy-seven-year-old grandmother was its steady and enduring pulse. The oldest of four siblings who'd all been fruitful, Loretta Torres was the family matriarch. Whether she was hustling around here or sitting serenely on her bar stool at home, Loretta drew people to her with her straight-shooting wisdom, her welcoming smile, and—if you were lucky—the incredible yeasty aroma of her just-cooked tortillas piled in a huge silver bowl on the open door of her oven.

Growing up next door to her grandmother, Alex had always been one of the lucky ones.

Right now, her Granmo stared up at her without expression from under her more-salt-than-pepper cloud of short, soft hair. Her eyes that licked down at the corners (they were the same shape as Alex's) assessed the three of them and her mouth didn't smile. Her brown skin stretched taut over the take-no-shit jut of her regal jaw. Loretta Torres never let her face tell you anything she didn't want you to know.

Alex hid her pang when she noticed the clunky walker. She leaned down to kiss her Granmo's papery-thin cheek. Loretta smelled like the sweet, rose-scented lotion she'd taught Alex to slather her hands in, but her indomitable shoulders felt too fragile beneath her blousy polyester shirt.

It'd been months since Alex had seen her.

Gillian swirled to take the free seat next to their mom and reached across the table to place a hand over Loretta's. "Granmo, we have some exciting news," she said, hazel eyes wide. Her actual eye color was the same dark chocolate brown as Alex's—they'd stared in the mirror and compared once as kids—but Gillian had taken to wearing colored contacts the instant she could afford them. "We know what a burden Loretta's has become. We'd like to take that burden off your hands sooner rather than later. It's a physical load and a financial sieve that someone of your years…"

Alex stepped back from the table as she saw the tick in her grandmother's unlined cheek.

Yes, Alex and her sisters had always thought of Loretta's as a pain that their asses would one day feel.

But you didn't insult Loretta's in front of Loretta. Sissy saw the tick, too.

"What Gillian means," Sissy interjected, putting her hand on top of her sister's, "is that we love you and we're worried about you. Since Loretta's is becoming more than you and Mom can handle…"

Alex rolled her eyes as her grandmother's back stiffened. Christ. Tell Loretta that she's not Wonder Woman and she'd lasso the world to prove you wrong.

Why were her sisters so bad at this?

"We want to buy the bar and the building," Alex said, arms crossed. "Buy it now instead of inheriting it later."

The bulb in the knockoff lamp at the front corner of the four-sided mahogany bar went out with a loud pop as her sisters swung their heads to glare at her. Her mother's mouth dropped open in surprise.

Her grandmother stared without reaction.

Alex hooked her thumbs into her oversized, stone-washed jeans. She'd worn her Stones' Sticky Fingers T-shirt with the cutaway collar, a wooly orange man's cardigan that hung to her thighs, a wrist-full of leather and silver bracelets, and an earful of studs. Her cat's-eye liner and burgundy lipstick were on point.

She'd driven ten hours last night believing that taking over Loretta's was going to be the easiest of her challenges. Now she was glad she'd come dressed for the contest of who was going to blink first.

Loretta scanned Alex and her sisters. "So the three of you are moving home?"

Gillian and Sissy looked down at their laps.

Alex cocked her hip. "I'm moving back."

For now.

Alex had been the first sister to escape Freedom, moving in with a distant cousin in Chicago after her sophomore year in high school. Gillian did it months later, sailing out of town as the Neewollah parade queen and class valedictorian with a full ride to an East Coast university. Sissy had tiptoed out, working in restaurants in Freedom, then Topeka, then Wichita, and finally landing in Kansas City and becoming one of the city's most sought after sous-chefs.

Sissy was better than Alex and Gillian about coming home for a weekend or the occasional holiday. But she still wasn't great.

Gillian jumped in. "Sissy and I will be part of major decisions. Mom can still work here. And you can be as much or as little involved as you want."

Sissy smiled. "It can be just like you and Granpo dreamed." She was the one who actually had hazel eyes, a mix of gray and light brown that sometimes looked violet. With those big doe eyes and bee-stung mouth, she was the beauty of the three of them. In blue scrubs, chef shoes, and no makeup, she was, as usual, doing nothing to help it along. "You can finally go fishing like you always wish you'd had time to do with Granpo."

Their grandparents opened Loretta's in the old Hugh Building forty years ago and operated it together for ten years before Granpo Salvador's death. His life insurance allowed Loretta to buy the building from a lazy landlord glad to be shed of it. She'd often spoke wistfully about her and Salvador's retirement dream: leaving the bar in the hands of their grandkids so they could go fishing.

Loretta frowned for the first time as she looked at Sissy. "Cecilia, you've never been in love, so you don't understand. But why would I do that without him?"

Sissy recoiled, blinking.

Alex studied her grandmother.

If Loretta was resistant to just them buying the bar from her—which was a huge fucking surprise since Loretta's had been the inheritance yoked around their necks their entire lives—then she was going to be super resistant to the radical changes Alex had planned.

"Alejandra," her grandmother said, her dark eyes serious and daunting.

Alex tried not to squirm in front of her like the time the drugstore owner had driven her to Loretta's instead of to the police station (which would have been preferred) after she'd been caught shoplifting.

"Why would I hand over this casa de mi corazon that I built to provide sanctuary and love and warmth to a granddaughter who can't even visit me when I break my hip? To a nieta who can't make it on time for an ambush?"

As her sisters began to deny that this was an ambush, Alex pulled her fingers from her belt loops and slid her hands into her big back pockets. She affected a smirk to cover her hidden clenched fists.

It was stupid, really.

This whole idea was stupid.

After the first tidal wave of fear when she'd heard about her grandmother being rushed to the hospital and then the sobbing-in-the-cooler relief when Gillian had called to tell her that Loretta was going to survive, Alex had babbled something about taking over Loretta's sooner than later. Her own instant excitement had surprised her as much as Gillian's quick agreement. Suddenly, she'd been having almost daily conversations with two people she usually only had a few awkward conversations with every year.

She'd asked to be taken off the schedule because of a family emergency but Randy, fucking Randy, had told her that they couldn't spare her. It should've triggered her spidey sense that maybe she didn't have as much power at the Fantasy Box as she'd thought.

All that—the panic and fear and guilt and reckless excitement and, now, the need to resurrect her reputation and career—had led her to why she was late this morning.

After her wham-bam-thank-you-professor, after she heard him close the door on the room next to hers, she'd snuck across the hall to her grandmother's office, moved the desk's stacks of paperwork and old menus to the floor—her grandmother had never been one for administrative work—and began setting to paper the ideas she'd already shared with her sisters. Open the building up to the empty side lot for a beer garden, change the layout of the bar for better flow, *finally* start selling the Mexican food her grandmother was known for instead of third-rate burgers and frozen pizzas, create a cocktail list that was special but accessible...

She'd startled awake this morning slumped over the desk. When she'd rushed into the bathroom, she saw that her pen scribbles for a beer list that would appeal to a college audience were imprinted on her cheek. She'd stopped rushing when she got her sister's irritating text that presumed Alex couldn't be relied on.

Now, as every female in her family looked at her with suspicion, it was so stupid that Alex was fighting to turn a dive bar in a hometown she'd scraped off her heel into a destination on the plains, a unique drink-and-food experience for the ritzy faculty from the college, foodies on road trips, and hipsters out of Tulsa, Wichita, even Kansas City.

She could explain all of this to the family.

But she'd stopped explaining anything—stopped sharing much at all—when she was forced to leave town when she was sixteen.

She gave her grandmother her smirkiest smile. "Why hand me the bar?"

Gillian glared a warning at her and Sissy's look pleaded caution.

"Because I'm your favorite."

It prickled her sisters, just like she knew it would, but instead of her grandmother listing all the ways she'd destroyed that first-place position, Loretta smiled placidly. "Mijitas, don't worry about me. Go back to your lives. I will be fine."

She gave a big, dramatic sigh.

"I've already had two offers for the building."

Shock stabbed through Alex. "What?"

Her sisters' eyes widened. It was the first time they were hearing this, too.

Loretta looked as serene as the chipped Virgen de Guadalupe birdbath in her front yard. "No one said anything to you? Oh. Maybe no one posted it on the Facebook."

"Granmo," Alex said sharply.

"¿Qué?"

"You put the building up for sale?" Sissy asked, horror in her voice. Sissy was endlessly loyal; for their grandmother to put the building—the bar—that their whole family called a second home up for grabs was a shocking betrayal. "Why?"

Her grandmother shrugged again. "For the reasons you said. I am old. Loretta's is a burden."

A second ago, it was the home of her heart. Alex clenched her hands tighter in her pockets.

"Who do you have offers from?" she demanded.

This wasn't fair. No one had let her know. Her mom hadn't even called her.

Alex glanced at Gillian. What they planned to offer for the bar and building—mostly money from Gillian's wealthy attorney husband combined with what Alex and Sissy had in savings—would comfortably set up their grandmother while leaving enough for renovations. Their plans would keep the bar in the family.

She expected her big sister, normally the nagging voice of reason, to argue this.

Instead, Gillian stared absently as her hand twirled a strand of caramelly hair. Seeing her childhood stress response while she wore diamond studs was jarring. Alex had assumed Gillian wanted to sweep in, save their grandmother, and add another halo to her heavy stack of them.

Now, she wasn't sure what Gillian had been getting out of their doomed plan.

As thunder rumbled outside, Loretta lifted her chin and sniffed. "I received an offer from Freedom Rings Development," her grandmother said. "They're a very important company. You know them?"

Alex shrugged and looked at her sisters, who shook their heads.

"They brought me roses," her grandmother said proudly.

"How much did they offer?" Alex asked.

Her grandmother said a number that had Sissy sucking in a shocked breath.

They could never match that.

Alex looked at her grandmother in confusion. "Why in the world would they be offering that for *this* building?"

"¿No sé?" Loretta shrugged, without a care in the world. "Perhaps they know something about the plant?"

The plant. Even Alex had heard about "the plant" during her few visits home. Rumor had it that the woman who kept Freedom limping along, billionaire Roxanne Medina—who'd been born in Freedom, wisely shed it the instant she could, and threw money at it whenever she had a guilt she needed to squash—was going to bring substantial manufacturing and its manna of good-paying union jobs back to town.

The ghosts haunting the town's many decaying mansions were more real than "the plant" dream.

Both sisters slumped in their seats.

This afternoon, Gillian and her kids would fly back to DC. Tomorrow, she'd get up, hand the kids over to the nanny, then spend her day at her tennis club. At least, that's how Alex assumed a wealthy DC stay-at-home mom spent her time.

Sissy would drive back to Kansas City and toque-up for her sous-chef job at a Michelin-starred French restaurant on the Plaza.

But Alex had nothing to go back to. Even if one of the bars who used to regularly try to poach her would still have her, she couldn't imagine going back under the heel of someone like Randy. Not after what had happened at the Fantasy Box. And her industry was full of men like Randy. She was so tired of seeing men—always men—who were less qualified and experienced being promoted over her again and again.

This, here, in a town she'd never wanted to return to, in a bar she'd have to wrench from her grandmother's hands, among family who trusted her as far as they could throw her, was the only way forward.

"You said there were two offers," she said, barreling on. "Who made the other one?"

The outside door opened, letting in a whoosh of cold and a pounding drumbeat of rain.

Her grandmother smiled like the first azaleas had just bloomed.

"Aquí está," Loretta said. "Mijitas, meet the next potential owner of the Hugh Building."

Alex turned as the cowbell clanged violently and the saloon doors smacked open.

His long trench coat dripped on the wood boards and he was removing a hat that made him look like some reporter from the 1920s. He adjusted his tortoiseshell glasses over his golden-green eyes, ran his hand through his thick brown hair, and then smiled at them.

His face was a mass of crinkles. "Good morning. Lovely day."

Standing there, dripping and delusional, was Mr. College.

Professor Josh Bigdick from the night before was trying to screw her. This time, not in the fun way.

Chapter Three

Jeremiah Post hid his gulp behind his smile.

In the year he'd been living above Loretta's bar, he'd become accustomed to the bold unfettered emotions of her infinite relatives: the boisterous humor and teasing he received from Loretta's brothers and elderly cousins, who occupied the same table five days a week drinking bottomless cups of coffee; the effusive affection and additional teasing he got from her daughters and their cousins, women his mother's age who brought their families in for dinner or came in after bowling night; the unreserved curiosity of the numerous children always underfoot who were fascinated by his height, bold about pleading to be picked up, and completely uninterested in the disciplines of introversion, timidity, or silence.

He'd sublimated his innate New England reserve in order to embrace the warmth this good family offered him, a stranger. A foreigner.

But even though he'd walked into the bar during the occasional passionate shouting match and had to break up a couple of fights—the uncles had offered him a seat at their table after he'd carried a patron outside by jeans and jacket—he'd never been the recipient of unrepentant hostility.

Not until he'd gotten Loretta's message after his first class, drove through the kind of rip-roaring spring thunderstorm he'd only encountered here on the Kansas plains, laughed in disbelief at the deluge as he'd leapt over puddles to reach the door, and barreled into his rented accommodations on the edge of his adopted home to find three beautiful women glaring at him.

The fact that eight hours earlier he'd been inside the one woman offering the most fiery-eyed hatred made the whole moment that much more surreal.

He was never one to inspire passion.

"Niñas, this is my tenant, Professor Jeremiah Post," Loretta Torres announced from her seat, with that raised chin and warm smile that curved her cheeks. She looked good. The best he'd seen her since her fall. "Jeremiah, you've already met Cecilia. This is Juliana y Alejandra, Mary's oldest and middle daughters."

He gave himself a moment by hanging his still-dripping fedora and soaked-through Burberry coat on the weathered coat tree.

Alejandra. Alex. Right.

He *had* heard of her before. Many times. She was a bartender in Chicago. Mary Armstead spoke of her with wistfulness. Loretta with pride. And whenever a certain era of cousins, the ones around his age, laughed uproariously as they retold tales of massive youthful indiscretions, Alejandra Armstead was always at the center of the mischief.

He turned, adjusted his glasses, then wiped his damp hands on his sweater vest as walked toward the women whose frowns hadn't eased.

"Juliana," he said, holding out his hand to the oldest daughter, fashionably turned out in cashmere and discreet diamonds as she sat next to her grandmother. "Nice to meet you."

She took his hand in a firm grip but said, "It's Gillian," without smiling.

"Okay." He shook her hand.

He leaned over the table toward the youngest sister. Even when she was frowning, she was very pretty. "Sissy, it's good to see you again." He'd learned his lesson from Gillian née Juliana: only family could assume the right to their birth names.

Sissy relented, giving him the smallest smile while she shook his hand.

He absorbed it, let it bolster him, before he straightened and turned toward the woman standing next to him.

Loretta's granddaughter. Mary's middle daughter. Alejandra Armstead. Alex Torres.

The woman who'd given him the quickest and most excruciating orgasm of his life.

He'd woken up slowly this morning, rain smacking against his window, thinking he'd enjoyed a fantasy-strewn wet dream the likes of which he hadn't had since he'd been a lonely and horny teen. A lush woman with full lips and a direct, dark-eyed gaze and bright flowers crawling up her arm had sprung to vivid life in the shadows of the bar, conquered him like a Valkyrie, then mounted him as her prize, spreading her legs and pressing a plush and perfect hind end into his hands.

Harsh reality had hit him like a crack of thunder when he realized that it had been real. She had been real, he had been really fast, and she was sleeping on the other side of the wall.

His mortification hadn't deterred his early-morning erection.

Apparently, her glare and the fact that he was standing in front of her sisters, mother, and grandmother wouldn't deter his late-morning erection either.

He cleared his throat. "Nice to meet you," he said, feeling the detestable heat crawling up his neck from under his collar as he extended his hand.

Her face was a solid mask of suspicion and hostility, without even a hint of a smile or familiarity to soften her full lips, wide jaw, strong cheekbones, and big, almost-black eyes with their thick lashes. He'd watched pleasure-shocked as those long lashes had clenched against her creamy caramel cheeks when she'd orgasmed around him last night. Her black hair was shaved close to her head on the sides then blossomed into thick wavy curls on top. It was a soft contrast to her sharp chin pointed belligerently at him. She wore a T-shirt that showed shining collarbones, a baggy deep-orange cardigan that hid her tattoos, big jeans, and huge black boots. Her clothes shouldn't have shown off how curvy she was, broad shoulders and big breasts and full hips.

But they did.

She seemed half his height, but the sense of her filled the room.

She crossed her arms under her breasts. "Yeah, great to see you again," she sneered, rejecting his handshake.

"Again?" Mary asked.

Alex didn't drop her bullet-tipped gaze. "He helped me out last night. With my stuff. He was super quick about it, too."

Jeremiah felt the flush he hated flare up his cheeks.

"It was the middle of the night," he mumbled. Heavy silver rings flashed on one of the hands propped under her breast; he'd felt that warm metal when she'd squeezed and stroked him. "I thought I'd dreamed it."

"He thought I was a ghost," she said without looking away.

He felt the humiliated flush up to his hairline.

"So tell me, professor," she said, tilting her chin up as she stepped closer, as if she would stab him with it. She smelled, confusingly, sweet and soft. Like a bridal bouquet. "Why would you want to buy a haunted building?"

"Alejandra, be nice," Mary chided gently.

The fifty-something-year-old woman's quiet manner and

reserved appearance—she wore a navy blue cardigan over a white T-shirt and her black hair waved down her back—made her easy to lose here in this place filled with Loretta's forcefulness and her family's verve. But Mary had been his lifeline in his first weeks of living here; her gentle smile from across the bar top had communicated that the family's jovial teasing was well-intentioned and inclusive.

He sought her corner of the bar to sit at whenever he wanted to do nothing more than read his book with the soothing murmur of Mary's bar work in the background.

Jeremiah took a discreet step back out of Alex's orbit to push his hands into his pockets and turned to address all the sisters. "I came home one morning and your grandmother was having a meeting with a developer. I told her that if she was putting the building on the market, I'd like to place a bid."

"Why?" Alex shot out.

"I…um…"

He looked to Loretta for help and got nothing but her placid smile. He soldiered on.

"I'm the head of the Freedom Historical Society. This building could tell the fascinating story of a small Midwestern town that once had more millionaires per capita than any place in the United States. Governors, senators, a Pulitzer Prize winner, even one of the first monkeys in space came from Freedom." He could feel the flush of excitement that sprang over him whenever he started in on this topic. "But more importantly, it could be the cornerstone to a new understanding of the evolution of Mexican-American communities in the Midwest. That's a fascinating story that's been unfolding since the early 1900s, but no one's told it properly. We could do that here."

Sissy furrowed her brow. "Granmo, what's he talking about?"

Loretta's eyes sparkled as she looked at Jeremiah. He wondered how she'd learned to do that.

"He wants to turn Loretta's into a museum," she said proudly.

The granddaughters' looks of shock explained why not one of the bar regulars or family members had protested the idea of the historical society setting up shop in their second home.

Loretta hadn't told them.

It had been…unpleasant to rush into Loretta's after his morning class to see three men in expensive suits hulking over the wan woman while another sat much too close, all but trapping her in her seat. She'd been on her own and just a week out of the hospital. He'd bumped into bar stools to draw attention to himself, then asked if Loretta needed anything. She'd announced without hesitation that the "nice men" were offering to buy her building.

Later, he'd researched the Freedom Rings Development group.

Then he'd come to Loretta with his own offer.

"The historical society would like to purchase the Hugh Building and transform it into the Freedom Historical Museum," he told her granddaughters now, focusing on all of them and not just the punk-rock beauty to his left. "We'll showcase the full story of Freedom's evolution but, most excitingly, we'll be able to tell the little sung story of the Midwestern colonias from Milagro Street, which was home to one of the first. This neighborhood, like other colonias throughout the Midwest, provided services, support, and a sense of home for Mexican immigrants arriving to work on the railroad. Even though few colonias still survive today, they are a large part of why you have pockets of fourth- and fifth-generation Mexican-American social groups in towns throughout the central states."

Jeremiah had gotten carried away. His hands were in the

air, and he could feel the pound of potential in his chest. This was *such* an important story to be told, not only about who Americans were but about who Americans are.

The granddaughters looked at him like he'd grown a third head.

"What do you do, Professor Post?" Gillian shot out.

"Please, call me Jeremiah," he said, lowering his hands. "I'm an assistant professor of history on the tenure track at Dupen College; I've been there five years. I teach US and European history but my area of focus has been pocket societies like those in Appalachia or the Louisiana Creoles who aren't indigenous but have sustained a community for—"

"You're from here?" the older sister asked skeptically.

"No, I'm from back East."

Back East. It was an entire swath of states that hid the background and people and numerous familial estates of one transplanted academic. Before he'd moved to Freedom, that was the most he used to say, and it had satisfied. But he'd learned quickly—at the bar, and in the grocery store, and getting a malt at the Rexall's—that you couldn't get away with that in a small town. In a small town, people kept digging, then filled in any holes you left behind with their own speculation and gossip.

The wild rumors he'd heard about himself couldn't match up to the truth.

"Where did you go to school?" Gillian demanded.

"Stop it, Gillian," Alex said sharply. "Even a rich professor can't live up to *your* standards."

The sister bristled.

Jeremiah felt for her, had borne the brunt of enough familial disdain to dislike it for other people, but he instantly had no thought for anyone but himself as Alex turned on him.

She looked toweringly angry.

"So, you moved upstairs to...what...study us? So you could press your nose right up against the glass when you watched the rats?"

His stomach fell right to the floor.

"Oh no," he said, feeling the wide-eyed shock on his face. "I would never..."

"Are you gonna use the museum to gain tenure?" Her eyes sparkled like glass shards.

"Well, yes, it will be part of a portfolio of work but..."

"What gives you the right to tell our story?" Her fists were clenched; she was truly furious. "A big wealthy man sneaks in, uses us for his promotion, steals from us the place where we come together, then turns it into a museum to let others applaud his white benevolence and gawk at our diaspora."

He sucked in a breath. "No, no, no. That was never my intention..."

"You swoop in and take advantage of an elderly lady, make good with the family just so you can—"

A hand slammed down on a table. "Parra," Loretta said, sharp and commanding. "Enough, Alejandra."

"But Granmo..."

Sissy was shaking her head quickly, her long, thick ponytail dancing behind her. "Alex, that's not... He was here. When she fell. He found her."

The mournful look on Sissy's face reflected the shadow that fell over the half-dark room, lit only by a few of the colorful glass lamps on the bar, as thunder rolled outside.

"He got her to the hospital," she continued quietly. "The doctors said that if he hadn't been here..."

He still didn't entirely understand why he'd woken up that Saturday night. She'd already been lying there an hour, so it wasn't her tumble down the five steps from the landing that did it. But he'd woken up with a sense of urgency. As if something was flicking the part of his brain that said *go, go, go.*

The way she'd looked at the bottom of the stairs was scarier than any ghost.

"I'm just glad I was here," he said cautiously.

"That's right, niña," Loretta said. "He was here. Where were you?"

Oh no. Alex kept her silence, staring at her grandmother.

"That's not what I—" he began.

"I am not a fool," Loretta barked. "I may be old. I may need this cursed walker." She flapped at it. "But no one takes advantage of me. Including you. You don't want to be in Freedom, you don't want to provide a haven in this neighborhood. So why do you suddenly want the bar so much?"

In a year of living here, he'd seen the occasional spat between family members or end-of-day tension between Loretta and Mary—of course he would. But he'd never seen this level of suspicion. Alex's belligerence seemed to bring out the worst in her family.

She lifted her sharp-edged chin. "Gillian is looking for an investment. Sissy would like to make changes in the kitchen. And I... I believe Loretta's can draw a bigger audience."

Loretta asked the question that Jeremiah was thinking. "What does that mean?"

"We'll attract people from the college."

Never. His colleagues laughed at his "eccentric" choice of housing.

"With the right changes, Loretta's could even become a destination for those outside the area."

"What kind of changes?" Loretta asked suspiciously.

"Improving the food." Alex met her grandmother's gaze head-on. "Diversifying the drink menu. Redecorating. Opening up the north wall and turning the parking lot into a beer garden. Renovating the second floor to provide more dining space and a private room for events."

"But you'd keep the tenant rooms?" Jeremiah blurted out.

Alex didn't even deign to look at him. "Changing the name," she muttered.

Gillian rolled her eyes and Sissy winced.

Loretta pressed her hands flat against the table. "These new menus mean you would have to raise prices, sí? Chasing away the family and friends who depend on Loretta's? How are they going to come anyway, since you've taken away their parking lot? And our tenants, the people who need a roof over their head and love around them. Where will they go? Y qué, you change the name your Granpo Salvador christened the bar with the day he gave it to me? ¿Qué pasa, mija? You hate your family this much?"

Alex shrugged. "No. Family can still come by. When they can afford to."

"Alex," Gillian groaned. Mary sadly shook her head as Sissy slumped forward to bury her face in her crossed arms and Loretta glowered. Alex stood unflinching on the firing range of her family's emotions, her chin up and shoulders back.

These women rejected the icy reserve and emotional deficiency his family had cultivated for generations.

Regardless of what Alex thought of him and his intentions, he had nothing but an intense respect for Loretta and Mary, the history of their family, and the bonds that tied them all so closely together. This bar was as important to keeping those bonds strong as the town, the local parish of St. Paul's Catholic Church, the Spanglish that many of them didn't speak but all of them understood, and Loretta's Sunday dinners at her home. Freedom Rings Development wasn't going to honor that. Jeremiah was beginning to believe that Alex wasn't going to either.

I like town. Don't you? he'd asked her last night.

Not particularly.

The historical society purchasing the building wasn't the ideal solution—ideally, Loretta had independently wealthy family who wanted to maintain the place as a profitless shrine for jovial family gatherings and a rooming house for one lonely professor. In lieu of that, Jeremiah believed he and the historical society offered the best option. He had plans for the lot next door as well. With the help of Joe Torres, also a member of the historical society and Alex's cousin, he'd been developing a way to ensure that Loretta's family always had a second place to call home.

He wasn't stealing anything from anybody. He certainly wasn't displacing friends and family to turn Loretta's into some hipster's retreat.

"You want this building, niñas?" Loretta asked, addressing all the girls but looking straight at Alex. "Prove it to me. Maybe I'll sell it to Freedom Rings Development for more money than I can imagine. Maybe I'll let it become a museum. Maybe I'll let you three claim it. But I've told the development company and Jeremiah that I won't be rushed, and I say the same to you. Alejandra, you think you deserve the bar? You have the spring to prove it."

Mary, Gillian, and Sissy all looked at the middle sister as if they were waiting for the shrapnel when she said one more explosive thing.

From where he stood, he could see Alex's bejeweled-and-white knuckles, buried in the folds of her oversized sweater.

"I quit my job in Chicago," she finally bit out. "This is important to me. I'll show you that. I'm moving in with Mom."

Sissy and Gillian looked nervously at each other as Mary looked down at her entwined fingers.

"What?" Alex asked.

Jeremiah didn't understand what was going on, but he envied the wordless exchange of info. He'd never had that kind of connection with his brother.

"Mom," Gillian said. "Tell her."

"It's not the time…"

"Mom."

Mary lifted her head, and took a deep breath. "I'm seeing your father again."

Alex went stiff from the tips of her inky black hair to the toes of her big black boots. Her full, burgundy-painted mouth fell open then closed. Twice.

Loretta and Mary had made a home for him over the last year, and he empathized with Gillian and Sissy's caution when confronted with their belligerent middle sister. He didn't trust Alex Alejandra Torres-Armstead and, apparently, neither did her family.

Still, seeing this blunt, fearless, take-no-prisoners woman left speechless was…uncomfortable. He squashed an instinct to do something, anything, to renew her ire.

"Fine," she finally said, lifting that sharp chin. "I'll stay here, then."

He startled. Her words shook him like a moan from the attic.

He'd have to share a bathroom. And a hallway. And a bedroom wall. With her.

He'd be alone in the dark with her every night.

She smiled cruelly when she saw his alarm. "You got a new neighbor, professor."

He didn't know if he'd survive it.

Chapter Four

After everyone left, Alex took her anger out on opening the decrepit old bar.

She'd still have plenty in the gun when her mom got back from saying goodbye to Gillian's kids.

She banged metal buckets she'd emptied from upstairs onto the raised bump-out in the back corner where bad cover bands sometimes played. How rain could wind its way to leak through a first-floor ceiling was beyond her, but she could probably blame the old Hugh Building's "eccentricities." She shuddered to think what was living in its guts. Something that sounded like more than rain tapped against one of the inset, stained-glass windows along the back wall and a cold spot followed her around as she swept.

The gong of drips against metal as she took the heavy wooden chairs off the tables got her eyebrow twitching. It didn't help that the thick chairs with their worn carvings of flowers and ivy and skulls and birds—her grandparents had bought them in Mexico and hauled them back here—kept thwacking her in the legs as she flipped them over, no matter how she tried to avoid them.

She shoved the last chair into place.

Next, she went at the large four-sided bar. It was made up of two long counters that had been original to the Hugh Building—her Granpo had cut them into four pieces, restored the thick mahogany, and refashioned them into the large square centered in the room. Alex had spent a lot of summer mornings and after-school afternoons sitting at the bar and marveling at the constantly changing tower of crap stacked precariously on the stair-step island in the middle: glistening bottles of liquor, jelly jar drinking glasses, rosaries, her grandmother's favorite milagros, Little League schedules, family photos, handwritten "thank you" notes, and a framed eight-by-ten of her Granpo, honored with an always-lit candle and always-full tequila shot. The island had been as fascinating as a treasure box when she was a kid, her sneakers kicking the carved wooden panel above the brass foot railing that read: *Hugh Apothecary. Proprietor, Wayland Hugh.*

Above the now-tarnished railing, that panel praising the building's original owner still gleamed as if the grandfather she'd never known had just refinished it and installed it at its place of pride—right at the front corner of the bar, where everyone who entered Loretta's could see it.

When Alex replaced the light bulb in the lamp above it, only to have it immediately short out again, she kicked the panel with more violence.

The bar got its revenge. When she had to duck under the pass-through because it was duct-taped shut, she felt a whisper of movement across her arm, jumped, and smacked her funny bone.

Howling curses, she swore she could hear an old man's chuckle.

What was she doing back here? The sure thing of Loretta's had turned into anything but. The bar obviously didn't want her here; everyone in her family knew how the building could be. Her sisters, her business partners, had run out with vague promises to talk later. Her mom... If Alex spent too much time thinking about her mom and her dad, she would break something.

And Loretta.

She'd actually deluded herself into thinking that her grand-mother would be glad she was back.

When scratchy Tejano music suddenly blared through the ancient speakers, Alex was glad to have another target for her mad. She charged back to the kitchen to tell Danny Marti-nez, her second cousin and Loretta's nephew, to turn it the hell down.

In his mid-thirties, Danny was determined to get a college degree, although he could never settle in on what. He totally ignored her anger to hug her close against his short, round bulk as he told her about his latest passion for anthropology. He liked his weekday job in the kitchen because it gave him time—so much time—for the coursework of his constantly changing majors.

He was a great guy. And a totally uninterested cook. Sissy had promised to develop new recipes for Loretta's to replace the menu of the-frozen-and-the-bland, while Alex hoped to inspire her to take over the kitchen completely.

Alex came out of the kitchen shocked by the state of it. Broken and outdated appliances, bad ventilation, inadequate storage, more leaks. They'd have to gut the whole thing.

How had the family let things get so bad?

Mary still hadn't returned by the time Alex turned on the Open sign in the front window at 11:30 a.m. and held the door for the five guys standing in the rain. Her retired tíos trucked in with water dripping off their ball caps and shed their wet gear onto the coat tree. Then they passed her around like the bat for a piñata: hugs, hugs, kisses, kisses, big smiles, back pats, shouts of "Alejandra!" and "You're back!", and bad jokes about Chicago (*Da Bears. Did you bring us any hot dogs?*). They settled at their regular corner table near the stage.

She gave them the same vague answer she'd given Danny when they asked what she was doing here: she was helping out while Loretta was recuperating.

As she took their order for five cups of coffees and a single plate of fries for the table (she'd be refilling those damn cups the whole damn morning), she realized not one of them mentioned the sale of the building. Neither had Danny. Not one of her boisterously emotional, familia-dedicated, and routine-loving tíos said a word about the end of Loretta's, the sanctuary for old men's gossip for forty years.

Alex jammed the carafe back onto the warmer when she saw her mom walking out of the short hallway from the kitchen tying a green server's apron around her waist. She slid under the broken pass-through to meet her.

"The family doesn't know Granmo's selling the building, do they?" Alex hiss-whispered.

Mary looked at her warily. "No."

"Why?"

"Your grandmother hasn't told them." Mary studied the table closest to them as if checking for condiments was the most important thing happening right now. "Thank you for refilling the sugar packets."

Her mom swept past her and Alex ground her teeth.

Mary always looked more like the teacher she'd wanted to be than a bartender. She was a couple inches shorter than Alex, with Alex's matching hips and boobs, and beautiful, thick black hair that fell to midback in a perfect wave.

Trailing in Mary's wake, Alex could smell the rose-scented hand cream that she also used. "*Why* hasn't she told them? Why haven't you?" After doing the bulk of the work to support their family as a bank teller, Mary had started working at the bar about a decade ago, after Alex had left. "Don't you care that you won't have a job anymore?"

Mary bent to get under the pass-through and then smiled at Alex absently. "Oh, mija, I'll be fine. I'll find something."

Alex had to stop, put her hand against the mahogany, and count backward from ten.

It'll be fine, was her mom's favorite statement. It could be printed across the blindfold her mom loved to see the world through: *I'll be fine. We'll be fine. Everything will be fine.*

When sometimes it just wasn't.

Alex also ducked under the pass-through.

Her family, the multitudes of people living right here in town, didn't know that Loretta was planning to sell the building. They'd just been okay with taking a paycheck from an elderly woman for half-assed work or kicking up their feet and asking for endless free refills while the building crumbled down around them.

She loved her tíos and Danny and all of them in that see-you-at-Christmas way. But, like her mom, they were just *everything's fine*-ing their time away while Freedom, Milagro Street, and the Hugh Building went to shit.

Everything was *not* fine.

"I can't believe you're seeing Dad again," she said low, feeling the burn of it like the last dregs of coffee boiling away on the burner.

Mary straightened from where she was pulling clean jelly jars out of the dishwasher rack. "We're just talking." She tucked her beautiful hair behind her ear—it was the first time Alex could see long, silver strands in it—and began to stack the jars on the island.

"Why?"

Alex was pretty fucking proud she didn't shout the question.

"He's still my husband." Mary kept her eyes on the jars. "He's still your father."

Pretty-and-proper Mary Torres, Loretta and Salvador's second child and oldest daughter, was diminutive in a way that Alex could never be, even if she'd been just as short. Mary had always been easy to miss. That fact roiled Alex up just as much as it kept her from unleashing the confusion, frustration, and anger that had been bubbling since she'd discovered that her dad was back in the picture.

Mary Torres and Tucker Armstead had been high school sweethearts, and nineteen-year-old Mary had put her desire to be a teacher on hold to support her husband as he pursued a creative writing degree. Tucker had always been the parent at home, working in his bedroom office on his latest novel or article for a magazine (which generally got nothing but rejection letters) or county fair reports for the *Freedom Gazette* (which at least brought in a paycheck).

Alex didn't know when he started drinking.

But she'd noticed the change in middle school when, instead of coming home to a slightly distracted dad who'd send them out to play, their dad would come running outside with them. He'd climb trees or dance with them in the living room. He'd been rambunctious in a way that their always-in-his-head father hadn't been before.

But then he'd get quiet. He'd get frustrated easily. He'd go into his office and not come out.

As the months passed, the joyful highs got fewer and fewer. And the silent, withdrawn low became all they knew.

She thought her mom had finally cured her *everything-will-be-fine* illness when Mary had kicked him out after Alex had moved to Chicago. But a born-and-bred Catholic, Mary wouldn't even consider a divorce. Alex had done more to break ties with her father than her mom had: when she'd turned eighteen, Alex had legally changed her last name from Armstead to Torres.

"Why would you let him back in your life?" she demanded as the gold ring and tiny diamond sparkling on Mary's hand mocked her.

"He's been sober for five years," Mary said. She finally turned to look at Alex from under her thick sweep of bangs. "I'm taking it slow. I attend Al-Anon meetings. You father goes to two AA meetings a week. All we've done is meet for lunch."

Alex's eyes widened. "Where do you meet for lunch?"

"At home. Here."

She hadn't seen her father in thirteen years and wasn't interested in breaking the streak now. She was surprised her sisters had made her mom fess up.

Gillian had always been on her dad's side. They didn't speak for three years after she once told Alex to *get over it.* Sissy hated the discord, thought forgiving and giving people multiple shots at hurting her was the solution.

Alex had hoped, maybe, with their dad out of the picture and the bar as a joint project, she and her sisters could put a few patches over the holes of the last thirteen years.

Of course her mom was seeing him again. Of course it would be now.

"I'm going to be sleeping here and staying out of y'alls hair," Alex said, not minding the flash of hurt in her mom's eyes. "I'd appreciate it if you can return the favor and keep him out of mine."

Her mother looked at her steadily. "Alejandra, the relationship between me and your father is between me and your father. But we won't meet here." Mary reached out a hand and squeezed Alex's. "And while I would love for you to stay at the house, I understand your decision." She stacked the last of the clean glasses. "At least you will have a nice neighbor."

Hell.

"Guapo pobrecito," Loretta had called the big, wealthy, PhD-flashing white dude who wanted to use her family like show ponies to gain tenure. The "poor handsome man" had gone back to his tony university with a tin-foil-covered plate of her grandmother's beef enchiladas in his Rolex-wearing hand. Tenants received one meal a day with their rent, which was usually fried food from the bar's kitchen.

That was Alex's lunch.

Dr. Hot-and-Rich got her Granmo's enchiladas and welcoming smile and warm regard, when all Alex got was her suspicion. This building was falling apart under their watch, and yet her grandmother glared at her like *she* was the problem.

Alex had known coming back to Freedom was going to be a battle, had even looked forward to butting heads with the town-dominating Hughs, her extended family, her sisters, her mom.

She ignored the existence of her dad.

But her Granmo was the only thing Alex had missed about Freedom. Until the day she'd left, Alex had seen her every day of her life.

Even when things had gotten bad in Freedom, when Alex had gotten bad in Freedom, if she hadn't caught her grandmother at the bar, she'd go to her back door, pick some of the fragrant cilantro planted by the porch, and spend five minutes with Loretta who'd be sitting on her stool in the kitchen, sometimes reading the paper, sometimes eating a quiet meal, sometimes chopping up something that inevitably needed cilantro.

She really had thought she was her grandmother's favorite.

Instead, Loretta had told Alex, who was a fucking bartender raised in this bar, that she had to "prove" she deserved it. Her own Granmo had put her at the starting line with a development company and a white, rich, dorky stranger.

A white, rich, dorky stranger she'd roped herself into sleeping next door to instead of with.

Professor Big Dick had looked like a pleasant distraction from all the stomach-clenching injustice before he'd opened his mouth. His moss-green cashmere sweater vest had highlighted the incredible plank of his chest. His face squinked up into all those wrinkles when he smiled. He had thin pink lips and pale skin and he was big and rich and gorgeous and entitled.

Just like the very best invaders.

Maybe she should sleep in her car.

"Alejandra," Martín, Loretta's oldest brother, called from their table. "You get into the ganja again, niña? No sleeping on the job; you got empty cups over here. Cuidado or we won't give you a tip!"

Maybe she should sleep back in Chicago.

Chapter Five

Jeremiah purposely stayed on campus longer than normal. He had dinner at the new vegan restaurant, then walked in the rain—the torrential downpour had slacked off to an on-and-off rain shower once he returned to Dupen College—to the coffee shop. The Salvadorean blend he sipped while he'd caught up on grading was a huge improvement over Loretta's acrid brew. But he would have happily traded in the balanced citrus-and-earth flavor if he could have been where he usually did paperwork: sitting in a pool of colored-glass lamplight while Loretta and Mary filled the cup at his elbow and shared tidbits of their day.

As people chatted with colleagues and friends and partners at nearby tables, Jeremiah sat alone, his mood descending with every drop of rain that ran down the window. Finally, he could resist no longer. He hauled out his laptop to research the reason he was sitting alone.

His graduate assistant would have been shocked; Jeremiah usually steered clear of the internet.

Alex Alejandra Torres-Armstead, he was horrified to discover, did not. In fact, she painted the internet in curses and escapades as wild and colorful as the flowers that decorated her arm. Her bartending awards and the reputable journalism articles praising her skills were drowned out by her antics and threats memorialized in video and on social media.

Jaw-dropped, he continued to scroll, his mood settling somewhere in the basement. No wonder her family didn't trust her. This woman who wanted to be in charge of a vulnerable and historically significant family institution was unpredictable, unreliable, and desperate for the fanaticism of online fans.

Alex Torres encouraged the kind of attention he'd changed his name to avoid.

Exhausted and overwhelmed by what the new tenant meant for his found home, Jeremiah pulled up to Loretta's late that night. As he looked through the rain pounding his windshield, a rain that had worsened on his drive, a rain he would never have been out in if it wasn't for her, he was glad to at least see that the Open sign was off. Hopefully, at this late hour, she'd done him the courtesy of finishing her nightly ablutions in the bathroom they had to share and hiding herself away.

Knowing Alex, she probably was dancing a naked conga line on the bar.

That thought—and the irritating, unflagging, low-simmering enthusiasm of his little brain for a woman he did not trust or like—hampered his run up the back stairs to the second-floor entrance.

By the time he shouldered shut the back door that always stuck, his fedora, trench coat, and everything beneath it were soaked.

At least the hallway was quiet. The bathroom door was open and her door was closed.

He huffed out a relieved breath, then quickly made his way under the light of the bare bulb to the bathroom, weaving around a couple of buckets Mary had set out. The warped boards of the hallway didn't need any more water dripping on them.

He flipped on the bathroom light. And froze.

She'd spread her things all over their shared bathroom, then declared her claim by hanging a blue sapphire robe on his hook.

He yanked the door closed behind him. He stripped down to his bare feet, wet slacks, and muscle undershirt, trying to look at anything but the robe shimmering against the white tile. When his hand brushed silk as he reached for his towel, he gave in to temptation.

The short, sapphire-blue silk robe had a—he tilted his head, verified, then huffed out a breath—had a dragon embroidered on it. The dragon snaked around the blue background in threads of orange and yellow and red, fire shooting out of its snarling mouth.

He could see the short robe wrapped around her curves. He could see the silky blue against her brown skin, the tip of the orange-and-red fire licking her deep cleavage, the dragon's loopy tail coiling around her soft, thick, strong thighs as he stroked his hands up...

He tore off his glasses and scrubbed the towel across his face.

He needed to brush his teeth and flee.

Righting his glasses, he stalked to the fifties-era pedestal sink, wrenched on the hot tap, then glared at a pink jar of hand cream squashed in next to the soap. The jar's shiny pink lid was askew; its squat packaging and flowery script made it look like a hand cream Loretta would wear, not her fifty-years-younger granddaughter.

When he reached for the soap, he accidentally knocked the lid to the floor.

He resented even picking it up.

The scent rising from the soft pink cream when he reached for the jar to screw on the top was uncomfortably familiar.

Uncomfortable because the powdery rose scent provided so much comfort when it drifted off Loretta and Mary. But last night, on Alex, and this morning, this scent had been intriguing. Beckoning.

Sensual.

Jeremiah closed his eyes and took a helpless inhale now.

The sense memory of this soft, rosebud scent trailing off the unfettered woman was like holding one of her heavy rings to feel her residual warmth. Reading a deleted line of wistfulness from her social media. Or bracing for the kick of her black boots and instead feeling the stroke of silk and dragons.

This scent spoke of secrets he didn't understand about Alex Torres.

"What are you doing?"

Jeremiah's eyes startled open to see his reflection in the mirror. Standing there with his wet hair shoved back, muscle undershirt sticking to his chest, and soaked slacks, he'd been sniffing her hand cream.

He quickly screwed on the lid as Alex glared at him from the doorway, large lime-green headphones pulled down around her neck, a toothbrush in one hand, and a cosmetics bag in the other. She still wore her clothes from today, and her ugly cardigan was sliding off one shoulder, revealing the torn edge of her sleeveless T-shirt and the top of her flower-stroked arm.

His Adam's apple felt like a bowling ball. He put the jar back on the sink. "I'm sorry—"

"Don't touch my shit." Her dark eyes could crucify him.

He bristled. "I didn't want to. The lid wasn't on—"

"You don't close the bathroom door?" Her eyes narrowed and her hand curled into a fist she settled on her hip. "Or you think you can flaunt what you got and get another round with me? Unlikely, Mr. Quick-on-the-Draw."

He clenched his jaw. "Of course not," he said, disgusted. He'd never once, in his entire life, used his advantages to gain sex with a woman. In fact, he'd actively resisted having sex with anyone who didn't want him for his burly, over-educated, overenthusiastic self.

That's what had led him to make last night's now-regrettable decision: she'd wanted him only knowing how he looked in his piped flannel pajamas.

Now she thought she was seeing a hand-cream-sniffing deviant in the mirror. He'd spent the first two-thirds of his life being weighed and measured against an unfair reflection. He would never let someone do it again.

He grabbed his toothbrush. "I closed that door." He wanted to be done in here, done with her. Still, he muttered, "How do I know you didn't open it?"

"What?" She marched in, her big boots pounding off the tile. "You got something to say, professor, don't whisper like a little baby."

"Just let me finish," he said between gritted teeth. He put toothpaste on his toothbrush.

She sidled up to him. "You're taking too damn long." She actually tried to hip-check him to get to the small sink. The move looked ridiculous in the mirror; he easily outmeasured her by twelve inches and eighty pounds.

He raised his chin, held his ground, and met her eyes in the mirror as he put his toothbrush in his mouth and started brushing.

She stood close to his side, glaring and brushing as well. He could feel her scratchy cardigan against his bare bicep. If he breathed deep, he'd stroke the left half of her curves.

He leaned over and spit into the sink. "I was at the very

least hoping we could be mature about this forced living arrangement," he said, straightening and brushing again.

She pulled out her hot-pink toothbrush. It was a novelty brush with a tiny decal of Scooby-Doo. "Are you calling me immature?"

"Would you prefer 'uncivil'?" he said around the foam in his mouth.

She spit like it was his bad taste she was washing out. She bent over to rinse.

He saw the indent between the strong muscles in her nape. The black hair there was shaved close and looked soft. When she straightened, he realized the extravagant pomp she'd styled her hair into that morning had softened, and she had to tuck the curls behind her ear to keep it out of her face.

She stared hatred at him through eyes smudged with end-of-day makeup as she wiped her mouth with the back of her hand. "You know what? You should move out."

"What?"

"Yeah." Her full mouth curved slowly upward and raised a surprising level of panic in him. "You living here…it doesn't work for me. You need to find somewhere else to go."

She turned her back on him and began strolling out of the bathroom.

Go. Where would he go?

He'd tried living on the Dupen College campus, but the transitory nature of academia—the constantly changing faculty and students—had left him feeling like a man with a shovel floating in the ocean. He'd rented a small house in town but that had been worse. The four quiet walls had given him nothing to dig into.

Only at Loretta's had he found a home and a community and place where he could sink in roots and grow something meaningful and valuable.

He rinsed his mouth in the sink and wiped his face before he called, "You—" His voice was strangled. He cleared it. "You don't have the latitude to kick me out."

She looked over her shoulder and yawned. The flowers on her skin were as bright as that man-eating dragon on her robe. "Now or later, one way or the other, I'll get you gone." She smiled patronizingly. "Look, Dr. Fancy Pants, I'll give you a week to find another place."

She turned and stepped out into the hall, her hips swaying, as if the matter was settled.

As an awkward kid growing up in an intimidating home, he'd tried to hide in the shadows of the library to avoid his family's calm contempt and surgically precise insults. Hiding hadn't worked.

Alex's contempt was anything but calm—she was a tornado who had wrecked her last job and now threatened to tear apart his found home. And Jeremiah was no longer that little boy.

Shoving back his still-damp hair, he followed her out into the hall. "I looked you up," he said. "I wonder if your grandmother has seen Saturday night's video."

She stopped dead in her tracks.

The most valuable piece of information about Alex Torres he'd discovered during his online search was a video of her departure from her most recent job. She'd assaulted her boss behind the bar of an upscale Chicago speakeasy during a busy Saturday night in front of dozens of customers. She'd shoved him into a row of liquor, sending several of the bottles crashing explosively, then, when she'd noticed the camera recording, she'd raised up his shirt, exposed his belly, and blew a raspberry on it.

She'd looked directly into the camera, raised both middle fingers, and yelled, "That's right, motherfuckers, eyes on me." She'd looked unhinged. "Shit's about to get wild."

Then she'd run out, throwing kisses with her middle fingers. He imagined that video, shown to Loretta, would put Alex out of contention for the bar. She couldn't be trusted with the low-risk responsibility of mixing cocktails. She certainly couldn't be entrusted with preserving the heart home of a multigenerational family she didn't respect in a town she didn't even like.

Someone would be leaving. But it wouldn't be him.

As Alex turned slowly to glare at him, all laziness lost, he set his jaw and squared his broad shoulders. He'd been a late bloomer and hadn't gotten his height until the end of high school, his width until he'd focused on it in graduate school. He'd learned to minimize his body in certain settings—say, when he was in a poorly lit hallway alone with a woman— and to manage the aggression his size sometimes engendered.

But Alex Torres wanted to brawl.

"Is that a threat?" she asked with a pugnacious thrust of her sharp chin. The hallway's bare bulb struck sparks in her eyes.

"I won't be bullied by someone who's using her family for personal gain," he said, lowering his face toward hers. "Even the best b-word in bartending would have a hard time finding work after Saturday night's display."

"C'mon professor, call me a bitch," she said, eyes flashing. "You want to talk about personal gain? Having a bunch of Mexicans as your lab monkeys sure will help with that tenure you brag about."

He straightened, feeling flames race up to the tips of his ears. "I— You— Your— I would never!" he finally got out.

She smiled cruelly at his stammering. Her lightning-flash eyes, her full mouth, her bobbing black hair…she was laughing at him.

He never lost his temper. He never made anyone else lose

theirs. He clenched his jaw and channeled every centimeter of his height and breadth into looming over her.

"You clearly don't appreciate this town, this bar, or your family. Why did you leave?"

Her smile dropped like a plate crashing. Anger tensed her body, causing the scratchy cardigan to fall to her elbow, displaying a plethora of blue, pink, and orange flowers over a strong, flexed bicep.

She raised her hand and rapped her rings against his sternum. "That's none of your fucking business," she snarled. "Why're you so desperate to hang on to a room over a dive bar in the ass-end of a dying town?"

Because he was lonely. Because he had no family of his own. Because he liked the way her people treated him like the six-by-four-foot space he occupied had value.

He grabbed her wrist to stop her knuckles from knocking a hole through his damp undershirt. "I could say the same thing—that's none of your damn business."

She tried to yank her wrist free. "What in the fuck could the east side offer a Richie Rich like you except a science experiment?" When he didn't let go, she raised her other bejeweled hand and banged him with those knuckles.

He grabbed that wrist, too. "Stop it," he demanded, glaring into her eyes. His ribs were going to bear the bruise of a skull ring. "You don't know me. Stop assuming the worst intentions."

"You stop it," she snapped back, bouncing up onto her toes to launch her words into his face. "The only thing you know about me is that I'm a great lay."

Oh. No.

He was restraining her. Handcuffing her wrists. Under her grandmother's roof.

He needed to let go. He needed to apologize.

What he really wanted to do was drag her closer.

His blood was pumping fast, making him swelter inside his own skin. He felt like his marrow was simmering.

He'd never been this exhilarated in his life.

Still holding her silky wrists, standing inches from the succulent curves of her body, he met her eyes. The bare bulb brought out the black ring of her pupils, the rich sienna brown. She didn't look away from his stare and she was breathing fast, exhaling soft huffs of minty breath between open, ripe lips. They were steps from a bed in a building where not another soul stirred. He could feel the heat pulsing off of her. She smelled like scattered flower petals.

He opened his mouth and inhaled deep.

Her thick lashes went heavy over her slopey, sexy eyes.

He eased his grip on her wrists but didn't let go, and she didn't pull away, relaxing the back of her hands against his chest.

The thunder of his heart beneath her hands could match the storm outside.

"Are you sure you want to live in a haunted building?" she said, low and slow. He watched her full lips move around the words more than he heard them.

"This building isn't haunted."

"Yes, it is," she replied. He didn't even try to hide his fascination as his eyes trailed over her face. "You know it is." She had thick, dark, perfectly shaped eyebrows. "You already sensed it—the creaks and the cold spots and the sense of being watched but you turn around and no one's there." The bridge of her nose was wide and had a ball at the tip. "You probably don't deal with the really irritating stuff: stuck faucets, furniture moving, tripping over nothing, light bulbs shattering." Her cheeks were prone to curve up into balls, too. "He likes white people. Especially rich white people."

Her skin glowed and she had a tiny beauty mark right where a dimple would be.

"Who?" he asked.

"The old guero who doesn't like a bunch of brown people in his building. Wayland Hugh." She met his eyes and said the words distinctly. "The man who built the building. He's the ghost."

Jeremiah needed to snap out of his haze. He held his breath for a second, tried to think without the smell of her. He knew a little about Wayland Hugh, a town founder who'd built his family's fortune here on the east side. How often had the toe of his loafer traced the man's name and *Hugh Apothecary* on the panel in the bar?

He frowned. "That's ridiculous."

"Yes," she said, drawing the word out so he felt it across the hard muscles of his stomach. "It's also true. Ask anyone in my family. Loretta never talks about it with the tenants. If word got around, who would rent the rooms?"

Lonely, gullible, horny history professors?

As if reading his mind, Alex smiled, those cheeks curving up. Her lashes were so lush he wanted to tickle his nose across them. She'd gone impossibly soft in his hold. "Don't you know, professor, things are a lot weirder in small towns than Andy Griffith and the Beaver would have you believe. You gotta've heard the rumors about all the weird crap in Freedom."

The stories that were true were strange enough: Freedom, with its oil-rich lands that had quickly gone dry, was once the summer playground of millionaires. A hometown boy turned Pulitzer-Prize-winning playwright had founded Dupen College. There was decent evidence that Freedom was the site of Quivera, the place Coronado searched for in his quest for cities with gold-paved streets. A mass-murdering family—one of the first recorded—had lived just outside of the town limits.

Jeremiah had heard of the millionaires that haunted the town's rotting mansions, La Llorona who cried along the Viridescent River, the crop circles and the jersey devil and the ghost truck and the thing that supposedly swam in the nearby lake.

But this...

"My family believes we go to Communion and put the actual body of Christ in our mouths." She looked up at him from under her thick, long lashes and swiped her tongue across her full bottom lip, making it shine.

Jeremiah's hands spasmed on her wrists, and Alex smiled wider.

She was doing it on purpose, her softening and her slow speech descending into a low drawl and her eyes and her lips and the way she said "body" and "mouth."

She was doing it for him. To him.

"The fact that we deal with a racist ghost is just not that interesting," she said with a lazy shrug of one naked shoulder.

He breathed slowly through his nose and raised his chin to look down at her. "I don't care if there is a ghost. I'm not leaving."

Her smile didn't waver. But he could feel her firm in his hands. "You've inspired me, professor. I'm not leaving either."

She slowly moved her wrists out from between their bodies, bringing his hands with them, widening his arms, and stepped in, gently pressing her breasts against him as she raised her chin, all but offering him her mouth.

"I don't care what I have to do," she breathed, gut-wrenchingly alluring as her eyes stroked his lips before meeting his helpless gaze. "You're not getting your hands on this place."

She was teasing him with all that he wasn't going to get his hands on.

He dropped her wrists. He stepped back from her then stalked to his door, shoved it open and slammed it closed behind him.

"Professor," she called, muffled, from the hallway. "You left all your stuff in the bathroom."

"I'll get it later," he shouted through the wood.

Discretion was the better part of valor and all.

Her laughter was her only response as he heard her open the door to her room.

He closed his eyes and breathed. Then startled when he heard a knock on the wall.

"'Night, professor," he heard, quiet but distinct.

The squeak of her ancient iron bedstead, shoved up against the wall like his own, was as clear as a bell as she settled on it.

He was never going to sleep again.

Chapter Six

Several days later, Alex grit her teeth into a smile as she re-filled her tíos' coffee cups for the fourth time while repeating to herself the order for three tables and balancing twenty pounds of dirty dishes in a bus bin on her hip.

"You let my coffee get so cold, I keep thinking I'm drinking that fancy ice coffee, niña," her great-uncle Martín said as he held out his cup. "No tips for the lazy."

Considering the change Martín had left her since Monday had barely amounted to a dollar, she wouldn't be missing out on much, she wanted to growl.

In Chicago, she would have. Without a pause. And a group of twenty-somethings would have howled and laughed and asked for selfies with her. The world expected an angry brown woman, and Alex had let it pay her rent.

But the other night's dust-up with the dude she was sharing a wall with inspired her to bite her tongue. Whenever she'd been tempted to mouth off over the last several days, she zeroed all her rage on his accusation: *I won't be bullied by someone who's using her family for personal gain.*

He'd accused *her* of using her family for personal gain when he threatened to tattle on her so he could turn Loretta's into a rich, white man's petting zoo.

You clearly don't appreciate this town, this bar, or your family.

Like his year of living above the bar trumped her twenty-nine years of being a Torres.

Focusing all her anger on the too-big, too-wealthy, too-white guy who tossed and turned too much on the other side of the wall had made it easier for Alex to be nice. Or at least, show Loretta—who was sitting at a table in line of sight of the tíos—that she was trying to be nice.

Alex lifted the coffeepot in an effort to wave back at her two cousins and their four little ones as they were kissing Loretta goodbye. She glanced at the disaster area of their table and could feel her smile turn into bared teeth.

"Leave Alex alone," Eddie scolded Martín quietly from the other side of the table. Eddie wasn't related, but he was so close with her family that he might as well have been.

Alex came around to his side of the table to refill his cup. "Just for that, you get free mozzarella sticks."

He patted his firm belly. "They're hell on my cholesterol. But I'll eat 'em." She didn't know how he found the time, spending so much time at Loretta's, but Eddie kept himself in better shape than the rest of the tíos. He was Black, with a full head of closely trimmed pure-white hair and a neat beard that was new since the last time she'd seen him.

He picked up his cup. "You need to get yourself some help."

Alex blew out an exhausted breath as she looked around.

Her mother was taking the order for the last lunch table willing to brace the continued rain. The several tables that had been filling up for lunch and dinner over the last few days would have been effortless for Alex to juggle at any other bar. But it was more difficult when every table needed hugs and kisses, a rundown of Alex's life, information about whether she had a boyfriend, and time to tease her about her tattoos, retell a favorite memory of her misbehavior, then poke and prod her twenty different ways to get to the bottom of why she was back in Freedom.

Loretta's had a new attraction and everyone in her family was coming to see it.

Alejandra is working at the bar!! was the news making the gossip grapevine run red-hot.

Why? What happened? And most importantly: *What did she do?*

With her grandmother studying her every move, Alex couldn't snap that it wasn't anyone's damn business.

Their lunch and dinner rushes were temporary. As soon as family had wrung Alex dry for info, Loretta's would go back to its "can't-pay-its-bills" ways. She'd been spending her nights in the office while the professor and his shoulders took up too much room at the bar, and she'd been shocked by what she'd found.

With the coffee cup at his lip, Eddie nodded at Loretta.

"How's your Granmo doing?" he said, muffling the words behind his cup and the overhead blare of synth and trumpets from Espejismo, Loretta's favorite Tejano band. Alex had added wiring the building with decent sound and trashing the hundred Tejano cassettes from the '70s and '80s that were Loretta's soundtrack to her infinite to-do list.

"She's doing fine," Alex told him. "Ornery."

"Let me know if she needs anything," he said quietly. The guys would razz him endlessly if they knew he was asking about their sister and cousin.

"She's got to let me know first," Alex replied.

She watched Loretta, who was dressed in a soft rose blouse and artificial pearl earrings, squeeze one of the grandkids close, totally unconcerned about the amount of ketchup all over the little kid's...everywhere.

The day after their confrontation, her Granmo had hob-

bled in from the back entrance using her walker, taken a seat
at a table, shrugged off questions about how she was feeling,
and barked instructions at Alex like Alex had never been recruited, wined, and dined (and felt up, before a finger was
broken) by the owner of one of the top ten clubs in Vegas.

Tip those beer mugs so they don't get so much foam.

Mijita, table 4 needs a refill. Did you forget about them?

Remember to wash your hands!

Loretta's pointed annoyance with her was almost better
than the moments when her grandmother went quiet, obviously in pain but denying it. Mary kept meeting Alex's gaze
with a big, forced smile, although she clearly wasn't happy.
And Alex hadn't been able to get ahold of her sisters since
they'd left. Their radio silence meant that Alex had to fake
enough enthusiasm for the three of them.

They were one big happy family.

With the edge of the heavy bin etching a permanent indent into Alex's hip, she hustled off, trying to remember if
her tías at table 9 wanted cheese on their burgers.

By the time her favorite cousin strolled in, shaking rain
off his canvas coat and hanging it on the coatrack that created a puddle and a slipping hazard right at the entrance, the
tables were back in order and her aunts were chowing down
on burgers that they, indeed, wanted with cheese.

Alex came out from underneath the bar to hug one of the
few people in Freedom she legitimately wanted to hug.

"Joe!" she cried as her cousin squeezed her in a bear hug
and rocked her on her feet.

Joe Torres was the oldest of all the cousins, the oldest son of
Loretta's firstborn, and he could have been a real prick about
it. Instead, he'd always watched out for all of them while allowing Alex to drag him into trouble. Now in his midthir-

ties, he was a successful contractor with the soul of an artist who never wanted to call anywhere but Freedom home.

The former state wrestling champ was five-ten, broad-shouldered, and built beneath his tucked-in plaid flannel shirt and jeans. He had dark skin and a wide bridge like hers, pretty hazel eyes like Sissy's, and thick black wavy hair he trimmed short. Joe's confident-but-kind brand of caretaking manliness would have slayed no matter where he was, but in Freedom, it meant that women had been throwing themselves at him since he could walk.

He had always made Alex feel interesting. And supported.

She squeezed him hard now before she let go. "Can I get you a beer?"

"Yeah." He glanced at Loretta. "Hang on."

Joe went over to kiss and check in with their Granmo while Alex ducked back under the bar and grabbed a jelly jar.

Every person in their family knew that you kissed and greeted the elders when you arrived at a place. It was a commandment. You gave thanks. You valued their presence because you never knew how long you were going to have it.

She filled the jar with Bud Light. "Your boss okay with you day drinking?" she asked as he walked back to the bar on steel-toed work boots.

"Let me check." He took his phone out of his back pocket. "Boss, you okay if I have a beer?" He switched the phone to the other ear. "Sure. Have two."

The joke shouldn't have made her laugh, but it did.

Torres Construction was the top construction firm in town.

She gave him a beer with a pretty head of foam. "How's it goin'?"

"Good." He toasted the picture of their Granpo Salvador and took a drink. The bulb in the front corner lamp flared then futzed out. They both ignored it. "Actually, Alejandra, I wanted to talk to you. You have a minute?"

He glanced over his shoulder at their grandmother, then signaled to the other side of the four-sided bar. Mystified, Alex followed him around the island.

She popped herself a cold Topo Chico while he settled on a bar stool.

"So... I'm on the board of the Freedom Historical Society."

She choked on her sparkling water. "No you're not."

His thick black brows scrunched over his eyes. "Yes, I am. Why wouldn't I be?"

"Because you're too—"

"Mexican?" he said, giving her that direct, hard-jawed look she'd seen him give members of the Hugh clan trying to fuck with their family.

She put down her bottle and waved him off. "Don't look at me like that. You're too young. Something called the Historical Society is for stick-up-his-ass guys in sweater vests."

"I build here, which means I also tear down. What I'm tearing down is important to me. What I'm building on top of means something, too."

He took a drink and so did Alex, giving herself a beat to think it through. Usually, she didn't mind pissing off her family. But she'd didn't want to be at odds with Joe.

"So..." She ran her hand over the short hairs at the back of her head. "Do you know about this plan to buy the bar?" She shook her head at him. "To turn it into a museum?"

"I hear you're not a fan," Joe said with enough sarcasm to host his own show. "Jeremiah said y'all didn't get off on the best foot."

Joe and the professor.

Her unwanted neighbor had just leveled up.

"He told me you and your sisters want to buy the building and take over the bar," Joe said carefully. "That came as a surprise."

"Why?"

He drank his beer and stared at her over the glass.

She could feel her chin jutting out.

It was a surprise because, until a few days ago, not one of the Armstead girls showed any inclination to return to town or any desire to be responsible for the bar.

It was a surprise because Joe knew that Alex spoke to him with an occasional text or phone call more than she talked to her sisters.

"Why y'all want to take over this place?" Joe asked.

"Is that my cousin asking or a guy working undercover for our competition?" She kept herself from rubbing a pang behind her breastbone.

"Hey." He reached across the bar to squeeze her fingers. "You know it's not like that."

"Dr. Dork thinks he's better than me."

"I doubt you did much to make friends."

"Make friends?" She yanked her hand from his hold. Joe might be her blood. But men always sided with men. "Why do I need to be nice to him? He wants to steal my family bar from me so he can turn it into a place where he pushpins all the Mexicans onto a board like we're dead butterflies for people to gawk at?"

"All of this came as a surprise," Joe said. "Granmo's fall, the development company's offer on the building, her willingness to sell… Jeremiah came to me and this was the best idea we could come up with quick. We didn't know you and the girls were also hatching a plan."

Alex hated that when he said "we," he was talking about him and the professor.

"But, the research on our family and Milagro Street and

the Mexican-Americans who've lived here for generations...
Alex, that's me and Tía Ofelia." Joe patted his chest. Alex
could hear the pride in the thump. "We've been working
on that."

Tía Ofelia was their mom's youngest sister and a popular
high school English teacher adored by her nieces and neph-
ews like a rock star.

"I told him about it a couple of years ago, and I was the
one who mentioned the vacant tenant room. He's focused the
historical society on telling our story, and he's connected us
with a Mexican-American professor at Drake University in
Iowa who's writing a book about a longtime Mexican community there but, Alejandra, he's following our lead. We're
the ones telling the story. Not him."

Alex dropped her eyes to the gleaming mahogany of the
bar as a Mexican grito wailed through the speakers. "So he's
got you wrapped around his finger, too," she said.

After the first night when the professor had stayed away
until late, he'd been making a point of coming home to
Loretta's early, taking up too much space at the bar and soaking up too much of her family's fawning attention as he ate
the meal that Loretta cooked for him. Alex ignored him during the dinner rush then, fed up with the smiles her grandmother and mother gave him that totally disappeared when
they looked at Alex, she'd take herself upstairs to dig out her
grandmother's desk from the piles of paper.

The number of unpaid bills in the piles were staggering.

But it was the unpaid taxes that truly scared her.

Before her favorite cousin came in declaring that he was in
cahoots with her enemy, Alex might have shared with him
what she'd discovered in the office. Instead, she said, "What's
happened to Loretta's, Joe? The roof's leaking, I'm terrified
the kitchen won't pass code the next time the inspector comes

through, basic maintenance isn't getting done." She motioned to the duct-taped pass-through. "This shit can't be blamed on Old Man Hugh. I'm surprised everyone let it get this bad."

Joe looked embarrassed. "You know how Granmo is. She insists on paying for work. And lately, when we offer, she says she doesn't need it."

Because she can't afford it, Alex thought.

"You keep her back turned and I'll take care of the pass-through before I leave," he mumbled.

Alex finally had an inkling why her grandmother thought selling the building was her only option.

"I don't know why you girls want this place," Joe said. "But I told Jeremiah that it was Granmo's decision. I'm not going to get involved."

Twenty pounds of tension dropped off her shoulders. She hated the idea of being on the opposite side of Joe. And she could never defeat the combined powers of the professor's goofy charm and her favorite cousin's goodness.

"That being said, he's a decent guy, Alex." Joe gave her his shiny, cajoling smile. She'd seen panties drop at that smile. "You should give him a chance."

Hell no.

"The chance to turn the bar into a museum? No offense, but it's not gonna happen. You say he's not appropriating our story for his own glory, and that's great. But what's he doing slumming it over here on the east side? Why isn't Mr. Rolex living on the west side with the Hughs and the other town bigwigs?"

Joe just shrugged. "I don't know, he doesn't talk too much about himself. But I get you don't trust him. You're protective of Granmo and this place. Thing is, so is he." He tipped his smug, handsome, oldest-cousin face at her. "Looks like y'all have something in common."

She rolled her eyes, but grabbed a jar and poured herself a beer, taking a midday break to catch up with Joe. She didn't want to keep arguing with him about how she had nothing in common with that too-big, too-rich, too-smart, life's-too-easy hand-cream sniffer.

His accusation that she was "using" her family when she'd thought he was the actual user had helped fuel her determination to claim the bar and keep it out of his hands. Now she knew that the professor's goal wasn't to turn the Hugh Building into a place where her family was displayed like specimens on a slide. Fine.

That didn't change the fact that the building was going to be hers. Even if the bar she envisioned looked unrecognizable from the current Loretta's, even if Alex planned to parlay the bar's inevitable success into a job and a plane ticket out of town, at least when she was done with it, it would continue to be a bar.

She still had plenty of reasons to steer clear of him. The fact that her pussy had shouted, "That!" when Dr. Feelgood had gripped her close in the hallway—his gold-green-brown eyes sparking temper and his soaked muscle tank showcasing his massive chest—was one of the main ones.

The clear creak of the old Hugh Building had made it easy to avoid him in the bathroom and hallway. But the building worked against her in her room, where the paper-thin wall between their bed frames made it seem like they were sleeping in one bed. She could hear the squeak of springs every time that hulking body turned over, feel the shimmy over her mattress. The heavy iron bed frame weighed a ton, but she'd managed to move it a couple of inches from the wall. When she woke up the next day, her bed was pressed back against it. The old creepy guero. When a hole in the blackout shade woke her too early with a shaft of light—goddamned guero—and she'd sleepily put her hand between her thighs imagining it was the professor's cleft chin, she'd been annoyed, shocked, and orgasmically thrilled to hear the repetitive squeak of the bed frame in the next room.

She'd finished before he had, then leapt to her knees to pound on the wall.

Having a good time, professor?

He was doing all he could to make her life hell.

As she chatted with her favorite cousin who'd declared himself a fan of Team Nerd, Alex was going to make sure she returned the favor.

Chapter Seven

Loretta closed the bar on Sunday so she and the other older aunts could serve up what sounded like an epic meal at her house to the family. People stayed and mingled and napped, Jeremiah had heard, while the kids ran around outside.

Although Loretta and Mary sometimes made him feel like an adopted son, Jeremiah still hadn't gotten an invite to Sunday dinner.

His meals at one of Main Street's four restaurants were generally less depressing than a Sunday evening meal on campus, when students were panicking over their unfinished assignments and faculty were dining with their families, but still his choices weren't great. He had to pick between the last, limping-along survivor of a long-gone pizza chain, an okay barbecue joint, a family-style restaurant that seemed to change ownership once a year, and the awesome-but-heartburn-inducing Johnny's Hamburger Stand.

This Sunday, with the ceaseless rain, unrelenting cold, and the early darkness brought on by thick, gray clouds, his bachelor's meal at Rickey's BBQ Pit could have been absolutely dismal.

Instead, sitting alone at a table against the rain-struck window looking out on Main Street, Jeremiah was glad for the day away from Loretta and her family.

He needed a break from Alex Torres.

She was like a slap of tar over the bar. She'd tarnished what was familiar and comforting, made it alien and unsettling. Her fumes were toxic, and yet he couldn't help but breathe her in.

Every time he stepped into Loretta's, she went right to his head.

He was usually confronted with her caustic remarks or pointed dismissal right away as she poured drinks, waited on tables, chatted effortlessly with family members as if she wasn't trying to ruinously change the place, and repeatedly bent over in bottom-defining jeans that lured Jeremiah's attention like fireflies.

Even when she hid herself in the office, even when he escaped to the college, he found her rose-scented fumes in his clothes. His hair. His hands. His every thought.

At work, he unwillingly daydreamed about her with equal parts frustration and fascination. In his car, he found himself arguing with the air, readying cutting remarks or revising conversations with quick and witty rejoinders.

In his bed, he lived the torture of all but sleeping with her. Her odd hours allowed him to fall asleep without the sense of her beside him. But the thin wall and the squeal of the old bedstead meant that, in the middle of the night, first thing in the morning, he heard her every movement, felt her fulsome body's every shift. He'd tried to relieve some of the tension early one morning. But she'd taunted him in his mind— full naked thighs and bright silky robe, the dimples of her butt in his hands, the hug of her warm wet vagina, the gorgeous ecstasy on her face—then taunted him with her mouth: *Having a good time, professor?*

He laboriously pushed his bed from the wall that morning. But when he returned that night, his bed was back in place.

Since a weekly dusting was part of his room rate, he imagined Mary had moved it. She'd hung a milagro of a dove holding an olive branch on his door.

As if peace were possible when one was haunted by the flagrantly rude, endlessly insulting, flamboyant, determined, straight-charging, sensual, lush, and ripe Alex Torres.

The only thing you know about me is that I'm a great lay.

An elderly waitress appeared to take his order.

Only the drape of the red-and-white-gingham tablecloth covered his tented khakis.

He shoved closer to the table, ordered, then gave a sharp nod and a forced smile to a city councilwoman dining with her Pentecostal pastor husband and their six children on the other side of the restaurant.

He hadn't been this out of control of his body and mind since he'd been a heterosexually inclined fourteen-year-old boy at an all-boys boarding school regularly receiving pornographic photos from strangers.

Cognitive calisthenics, he berated himself as he took long, cooling gulps of his iced tea. He'd been getting up earlier, running further, working out harder. Now his brain just had to do those same push-ups. He needed to shove away thoughts about one angry, luscious bartender until the muscles were strengthened and the move was effortless.

He looked through the front window and the evening rain to focus on Main Street, that dividing line between the east and west sides. The difference between the two was negligible compared to the kind of wealth he'd grown up with. But even with the gloom of the rain and the glaring *Close-Out Sale. All Must Go!* sign across the street, a quick glance proved that Main Street was faring better than Milagro Street. Retail and offices kept Main Street's four-block-long string of neoclassical and Classic Revival buildings at an okay occupancy rate. The street was anchored by the pretty Carnegieendowed library on one end and the Art-Deco-styled city hall on the other, and a billionaire-funded soda counter and movie theater kept it active after business hours.

On Milagro Street's two blocks, the few nineteenth- and early twentieth-century brick buildings not boarded up or condemned had businesses that barely limped along; the owners had Loretta's to thank for the customers they were able to drum up.

Jeremiah believed the historical society's plan for the Hugh Building could change that. That's what was so frustrating about Alex treating him like a bucket of rancid cooking oil.

The Freedom Historical Society had always planned on locating the Freedom Museum on Milagro Street. Its rich cultural past, historic buildings, cheap real estate, and plentiful parking made it a slam dunk. They also hoped that anchoring a historical museum there that told a little-known but significant aspect of American history would help re-energize the economically depressed east side. Far-off dreams included renovating the beautiful-but-shuttered train depot across the street from Loretta's into a community space, restoring some of the buildings like the one that housed the Spanish-language newspaper, and restarting some of the businesses—the tienda, the bakery, even the three-story hotel on the opposite end of Milagro Street.

The fact that the museum would be part of his portfolio for tenure was incidental. Jeremiah fundamentally believed their plan could benefit Loretta's family, the east side, the entire town of Freedom, long-standing Mexican-American communities throughout the Central Plains, and, ultimately, all citizens who had limited their understanding of what made an American.

Alex's plan would benefit Alex.

Under reasonable circumstances, he would have offered to

show her the excellent slideshow presentation he'd put together about the museum. But nothing was reasonable about
her determination to turn her back on her family, hometown,
and history in favor of currying "likes" from strangers on social media. Joe Torres, his fellow board member and friend,
had been shocked the Armstead sisters wanted the building.
Loretta and Mary were still suspicious of her. Instead of using
Jeremiah's name, Alex continued to mock him with childish nicknames about his career, his financial status, and his
rapid orgasm.

There was no reason that she continued to fascinate him.

"Professor Post," a voice boomed behind him, startling him
out of his Alex-induced fog. He slammed his thigh against
the underside of the table, slopping iced tea onto the ging-
ham surface. He quickly grabbed paper towels off the roll in
the center and sopped up the mess.

He had the cognitive push-up ability of the brown, dripping clump in his hand.

"Smooth move," the man jeered, chuckling, as he came into
view.

Jeremiah's hackles went up as he finished wiping up the tea.

"Looks like this seat is empty." Beneath the dripping rain-
coat that he flung onto an unoccupied table, the fit man wore
a sleek gray suit. It was a bit much for a Sunday night dinner
at Rickey's BBQ Pit. He pulled out the chair on the other
side of Jeremiah's table and sat.

"Thank God for keto, am I right?" he said, waving at the
occupied waitress until she had no choice but to immediately
come over. "Get me ribs and brisket. And a beer. Make sure
to put his order on my bill. You want a beer, Jer?" His blue
eyes looked at Jeremiah for less than a second before he dismissed him with a wave. "He wants a beer. Actually, bring
us a bucket of beers."

The waitress scooped up the sodden paper towels and hurried away as the man settled a designer shoe on his knee and sat back in his seat. His blond hair was gelled into a swoop back from his forehead. "Sundays, am I right, Jer? A man needs to take a load off."

Jeremiah felt the flush crawling up his neck as he stared at the head of Freedom Rings Development, a man he absolutely did not want to share a meal with.

"Mr. Dutimeyer," he said, exhaling through his nose. "I would prefer you call me Jeremiah. Or Dr. Post."

Lance Dutimeyer's toothy smile didn't flicker. "Sure, no problem, professor." He leaned forward. "You make sure to call me Lance."

The derisive nickname reminded him—again—of Alex. Jeremiah had never had his hard-earned degree used against him so relentlessly.

"Mr. Dutimeyer, what are you doing here?"

The waitress put a silver pail filled with ice and beer bottles on the table. Dutimeyer leisurely lifted one out of the ice, popped the top, and took a long drink. He never moved his eyes off Jeremiah.

Jeremiah had been dealing with far-superior bullies longer than Dutimeyer had been alive.

"You and I got off on the wrong foot," Lance drawled, motioning expansively with the bottle. "It's easy to see why you'd be intimidated by me—Freedom's top developer must seem like a natural-born enemy to the head of the historical society. Predator to prey. But there's no reason it's gotta be like that."

Jeremiah channeled his brother's glacial look. "Freedom Rings is not Freedom's top developer."

"Yet," the man said, greedy grin growing.

It was the same grin he'd been directing at Loretta, an

elderly woman a week out of the hospital, when Jeremiah found him gripping her hand while three large men in suits surrounded them. Now, Dutimeyer thought he'd trapped Jeremiah here with his dominating entrance, grin meant to intimidate, and a bucket of beers. Jeremiah might as well use it to his advantage.

"Why is Freedom Rings purchasing abandoned properties on the east side?" he asked.

Dutimeyer's smile didn't waver. But his eyes flickered like a shark's.

After meeting Dutimeyer and his flunkies, Jeremiah had spent the afternoon in the city clerk's office looking up property records. There, he found that Freedom Rings Development had been quietly scooping up abandoned buildings on Milagro Street and foreclosed homes in the surrounding eastside neighborhood where Loretta and Mary lived.

The fact that the properties were empty was why the development company had been able to keep the dirt-cheap purchases quiet in this gossip-rich town.

"We're doing our civic duty," Dutimeyer said, opening another beer.

He offered it to Jeremiah, who shook his head.

"Watching your girlish figure?" Dutimeyer smirked, leaning back in his chair.

His eyes grew crueler when Jeremiah didn't rise to the bait. "The east side's a shithole," he declared. "Let's get rid of some of those eyesores. Build a few properties that'll make that side less of a blight on the whole town. That's why I want to buy the Hugh Building. Bring it back into the family fold, wash out the trash, then put the Hugh shine back on it."

Jeremiah squeezed his fists in his lap to keep the disgust from showing on his face.

Dutimeyer's father came from Texas ranchers, but his

mother was a Hugh. The Hughs' declining fortunes since the days Wayland Hugh had built his wealth on the success of Miracle Street—then abandoned the street when it became Milagro—hadn't diminished their willingness to throw around their name.

The mayor's office had been saddled with one ineffective Hugh descendant after another for decades.

Dutimeyer's branch had over-ranched their land. Lance Dutimeyer, who Jeremiah discovered had been a poor student, a blue-ribbon county fair winner, and a grade-A bigot, was now determined to make his own fortune with his daddy's remaining money.

"I'm no expert," Dutimeyer said, waving his beer bottle around, "but putting a museum over on the east side seems like you want to flush your good idea right down the poopchute. Tourists aren't gonna wanna deal with that element over there."

Jeremiah felt like steam was coming out his ears.

He was getting sick and tired of his extremity of emotions.

Dutimeyer leaned back in his seat and took a deep drink. Finally, he said, "But I like you, professor. You want a museum? I'll give you a museum." He tipped his bottle toward the window. "You tell Loretta you're no longer interested in the Hugh Building and I'll get you something right here on Main Street. Prime location. Right in the thick of things. Put up a nice plaque thanking Freedom Rings Development, then you can keep all your money for exhibits and whatever."

Dutimeyer's hammer-hard blue eyes belied his good ol' boy tone.

Jeremiah gaped at him. "Why would you do that?"

"Just doing my civic duty." Dutimeyer finished off his beer. "You're going to want to jump on this bandwagon, professor. I'm looking to make a big impression."

The waitress arrived with their plates. As Jeremiah watched Dutimeyer flip his silk tie over his shoulder and pick up his knife and fork, he wondered if the infamous "plant" rumor was starting to have more than coffee-shop whispers and city council prayers behind it.

Freedom, the county seat of ten thousand souls, was dying for the same reason many small towns throughout the Midwest were dying: the collapse of manufacturing, the dearth of new opportunities, public educators forced to do more with fewer resources, and a conservative state leadership more focused on maintaining their moral agenda than doing the hard work of bringing jobs to their communities. The last remaining manufacturing employer, Liberty Manufacturing, had downsized drastically since its heyday and was struggling to stay alive.

The only reason Freedom still had its downtown theater and its soda counter at the Rexall, its stellar hospital and its thriving Parks and Recreation budget was because of the town's benefactress, billionaire Roxanne Medina. She'd grown up here and stayed engaged because of her connection to the charismatic priest of St. Paul's Catholic Church. She and her family even visited every so often, which lured die-hard fans to town in hopes of a glimpse. The going-out-of-business gift shop across the street had stocked itself with billion-dollar-bill tissue packs, fake plastic crowns, and stand-up cutouts of Roxanne Medina and her husband, the king of a small Spanish principality.

Jeremiah had always rejected the rumor that the billionaire was going to save Freedom with a new manufacturing plant. He knew from experience that the altruism of the wealthy only went so far.

Now, Dutimeyer's greed cloaked in generosity made him

wonder if he was missing something at the many city government meetings he attended.

Dutimeyer pointed his knife at him. "You and me, we're smart men. We know how the world works. Some people are winners, and some—they're just losers, am I right? I pledged Sigma Chi. You?"

Jeremiah just shook his head.

He saw the first flare of annoyance in Dutimeyer's smug gaze. The man stabbed his meat and began to saw. "Let me get you a membership to the country club. Introduce you to the right kind of people."

"I don't have any desire to—"

Dutimeyer's knife made a sharp clack against the plasticware beneath it. "Look," he spat. "This is going to turn out best for you if we're friends."

Jeremiah's ears were red, and his knuckles were clenched white under the table. He wouldn't mind if this altercation turned physical. He pulled a trick he'd learned from the woman harassing his thoughts: he raised his chin and gave Dutimeyer a stony glare.

Rather than inciting him, Dutimeyer's gaze turned calculating. He rested his suited forearms on the tablecloth, both utensils pointing at Jeremiah. "I looked you up, professor," he said, low. "Couldn't find out much about you before your grad school days." He leaned over his plate. "It's like you sprang to life when you turned twenty-one."

Dread sprinkled over Jeremiah.

Dutimeyer got back to sawing. "Couldn't find much about your family or where you grew up," he said in a normal speaking voice. "Where was that again?"

He was grateful Rickey's BBQ Pit was sparsely filled. He didn't want other people latching on to Dutimeyer's curiosity. For the last five years, he'd been trying to make friends and build a home in this town. He was the only one who knew he'd been doing it from hiding.

The pleasure of his bomb landing showed in Dutimeyer's self-satisfied smile.

"You know I'm right, genius," he said, swallowing and taking a triumphant drink of his beer. "This is gonna work out best for you if we're friends."

A slam against the window made them jump. Jeremiah looked out and saw Alex Torres standing in a figure-hugging jean jacket as rain cascaded down her. She glared accusingly at him through the glass as mascara streamed down her cheeks in inky lines.

Chapter Eight

Standing in the downpour sheeting off the building, Alex stared through the window, stunned. She couldn't believe her eyes. It was like seeing a ghost.

Dr. Dickhead was having dinner with fucking Doodymeyer.

Enraged, she hauled back and banged the window again. But the glass was too hard, too slick, too resilient. She wanted to sink her fist into flesh.

She turned and charged for the door.

At Sunday dinner, where Alex finally had the opportunity to inhale her weight in her grandmother's sopa and frijoles, Mary had offered to let her store all the stuff overfilling her single room in the family's garage. When Alex declined, her mom had flinched back and her Granmo had given her a look of pursed-lip disapproval.

Alex had put her head down and grabbed another tortilla.

Mary had made a choice about letting her husband back in her life. Alex had made one, too. Why couldn't her grandmother understand that? Her dad hadn't made any unexpected appearances during the week, but he didn't need to be around to make Alex's life more difficult.

Alex had been going it on her own for thirteen years, and she definitely hadn't wanted this long-term layover in her hometown to change that. But she'd been driving back from the self-storage complex on the edge of town with plans to throw herself a good pity party when she'd glimpsed them through the restaurant window. She'd braked hard in the middle of Main Street.

Goddamn them! Of course, the professor and Doody-meyer were pals. Rich, white, and entitled; they had so much in common.

She'd screeched her car into a parking space determined to...to...

The one thing Alex was good at was delivering punishment.

She stormed inside the restaurant and toward them.

"I knew it," she yelled, flinging her arm and splattering them with rain. "I knew you were a piece of shit."

Jeremiah shot up platter-sized hands. "It's not what it looks like." His rich brown hair fell onto his forehead. He was wearing a white shirt, blue sweater vest, and a goddamn green-and-blue bow tie that brought out the hazel in his eyes.

A fucking bow tie.

Doody-meyer smiled. "Alejandra," he drawled, bright and slow. "Been a long time, girl."

She hadn't seen him since they were both sixteen but his oil-slick good looks hadn't changed. He'd matured into the exact manner of asshole she'd expected.

"Go fuck yourself, Doody-meyer," she growled. She heard shocked gasps behind her.

Loretta was going to love it when this got back to her.

Alex cast a disgusted glance at Jeremiah. "Of course you two are friends."

She didn't know why she was surprised.

She knew less why she was hurt.

She'd never trusted him. But Joe and Loretta and Mary did. He occupied so much space she couldn't help but see him laugh at her tío's bad jokes and gently get her grandmother to open up about how she was really feeling and adeptly rock her cousin's squalling baby when her cousin had been hunting for her keys. She'd let herself believe that he maybe kinda actually cared about Loretta and the family. That maybe he could be an okay human being when he wasn't a mountain standing in her way.

Like a fucking idiot, she'd relaxed into the belief that he was the kind of decent that would never allow him to hang out with a racist, misogynist scumbag like Lance Doody-meyer.

How many ways had Jeremiah betrayed Loretta in the guise of being someone she could rely on?

The thought added gas to the fire, and Jeremiah's eyes widened as he saw her flare up.

"He and I are *not* friends, Alex," he said quickly. "He just sat down to...to..."

"To offer the historical society the best damn deal it's ever going to get," Doody-meyer said, smugly.

Jeremiah shot him a glare through his round, tortoiseshell glasses that was...something. Alex felt the impact of that hard look in her chest.

The look was probably fake.

"He's trying to bribe me," he said. "He wants the historical society to bow out of contention for the Hugh Building."

Alex was confused. She was wet to the skin and dripping on the floor of a crappy barbecue restaurant and clueless. "He... What?"

"He wants me to abandon the field so that he can buy the building." Jeremiah looked closely at her. "You know he's head of Freedom Rings Development, right?"

A rush of shock whistled through Alex's ears.

"Wait..." She looked at Dutimeyer. "*You're* Freedom Rings

Development?" Her eyes went wide and her stomach knotted. "My grandmother is willing to sell our bar to *you*?"

Her grandmother, the woman she loved most, was contemplating selling Alex's bar to the boy who'd tormented their family then rained hellfire down on Alex.

Dutimeyer openly gloated now, blue eyes lazy and smile wide as he leaned back in his suit, ran a hand over his blond hair, then rested his enmeshed fingers over his tight abs.

She eyed the knife sticking out of the pork ribs on his plate.

"You didn't know?" Jeremiah said, confusion in his voice.

"That offer will set up your grandma for life," Dutimeyer said, picking up his bottle and pointing it at her. "Let her spend her days playing those slot machines she likes to visit in Kansas City." He took a got-all-day drink, swallowed, then tipped the bottleneck at her again. "You'd better say yes soon. That's my nice offer. You don't want to know what I've got up my sleeve for the mean one."

Alex's anger usually got her through anything. Right now, she was in the eye of a tornado of rage and frustration and helplessness and could get nothing out.

She'd felt this way before. Thirteen years ago.

Dutimeyer had gotten to watch it then, too.

Pleased as punch, he turned back to his meal. "I heard Freedom's number one bitch was back," he said as he cut a piece of brisket then stabbed it. "Alejandra, you're not gonna try anything stupid, are you?" He put the meat in his mouth, closed his eyes, and chewed. "You know how it turned out the last time you tangled with me."

He savored the bite like Rickey's stringy brisket was Alex's blood-rich heart.

The last time she'd tangled with him, Alex had ended up in jail. Unless she left right this second, she'd end up there again.

Murdering him quick wouldn't give her back what he'd taken from her.

She had to get out of here. She turned on a heel.

"Alex," Jeremiah said.

Her Converse landed in her trail of rainwater. She slipped and nearly fell, slammed her hand down on a table.

Thirteen years later, Alejandra Armstead was still making a useless racket.

Conscious of Dutimeyer's eyes, of Jeremiah's eyes, of everyone in the restaurant, she got her feet underneath her and raced for the door.

"Alex!"

She shoved the door back and ran out into the storm.

Rain bombarded her as she sprinted to her car and fumbled at her pockets. Her keys... Her hands flew wildly over her pockets. Goddammit. Where were her keys?

"Alex, wait!"

Jeremiah was racing toward her, wearing his ridiculous hat, his trench coat flapping.

Her teeth were chattering. Her whole body was shaking. She wasn't cold.

No one could see her like this.

She turned and ran.

"Dammit, Alex," he yelled behind her. "Please!"

She sprinted across the street, rain a curtain between her and her next step. She knew downtown, every inch of this godforsaken town, like the back of her hand. She ran down the opposite sidewalk—folks in the restaurant were going to have to get wet to keep watching this show—to put real distance between her and Jeremiah.

People were always surprised how fast a woman with thighs and an ass like hers could run.

A block and a half down, her heart in her ears pounding

louder than the storm, she slipped into the two-person-wide alley between Waslow's Furniture Store and a shuttered building. Her speed, the narrow space between the buildings, and the rain blanketing the glow of the streetlamps had helped her pull her disappearing act.

The next time Jeremiah got a look at her, she'd be snapping a Master Lock on his tenant door with official notice to vacate the—

A warm hand grabbed her arm. "Alex, please, let me..."

Shocked, she whirled to face him.

He no longer wore his hat or glasses and he was drenched. His shoulders filled the narrow alley.

"Are you okay?" he yelled. The rain came down on them like it was pouring through a spout, over his dark hair, over his broad forehead and hard cheekbones and wide shoulders.

She wanted to struggle away from his bicep-engulfing hand. But she didn't. Her mouth opened, but no words came out.

"Do I look okay to you?" she finally yelled back.

It was all she had.

"This rain..." he muttered, astonished, squinting as he looked up at it then behind her. "Let's..."

He grabbed her other arm and then maneuvered her backward. He pushed her against the brick wall, into a tiny rain-free space beneath a second-story window ledge. He tucked in close to share it with her, put a forearm by her head. Rain cascaded down his back while his big body shielded her from it.

She stared stupefied at his bow tie and wondered why she'd let him push her here instead of fighting her way free. The dorky professor had just manhandled her.

It was quieter in this chamber he'd created with his body and coat. Alex could hear them both panting from their run. His breath huffed against her wet hair. Her breasts kept brushing his chest. Their little space, she realized, was shockingly warm in contrast to the arctic freeze of the rain. He smelled like…like good coffee and a hot shower.

He smelled like comfort at the end of a long day.

"Alex." He shifted, and then his blunt fingers circled her ear, pushed her wet hair back behind it. The cold top of her lobe tingled as she felt his warm breath against it.

"Alex, look at me."

She wasn't a coward.

She had to tip her head back. Way, way back. Looking up at him, with an alley light giving him a hazy outline, it struck her again how fucking ginormous he was.

How achingly, gorgeously big he was.

He shoved his dripping hair back from his forehead. "I wasn't having dinner with Dutimeyer," he said. If eyes could beg, his were down on their knees. "He sat down, uninvited and unwanted. He's a horrible excuse for a human being."

To ease the strain on her neck, Alex squeezed her hands between them and placed them on his vaulted chest. "He really is," she said.

She felt his relieved sigh.

She felt his hand settle on her waist. "Inadvertent or not, I'm sorry I upset you." The hand rubbed there, through her wet jacket and in the bend of her, as his line-straight eyebrows crinkled. "I'm not actively trying to upset you."

Her eyes fell to the divot in his chin. She wanted to lick the rainwater out of it. "I… I know."

He dropped his forearm to squeeze her waist with both hands. "You do?"

She met his eyes again. He was older than her but sometimes seemed so young. Not in a bad way, but like he still held on to all his kid dreams.

Alex nodded. "Joe came in," she said. "He told me that

you and him and Tía Ofelia were all working together. That the idea started with him and tía."

Jeremiah's gorgeous, too-young face gave an expression like the sun had come out.

His thumbs slipped under her T-shirt to stroke the skin at her waist. They took too much advantage, were too hot, and felt too good.

They made her arch up against his chest.

"You don't know me," he said, urgent as he searched her eyes, those thumbs caressing. "But please believe that the idea of me playing white savior to your community is anathema to everything I believe in and everything I've built my career on. I want who's perceived as the winners to change. I want people to know that there's a truer, richer story to our past than what they've been told. All I want here, all I care about, is that your family's important story is heard."

His passion, academic and nerdy, was like a flame between her legs. Her blunt nails helplessly kneaded his chest. "I believe you."

Both of his hands dipped under her shirt to hold her, bare palms against naked skin, and he stepped in to press his whole body against her, tucking his chin to keep hold of her eyes.

She grabbed his sides. "I still don't want you—I mean, the historical society—to get the bar," she said, rushed and breathy. "I still want it to be mine."

"I know," he said.

Then he bent down and pressed his hard, thick erection between her legs. He rubbed up and it felt so good, so warm, so mind-emptyingly pleasurable that Alex clenched her fingers into his sweater vest, canted back against the wall, and widened her thighs.

He angled her hips and pressed up in long, slow, indulgent strokes against her pussy. The gold and green and browns of his eyes snatched up every bit of light. His narrow lips pressed tightly together as he watched her mouth fall open.

Every inch of her throbbed.

Then he stepped back and let her go.

"I'll walk you to your car," he said, turning from her to face the street.

She swallowed and leaned on her snark as heavily as she'd been leaning on the wall. "Nervous about gettin' caught, Jeremiah? Don't worry. This wouldn't be the first time I did it in this alley."

He tilted his chin to look at her before he again looked forward. "It's not that," he said. "I want to savor the fact that this is the first time you've used my name."

He held a big obnoxious hand out in front of him.

She shoved away from the wall and marched down the alley without looking back.

They were silent, walking side by side and halfway to her car before Alex realized that—for the first time since she'd arrived in Freedom—it had stopped raining.

Chapter Nine

Alex woke up early the next morning to pay her grandmother a visit. The lunch and dinner rushes she expected to die down hadn't—yet—and her cousins who worked weekends at the bar all told her that they couldn't step away from their weekday jobs in order to lend a hand. Alex needed to get back to the bar to help her mom and Danny handle the lunch crowd.

But it was time she and Loretta had it out.

She parked her restored cherry-red '69 VW Beetle in front of her grandmother's house then took out her phone to take a picture. The sun was finally out, and the warmth of it in the cool early-spring air was creating bars of touchable-looking sunlight that poked through the branches of a huge oak. The gigantic, many-limbed oak trees that lined the streets in Freedom were as old as many of the moldering mansions.

She applied a filter and then posted it to her feeds. There. It was pastoral. All back-to-nature and organic. Her followers would eat that shit up.

Over the weekend, Alex had been refilling the tea of an older third cousin when the woman had grabbed Alex's cleaning-cloth smelling hand.

"I remember you carrying around a pitcher when you were little, asking everyone if they wanted more tea while you were wearing the apron tía made you." Her grandmother had embroidered *La Reina de Loretta's* and a crown on the small pink apron.

"She's so glad you're home." Her cousin had wiped tears from her eyes. "She's so glad you've come back to take care of Loretta's with her."

Alex had given her cousin her best bartender's smile and thought of the scribbled list of new names for the bar that she had in her notebook upstairs.

Hiding behind mirrored aviator shades, an oversized black sweatshirt, and ripped leggings, and hauling a Big Gulp of coffee, she opened the squealing gate of her grandmother's chain-link fence and walked past the front door and around the side of the house. She kept her eyes averted from the little abandoned house across the street and the white, two-story house she'd grown up in next door. If she saw a car that wasn't her mom's parked in the carport, it would tank her whole day.

Past the empty, brick-lined beds that would be thick with cilantro, tomatoes, and chiles in a couple of months, and up the cement steps to the porch, the back door was open. Her grandmother was awake.

Alex had spent half her life glancing for that open door. She'd used the side gate between their houses almost every day until the summer after her sophomore year.

Now, she opened the screen door and walked through.

She'd never considered asking to move in. Loretta balanced the open-door policy at her house and the welcome she provided at the bar with a surprisingly firm resistance to people occupying the spare bedrooms she and Salvador raised six kids in.

Houseguests were como peces, she liked to say. Smelly after three days.

Her grandmother turned on her counter stool, her black-framed readers on and the *Freedom Gazette* and a half-eaten sweet bun on the peninsula in front of her. A morning talk show was turned low on the small TV in the corner.

The kitchen smelled of coffee and canela, and sunlight came through the lace curtains.

"Morning, mija," her grandmother said as if Alex showed up there every day. She turned back to her paper as Alex shoved her sunglasses up. "Get yourself some coffee."

Alex put a hand on her Granmo's back and kissed her soft cheek, got a scent of her flowery perfume. "Got some," she said, lifting her giant cup.

"You have breakfast? There's eggs and bacon in the fridge and some enchiladas left over from yesterday."

"No," Alex said, the corner of her mouth beginning to lift despite the reason she'd come. "I'm good."

"Eat this roll," her grandmother said, not taking her eyes off the paper as she lifted the plate and put it closer to where Alex stood. "I don't need it."

Her Granmo and food. Everyone who entered through that back door did this dance with her, accepted the food if they were hungry or cried off until they pretended to eat if they weren't. Her grandmother had a lot of love languages, but food was her most precious one. Which is why it mystified Alex that Loretta had always refused to serve her food at the bar.

At that sobering reminder, Alex rubbed her grandmother's back once—Loretta was in a soft orange T-shirt with a flower on it and softer-looking denim pants—then stepped away to pull up another stool and sat.

The stool was just shorter than her grandmother's and forced anyone sitting on it to look up at her. Alex always believed she'd done that on purpose.

"Hey," she said, drawing her grandmother's attention.

"How are you feeling?" She saw the medication bottles and the half glass of water near her coffee.

Her grandmother tilted her head to look at Alex over the top of her glasses. "Fine. Why?"

"Because I need to talk to you."

Her grandmother stared at her for several beats longer and Alex stared right back, determined brown to determined brown. Finally, Loretta took off her glasses and let them hang from the bejeweled chain around her neck.

"Bueno, dime."

Alex plunged right in. "I ran into the professor and Lance Dutimeyer last night."

Loretta blinked and hummed noncommittally. It was as big of a reaction as Alex could have expected.

Cálmete, Alex coached herself, hearing her grandmother's soothing voice from when Alex was twelve, thirteen, fourteen, coming in to sob frustrated tears at her father's behavior and continued withdrawal into alcoholism. Cálmete.

"Right. Hmmm?" Alex said with the barest hint of sarcasm. "What could my worst enemy and your new best friend have to talk about?"

Loretta said nothing. Under her soft helmet of salt-and-pepper curls, she had the look of a gunslinger.

"Turns out, Doody-meyer was trying to bribe Jeremiah to give up the Hugh Building," Alex barreled on. "You know, since Doody-meyer is desperate to own our family's building even though he treats us like dirt."

Loretta's brow furrowed. "Mijita," she lightly scolded. "You're an adult now. You don't need to use those baby nicknames."

Alex felt the fiery rush in her chest. "Granmo, I get to call that asshole whatever I want until the day I die."

Her grandmother considered her for a second. Then nodded.

That was why Alex loved her so fiercely. She trusted that, even with Loretta's titanic might and pride, her grandmother would be willing to listen to her, to concede to her if Alex was upfront with her. That was why Alex hurt so bad now.

"How could you not tell me that Lance Dutimeyer was head of Freedom Rings Development?"

Alex felt the burn of helpless tears in her throat. She ran her tongue over her teeth, looked away for a second, rubbed a hand over the back of her hair, blinked.

She was *not* going to cry.

That wasn't the real question. That wasn't the most important question. If they were going to have this conversation, if they were going to get past this, she had to ask the question that had kept her up for most of the night, tossing and turning like a ghost trying to shake off its chains.

She looked back at her grandmother and felt the tears trying to regather in response to her elderly grandmother's forlorn gaze. Loretta never looked regretful.

"How could you even consider selling the bar to him?"

Him came out on a teary, stuttered breath. Dammit!

"Mijita," her grandmother said, reaching out a hand to rub her shoulder.

Alex reached across herself to grab Loretta's hand. She squeezed the soft skin and fragile bones and ivy-carved gold ring that was an anniversary gift from her grandfather. Then she stood, she couldn't sit any longer, and walked around the side of the peninsula so she could look her grandmother in the face and at the same height.

She hated this feeling that Loretta had betrayed her and she wanted it gone.

"Granmo, what is going on?" she implored, her hands gripping the fake butcher-block laminate counter.

Loretta looked down at her paper, at the bun, at her coffee.

"Nothing, mija," she said, looking shrunken and unconvincing. "They made me a good offer and I'm getting old and—"

"No," Alex said, cutting her off in frustration. "I don't believe that. I don't believe you would just hand over the bar to the Hughs and let them do whatever they want with it."

The fertile Hugh clan clung to their kingdom of Freedom, Kansas, with everything they had. They'd all discovered that their abilities to intimidate, tyrannize, and awe didn't extend beyond the town's borders, so they'd burrowed in and infested.

The Hughs liked nothing better than to show off their power by bullying easy-to-spot brown people. Every León descendant had their Hugh antagonist, and Dutimeyer had been Alex's.

No way would Loretta let him or his family make themselves at home in the middle of their community.

"Selling the building to the historical society is one thing. But Dutimeyer?" She sneered his name. "What about the family? The street? The neighborhood?"

Loretta got a focused frown as she looked at Alex.

Uh-oh.

"So now you care about the family y la comunidad?" Loretta asked carefully. "Or are you mad because you don't want him to have the toys you threw away?"

Alex huffed. "That's not fair."

Loretta's glare grew sharper. Alex had gotten her good, good temper from someone.

"No. Lo que no es justo..." Oh no. Her grandmother was speaking in Spanish. "...Is you accusing me of doing something wrong when you haven't wanted to be part of the picture." Her English was building in speed and volume. "What's not fair is you girls showing up like your plans were a done deal without considering me at all. I'd given up praying that you'd come home. Then you three ambush me with this *you're-too-old* and *it's-a-burden* crap and tell me you're going to ruin the sanctuary I built."

Crap was the foulest word her grandmother used, and when she said it, she was truly pissed. Alex realized this tirade had been building for a while.

"You couldn't even do me the courtesy of picking up a phone and talking to me. No, Granmo's so old she's just going to roll over and do what we say." Her Granmo's hand flapped anger in the air. "At least I expected to get bullied by Lance. He brought me flowers."

Loretta wasn't wrong. Alex and her sisters had made assumptions. That their grandmother would be relieved. That she'd be grateful.

That she was getting old and therefore less...necessary. That she'd shuffle off.

Alex wasn't the only person in the room who felt betrayed. Why hadn't they just called and asked her what she thought? Hell, they could've texted her. Loretta was a whiz with her smartphone.

Loretta was on a roll. "Since you've been here, you haven't asked me *one* question about the bar I've run for forty years even though I'm sitting there every day. No, no, Granmo doesn't need to be included in your big plans; Granmo's just a pothole you're going to drive over."

Alex thought her grandmother had come stumping in on her silver walker every day to judge her. To prove to herself that Alex wasn't worthy.

Alex had never thought that Loretta was there to lend a hand the only way she could right now: by sharing her experience with her.

"Granmo..." She tried to ease in with an apology.

Loretta was on full steam. "And what about your sisters? Where are they? Are you even talking to them?"

Alex blew out a long breath. No, she wasn't. She still needed Gillian's money and Sissy's help in the kitchen. But after days of silence, they'd both texted with a cautious "How's it going?" that she'd been too irritated with to answer.

Still, her Granmo's rightful anger didn't erase the out-of-character fact that she was contemplating selling her life's effort and her family's second home to a racist man who treated them like trash.

"Did Dutimeyer threaten you?" Alex asked. "Because of how much you owe?"

Loretta's chin shot sky-high. "That's none of your concern."

Talking about money in her family ranked right up there with talking about abortion and whether someone cooked with lard—you did not mention it. Which was why, with a multitude of family members who would help Loretta with accounting, repairs, and loans, her grandmother had managed to rack up debts that equaled a terrifying amount in Alex's notebook.

Loretta's expenses had been outpacing its profits for years, according to the past due notices and IRS warnings that Alex found. But what her grandmother owed had risen sharply in the last six months. And Doody-meyer had mentioned her enjoyment of the slots on the gambling riverboats in Kansas City.

Alex put a hand covered in thick silver rings gently on top of her grandmother's. "I don't believe for a second you would consider Dutimeyer's offer unless he was holding something big over your head. The sooner we're honest about that, the sooner we can deal with it."

Her grandmother's stony expression made Alex work to breathe in some of that maturity everyone kept talking about.

"And you're right. We should've let you in on our plans."

Loretta's eyelashes jumped. Alex admitting that someone else was right was like the sky going plaid.

"We should've called you. And…and I'm sorry I didn't visit you after your fall." She could blame Randy—fucking Randy—for not giving her time off. But she could have pushed, talked to her bosses, or left anyway and asked someone to cover her shifts. She hadn't.

Fixing things with her grandmother had always been something she would have time to do in the far-off future. Seeing her in a hospital bed would've put too much pressure on the present.

The future, Alex realized as she stood in the kitchen that was as much an embrace as her grandmother's hug, was right now.

"I'm sorry I didn't come to see you until…until it looked like I wanted something for me."

Loretta studied her and Alex let her look. She loved her grandmother. She had to hope her Granmo, regardless of everything, believed that.

"What do you want for you, mija? You threw away that job in Chicago."

Of course she'd seen the video.

"You don't want what Loretta's can give you: a home. Your family back." Loretta had never shied away from saying what was hard. "Why do you think I'm considering Jeremiah's offer? He wants those things. He needs them."

Jeremiah had a doctorate and a prestigious job and enough wealth to wear a Rolex and park an older Mercedes in the lot.

Alex had a GED and might have to work at a chain restaurant where she'd ask customers if they wanted a blooming onion with their drink if she couldn't convince Loretta that she was the next best owner.

"Why do you trust him so much?" she asked. That was the true difference between what Jeremiah had and Alex didn't. "What do you even know about him?"

"Not much. He doesn't say much about himself." Loretta shrugged, as if maybe hiding a serial killer or a mob informant in their bar wasn't important. "I know he's passionate about his interests. He's quiet but not shy. I know he's kind. And very lonely." Her dark eyes sharpened on Alex. "I know he loves our family. He plans to create a coffee shop at the museum where your mother and I can work and the family can still gather.

"*He's* going to keep the name Loretta's for it," her grandmother said archly.

Alex looked down at her coffee cup.

"I know he's never lied to me."

Alex snapped her head up. "Neither have I."

She was surprised by her Granmo's chuckle. "That's true. When sometimes it would have served you to be quiet."

Loretta brushed her hand over hers.

It was the soothing Alex needed. "You're mad at me," Alex said gently, "and I'm mad at you. But... I've missed you. I'd rather hang out with you than be mad at you all the time."

Her grandmother's small smile was like the first spring flower. "Me too, mija."

The days since her return to Loretta's couldn't have been more miserable. Being at odds with her grandmother and mother and sisters, constantly wrestling with the building and its racist ghost, the terrifying bills on her grandmother's desk, the unexpected crowds, the lurking non-presence of her dad, and the distracting shoulders of one cleft-chinned professor had left her little time to plan her takeover of the bar.

But she wanted Loretta's now more than ever.

Maybe it was possessiveness, as her grandmother suspected.

But she'd started looking at all of the building's detriments—its creaky floors and old jelly jars and broken stained glass and flickering lights and oversized, mellow-wood bar—as part of its potential. She'd been exploring ideas that were less about making money and more about making it hers: getting staff aprons with her grandmother's tea-towel embroidery instead of the hipster-y denim-and-leather aprons she'd planned, seeing if the cousin in Wichita who'd opened a microbrewery would be up for making a Loretta beer, talking with Joe about turning the ramshackle island into an altar—which it already kind of looked like—that was functional with liquor and glasses but also better displayed the milagros, picture of Granpo Salvador, and community notices.

She would show them. Show them all. She had a vision and she would show this town and Randy and her sisters and her mother and fucking Doody-meyer that she could transform a nothing bar in the middle of nowhere into a destination on the plains. Show influential bar owners and restaurant group presidents that she had what it took to helm a top-tier establishment.

Show Jeremiah that maybe he'd read her wrong, too.

She'd tossed and turned most of the night, but he'd stayed still. There'd been no squeaks or mattress shifts coming from his side of the wall. At one point, she'd put her hand on the plaster and wondered how close his body was. Wondered if he'd offer anything to help her sleep. When she'd gone into the bathroom this morning, she walked into the still-lingering steam of his soap and evergreen-smelling shaving cream.

Her big, nerdy neighbor had chased her down, manhandled her against a wall, and protected her from the rain to convince her that he wasn't trying to be her enemy. Then he'd sexed her up.

Everyone wanted a piece of this ass.

Maybe Dr. Jeremiah Post wasn't as fumbly as she'd first thought. Maybe he wasn't her enemy, and maybe he wanted her bad.

That still didn't make him her friend.

He thought she was bad news for her family and this community he admired, and he believed his purpose for the Hugh Building was more noble than hers.

He had a lot of buildings he could choose from on Milagro Street.

She kissed her grandmother goodbye with a promise to have a list of irritating questions for her when she came in later.

When she went through the front yard, she paused to snap a pic of some sparrows making use of the Virgen de Guadalupe birdbath, her chipped blue robes a contrast to the sparkling water drops Alex caught in the frame.

It looked like it was actually going to be kind of an okay day.

Chapter Ten

Several nights later, Jeremiah stared at Alex's bedroom door as he bolstered his nerves. The plain wooden door with a dime-sized milagro of two eyes—I'm watching you—pulsed with spine-tingling possibility.

Every morning, he sped past this door to avoid a just-woken-up view of her. That damn sapphire robe always startled him in the bathroom. He'd stroked it with one finger—once—and it was as liquidly silky as he'd feared.

In the evenings, he contemplated the door while her room was unoccupied. Imagined what secrets it hid.

Every late night, the door beckoned like a sound in the basement. Living with her was like constantly being on edge that a heart-stopping creature was going to burst out of the dark.

Since those moments in the alley, there'd been a cautious détente between them that he didn't want to disturb. He didn't trust her. Her wishes to transform this cultural institution into an Edison-bulb-lit speakeasy that attracted the ugliest of publicity mongers on social media hadn't changed. She was still that unpredictable woman who seemed proud to memorialize her bad-tempered, foul-mouthed displays on video.

She was also that woman who'd looked at him—open and vulnerable—and yelled, *Do I look okay to you?* Her honesty while rain rushed over her had knocked him off-kilter. Protecting this fierce, fleet-footed woman and giving her some honesty in return had been all he'd wanted to do.

Then he'd fondled her in a public alley.

He didn't have sex with women he didn't trust. So why was the need to touch her again so imperative?

Their interactions in the bar had been few, but polite. He'd greeted her with a simple, "Good evening, Alex," the next night, wanting to test the atmosphere.

"Evenin', professor," she'd replied, instantly raising his hackles. Then she'd given him that slight tilt of a smile, the sweetest uptick of those slopey eyes, and Jeremiah felt it like the time one of her little cousins had asked to be picked up.

For all of their limited conversation, Jeremiah was perversely pleased to see that Alex was talking to her grandmother more comfortably. After one evening's busy push of patrons, Alex had sat down with her grandmother and asked her about a stuck gas valve in the kitchen, a cranky beer tap behind the bar, and Danny's dedication to sending out limp and cold French fries.

Jeremiah had smiled down at his stack of unread midterm essays and castigated himself for cheering for the increased advantage of his competitor.

What, truly, did this fierce, bad-tempered, world-dominating woman want with this place?

Right now, it didn't matter.

It was late and he'd come straight from the bowels of city hall to her door. He had to put his daydreams and nighttime fantasies aside to share with her what he'd discovered.

He had to tell her this immediately, regardless of the hour. They might already be too late.

Jeremiah raised his knuckles to knock.

And was horrified when the door swung silently open.

Dumbstruck, his fist in the air, he stared at what the door revealed.

Alex was in bed. Rather, she was on her bed, sitting on top of her sheets and old quilt and coverlet. She was naked. No, not naked. Worse than naked. She had on a loose, pastel-pink tank top, its straps hanging onto her strong shoulders while the front of it gaped low, low enough for him to see deep cleavage and the golden-brown tops of her heavy breasts, the curve of their succulent shape pressing up against the cotton. She had one brown, naked leg bent in front of her—a thick, scrunched-down blue sock tapped on the bed—and the other leg was bent beneath her. Was she wearing underwear? Why did she have such pretty knees?

Papers and sketches and lists were spread all over the bed, and she was bent over a notebook propped on her knee, her pen moving quickly with that energy that was inherent to her, her head bobbing to whatever music was coming through the large green headphones she'd popped on over the wild peaks and curls of her dark, high hair.

Suddenly, she sang under her breath, off-key and diva-ish. *Tell mama…all about it. And I'll make everything all right.*

The bright flowers on her right arm bent and wove as she wrote.

Jeremiah wanted to go to her, take her pen, slide it behind his ear so she could get right back to work when he was through, and press her back to the mattress.

Alex looked up. Her eyes went shocked wide.

"What the hell," she roared instantly, appropriately, as Jeremiah stood in her doorway with his fist still raised to knock.

"I…uh… I…." That was the intelligence this Beinecke Scholar was able to get out.

"What are you doing?" she shouted, throwing off the headphones, leaping from the bed, looking wildly around until she

grabbed the pearled coverlet she'd been sitting on and pulled it over the papers like a magician's cape.

She was all flashing skin and flexing muscle and vibrant color. She was wearing underwear. Her panties were blue and had tiny terrifying clowns all over them. They outlined the very tops of her rich, gorgeous thighs and cupped her large, heart-shaped bottom like his best, dirtiest dream.

He loved clowns.

She swung back around on him, her face mobile and astonished. "What the fuck, Jeremiah? Don't you knock?"

She put her fists on her hips and there wasn't a drop of makeup on her face and she'd said his name and her hair was shiny and curly and she was all skin and big breasts and grabbable hips and he—he—

He put his hand out as if it could save him from this nuclear view and turned away.

"I was going to knock," he said, blinking to clear the contrails. "But the door, it opened without me touching it. I'm so sorry. It just swung open. I don't know—"

"Fuck," he heard her say. He didn't dare look. "Fuckin' Old Man Hugh. I know I locked that door."

"Really?" he asked, keeping his eyes away from her and her bed. She'd cared more about covering the papers than herself. The other side of the room, with its open shelving and old armoire, was neatly arranged, showed her same penchant for neatness and organization he'd noticed slowly taking effect downstairs. His eyes wandered over a few mismatched candles that had left the scent of ambergris in the air, a basket of bright scarves, a mannequin hand decorated with her many rings, and another jar of her rose-scented cream. He felt a bubble of warmth percolate to the surface at seeing her intimate things, the things that made Alex.

Then he realized what she'd said. She'd locked her door although both the outer doors were bolted.

"Alex, do you feel…" He wouldn't look at her. "Do you feel unsafe sharing quarters with me?"

"No," she said, immediate and serious. "You mentioned hearing someone jiggle the entry door after hours. Locking my door is a habit. I lived in Chicago for the last thirteen years."

"Oh." Thirteen years? How old had she been when she moved there?

"Yeah, oh," she replied. "You believe in the ghost now?"

He was certain he'd closed the bathroom door when she'd caught him sniffing her hand cream. "I… I'm growing less skeptical."

"What the hell are you doing here?"

"I wouldn't bother you if it wasn't urgent." He put down his hand but didn't look at her. "Would you mind putting on some pants?"

Her lack of response, the long then longer quiet of it, made the air throb.

Finally, she said, "Getting a little worked up, professor?"

He adjusted his glasses and refused to cover his crotch.

"This is serious," he said. "I need to talk to you."

"Fine," she huffed with laughter in her voice. The sound was titillating and humiliating. She could make him feel both and, for some asinine reason, one enflamed the other.

He heard her walk to her bed then shuffle around. "This better?"

Jeremiah dared to look. She'd engulfed herself in an oversized black sweatshirt he'd seen her wear before. It covered the full hourglass of her—mostly, little could hide those phenomenal breasts—but her legs were bare from midthigh down to the thick scrunched socks and she was still achingly accessible.

The mighty brain in his pants, thankfully, seemed to think it was relief enough.

"Thank you," he said, dropping his hands and straightening. "I've just come from city hall and made a discovery that I believe is imperative to communicate immediately."

She grinned with raised eyebrows—her full eyebrows would be mink-soft under his thumb—and he shut his mouth. Gripped his jaw.

Over a hard-fought thirty-two years, he'd come to prize his intellect, curiosity, and enthusiastic fascination when others would have had him temper those qualities or corral them into an appropriate mold. But even he recognized that Alex's presence sometimes made him into a caricature.

He rubbed his forehead and started again. "I've been researching Lance Dutimeyer and Freedom Rings Development," he said. "Why is he going to such extreme lengths to claim this building?"

Lance's outsized offer for the building, his effort to bribe Jeremiah with a Main Street address, and, most pressingly, his threat—*That's my nice offer. You don't want to know what I've got up my sleeve for the mean one*—had lent a sense of urgency to Jeremiah's research.

Although Alex's dark eyes were shuttered now, the naked pain and shock on her face at the restaurant had made Jeremiah want to reprimand everyone to look away. *You're Freedom Rings Development? My grandmother is willing to sell our bar to you?*

No one—not Jeremiah, certainly not Lance Dutimeyer—deserved to see her that vulnerable.

He didn't know what happened in the past between Dutimeyer and Alex, and she didn't owe him that story. But Jeremiah felt a growing duty in the present to make sure that slimy narcissist didn't hurt her and her family again.

"Lance Dutimeyer established his company a year ago, but

he hasn't bid on any city or county projects." They both knew he'd be a shoe-in to get them. Nepotism ran rife in their community and half of the city council and county board were made up of his family members. "All he's done so far is purchase abandoned properties on the east side."

"Alex," he said, drawing her eyes back to him. "If he wants a large swath of land that's undervalued and already equipped with city services and infrastructure, this would be it. Loretta's is the most prominent entity on the east side; getting rid of it would make buying up other properties much easier, both financially and politically. Some people already believe there's nothing on the east side worth preserving."

Alex looked at him in confusion. "Why would anyone need a big piece of land in Freedom?" She put a hand on her hip. Her sweatshirt hitched up. "Doody-meyer's going to build a sports coliseum? They finally get that baseball franchise the town's been aiming for?"

She was mocking him.

Jeremiah's flare of annoyance helped him ignore her thighs. She didn't value Freedom, and Freedom was the warm blanket he'd wrapped himself in. "A plant would benefit from the east side's access to the railroad and a highway."

Alex scoffed at the tired rumor. "Look, I wouldn't put much past Doody-meyer." Her eyes narrowed with skepticism. "You just seem a little paranoid."

Alex Torres knew how to push every button he would have sworn he didn't have. There was a physicality to his every reaction to her—to take her in his hands and shake her, to push her up against a wall and kiss her—that made him alien to himself. That made him glad he was across the room from her.

He straightened his glasses. "Well, how's this for paranoid," he said steadily. "Lance Dutimeyer might be able to claim the Hugh Building without paying Loretta a dime."

That sobered her up. "What?"

"Yes," he said. "There's a second deed out there. And it may supersede the deed your grandmother has."

He shouldn't have felt satisfaction at the gathering look of shock and denial on Alex's face, but it was difficult to reconcile how badly he wanted to get under her clothes with how frustratingly she got under his skin.

He wanted her to appreciate her hometown the way he did. He wanted her to understand that the home and family she took for granted didn't come so easily to everyone.

"What the fuck are you talking about?" she said, finally outraged. "How in the fuck is that possible? How is that legal? She owns the building."

"Dutimeyer mentioned wanting to bring the Hugh Building back into the family fold and it jogged a memory loose. A couple months back, our historical society assistant mentioned getting a call from someone looking for Wayland Hugh's will." Jeremiah had just enough room between her small bistro table and her door to work up a good pace. He wondered if the building's former owner and (according to Alex) racist ghost was listening in. "Our assistant told them we didn't have it and that the information was stored at city hall. Earlier today, I talked to the part-time clerk who works down there."

He'd been shocked by Natisha's frantic whisper as she'd shared everything she'd been through. He spent more time in the archived records room in the basement of city hall than the young woman did. The dust bothered her allergies. But a sudden flurry of visitors from men in suits had made her curious about what they were researching, so she reviewed the records they'd pulled.

"According to what she read in the will, Wayland Hugh created a second deed that will allow a descendant of his first son to claim the building. It appears Lance Dutimeyer is going to say that he's an heir."

Natisha had sounded like she'd been whispering from inside a closet. From their significant roles within city hall, the Hughs had been running Freedom into the ground for years.

"But…" Alex ran both hands over the soft hair at the back of her neck. He would find that comforting, too. "Are you saying he could use some old deed to claim a building that Loretta paid a mortgage on for a couple of decades?"

"The law legitimizing dual deeds is still on the city books," Jeremiah said. "So is the law that makes it illegal to drive a mule through the streets faster than a trot. If Lance finds the deed first, you can fight his claim in court, but can your family afford a legal fight?"

He could see the gray cloud of her answer on her forehead. "This is…" Then she squinted at him. "Wait…you said, 'if they find it first.' They don't have it?"

"He offered your grandmother a fortune, bribed me, and threatened you. Do you think he'd wait a moment to lord it over us if he did have it?"

Us.

"Our only option is to find it first to keep him from using it."

Our.

She seemed to hear it at the same moment he realized what he was saying. Her dark eyes narrowed as she slowly crossed her arms under her breasts, hitching the sweatshirt further up her thighs.

"We're going to have to search for that deed." He had to soldier on. This was the only reason he'd come to her door in the middle of the night. "Together. Immediately."

Her pink tongue licked her full bottom lip while her eyes peeled him apart. "Why would we do that?"

"We both have something at stake. We both want this building. We both want to protect Loretta." Searching together made sense. "I have an encyclopedic knowledge of the history of this town. You're a bartender and a local. You know everyone. People tell you things. You can get us entry into places I can't."

She rocked back on a blue-socked heel. "Right," she drawled. "I'm a townie bartender with a criminal past. With your 'encyclopedic' knowledge, you must have heard of that. No one's gonna open doors for me the way that they'll hold 'em open for you, but I can always break us in through the back."

Jeremiah realized he could have better chosen his words. Or told her that, for all of his desire to be a part of this town, he would always be an outsider.

"I didn't mean—"

"Why would I use my zero amount of free time to hang out with someone who thinks he's better than me?"

He never—

"You want me to believe we should go poking around for a hundred-year-old piece of paper?" She threw out a hand as she mocked him. "That's there a big bad developer breathing down our necks? This sounds like the make-believe of a guy with too big of a brain, too much in his wallet, and too much time on his hands."

Every scathing word was a stab to his honesty, his integrity, and his good intentions.

"If you're looking for another fuck, Jeremiah, you don't need to make up stories." She actually ran her hands over her coveted breasts before she propped them on her hips and jutted up her sharp chin. "Just promise you'll last longer than thirty seconds and we're good to go."

Damn her. He wanted to stalk close, put her in his shadow,

make her feel his heat. He wanted her to understand that he wasn't always that man she'd upended in the bar.

But he was in her room and she wasn't wearing any pants.

He straightened and worked to keep his fists relaxed at his sides. "The night guard who spent two days in the hospital doesn't think it's make-believe." He was glad to make her blanch. "He was knocked out and boxes of information about the Hugh clan were stolen out of the archives. I just came from verifying for myself. The copy of the will, the birth records of the prolific family, documents that could help prove or disprove whether Dutimeyer has a legitimate claim…it's all gone."

Some mechanism had been started and he couldn't see its purpose.

Her chin jutted out mulishly. "If all the info's gone then…"

The raising of his own chin was slow and proud. He'd never been more glad to be a nerdy professor. "Our historical society assistant doesn't know our records the way I do. We have the original last will and testament of Wayland Hugh."

If her blink was the only response he was going to get, he'd take it.

"I don't doubt a word the clerk has told me, but I'm going to review the will. Without the rest of those records, though, I'll have to discover what Lance is up to some other way. That'll go easier with your help. With or without it, I'm pursuing this. Come look at the will with me; decide for yourself.

"Regardless, know this." He lowered his chin and put every drop of his desire and frustration into his gaze. "Wanting you is a distraction I don't need. When I want to be inside you again, I'll make it crystal clear."

Her full mouth dropped open, just for a flash of a second, before she closed it and pressed her lips together.

All of her teasing and taunting and allusions to their first time—it was as if *she* was the one who couldn't let it go.

"You and I have a common enemy," he continued, less stridently. "Ultimately, we don't have to convince each other of the superiority of our plans for the building. Loretta will make the final decision; she's the one we'll have to convince. She's the one we have to protect."

All that defiance in her face softened to something like confusion.

Despite himself, he moved closer to her. "I'm not trying to deceive you, Alex. I want to be relentlessly honest about my intentions. I still believe that if Loretta's cannot continue as is, then the historical society's plan is the best next incarnation of this building." He had a ridiculous urge to rub her stiff shoulders in her sweatshirt. He saw how much lifting and carrying she did. "If you'll allow me, I'll show you our plans."

"No," she answered. Her denial was soft as she tilted up her chin to keep her eyes on him.

For an instant, the ferocity of her mistrust struck Jeremiah. She had a huge family in a close-knit hometown. There were as many people in Freedom willing to help her as there were new stalks of spring wheat in the surrounding farmland.

"Let me show you the will on Friday," he urged. Standing this close to her, her soft, rosy smell defied all of her hard edges. "Come to the historical society office."

"I don't know," she murmured.

"I'll be there at two. After the lunch rush."

"That…could work," she said. She bit her lip, like she wished she could take the words back. "I guess Old Man Hugh would love it if his great-great whatever could steal the building from a Mexican."

There was no logic in the long hours that he could stare at her.

"Do you truly believe he haunts this building?"

The bulb in her lamp went out with a pop.

"No," she deadpanned in the dark. "Not at all."

He was standing in the pitch-black with a half-naked Alex Torres. With one step, he could lean her back on her bed, get down on his knees, pull her thighs over his shoulders, and nestle his face into blue cotton and clowns.

He staggered back.

She laughed nervously and it was a sound that usually came from him, never from her—bold, confident, arrogant her. "Looks like Old Man Hugh might want us to be distracted, huh?"

He turned on a heel.

"I hope you come, Alex," he said over his shoulder, putting his hand out and feeling the doorknob in his palm with relief.

If he waited a moment longer, he couldn't blame a ghost for what he did to her.

Chapter Eleven

Alex's mother and grandmother believed the wildest things. They believed that telling a person on the other side of a wooden phone booth how many times they said "damn" that week would ensure their soul's entry into heaven. They believed in souls and heaven.

They believed that a house on the lonely stretch of road between Milagro Street and the cement plant once held a demon child so horrific that it lived for years screaming behind the brick walls its parents and a traveling priest had imprisoned it in. They crossed themselves every time they drove over the Viridescent River to prevent the spirit of La Llorona from following them home to steal away one of their children to replace her drowned ones. They lived peacefully and contentedly with a long-dead racist who tripped them, locked them out, and forced them to stock up on light bulbs—they even defended the old bastard when Alex asked if he'd had anything to do with Loretta's fall.

Her mother believed that a man who repeatedly turned his back on her and her daughters deserved another chance to hurt them again.

So their hilarity when Alex tried to explain Jeremiah's wild conspiracy theory—second deeds and stolen documents and Doody-meyer's dastardly plans—made Alex feel even more ridiculous for the brief second when she'd half believed him.

The lost files hadn't been reported in the local paper, but they'd read about the injured security guard. The man hadn't seen who hit him and the cops blamed "kids."

"His imagination is as big as his shoulders," her grandmother had chuckled before the bar opened, sitting at her designated table with her cane propped next to her and her readers on as she looked over the ordering invoice for next week. Alex had recommended increases to the beer and pop supplies since the rush of customers still hadn't died down. "Déjalo todo en manos de Dios."

Mary's response, while not advising that all should be left in the hands of an uncaring God who'd tossed Loretta down the stairs, wasn't much better.

"Alex, that could never happen," Mary said as she poured a trash barrel of ice into the ice bin. Her mother dressed like an elementary schoolteacher and carried loads like a stevedore. "The people of this town wouldn't allow it."

Her mother gave the "people of this town" more credit than they deserved. And all too often, her mother's pacifying point of view had been in the direct face of things she needed to worry about.

Still, Alex had no time for a two-ton-geek's paper search. Word that Alex was back in town had now filtered beyond family, and the unending meal rushes meant that she had little free time to work on her own plans for the bar. When the professor had barged in on a couple of hours that she'd finally carved out to develop the cocktail list, event schedule, and renovation plans that she would share with her grandmother, he sounded like he already had a frigging Power-Point ready to go. He had the help of an entire committee and her favorite relatives. Alex was doing it all on her own. Although the clutching band around her heart had eased as her relationship with her Granmo had improved—Loretta did know a lot of tricks about this ornery old building—she knew her grandmother was still suspicious about the absence of Alex's "partners." In her few spare seconds, she'd been trying to rouse Gillian and Sissy with texts and phone calls. But the competition for the building had erased their excitement for taking it over.

Or maybe they just assumed Alex was going to lose the fight.

She didn't have time to be rooting through Freedom's hidey-holes looking for a piece of paper. Still, it *was* weird how much effort Doody-meyer was putting into owning one run-down building.

Before the Friday lunch crowd started pouring in, she figured she could at least ask her tíos if they'd ever heard of dual deeds.

"Remember that big ol' house over on Poplar," her Tío Pepe said to the others at the table as he poured more sugars than his diabetes recommended into his just-filled cup. Pepe had three grown and successful kids and a good pension after retiring as a foreman from Liberty Manufacturing when the after-market car parts maker had still been thriving. Now, he felt that a good life, hard work, and the too-soon death of his much-loved wife dictated that he got to do what he wanted. "Couple of hippies from Montana claimed it with a second deed passed down to them."

"Sí, sí, sí, that's right, compadre," Tío Martín said with a scowl. "Tried to turn the house into a watchucallit…"

"A commune," Eddie said with a chuckle and a stroke of his trim, white beard. "They tried to pack thirty people into the house."

"And the city let them get away with that?" Alex asked, eyeing her mother who was ignoring her from behind the bar.

"You know white people," Tío Pepe said, clicking his coffee cup with Martín and creating a sloshing mess that Alex was going to have to clean up. "They get what they want."

"It was a foreclosed and falling-apart property," Eddie said, his legs crossed and his coffee cup lazily held on top of his knee. "The bank was happy to relinquish it. Ultimately, the city got the new owners for trying to house livestock within city limits."

"Those gueros and their chickens," Tío Pepe said, shaking his head. "I'm not my grandfather; I like my eggs to come in a carton."

That would be Alex's great-great-uncle, a man too obscured by the years for Alex to have spent any time thinking about.

"Why did he come here?" Alex asked. She didn't even know the man's name.

"Who, Francisco?" Pepe asked. "He lived with his tío and tía, your great-great-grandmother, to work as a traquero and send money back to Mexico."

"A traquero?"

"Sí, a railroad worker. He laid track. He started when he was eight."

"Eight?" Alex replied, horrified.

Pepe grinned at her. "Yeah, he would keep the tracks clear of weeds. He lost two toes. They were lifting a rail to rebalance it and it came down on his foot. When we were little, he would take off his sock then chase us around the house rattling a cup he said had his toes in it."

Martín started to laugh. "Remember when I dared you to open the cup and touch them?"

The whole table started chuckling. "I thought I was going to be sick," Pepe said. "The biggest disappointment in my life was when I opened that cup and saw that it was just two pinto beans."

The men's laughter rose to the dusty, dropped ceiling.

"But that pendejo didn't tell us the truth," Martín told the others, grinning and flinging out an accusing finger at Pepe. "Walked around all summer like a big man, and I had to let him ride my bike for a month!"

Pepe pointed back. "What about the time…"

Realizing that any opportunity to learn more about their family's history was over, Alex turned to move away from the table. She caught Eddie watching her a little too closely.

"Why do you want to know about dual deeds, Alex?" he said quietly, under the men's roaring laughter and accusations.

Nothing escaped Loretta's eagle ears. "Callate, viejos," she called from across the bar. "You talk and talk and talk and keep my granddaughter from doing her work."

"Ay, prima, you wound me," Tío Pepe called back, hand over his heart.

When Loretta met Eddie's eyes, her chin went up.

Alex moved away before the man could sniff out anything else. The sale of Loretta's was still a secret no one in the know was sharing. But Alex had made a decision.

She went behind the bar (now with a fixed pass-through thanks to her cousin Joe's surreptitious labor) where her mother was looking for a pen as the first table of lunch customers walked in.

"I'm going to need to take a couple of hours off this afternoon."

Mary looked at her in exasperation. "Gina said she was going to be late today." Alex's cousin worked as a bartender and server on Friday nights and Saturdays.

Alex poured water for the two-top. "I'll be back in time for the dinner rush."

"If you're already thinking about leaving town, let me

know." Mary had lowered her voice. "I'll find someone who can help me."

Alex looked at her with a scowl. "I'm not." She'd been about to tell her that she was going to find out more about the second deed—though she was not going to mention the professor—but her mother's skepticism shut her up.

Mary pursed her lips together then said, "I'm sorry, it's just... I can't manage the bar by myself. I need someone who's reliable."

"Oh, *now* you need someone who's reliable," Alex snapped back. "Then maybe you should reconsider who you're having coffee with."

No one had mentioned a peep about her dad, and Alex figured her mom had had about as much spare time for a betraying cup of coffee as Alex had. But the jagged sense of injustice that her mom was seeing him again hadn't gone away. It just sat there, knife-sharp and deadly in the back of Alex's mind.

It stabbed with the suggestion that *Alex* was the one her mother couldn't count on.

She went to take orders without looking back or apologizing.

After a hectic lunch, several sent-back plates of food (Danny had a midterm, so was trying to work the burger grill with a textbook in his hand), and a "drop by" from a woman from Alex's year who wanted to giggle about the video and get all up in Alex's business, she'd not been in the greatest of moods when the message she texted Jeremiah after sneaking his number out of her grandmother's phone bounced back.

His number was a fucking landline.

When she'd reached his voice mail at the college, she'd snarled into it, "Meet me in the lot behind city hall. I don't want anyone seeing us together."

The cool, spring-bright day, the eggshell-blue sky, and the yellow daffodils poking out of the new grass in front of the barbershop across the street mocked Alex's coal-black mood. She snapped a pic that framed the flowers in front of the old-fashioned barbershop pole, wrote a trite sentence about new beginnings and tradition, posted it, then leaned back against her Cherry Bug as she watched the professor pull up in a gold, older-model, two-seat convertible Mercedes.

Her mom probably thought he was the top dog of reliability.

She kept her aviator shades on, her chin down, and her hands buried in her black bomber jacket as he bounded out of the car like a big, shaggy Lab, tail wagging as he held a file folder and looked wide-eyed at her Bug.

"This is yours?" he said. "What a beauty!"

Alex scowled at him. Her Cherry Bug was a splurge after the article came out and her tips went astronomical. She'd personally overseen the renovation. She didn't want him to love it the way she did.

He didn't have on a coat although the day was chilly, and his forest green suspenders hooked onto checked pants should've made him look stuffy and ridiculous, like a Brooks Brothers circus clown. Instead, with his white rolled-up sleeves exposing his muscular forearms and the pants clearly outlining his firm waist and the broad bands of the suspenders smoothing over the well-defined torso...

"This car's been sitting at Loretta's since I moved here. Who the hell else's would it be?"

He just shrugged as he ogled. Alex refused to find him adorable.

She shoved her sunglasses up onto her head. "You walked me to my car!"

He ripped his eyes off the shiny chrome bumper to give

Alex his biggest, goofiest, crinkly-eyed-with-dimples smile. "I've been told I have tunnel vision."

"Ya think?"

She felt that tunnel vision suddenly focus on her. His smile softened. It was like he added height and width, standing in the parking lot near a dumpster that hid them from the street, staring at her through his tortoiseshell glasses.

"You look nice," he said. His spatula-sized thumb rubbed softly, back and forth, over the manila folder. "I'm glad you came."

She was wearing steel-toed Doc Martens and tight ripped jeans an artist friend had spray-painted and a zipped-up black bomber jacket and almost-black lipstick and heavy eyeliner because, when she'd been changing after her shift, all she could think was *fuck these people and fuck this town.*

She swallowed the *thank you* in her mouth.

"How come the only number Loretta's got for you is a landline?"

"I don't have a cell phone," he said as he walked toward her and gingerly put the file folder on top of her hood. He opened it and began flipping through papers.

"You don't…?" She watched him brush the thick hank of hair that always fell forward off his forehead. "How is that possible?"

He rejected a couple of sheets then brought one to the top. "I don't have anyone who needs me immediately," he said absently as he read over the paper.

He could write a textbook about her, her professional background, her family history. Hell, he could probably draw her family tree. It'd been sticking in her craw that she knew next to nothing about him, where he was from, who his people were: his coworkers, friends. Family.

Right now, squinting at the hot, nosy, Mercedes-driving

professor who was hijacking her bar, she could kinda see a lonely nerd who rented a room on the run-down side of town.

"What do you watch porn on?" she jeered.

Instead of ruffling his feathers, he turned slowly to consider her through those lenses, his thick hair failing forward again, and just silently looked his fill.

When I want to be inside you again, I will make it crystal clear, he'd told her. She'd felt his words like a lick at that sensitive spot in the small of her back.

She glared at the papers on her car. "You got me here. Convince me."

Without a word, he handed her a few sheets. On top was a photocopy of an old-timey document. *The Last Will and Testament of Wayland Edgar Hugh*, it said in an elaborate scroll across the top. The next piece of paper—thank God—was a transcript of the tiny, curlicue script. Alex started reading.

"How much do you know about Wayland Hugh?" Jeremiah asked her.

Alex shrugged noncommittally as she continued to read.

"He was one of original founders of Freedom; his name is on the incorporation papers from 1870." Alex snorted. *That* she knew. The Hugh descendants walked around town like they made Freedom from one of their ribs. "Wayland was an apothecary from Ohio and operated the town's first drugstore out of a clapboard building on Main Street. In 1890, when Freedom finally won a railroad line, Wayland saw an opportunity. He stumped for the line to run through the empty land east of town—land he already owned—and for Freedom to create a second business district. With the discovery of oil in the county, people were talking about the population growing to 100,000."

Alex snorted again and kept reading.

"With his campaign a success and the construction of a

state-of-the-art train depot underway, Wayland built his crown jewel: a brick building with a parapeted roof, two lovely bay windows, and his name emblazoned across the top in a faux brick scroll." Alex finally had reached the part about a second deed. "Hugh Apothecary anchored the new street that he'd cajoled city planners into naming 'Miracle Street,' and all of the business owners who'd believed his talk of explosive growth and riches waited for the crowds to come."

Alex had finished reading. She put down the paper and turned to watch Jeremiah, who was looking absently at the documents as he spoke. "The crowds did come. Mexican immigrants fleeing peonage, economic instability, and revolution were recruited to maintain railroad tracks, and they came in droves. They lived in boxcar settlements surrounding the depot, then began to build homes."

He grinned down at the sheets.

"Wayland was furious. That wasn't what he'd wanted at all. His neighbors began to walk away from their fine brick buildings, and Mexicans eager for a sense of home snatched them up and began businesses of their own, establishing a thriving *colonia*. Wayland had sunk his good name and every penny he had into the success of the east side; he couldn't afford to walk away. Ultimately, the Mexicans who frequented his apothecary and general store, paid him rent on other buildings, and built homes on his land, made him rich."

Finally, he looked at her. "He cursed every one of them."

Alex gave an involuntary shiver. She remembered the first time she tripped over nothing in front of the panel carved with Wayland Hugh's name. A splinter had wedged so far in her hand her grandmother had had to carefully slice her soft, eight-year-old palm to remove it.

She remembered the first time she changed the bulb in the

lamp over the panel, only to watch in fascinated horror as the new bulb flared furiously then sizzled out.

She flicked the paper with her nail. "This says Wayland parceled out all his stuff to a bunch of kids, but that he created a second deed for—" She looked at the sheet again. "Edward Hugh. Wayland's firstborn. And that if Edward or his descendants wanted the building, he could have it. Wayland wanted to 'sow the seed at the beginning to right a great wrong.'" She said it in her best *Downton Abbey* voice. "What's the wrong? Why's Edward get dibs?"

When Jeremiah didn't respond, she looked to see him staring at her. His eyes were as green as summer grass.

"What?"

"You're listening."

She scowled. "Of course I am." She scowled at herself, too. She'd been caught up in the drama of his story. It was like he was filling in missing concrete in her foundation. "Why else would I be here?"

"I... Sorry," he said, shaking his head. The sunlight gleamed off a couple strands of auburn in the dark, rich brown. "I couldn't find anything else about Edward in our records. But the Hugh clan is famously prolific, with lots of descendants. Without those documents from city hall, it's going to be difficult to disprove Lance's claim. We need to find out more information about Edward, the second deed, and what Lance is up to some other way."

"How..." She scrubbed her hair. She couldn't believe she was contemplating this. "How do you know the second deed wasn't used for kindling? Or toilet paper? How do we know it still exists?"

"We don't." Jeremiah shrugged. "But it's the most valuable piece of paper in Freedom if it does."

Alex scoffed. "Because whoever has it gets to own a building behind on its taxes?"

"Loretta is behind on her—"

Alex frowned. Why did she tell him that?

Jeremiah frowned back before he went on. "The will specifies that the second deed can be used to claim the Hugh Building and all of Wayland Hugh's holdings. When he died, Wayland Hugh owned most of the land that makes up the east side."

Alex started shaking her head. "No. No way. No way Doody-meyer can use a lost piece of paper to claim half the town!"

Jeremiah shrugged those meaty shoulders. "How many people could afford to fight him? He's got a couple of uncles who are judges. But you're right, Alex, all of this is conjecture. That's why I need your help."

He turned from her, gathered up the papers, and began tapping them together against the cherry-red of her hood. "Dutimeyer is putting time, resources, and a possible assault into this search; that tells me he believes a second deed still exists and that it's valuable. Edward Hugh is the firstborn son of a town paragon, and yet he's been scrubbed from the historical record. That denotes a family scandal." He finally stopped tapping the papers and returned them to his file folder without looking at her. "Descendants are happy to talk to the historical society about their family's glorious achievements, but they're less enthusiastic to share details they've swept under the rug."

"You need me to help sniff out the Hughs' dirty laundry?" It was the first happy thought she'd had all day.

Jeremiah looked at her, surprise licking into his dimples. "You know everyone," he said. "You know how they behave when they're not on their best behavior. You know how people are interconnected and what's whispered about them."

She'd never thought of that useless knowledge of her hometown as an advantage.

She handed the will back to Jeremiah. "I'm not saying I'm convinced." His conspiracy theory was just getting more and more wild. "I'm saying… I'm willing to turn over a rock or two with you. Just to see if anything crawls out that I can squish."

One of his knock-her-on-her-ass smiles grew over his face. "Great," he said. "You're driving."

He went around to the passenger side, creaked open the door, and carefully curled his gigantic body into her tiny car with the expression of a kid buckling into an amusement park ride.

Chapter Twelve

Jeremiah sat with his knees almost up to his chest in Alex's beautiful, mint-condition car as he gave her turn-by-turn directions and fought to hide his excitement about embarking on this adventure with her.

Cool was never his forte.

Alex was fascinating. He was fascinated. The other night, his catalog of her—a blue silk dragon robe showing up in his dreams, a haunting rose-and-baby-powder smell, the creak and shift of her in his bed—expanded to include the neat and evocative details of her room. Now it included a car that had taken an exorbitant amount of time and money to make so precious and pretty.

The soft croon of Etta James came through her speakers, surprising him. He assumed she only listened to music that roared. Hanging from her mirror was a medal of a sanctified woman with a dragon curled at her feet. *St. Martha, Pray for Us*, it read. In the plastic console she'd jammed in between the seats were oversized, polka-dotted sunglasses, hand sanitizer, a roll of quarters, a half-smoked joint in a sealed baggie, and a large pastel-pink tube of hand cream.

Her orderly contrariness captivated him. He wanted to touch each item. He wanted to ask her how she could be such a conundrum and yet be so consistently straightforward.

When she'd stared at him as he told her the abbreviated

story of Wayland Hugh and his Miracle Street, he'd known with confidence that she was absorbed and interested. That wasn't the polite look of colleagues or the struggling-to-stay-focused glazes of students or the tight smiles of family members embarrassed by his enthusiasm.

Alex Torres didn't do polite. She had no use for shielding her true thoughts with social niceties or good manners. She'd exposed herself and her thoughts of him nakedly and blaringly in every question she'd ever asked of him—*Want to help me blow off some steam? What gives you the right to tell that story? Do I look okay to you?*

She was honest when she wanted him and when she hated him. The way she'd looked at him as he told his story had been honest, too. She'd been engaged in his work and words, his efforts. It was an unvarnished appreciation that he could believe.

As Etta sang about a Sunday kind of love, they crossed out of downtown into the neighborhood of large turn-of-the-century mansions shaded by ancient oaks. After gas and oil was discovered in the county in the later part of the 1800s, the oil barons of northeast Oklahoma decided to make the little town with the pleasant breezes coming off the Viridescent River their weekend and summer retreat. Although the county saw many of its wells dry up by the 1920s, gas and oil continued to be a primary employer in Freedom until the industry contracted in the early '80s. Jeremiah was still surprised how many former refinery draftsmen and retired oil executives he met in town. The last remaining headquarters—five stories tall, with 55,000 feet of office space and an unfortunate lime-and-beige exterior—had been condemned several years ago.

Many of the mansions of Freedom's former oil wealth weren't faring much better. Built in the late Victorian and early Classic Revival style of large wraparound porches and gabled roofs, a multitude of rooms separated by French doors, and full basements and attics, many of the old girls had now been broken up into apartments. Some had been bought by antique-loving homeowners who had construction skills and a desire to own a mansion at the fraction of a mansion's price. Others had simply been left to rot.

According to town lore, they were all haunted.

It was easy to believe Freedom was a ghost town. The day was pretty, but the wide, potholed streets were empty of cars and people, and the bare limbs of oak trees created jagged black lines against the cool blue sky.

"Where're you from?" she asked.

He pointed her to a right turn. "Out East."

"That's it?" she asked. "East is a pretty big place."

He felt a prickle over his shoulders, anticipation balanced with alarm. Was she curious about him? "Connecticut mostly," he hedged. "I did my undergrad and master's work at Columbia, got my PhD at Brown. You'll take a left here."

"Fancy," Alex said. "Are you close with your family?"

The prickle turned into porcupine quills. "No."

"Why? And ease up on all the explanations. You're about to talk my ear off."

He should have been used to the invasive questions of the folks of Freedom. He'd handled them plenty of times before.

But he didn't want to lie to Alex.

"We don't have a lot in common," he said.

They passed a house he'd always appreciated, big and made of still-bright brick with a cupola that had a small round window, like the builders had created it for a plains princess who needed a tower to dream out of. As a child, observations like that used to roll off his tongue until he'd encountered a heavy sigh and awkward silence once too often.

"That's why they never need you in a hurry?" she asked. "Or do they just not know how to use a cell phone either?"

Ah. She was teasing him. That he could handle.

"I'm not a Luddite, Alex," he said as he turned to look at the cruel aviator sunglasses that hid her eyes, her high and artful hair. He could imagine how such a woman who shined her bad and glorious all over the internet could find his unwillingness to attach himself to such a tool bizarre.

He told her to make one more right. "I don't have a mobile device because I'd never take my eyes off of it. I can't have an open window to all the world's knowledge in my hand." He studied the variety of studs in her lobe, the silky black of her hair where it was shaved close to her head, the precise line of black lipstick that made the bow of her mouth that much more devastating. "When I become fascinated by something, I want to learn it intimately, inside and out."

Why hadn't he been staring at her all this time? She was a foot away and there was no wall between them. She smelled sweet and soft.

She tilted her mirrored shades at him, allowing Jeremiah a distorted look at his bedazzled expression, before quickly looking back out the windshield. "Are we getting there soon? Freedom's not that big."

"Here," he said, pointing.

Jeremiah didn't want an open window to the world. More importantly, he didn't want the world looking back.

She pulled up in front of a big, flat-fronted home with five two-story columns. "You could have just told me to drive to the mayor's place."

Jeremiah opened his door and got out.

Bernie Hugh Mayfield had been the town's mayor for four terms and showed no interest in giving up the throne anytime soon. Jeremiah found the man's conservative politics offensive, but for the sake of the historical society and the tiny bit of influence Jeremiah had with the city council, he kept his opinions to himself. Mayor Mayfield slapped an American flag on anything that stood still and loved having Jeremiah around to point out East Coast elitism. But in truth, the man enjoyed the whiff of pretension Jeremiah gave him and city government.

Jeremiah was counting on Mayfield's haughtiness and his willingness to be manipulated by a constant flow of meaningless compliments to help him discover what had inspired Lance Dutimeyer's city hall crawl.

They had to walk up two levels of stone steps to reach the door of the garish, plantation-style home lording over the street. It stood on the bones of the original Hugh mansion, a lovely affair (according to the pictures Jeremiah had seen) before Bernie built this monstrosity that looked ripped from the pages of *Gone with the Wind*.

Jeremiah pressed the doorbell. Inside, they could hear an elaborate version of Lee Greenwood's "Proud to be An American" played out in door chimes.

"Don't think I can help your cause here," Alex grumbled from just behind him. He turned to look at her, at her mirrored shades, the side of her mouth drawn up skeptically. He was starting to like the rolling, throaty drawl of her grumbles.

"Our cause," he told her. "Dirty laundry."

The door opened and Jeremiah smiled at Bernie Hugh Mayfield like he was one of the five people who'd bought, read, and enjoyed his published thesis paper.

"Mayor Mayfield, wonderful, you're home!"

Big and broad and yellow haired with a gleaming set of dentures, the mayor returned his smile with delighted eyes, unused to this level of enthusiasm from the historical society head.

Then his eyes slipped over Jeremiah's shoulder. His smile dimmed.

"Well, well, girl," the man said, drawing himself up like he needed to tower over Alex's five-foot-nothing. "You finally here to apologize for what you painted on my columns?"

Jeremiah's smile froze.

"Bernie, like I said before, I have no idea what you're talking about. You finally payin' my cousin a living wage?"

The mayor's face flushed a florid red and he turned to glare at Jeremiah. "Dr. Post, I know this isn't PC to say, but there are good ones and bad ones. It would be best if you could figure out the difference."

The man stepped back and slammed the door shut and—in the span of twenty seconds—Jeremiah Post found himself steeped in the most disgusting racist incident of his life. He turned around to find Alex casually jogging back down the steps to her car.

"Told you I wasn't going to be any help," she called back to him.

Every bone in his body felt weighted with shock and disgust and ineffectiveness. He shoved himself forward and hurried after her.

"Alex…" he called. "I'm… I'm so sorry."

She glanced at him as she reached the sidewalk. "No worries, professor."

With her glasses hiding her eyes and the lazy smile on her face, he might have believed her nonchalance if she'd ever shown a drop of it before.

This was the first time she wasn't being honest with him.

"I…" He could feel Hugh's eyes on his back through the curtains. "Get in the car."

She circled the car and got in the driver's seat as if she was fine with Jeremiah ordering her around.

He settled in her car with a loud creak. He was afraid he was going to break the toy automobile with his giant uselessness and impotent anger.

"Good ones" and "bad ones." As if Alex's skin color and ethnicity gave Mayfield the right to line her up and judge her.

"What did you paint on his columns?" he asked.

"Slave labor," she said, not denying it as she looked out the windshield and kept her hands on the wheel. "He was paying my cousin pennies an hour to take care of his mom and work overtime. It took forever to figure out a good message for five columns. With the way his house is all raised up, you could see it from three blocks away."

"That must have felt great."

She huffed and looked at him. He wanted to take her glasses off, but didn't dare.

"The *Freedom Gazette* did an 'exposé,'" she said, drawing air quotes. Then she pointed at an older model Chevy Malibu parked a half block down the street. "That's my cousin's car. He makes her park down there so she doesn't spoil the view, doesn't even let her park in the driveway. But he gives her a raise before every election."

"I'm sorry he said what he said." His fingers flexed on his knees. "I'm sorry I didn't respond."

How did he focus on her and not on the heavy weight of ineffectiveness he felt? How did he apologize for the centuries of entrenched other-ism based on the melanin in an American's skin?

"It's hard to snap back quick, isn't it?" she murmured, still looking at her cousin's car. "Punching people stopped being an option when I turned eighteen." She straightened in her seat and got out her keys. "What time is it?"

He blinked at the non sequitur.

"C'mon," she said. "Put that fancy watch to use."

He glanced at his Rolex then told her.

She looked again at her cousin's car. "I think I know where we can get some answers."

Just like that, they were pulling away from the curb and sweeping what had happened under the rug.

"Wait," he said. "Alex, I—"

"Look," she interrupted. "I swore to myself a long time ago that I wouldn't be embarrassed by other people's racism. I'm not the one who should be ashamed. But, in front of you...yeah, that was embarrassing. So can we please drop it."

He wanted to pull her into his lap. Not in a tender way. He wanted her to straddle him so he could show her how hungry her bold, bare honesty made him.

His admiration for this woman he couldn't trust made him want to eat her alive.

"Of course" was all he said.

Twenty minutes later, after a quick grocery stop, Jeremiah found himself trailing behind Alex at the Riverview Park Zoo as she circled Monkey Island, a fenced-in knoll and moat with a castle playland for a group of capuchin monkeys. Monkeys had populated the space since the zoo was built in the 1920s, and a faded sign trumpeted how the famous Miss Able, a rhesus monkey from the zoo, had been the first monkey in space.

Periodically, her preserved form was shown at the Smithsonian's Air and Space Museum.

This wild little town.

Alex paid no attention to the scampering monkeys or the sign as her face lit up when she saw a middle-aged woman in green scrubs sitting on a park bench reading a paperback.

"Linda," she called, waving and rushing forward.

The woman looked up, a wreath of instant and surprised welcome on her round face. "Alejandra," she said, standing and hurrying to meet Alex halfway. The two women hugged tightly. "I heard you were back in town. I'm sorry I haven't had the chance to come by Loretta's."

Linda was several years older than Alex, short and round with her hair pulled back into a thin, brown ponytail. She had Alex's glamorous smile.

Alex answered Linda's curious look at Jeremiah with an introduction. Then she said, "Mother Hugh still running you ragged?"

Linda shrugged. "At least they're paying me good for the work." She reached out and squeezed Alex's hand. "Thanks to you. Bernie can't wait for her to die. That's how I get her to take her meds; we're both happiest when we're irritating her son."

Alex laughed with her cousin. "Can I speak with her?"

Linda's eyebrows quirked and she glanced at Jeremiah. "Of course."

Alex kissed her cousin's cheeks before she and Jeremiah walked toward a grove of willow trees.

"Do you know about the peacocks?" she asked him.

"I know my blood curdled the first time I heard them screaming."

Legend had it that in Freedom's heyday, a millionaire brought two peacocks to town to adorn his lawn, but after finding them unruly, he let them run wild. Now, cries of the plentiful flock echoed all over town. They were like Freedom's roosters, a harrowing alarm clock to those who'd never heard their call.

Jeremiah cleared a path for them through the budding fronds as they walked through the willow trees.

"Every few years, a pissed-off citizen tired of cleaning up peacock poop or being chased down a sidewalk tries to get the city to cull the herd," she said. "But the city can't. Not while Bernie's mom is still kicking. There's only one thing she loves in this world, and that's those peacocks. She comes here every day at this time to feed them."

When they exited the low-hanging branches of the trees, Jeremiah saw a magnificent sight: a flock of brilliant male and plainer female peacocks filled a scraggly patch of grass. Two of the males had their feathers fanned, shaking big eyes of deep royal blue surrounded in emerald green. They weren't trying to seduce the ladies. They were, instead, shaking them at an elderly woman in a wheelchair who was tossing bread crumbs with an arthritic hand.

"A Hugh descendant who only loves birds?" Jeremiah murmured as they approached her, her wheelchair turned away from them. "Usually, all a Hugh loves is their family name and past accomplishments."

"Not this Hugh," Alex whispered, taking her sunglasses off. "She married Mayfield for his money, thinkin' he'd get her out of Kansas and away from them. Unfortunately, Mayfield married her for her money, too."

They were still a few yards away when Mother Hugh squawked, "Who's chittering back there? You're gonna scare my babies. If you're here to mug an old woman, get it over with."

Alex pulled a container out of her bomber jacket as she came within the woman's view. She showed her a pint of blueberries. "Can I feed your peacocks?"

The elderly woman glared through her glasses. "You won't get any money off me!"

Alex stayed silent.

The woman sniffed. "Well...they do love their berries."

Jeremiah stood quietly by as Alex began to toss blueberries to the wildly interested birds.

Mother Hugh was tiny and bundled up, wearing a coat, a

knit cap, and an afghan across her lap. Even swaddled, wearing glasses, and with white wisps escaping her cap, there was something about the woman that warned you not to get too close to her chair. She could bite.

"I know you?" Mother Hugh asked.

Alex tossed a berry while Jeremiah took a slow step back from a waist-high male giving him the evil eye. "My family owns the Hugh Building over on Milagro Street."

The older woman gave a grunt of disapproval. "That horrible name."

Over the century of their dominance in Freedom, the prolific Hugh family had enjoyed emblazoning their name around town: on the now-decrepit Hugh Amphitheater in the park, on the Hugh Gym at the high school that was now in need of a renovation, on the Hugh Family Charity Golf Event that had raised some eyebrows about where the money actually ended up. But, until Dutimeyer's interest, they'd all eschewed the Hugh building and the east side, seeming to want to forget that the seed of their wealth had been planted on Miracle-turned-Milagro Street.

"We've been looking into the history of the building," Alex said simply. "I was wondering if you could tell us about Edward Hugh?"

Mother Hugh cackled. "You Mexicans know about the family curse?" Her white hair shivered as she laughed. "Wayland is flipping in his grave."

Alex shot a quick glance at Jeremiah, then scattered the rest of the berries to the eager birds, put the container in her pocket, then turned to face the woman.

"Curse?" Alex asked.

Mother Hugh narrowed her eyes at her. "You thought you could come out here and bribe an old woman with blueberries?"

Remembering how everything fell apart with Mother Hugh's son, Jeremiah was about to intercede with some of that charm elderly women loved when Alex said, "Do you want me to lie to you?"

He closed his eyes.

"The firstborn of Wayland Hugh was a disgrace and a disappointment from the instant he slid out of the womb," he heard Mother Hugh say. He popped his eyes open. "Was about as useful as my worthless son. Edward was rich with all the advantages in the world and a town at his feet and what did he do with that apothecary education he learned on his daddy's knee? He became..." She leaned over the arm of her wheelchair. "A bootlegger!" Her eyes were a delighted blue behind her silver-rimmed glasses. "Got himself arrested, would have ruined the family name and all Wayland had worked for if his daddy hadn't covered up his mess. You know what Edward did for a thank you? Knocked up some slut, jumped into a sidecar, and stole out of town. Lucky son-of-a-gun."

The wind whooshed out of Jeremiah. Was their search over before it had begun?

"If Edward's the family curse who left town," Alex asked, "then why would Wayland try to give everything to him in his will?"

Mother Hugh peered at her. "You Mexicans are smarter than you look."

At that moment, Jeremiah swore to do everything he could to loosen the Hughs' blithely racist leash on this town.

"The curse began..." Mother Hugh's voice dropped to a whisper "...when Edward came back."

Edward Hugh had returned to Freedom. Jeremiah's heartbeat kicked up.

"What happened?" Alex asked.

Mother Hugh settled back against her chair. "Why would I tell you?"

"Because you like my cousin more than you like anyone in your family. And you hate her," Alex said. "I'll bring you a pint of blueberries once a week and you can spout off about any number of things that make you unhappy."

Squaring off with this lonely, spite-filled old woman, Alex had the bigger piece of cheese. He was so glad—so glad— he'd begged her to join this hunt.

"Come twice a week," Mother Hugh snapped.

"Fine."

Mother Hugh sunk her hand into her bread bag of crumbs, but all black-and-beady eyes were still on Alex.

She had that effect on everyone.

"Wayland Hugh, stark raving mad on his deathbed, cursed this family when he declared his chosen one was the one he'd disowned, a degenerate criminal who wanted nothing to do with him." She said it with gleeful malevolence as she slowly sprinkled out crumbs for the peacocks. "If not for the curse, my family used to say, the Hughs would have had dominion far beyond the borders of Freedom. But we can't escape this horrible little town; whenever someone tries, we fail spec- tacularly."

The delight on the woman's wrinkled face made her look years younger.

"Used to be whispered you could break the curse if you found what Wayland had promised his dishonored firstborn. Most of the Hughs—like my good-for-nothing son—are too lazy to look or too stupid to remember. They're happy for the little bit of blood they can still squeeze out of Freedom. But you're not the only young person who's come to visit me recently."

Mother Hugh set her cold eyes on them. She'd been bait-ing them all along. She'd wanted to tell this story. The kill was only good if you got to play with it first.

"That loser Lance is looking to snatch what Wayland promised his firstborn. He's thinking he can grab the east side and the treasure along with it."

"Treasure?" Alex asked.

"You Mexicans don't know everything, do you?" the old woman cackled. "Family legend has that Wayland hid a fortune with the second deed. Find it, find what the family has lost."

"Where would Lance look?" Alex asked.

That made her hoot harder. "You're the smart one. Just make sure he doesn't swipe it out from under your little brown nose."

Ghosts, curses, and treasure.

And wicked old witches.

The hunt to find the second deed before Lance Dutimeyer did was on.

Chapter Thirteen

Alex screeched into one of the few remaining spaces in Loretta's parking lot, still shaking her head.

Curses? And treasure? Actual treasure?

She felt like Short Round to Jeremiah's Indiana Jones.

"You said Dutimeyer wants the deed to complete his evil plan to claim the east side," Alex had argued as she drove him back to his car. "Now we're gonna believe there's a treasure, too?"

"Our skepticism doesn't matter to Dutimeyer," Jeremiah had replied, the gold in his eyes sparkling behind his glasses. "It certainly gives him extra incentive. And isn't he the type to want it all: the building, the east side for whatever he's planning, and the fabled treasure of family legend?"

It had taken a couple of minutes to even get a word in edgewise, he'd been so over-the-top about how she'd done it and how horrible the Hughs were and how systemic racism was the cancer that blah, blah, blah... The rosy flush had been high on his marble-carved cheekbones; he'd looked like a rocket about to ignite.

Alex had gone back and forth with him as they leaned on their cars behind the dumpster at city hall until she'd seen the time and freaked. She was going to be so late. Jeremiah had to return to his office. But he hadn't even tried to hide the smug look on his face as he got into his Mercedes.

He knew he'd roped Alex in good and tight to his treasure hunt.

She ignored her own ember of pride that she'd dug something up, dug up the fact that the Hughs—for all of their advantages and the way they lorded those advantages over the whole damn town—considered themselves cursed.

What assholes.

One of them had to keep looking at this whole deal with a side-eye. It wasn't going to be Jeremiah. The big, eager puppy.

The big, goofy, hot, brainy, kinda sweet puppy. Alex had served drinks to thousands of people, but she didn't think she'd ever served anyone like Jeremiah Post. She'd had the stupidest impulse to lean over her stick shift and against those heavenly suspendered shoulders after Bernie shot his shot. He would've let her.

You didn't look like her, as Latina as her, without dealing with racism in all its glorious forms. Although most people would assume she'd jump straight to mad, she'd actually greeted it with every color of the rainbow—shock, a snappy comeback, a punch, a blank look and a hollow ache, ignoring it, losing her fricking mind. At twenty-nine, though, and coming from Bernie and his old, sad, angry mother, it just made her so exhausted.

She was grateful Jeremiah had followed her lead. She'd never wanted a man to take care of her problems. That the brainiac had been as flabbergasted as she sometimes felt—and that he'd had her back—was enough.

She waved at a couple of folks leaving Loretta's as she ran around the back so she could enter through the back door and get right into the kitchen. Her mom was going to be so pissed.

The weekend crew yelled at her as she flung off her coat and tied on an apron.

"What the hell, Alex," shouted Barbara, the weekend cook

and a longtime friend of her mom's. "Plates are backing up." Alex did a visual check—food on the grill looked manageable and Julio was keeping up with the dishes. Barbara and Julio ran a tight ship over the weekends and the marginal improvement in food had helped to keep Loretta's limping along. But the plates under the warmer were stacked two deep.

"I got it," Alex yelled back, grabbing the orders for two tables. Every decent service industry employee eventually learned to have eight arms and twelve hands.

When she came through the hall, the main room was already three-quarters of the way full, and the setting sun was shining through the front bay windows making all the worn wood glow pretty and orange. It was mostly family on this early Friday evening, but Alex saw a group of ladies at the bar celebrating happy hour and she knew they were supposed to get a post-Little League-practice group of parents and kids soon. The number of customers was startling, and Alex couldn't blame it all on the magnetism of her presence.

The best bitch in bartending had made a few changes that were already shining up the place.

She just hoped her grandmother noticed.

She barely missed getting mown down by a sprinting three-year-old—"Patty, don't let him run around in here!"— as she delivered the first set of plates with a murmured apology and a promise of free beer refills.

She grabbed the table's empty mugs and spun around.

She locked eyes with her father.

Tucker Armstead was stacking dirty plates into a bin at a close-by table. His true-blue eyes were magnets on her.

Three full plates slipped from her left hand. They crashed explosively in the echoey space, startling a few people into screams.

"Dad!" she exclaimed. The room was shocked into silence.

The Tiffany lamp at the front corner went out with a tiny pop. "What are you doing here?"

"Are you okay?" Tucker asked, rushing forward with the bin, a white apron tied over his jeans and shirt. "Did you hurt yourself?"

Alex realized she had Velveeta-cheese queso dripping down one leg of her jeans. She was standing in a heap of broken plates and Friday-night burrito specials in the middle of a silent and crowded dining room looking at a man she hadn't seen or talked to in thirteen years.

Everything in her went cold and hard.

She raised her chin and blinked away her tears. "I said what the fuck are you doing here?"

"Alejandra," her mom hushed as she hurried across the room toward them.

Her father bent down on a knee and started to pick up the shattered plates. "I heard you needed some extra hands," he said, putting the mess in the bin.

"You heard wrong," she said, staring down at his pale blond head. He hadn't lost a strand of that thick head of hair; her dad was as handsome as ever. Maybe even more handsome. He looked trimmer and healthier than he had before she left. He still had his full, blond moustache; he'd had it for so long that it had circled back to trendy. She could see strands of white in his hair as he kneeled at her feet.

"Alejandra," her mother said, now next to her, dark eyes wide. "I called him."

Alex savaged her with a glare. "Of course you did."

She should have gotten out of town the instant she knew her mother was seeing him again.

"Stop it," Mary hissed, pulling her gorgeous hair over her shoulder. "You weren't here. I didn't know if you were coming back."

Of course. Of course. Because the last weeks of sunup-to-midnight effort on Alex's part wasn't enough to prove to her mother that she cared, that she was putting in the effort to make this work, that this meant something to her.

She was never going to get her mother's support when her father was in the picture.

Alex saw Gina and Matthew, the weekend help, give her twin looks of sympathy. The entire quiet dining room was taking in the Alex show.

She looked at the table whose food she'd dropped. "I'm gonna have to put your order in again. It's all on the house, of course. I'll grab you a plate of French fries."

Head held high, she put the empty beer mugs on the bar, requested that Gina deliver another round, then walked to the kitchen.

Mary followed on her heels.

"Mija," her mother said as Alex slapped through the kitchen doors.

"Sorry, Barbara," Alex said. Through the roar of the corrido music, the sizzle of the grill, and Julio's blast of the dish sprayer, she doubted Barbara heard all the commotion out in the bar. "You're gonna have to redo table 15."

"What?" Barbara yelled.

"Alejandra," her mother said again as Alex went over to the fry bin. She heaped a bunch on a plate and salted them. "He was the only one I could think to call at the last minute—"

"Right," Alex said, slamming the plate down. She whirled on her mother. "Right. In a town where you can't throw a rock without hitting family, the only person you think to call is the one person I explicitly told you not to bring here."

Tucker came through the swinging door with the bin. Alex was shocked again by his presence. He wasn't a big guy, only about five foot eight, and his button-up shirt was tucked in neatly, his buttons done at the cuffs. She'd once appreciated his neat, bookish appearance, the way he always tucked in his shirts and kept a little moustache comb in his back pocket that she'd steal to brush her hamsters. He'd been so different than many of the loud, brash, gotta-prove-something dads in town.

Then he'd started drinking and became a stranger.

He put the bin down and came toward them.

"We knew you were going to be angry," he said. "We didn't see another way to get through the evening rush."

We...we. She focused all her anger on her mother.

"I said I was coming back," she said through gritted teeth.

"I know," Mary said. "I'm sorry."

Alex breathed out a huff. "Then he can leave."

Her mother looked at her steadily, her hair trailing down her soft pink shirt. "Until...until your grandmother is back on her feet or we can hire someone else...we need the extra hands."

Thank God her grandmother hadn't been there to hear Alex drop an F-bomb in front of the early evening families. She'd had physical therapy that afternoon, which usually wore her out, so she was home.

"What are you saying?" Alex demanded.

Mary took a deep breath. "I'm saying your father has offered to help." She crossed her arms under her ample boobs. "I'm going to let him."

Alex's mouth fell open. "No. That's not fair. You have no right to—"

Mary drew herself up as much as her five feet would let her. "I have every right, Alejandra. Your grandmother isn't doing me a favor by letting me work here. This is my bar, as much as hers, something you and your sisters fail to acknowledge."

Startled, Alex said, "That's not—"

"You girls overlook and dismiss me except when you're

angry with me." Mary put her hands on her hips. "Let me make this clear: my decision to start seeing your father again was not to hurt you. In fact, it has *nothing* to do with you. *I* didn't know you were coming back. *I* didn't know you were interested in taking over the bar. Why? Because you don't talk to me."

Over the last thirteen years, they'd talked. When Alex came home for the occasional holiday, they'd talked about Loretta or the family or what Mary was growing in her garden. They'd talked over the last few weeks about inventory and the schedule and who was going to open. Observing Mary at the bar, Alex had acknowledged that her mother was an octopus-armed multitasker who maintained her cool during a rush and kept Loretta's running as best as a car dragging its muffler could.

But her mom's calm and contained had driven Alex batshit crazy when she was young. So many evenings, so many weekends, so many Christmases and Easters and Sunday dinners, Alex would see that little frown between her mother's brows as she tried to smile away their dad's behavior and absence, as she made excuses for him without showing how much it hurt. How unfair it was.

Mary had never insisted on anything for herself until now.

"He is trying to make amends to me." Mary shoved a thumb at her husband. "If one of the ways he wants to do that is by offering my business free labor, I'm going to let him. We need the help around here and he's going to stay. I don't know what your plans are, but if you want this bar to be part of your future, you better get used to it."

Alex swallowed down her howl of denial as Mary put her soft, rose-scented hands on her, her brown eyes full of love and frustration. "I let you down, but I have tried and tried and tried to make it better for years. And what has it gotten me? You ignore me except when I'm your punching bag. Well, I'm *tired* of it." Her mother squeezed her biceps. "You're a grown woman now, not a teenager. When you're ready to have a real conversation with me, I'm here."

Her tiny, kindergarten-teacher-of-a-mom walked out of the kitchen—not one beautiful black hair out of place as it trailed down her back—with her head held high.

If the speech had been aimed at anyone else, Alex would have applauded her for it.

She turned to the plate of fries.

"I'm sorry," her dad said from behind her. "That was the worst possible way for this reunion to happen."

Alex turned further away from him. "There is no reunion. I don't want to look at you, I don't want to listen to you. I don't want you here."

"I get that." He had a light Midwestern drawl. She once thought he was the smartest man alive. "I'm so sorry." He stopped for a second. "Lord, I've missed you."

The hurt twisted inside her like a tornado.

She grabbed the plate of French fries and walked the long way around the kitchen so she could exit without having to look at him.

As the doors slapped closed behind her, she stopped just outside of the view of the dining room and swiped at an angry tear that had the fucking fearlessness to escape.

At their dinner table, her dad had once provided a quiet humor, the weird and interesting thoughts of an artist, and a rock-solid assurance that she and her sisters were the most interesting, smart, and capable daughters a man could be blessed with. She'd believed in Tucker Armstead—with his yellow pads and pens and clunky computer—as passionately as she'd believed the Earth circled the sun, Freedom was a great place to live, and Loretta was the world's best tortilla maker.

Then her dad had stopped believing in anything but the bottle.

Now her mother thought an alcoholic was more reliable at the bar than the best bitch in bartending. Just like her grandmother thought letting a wealthy East Coast intellectual erase the bar was better than giving it to her own flesh and blood.

What was Dr. Big Dick's story anyway?

It was time she found out, she thought with angry determination as she strode back out into the dining room.

Maybe she couldn't stop them from welcoming her father back to destroy their lives. But she sure as shit could make sure the professor didn't do the same.

Chapter Fourteen

It was late when Jeremiah parked at Loretta's feeling equal parts terrified and triumphant. The Open sign was off, but a light on the ground level was still glowing. He slung the white button-up shirt he'd taken off while moving boxes in the historical society's storage room over his shoulder; he didn't want to waste the seconds it would take to put it on and risk that light going out.

He couldn't wait until morning to tell Alex what he'd learned.

With his suspenders dangling around his waist, he grabbed the fax from Natisha, the rolled-up blueprint, and his briefcase and hurried to the entrance, planning to knock.

But the front door was still unlocked. He frowned.

With what he'd learned, they couldn't afford to leave doors unlocked after hours. He locked the door behind him, pushed past the saloon doors, then stumbled to a stop as the welcome cowbell clanged overhead.

Only one lamp on the bar was on. It created a sphere of liquid, multicolored light that surrounded one bar stool left on the ground.

The light also captured Alex, behind the bar, watching him with darkly lined eyes, slickly painted lips, and an artful curl to her hair. Her T-shirt had slipped down her arm. He could see one bare, mouthwatering shoulder tattooed with a bright magenta flower. She held a glass of something amber.

"Come here," she called, her voice low. Ice tinkled in her glass. "Come take a load off, professor."

As a man whose size sometimes provoked others, he'd developed a sixth sense for danger that now sent up a warning flare.

"Alex?" He glanced around the bar. The hall leading to the kitchen was dark. No one else was around.

"Come 'ere," she said again, this time with a curve of her cheek and a tilt of her mouth. Her lips were a deep bloodred. "If I was gonna bite, don't you think I would have done that already?"

The elation he'd been feeling plunged like a cut elevator. He'd thought…he'd hoped…

He'd foolishly believed that, after their compatriotism of today, she would finally put away the sexual innuendo that she used against him like a shield.

He slowly crossed the room toward her. In the provocative light, he saw she was wearing one of her cut-up T-shirts, this one in a washed-out lilac with The Queen is Dead written on it in hot-pink scroll. He could see skin: a smooth strip of belly above her jeans, the glisten of her collarbones beneath the stretchy black lace straps of her bra.

Was this what she'd been wearing under her bomber jacket when he'd been alone in a car with her? Without a protective cover—protective for him, not her—she looked like the worst idea he could have.

He reached the bar stool as mesmerized as some cartoon cat floating toward her on the scent of the dining room's rosemary, vinegar, and lemon perfume.

Her alluringly lined eyes were lazy and luminous. "What do you want to drink?"

"Drink?" What a horrible idea. "I should…" He glanced at the stairs, then gripped the papers he'd been so eager to show her.

Without taking her eyes off of him, she reached into the cooler, pulled out a beer, twisted the top off, and put it in front of the bar stool.

He could share one beer with her. Then he'd tell her what he'd learned. He'd rushed in with a purpose.

He laid the papers on the bar, put his belongings down, and took a seat.

The shock of the beer's chill made him realize how hot he was. How flushed. He took a drink then pressed it to his chest, above his undershirt, where he could feel perspiration gathering.

"You look like Marlon Brando," she said, her own drink near her mouth.

Jeremiah choked and coughed. "Excuse me?"

"In *Streetcar.*" She smiled a beguiling smile that included him in the joke. "I thought you were going to yell 'Stella!' when you came in. What've you been up to?"

He looked down at himself—the white undershirt, now dirty with storage room dust, his hanging suspenders. There was a streak of grime down one bicep. "I found something you should see."

When he looked up at Alex, her long-lashed eyes were stroking over him.

"Let's talk about that later. I'm more interested in gettin' to know you better." Her drawl dripped over his skin, as sticky as honey. "Where're you from?"

"Out—"

"Out East," she bit out. The *t* stung. "Yeah. You said that already. Mostly Connecticut. But what's your story?" Her voice went lazy again. "Who are your people?"

His heart rate was trying to kick up through the soporific effect of the low light and her lush beauty and her purring words. "Just…people," he said, the beer cold in his sweating hands. "There's not much to say. I don't have a lot in common with—"

"Yeah. You said that, too. Give me some details. Maybe *I* can tell you if you're anything like them. A history hound like you, who likes to sniff everyone's butt, you understand the importance of the specifics."

"I don't really want to get into all of—"

A knife-sharp gleam jumped into her eyes. "Oh," she laughed. "It's okay for you to Google me so you can judge me unfit to run this bar. But if *I* want to know more about a guy getting all up in my family's business so he can play Lord and Savior to a bunch of dirt-poor Mexican-Americans then that's—"

He put down his beer with a *thunk*. "Alex, what's going on?" What had happened since they'd parted? "Why are you doing this?"

"Just tryin' to get to the bottom of things." She shrugged with zero nonchalance. "You're so rich you barely notice the Rolex on your wrist or the ten-dollar words falling out of your mouth. Why're you here instead of hanging with the country club crowd, professor? You wanting this building makes about as much sense as Doody-meyer wanting it."

Jeremiah's temper flared at the comparison. "I'm nothing like him. I want to make sure your grandmother and mother are treated fairly."

"Uh-huh."

He felt the burn of frustration up to his hairline.

"Why do you give a fuck about them?" she demanded. "Being a big man with a fat wallet not enough to make you feel important?" She twisted her lips into a bloodred pout. "Or loved? Poor little rich boy."

He straightened at the double-barrel blast of her words. This wasn't the first time that he was accused of being desperate for affection. *Your neediness is cloying.* He should have been accustomed to the embarrassment others felt about his desire for connection.

"You know they're not going to adopt you, right?" she sneered. "They're *my* family. Not *yours.*"

Was she *jealous* of him? When he was so envious of what she had? He tried to take a sip of calm. "Alex, of course I know that—"

"I'll ask again. What's your story?" She hammered at him. "Why don't you go obsess about your own family and leave mine to me?"

She was ringing him like a gong. "Why is this so hard for you to understand? I don't get along with my family."

"Why?"

He snapped. "That's none of your goddamn business."

She burst into a full laugh, her silver-decked hand on her chest. "You've got to be kidding!" she declared, eyes wide and blazing. "It is my business. I trust you as much as I trust the other white man harassing my family. What deep dark secrets are you hiding, professor?"

He jolted off the stool and it toppled with a bang to the floor.

He had to go. He was furious.

"I'm not participating in this with you," he gritted out as he turned and headed for the stairs.

"You coward!" she shouted after him. "God forbid one of the Torres women refuses to bow at your feet. You say you want to protect my family, but when I'm trying to do the same, you run away." He could hear her coming after him as he took the stairs two at a time, only the moonlight coming through the stained glass on the landing lighting his way. "You're as fragile as a fucking daisy. No wonder you're so lousy in bed."

Enraged at that tired taunt, he spun in the middle of the hallway. She was right on his heels.

He shoved his face into hers. He wanted his scorn to burn her skin.

"Unlike every idiot you've been with, I don't have to base my worth on my sexual prowess."

"Good thing." Her eyes flashed. "Since you don't have any."

He set that up and she knocked it home.

"Damn you, Alex," he said, grabbing her.

Her shoulders were hot and strong in his hands. A sudden moonbeam, as clear as a spotlight shining through the stained glass, showed him her face.

Showed him the angry desire in her eyes.

He searched them, awestruck. "You want it like this," he breathed.

Her sharp chin shot up. "I don't want dick." She licked that fat, glistening bottom lip and didn't pull away.

Jeremiah slowly straightened. Refusing to apologize, he loomed over her while he pulled her close.

"You want this dick," he told her.

For an instant, he absorbed her shock and lust: her wide eyes, the gasp of her breath, the arch of her breasts. Never had he felt a further distance between his primal instinct and his wish for harmonious conformity.

Then her dark-side-of-the-moon eyes went calculating. She lifted her hands and spread them possessively on his chest.

She pushed and he let go. "I want you to understand something." She followed as she shoved him again. "My pussy...

she's not very discriminating." His back banged against the wall. "If we do this, it'll be hot." Her fingertips kneaded into his pecs. "It'll be memorable and interesting." Her palms pinned him to the paneling.

"But it won't be special. It won't be about you."

Her eyes were diamond hard. So was he.

Anger gave her permission. He wanted it, too. His fingers clung to the wall at his hips as he searched her: her heavy-lashed eyes, her ripe-plum mouth, the tight peaks of her nipples he could see through bra and T-shirt.

"Okay. Okay," he said, nodding quickly. Whatever. Whenever. However. "I accept your terms. I want to do this. Can we do this?"

She smiled and she was the winningest wicked witch, the black cat with a whole dairy of cream, his whip-cracking Cruella soul mate. "Okay," she said.

Jeremiah picked her up. He wrapped her thighs around him, grabbed that fabulous ass, and thrust his tongue into her mouth. He kept going until he thumped her against the opposite wall. He planted her against it so he could finally savor the infuriating, exhilarating, undeniable taste of Alex Alejandra Torres-Armstead.

She gave a shocked moan-gasp around his tongue.

He licked and nipped the sound off her lips. God, her lips. So ripe and pillowy. But she tasted of lipstick and that wasn't…he needed to get to the flesh of her. He leaned back and swiped the heel of his hand across her mouth, smearing the red, streaking it across her creamy brown skin. She moaned when he dove back in and there…yes. That. He nibbled on her naked tender lips, tasted and savored where her heat ran close to the surface.

Her plush, warm bottom squirmed in his hands as her

thighs squeezed him closer. When he fed her his tongue, her nails dug into his chest.

Pressing all of her against him, he slow plunged into Alex Torres's mouth, imagined entering her below with the same rhythm, slow in and slow out right up against the wall, so she felt him deep, so he could feel her everywhere.

She tasted amber-gold. He sucked on her tongue, sucked her flavor right off of it, and she gave some kind of helpless sound right into him. Their mouths were an infinite loop of pleasure and he wanted to slide her to the floor, open his pants, and feel that pleasure around his hard penis.

Feed that pleasure into her soft, wet, amber-tasting vagina.

He hefted her higher so he could press between her legs, squeeze her glorious temple of an ass, rub along the seam of her with his pinkies. She gave a little "gah" against his mouth and bit his lip. Her hands were trapped between them.

"Touch me, Alex," he demanded, sliding his mouth over her jaw, setting his teeth to the sharp chin she was always jutting at him. "You said you wanted… Touch me."

When she still didn't, he pulled his addicted mouth off her.

Her mouth lurched for his before she realized and pulled back. Her eyes were dazed; she looked like she could barely keep her heavy lids open. She was breathing fast. Framed against the old paneling, she looked impossibly young.

His grin grew wolfish.

Mr. Quick-on-the-Draw. Lousy in bed. Last longer than thirty seconds. She'd taunted him relentlessly about his fast orgasm.

Jeremiah had never had sex with a stranger before, although he'd had countless invitations from them when he was young: nude photos coming to his email, people he didn't know approaching him in the school cafeteria. He chose bedmates he could trust, who wanted him for him. And while—as he'd told her—he'd never based his self-worth on his sexual prowess, he put all of his innate enthusiasm, skills at research, and training as an observer into ensuring his partners felt as much pleasure as he did. Normally, no orgasm went untended.

He believed the interaction of the spiritual, metaphysical, and primal during sex created something sacred. He'd even co-authored a paper about how such a philosophy impacted the lives of early Creole settlers.

As he carried the whole of her in his hands, as he gloried over her heavy, slopey eyes and eager panting mouth, as he shifted his penis against where he wanted to be again even though it would be declaratively disastrous, there was nothing scholarly or virtuous about what he wanted to do to Alex Torres.

He bent toward her neck, inhaled the spice and baby powder scent of her. "Keep going?" he teased, low enough for her to feel the grate of his voice. He remembered how she'd taunted him. He remembered how she'd pushed.

He remembered how angry he was with her.

This was a horrible idea.

But at the feel of her frantic nod, he hoisted her higher up the wall so her big breasts were right in front of his face. She gave a whimpering gasp that shut up all of his better intentions.

"Take your shirt off," he said, and he nipped the hard nipple right in front of his mouth. She shuddered. "Alex…get rid of your shirt."

Her bottom danced in his hands as her pelvis moved like she would get herself off on his ribs.

Then she was struggling out of her T-shirt and she flung it away and Jeremiah got to watch it, his eyes, his nose, his mouth, right in front of her luscious body, watch her breasts move and bounce, releasing a cloud of her sweet scent as her breasts settled in black lace.

Her bra was stretchy, barely containing her in a pattern of interconnected roses and thorns. Her nipples were deep brown and large, tight at their tips. His imagination was extraordinarily good, but she was prettier than anything he could have dreamed up.

He sucked in a breath to calm himself.

"Do you like to have them touched?" he asked. His obsession didn't have to be hers. "Do you like to have them licked?"

She moaned and nodded, her breasts trembling right in front of his face, and at last, she touched him, her fingers twisting into his hair and pulling him toward her breast.

With a starving smile, he let her guide him to her flesh and sucked her nipple, her body, the essence of Alex, into his mouth.

She twisted the hair in her hands with a hiss and he sucked harder, flicked her with his tongue, propped her up on one forearm while wrapping the other around the small of her back, forcing her to arch and give him more, offer up that beautiful boob for him to devour. He stroked over the lace with his tongue, nipped at the nipple, sucked it in again deep as her strong fingers urged him closer. Her fingers were desperate in his hair. He let her nipple go with a dirty pop and nuzzled across to the other boob. Succulent heavy flesh. Baby sweet with the warm tinge of her salt. He flattened his tongue, stroked and memorized, felt the silk of her between the fine threads. He lightly took her nipple between his teeth and glanced up.

Her head was arched back against the wall, eyes clenched and mouth wide, gasping into the air of the hallway. He was about to take her in her grandmother's building.

He didn't want... Well, he did want...

Alex Torres made him contradict himself. Everything he prided himself in, she turned on its head.

"What do you want, Alex?" he groaned against delicious skin and lace.

"Inside," she gasped into the haunted, historic air. "Fuck me."

They were the first words she'd spoken since she'd given him permission.

It'll be hot. It'll be memorable. But it won't be special. It won't be about you.

He'd never so desperately wanted to mark a woman.

He slid her down to her feet before he could convince himself that he shouldn't, stroked his hands over her round hips and the smooth skin in the curve of her back, up over the flowers on her arm and into the shorn hair at her nape. He tilted up her head and claimed her mouth, kissed her deep enough to forget that this was a bad idea, deep enough to give him something to remember after he regretted it. As he tongued at her, he undid the top button of her jeans and pulled down her zipper.

Her hands slid over his biceps.

"Your fucking..." she gasped against his mouth. "Your fucking arms."

He grinned like an outlaw and flexed his muscles like the worst of showoffs.

He gripped her neck tighter as he smoothed his free hand down her soft belly and into her panties.

"Oh God," she sputtered, lurching against him as she grabbed onto his arm.

"Should I stop?" he breathed against her mouth. He lightly stroked his finger back and forth across crinkly hair.

"Nonononononono," she said, clinging to him like he still supported her weight.

He grinned like an outlaw looking down the barrel of a gun.

He slid his finger into the heat and wet between her folds and watched her face, that lipstick he'd smeared, as he did it.

His bad decisions were going to get worse if he kept looking at her desperate in pleasure; he tilted her head up to devour her mouth while he caressed her clitoris.

She whimpered and sagged against him.

He never expected this. He never expected her to be soft and acquiescent and swept away. He thought making love to Alex was going to be a war. Instead, her surrender was the sweetest, most addicting aphrodisiac.

It was turning him feral.

He wanted her naked. He wanted her thighs wide, around his hips, planted on his mattress, over his face. He wanted to lick up what was soaking his hand, then stroke his penis inside this hot, wet Alex place, inside all of her hot, wet places.

He wanted her to remember him.

He shifted his hand to stroke at her entrance while he circled her, ripe and hard and juicy, with his thumb.

"Alex," he said, holding her head, kissing her mouth. "Sweetheart, can you come for me?"

"Oh god." It came out like a sob.

He was about to lose his mind. He thrust against her hip. He entered her with the tip of his middle finger and played at her there, his thumb vibrating.

"Alex, Alex, can you come for me, honey? Please?"

She groaned and shoved her hips against his hand.

He slowly pushed his big finger into the tight heaven of her. He pushed it as deep as he could go.

"Now, Alex." He began to shove his palm against the cradle of her, hard as her pelvis rocked against his hand and his finger fucked her and his thumb circled and flicked and stroked. He held her head and kissed her deep. Then he dragged his mouth to her ear. "Now, dear," he whispered into it.

"Come."

Her vagina clenched hard and mind-emptyingly good on his finger as she cried out then gripped him, there would be bruises left on him, her mark on him, as she came wetly into his palm, and he took her, kept rubbing and flicking and fucking until she twisted to the side but he wouldn't let her go, pulled her close and buried his head in her neck, and she called out and came again, the squeeze just as strong, just as much temptation, and he groaned, long and frustrated and so, so, so tempted, and jerked his hips away from her because even a featherlight touch from her right now would give her more ammunition to mock him with.

He flipped away and slumped back against the wall, let her cling to his arm and lean on his shoulder as the wall supported her side.

He pulled his finger out and held her, warm and wet, in his hand.

They stood there together for several minutes in the dark hallway, barely visible to each other, as their breaths evened out. He could feel the softness of her breasts and her slowing-down heartbeat against his arm.

"I want you, Alex," he said when he could delay it no longer. His voice echoed hollowly in the hallway. "You've known it from the start and there's nothing I can do to hide it. But you want me, too."

He gently pulled his hand from between her legs. He gave her a moment to untangle herself from his arm then he straightened from the wall and stepped away. He turned his back to her, ignoring his bellowing erection.

"The fact that we both feel that way makes us doubly damned."

He opened his bedroom door; the milagro of a burning heart that caught the dregs of moonlight mocked him.

"Wanting each other is the dumbest mistake we've ever made."

He stepped into his room and closed the door behind him.

Chapter Fifteen

Too early the next morning, Alex jogged along the banks of the Viridescent River, scanning the next curve through the overhanging trees rather than watching out for snake holes, crab grass, and mud puddles on this unmaintained trail that seemed certain to grab and twist an ankle.

She was looking for Jeremiah. She was literally running after the professor.

She rolled her eyes and picked up her pace.

The slam of the back second-story door had woken her from where she was slumped over her grandmother's desk. She knew he ran along this trail, just a couple blocks from the bar, most mornings. The riptide of guilt she'd felt in the next instant had had her lurching to her room, struggling into her tights and running shoes in the bathroom as she rushed to pee and brush her teeth, hurrying downstairs to the bar, and now freezing her ass off in the early morning sunrise as she searched for him.

She'd fucked up. She needed to tell him that.

Alex accepted that she regularly pissed people off. Liked it, even. Usually. She saw no value in undermining herself to please, make peace, avoid, or acquiesce to people whose expectations, morality, or basic human decency conflicted with hers.

But every time she'd taken on someone, taken on a man,

she'd actually had a good reason. Sometimes she came up with that reason in a split second.

Generally, she didn't share that reason with anyone else.

Like when she spray-painted the mayor's house. She wasn't going to let him mistreat her cousin without answering for it. And she'd been more than justified when she stole Doody-meyer's calf out of his barn. He'd earned his nickname long before he learned the Spanish word for "cow" in the fifth grade, but the way he snickered with his friends as he called her and her brown classmates *"vaca chocolate,"* the way he'd sneer worse under his breath when he was surrounded by his family, had branded the *Doody* into him. When he'd harassed her cousin right out of town—the worst punishment Alex could have imagined at the time—Alex had known what she had to do.

In Chicago, there'd been a reason she'd stood up to Randy. Unfortunately, getting her ass fired hadn't helped the waitress and other female staff she'd been trying to support.

Maybe sometimes Alex's mouth and her elbow-to-the-throat impulses got her into more trouble than she'd intended, but she'd almost always felt that her why—even if no one else understood—was justified. Righteous, even.

Until last night.

There was nothing just or righteous in the way she'd treated Jeremiah.

She'd rushed out of her room before she'd remembered to grab her sunglasses, so when she turned the corner and was blinded by a sparkle of sunrise off the swiftly running river, it took her a moment to blink it away enough to see him.

Or rather, see his broad, beautiful, naked back.

Someone had tried to maintain the rut of bare dirt that ran alongside the river as a real walking trail, and they'd set up boards and pipes as exercise stations. These days, most of the stations were piles of splintered and rusting debris, but—of course—Jeremiah found one of the few sound pieces of equipment.

With his strong, pale back to her and wireless pods in his ear, he was smoothly performing pull-ups on a bar that squeaked every time he got his chin over it.

The squeak was as syncopated as a heartbeat.

He was a long streak of naked skin and hard muscle interrupted by light gray running shorts; his T-shirt waggled as it hung from his waist from where he'd tucked it in. His knees were bent and crossed at the ankle. His biceps and shoulders were as seductive as belly dancers as he lifted and lowered all his weight. His back was surprisingly pretty for the barbarian size of it: smooth, flushed, a few moles, a sweaty sheen running down his spine and into his shorts.

The look of him was more blinding than the sunstruck river.

She was as jaw-dropped and stumbling around concussed now as he'd made her last night.

Last night, Dr. Jeremiah Post had picked her up and knocked her socks off. He'd spun her and now, with two feet planted beside a river whose secrets she'd known since she was a kid—she knew the best fishing spots, where blackberries hid, and the bends La Llorona haunted after dark—she couldn't get her bearings.

It started the instant he'd barged into the bar.

She'd seen him in a muscle shirt before, but last night, a streak of dirt had licked down the bulge of one hard, gleaming bicep, and his goddamn suspenders had created "look at me!" loops around his round, tight butt. It wasn't fair that an academic who sat around on it all day had such a great ass.

The look of him had whipped hard at her eagerness to be cruel. The gorgeous beefcake professor deserved to be taken down, she'd told herself.

If we do this, it'll be hot. It'll be memorable and interesting. But it won't be special. It won't be about you.

The joke had been on her.

In the darkness of the hallway she'd grown up in, she hadn't had a whisper of breath or a flick of pleasure or one half-formed thought that wasn't steeped in him. From the instant he touched her, she'd been unable to get a bead on him, and it had left her reeling.

He'd been an eager puppy one minute—*Can we do this?*—and a red-room dominant the next.

Get rid of your shirt, Alex.

He grabbed and commanded her, swiped away her lipstick like it offended him and he had the right, then begged for direction and consent. *Do you like to have them touched? Do you like to have them licked?*

He kissed her like he'd be happy taking a two-week vacation in her mouth. Then he demanded her orgasm within moments of touching her clit.

To her shock, he'd gotten it. Other men had tried that annoying countdown-to-orgasm thing with her before, and by the time they'd growled "four," she'd been ordering an Uber and fantasizing about her vibrator.

But Jeremiah, with his *sweetheart*, and *dear*, and gentle request...

Can you come for me? Please?

He'd torn her apart—twice—then held her pussy in his hand as she'd put herself back together. He walked away without taking any pleasure for himself.

It had been embarrassing. It had been humiliating.

It had been exactly what she deserved.

Well, exactly what she deserved except for the mind-blowing orgasms.

Wanting each other is the dumbest mistake we've ever made.

Even cruel, he was too kind to say what he'd really been thinking: that it was the dumbest mistake *he'd* ever made.

Alex had learned good Catholic guilt just like everyone else in her family, but she couldn't blame a dead religion for how bad she felt now. His back glowed like pink marble in the morning sunlight. For such a big, strong back, it looked surprisingly vulnerable.

"Hey, profe—Jeremiah," she called.

He kept performing pull-ups like he was the Terminator. The sudden glowing-hot thought that he would have this kind of endurance on top of her, inside her, wasn't helping her find her feet.

Damn, high-end, noise-canceling earpods. Wait... Earpods? She tromped through the spring grass toward him.

She reached out to poke his sculpted, sweat-sheened back. "Jeremi—"

With a garbled yell, he arched his body away from her and swung himself up and out, launching off the bar. He landed nimble as a cat and spun to face her in a ready position, hands out like he was going to Greco-Roman her to the grass.

Her jaw was already there.

How did such a big guy move so fast?

"Alex," he shouted, multicolored eyes wide and accusing through his glasses. "What are you doing?"

He was overloud thanks to the pods in his ear.

Alex bit her lips. Even with everything between them, even taking into account how his chest and abs looked every bit as lickable as his back, his goosed reaction was still the tiniest bit funny.

She pointed to her own ears.

With a scowl behind his glasses, he pulled his white pods out.

"You said you didn't have a cell phone," she said.

"What?" His sweaty brown hair flopped onto his forehead.

"A cell. You have to have a phone to…" The rest of her words were burned away by his astonished, angry glare.

"My graduate assistant uploads lectures to an MP3 player for me," he bit out.

"Oh." She gave him a weak half grin. "I guess I finally got you back for all the times you've surprised me."

Sneaking up on each other was their bad comedy routine.

His scowl went deeper. It pulled out those deep crevices around his eyes and mouth just like his smile did. He shoved his pods in his pocket and grabbed his blue T-shirt out of his waistband to struggle into it, ruffling up his hair.

Covering up was good.

Then he tried to stalk past her.

Her and her mouth. She was going for contrite, she reminded herself.

"I'm sorry," she said quickly, touching his forearm but then snatching it back when he glared at her hand like it was radioactive. "I came to say I'm sorry."

He looked at her like she'd babbled in alien. "What?"

"I'm sorry. For last night."

He was close, too close, right at her shoulder, and she could see his dark morning stubble and the blue-gray smudges in the valley of his glasses. Even though she hidden herself away in her grandmother's office—she'd told herself that she had work, that the physical sense of him on the other side of the wall wasn't why she was avoiding her own bed—he hadn't gotten a good night's sleep either. She wanted to run her fingers through her hair or cross her arms or fidget. But her hair was held back with a runner's headband and she knew better than to strike a defensive pose. She had no right to it.

"I'm sorry for the mean things I said to you. For…insulting you. I'm sorry for taking my bad night out on you."

He frowned at her apology. "A bad night," he said. "Is that what you're going to blame your mistreatment of me on?"

She quickly shook her head. "No. I mean, I'm not saying it excuses it. You shouldn't let me off the hook. I'm just…" She looked around but then remembered to keep her eyes on him. "I'm trying to be upfront about what happened." She couldn't hide from how she treated him. "It was my fault. Not something you did."

"I have no doubt of that."

All his good-humored kindness had disappeared. She'd erased it. Her goofy neighbor was stiff and hulking and so, so angry.

She nodded. She'd said what she wanted to say. Nearly scared him out of his skin to say it.

She should go.

"What are you doing here?" he said. It sounded like an accusation. "Did you follow me? Why couldn't this wait until I got back to Loretta's?"

She tapped her fingers against her running tights and gave herself the tiniest bit of cover by staring at the indent in his chin. "I'm impatient. I wanted to give you this." She reached into the front pocket of her hooded, black sweatshirt and pulled out the folded document he'd said he'd wanted to show her last night. She held it out to him and again met his gold-green-brown-gray eyes. "I haven't looked at it. I put that rolled-up paper and your stuff in your room."

It was a little pathetic, the way she was holding the paper out to him like it was a bunch of dandelions she'd picked from the riverbank.

Jeremiah didn't pay any more notice to it now than she had last night.

"What caused your bad night?" he asked. Demanded, really. That gray in his eyes had gone to steel.

She put the document back in her sweatshirt and kept her hands in the pocket. She could say it was bad customers or overwhelmed staff or the Hugh ghost throwing wrenches into the works... Come to think of it, that old fucker had been surprisingly silent through last night's chaos. No wonder. Things had been going pretty bad without his help.

She could tell Jeremiah that it wasn't any of his damn business, just like they'd told each other multiple times, but that was a trip that was getting boring and going nowhere good. After the way she treated him, she owed him a little uncomfortable truth.

"You were there when my mom brought up the fact that she is seeing my dad again. You know we don't have a good relationship?"

He gave one sharp nod. His dark hair had a lot of copper in the sunlight.

"My dad showed up last night. At Loretta's. He's going to work at the bar."

Jeremiah kept his firm, multicolored gaze on her. His glasses were like a magnifying glass, and she was the ant.

"It's the first time I've seen him or...talked to him in a long time." Over the years her dad had written and called. She'd never read his emails or listened to his voice mails. "I was upset and angry and... I wanted to take it out on someone."

"And you knew I'd take it because I've been taking it."

Shame ended her pity party. "Probably." She looked down at her running shoes. "Sorry to bother you. I'm just...sorry. I said the worst things I could think of. Like...comparing you to Doody-meyer."

It had made Jeremiah flare up the way nothing else had, and she'd grabbed on to the angry heat, wanting something to burn away all the frustration she felt about her dad. "I know you're nothing like him, and I'm so sorry I said it. You've been a good tenant and friend to my grandmother and mom. That's what I really believe, no matter how irritated I am about it sometimes. I appreciate that you've been there for them. I'm sorry I treated you last night like I didn't."

She could move in to a cheap apartment if she decided to keep fighting for the bar.

"I definitely didn't expect or deserve to be attacked last night," he said.

Alex stared at the edge of a purple crocus that she'd accidentally crushed under her shoe.

"But I didn't expect to be chased down and apologized to this morning either."

She looked up and met his eyes.

His thick brows scrunched over his glasses. "You said last night that your family is yours and not mine. Are you jealous of me?"

"Maybe a little." She shrugged. She turned and looked at the rushing rain-flooded river.

Maybe a ton. "They all really admire you. Especially my grandmother."

He was silent and it made Alex want to throw something.

Finally, he said, "I don't think I'm better than you."

In the heart of her, she knew that.

"I don't think I'm better than them. Your grandmother has given me a home. All I want to do is make sure she's not bullied out of hers."

Birds swooped across the water and away. "You genuinely care about this whole bunch of Mexicans, don't you?" she asked.

"Yes." She could hear the hint of a something not-as-angry in his voice. "Not everyone gets a family like yours."

After what she'd done last night, she'd lost the right to

probe. She'd also lost the right to point out that there was some truth in her outrage.

"You're right, though," he said like he was reading her mind. "It's not fair that I've delved so deep into your personal life while offering so little of my own past. It's not fair that I've used what I've learned online to assess you, then gotten angry when the lack of what you know about me has made you suspicious. We've both misjudged each other."

She turned carefully to face him again. He admitted he'd misjudged her.

She didn't want to disturb this moment.

"My family is a sore spot," he said. He met her eyes with a troubled frown. "The difficulty is—and I don't say this to be cruel, Alex—I don't trust you enough to expose that spot to you."

She ignored the pang caused by his clear, honest words and nodded.

"But I do like you." There was even more gold in his eyes now. His little side grin looked like it was there without his knowledge. "It's innate. I can't seem to help it."

"You sound like you want to."

"Wouldn't it make things easier if I could? If we could? If we weren't so drawn to each other?"

His hair was a sweaty mess and she figured he hadn't brushed his teeth yet and he had that dense smell of a man's night sleep and morning exercise. And yet, she wanted to step closer, not away. She wanted to press herself against his broad, sweaty chest.

"Do you want to keep treasure hunting with me?" he asked, his smile crinkles going deeper at his choice of words.

"I do." The whole story was so over-the-top—disowned sons and deathbed curses and dual deeds and a villain's plan to claim half a town.

But this was Freedom, after all, and Alex believed in ghosts.

"Then give me a little time to get to know you," he said, looking down at her, all of his earnestness in his shoulders. "To trust you. Give me time to tell you about me. I swear to you, I won't do anything to undermine your family or you. Loretta has her decision to make but, you and I, we'll find that second deed and keep Dutimeyer from using it together. Okay? Maybe give you a chance to learn to trust me, too."

There was a loud clash and clang inside her. She wanted that. As unlikely—as unnatural—as the two of them hanging out was, she couldn't help wanting it.

She also wanted to kick him in the shin and run.

"Okay." With her now sweaty hand, she again pulled out the paper from her hoodie. "What is this anyway?"

"Proof that Lance Dutimeyer believes the second deed and Wayland's treasure is hidden inside the Hugh Building."

"What?"

A caw echoed back from a far-off field.

Jeremiah's half-mast smile grew into all of its squinky lines and dimples. "I anticipated your skepticism. It's why we'll make a good team. The city permit office logs requests for blueprints. That's a record of Dutimeyer requesting the blueprints to Loretta's."

Alex was just wasting breath being shocked all the time. "Why would he think it's there?"

"The will says Wayland would *sow the seed at the beginning to right a great wrong.* It's natural to assume the beginning is Edward, his first son, the son he trained as an apothecary in the Hugh Building according to Mother Hugh. But think about the circumstances Wayland would have written the will under. He had eight other children who could lose everything to Edward. Like us, they'd want to destroy the second deed."

Jeremiah used his big hands when he talked. She bet his students had a hard time taking their eyes off him.

"So maybe *sowing the seed* wasn't just overwrought language," he continued. "Maybe it was a clue to Edward. Wayland intended to hide the *seed*—second deed—*at the beginning* of his empire, in the Hugh Building, a building his oldest son, the son he wanted to follow in his footsteps, would know best."

He stopped and slid those wild hands into the pockets of his running shorts. Did he know how hot he looked when the color was high in his cheeks?

"It's certainly what Mother Hugh believes." He shrugged. He was not good at casual. "That comment about finding it under your nose is what led me down this path."

"Good to know it was more than a racist jab."

"The racist part was just for her fun." His brow wrinkled. "We need to take this seriously, Alex. Lance has shown he is. You should upgrade the locks. I'm concerned that the times I heard someone messing with the doors might be something more malicious than kids."

"Jesus." She'd call Joe the second she got back to the bar.

She suddenly remembered that the building did have secrets. She opened the paper. Next to Doody-meyer's signature and the Hugh Building's address was neatly printed: *Document Not Available.*

She exhaled. "I guess the city wouldn't hang on to ancient blueprints of a building no one cares about."

"Well," Jeremiah said. "The *city* wouldn't."

She looked into his smiling face and thought of the rolled-up paper she'd put in his room.

If the building was hiding a treasure, what she knew and what the blueprint showed could help them uncover it.

She smacked him in the bicep. "Nice job."

He huffed a laugh as he winced. He probably hadn't grown up with a pack of demonstrative cousins like she had. Then she saw the bruises.

Purple-ripe ovals marked his pale, marbly skin. They were the size of her fingertips. She'd gripped his bicep hard last night as he'd made her come. Repeatedly.

His smile disappeared. "About trusting each other. We're only going to be able to do that if you stop using sex against me."

That was…harsh.

She just nodded again because what else could she…

"I mean it, Alex. Stop teasing me about the first time, stop the innuendos—"

"Hey," she said. "Sometimes that's just the way I talk…"

"You know what I mean."

She blew out a breath. "Okay. You're right."

The set of his meaty shoulders, the intensity of his gaze, the whole presence of him, warned her he wasn't done. "Regardless of this…draw between you and I…regardless of how… good it is." The gold in his eyes felt like the sun. "It's not good for us."

He blinked his eyes as if to clear them. "So, no sex while we're searching for this deed."

She wondered if he heard his caveat as clearly as she did. No sex *while we're searching for this deed*.

"Okay," she said. "No sex. No teasing about sex. I promise."

She wanted to protect her grandmother, make sure Doodymeyer could never hurt her or her family again, and learn the history that hid in the building she wanted to claim.

She wanted to guarantee that, whatever the future of the building was, it was a choice that was in Loretta's hands.

She wanted to understand why she was so fascinated by this guy.

With a declaration to stop teasing him with their desire so they could learn to trust each other—for the good of Loretta and the family, of course—she stood in the rising spring sun with him, staring into his absurdly handsome face and smelling his clean sweat and wanting him more than any man she'd ever known.

Chapter Sixteen

The bar was busier that night than Jeremiah had ever seen it.

The pure number of Saturday night revelers was unusual enough: some were up on the corner stage that had been cleared of tables to make a makeshift dance floor, dancing to the '80s and '90s music coming through the speaker system; some were in clumps around the crowded bar, laughing and talking as many drank dark orange slushies out of Loretta's jelly jars; and some were gathered around a dartboard bathed in sparkly lights that had appeared in a formerly ill-lit corner.

Even more unusual than the size of the crowd was its makeup. There were as many people from town as family; the dart players were a group of nurses from the Freedom Medical Center. Jeremiah had only seen that happen when Loretta's had been the unfortunate recipient of a bachelor-party crawl. Even the family here was out-of-the-ordinary. Alex's cousin and Jeremiah's compatriot on the historical board, Joe Torres, sat on his left side at the bar, flashing his dazzling smile at one of the nurses. Joe usually reserved his Saturday nights for bars where there were fewer family members among the clientele. Loretta, who usually spent Saturday evenings going to mass and preparing food for the next day's luncheon, sat on his right.

Alex's father, the never-before-seen Tucker Armstead,

floated through its crowds, wearing an ironed bar apron and quietly clearing tables, refilling waters, and carting ice from the kitchen.

Jeremiah wondered if Tucker's presence explained Joe and Loretta's appearances. Alex had put a beer down in front of him the instant he'd sat—they'd nodded to verify the maintenance of their fragile peace—then hurried off to make drinks. She declaratively stayed behind the bar while the weekend bartender and wait person managed the tables and any interactions with Alex's father.

She seemed to have a sixth sense when her father was entering the confines of the large square bar; right now, she made herself busy checking on customers on the opposite axis from where her father cleaned trays.

Drinking from his beer, Jeremiah surreptitiously watched the neat-and-trim Tucker Armstead spray off a tray then fastidiously scrub it clean. He'd noticed Tucker give a smile and say a word to a few of the customers, but he seemed intent on his job.

This blond and mustachioed man had fathered Alex.

Realizing he was staring, he lowered his beer and straightened his glasses. "I ran into Alex last night. She was upset." That was like calling the eruption of Mount Vesuvius a warm day in Pompeii. "About her father."

Loretta gave a noncommittal "Hmmm..." as she blew on coffee through lips painted a bright peachy orange. It was great seeing her sitting at the bar next to him. Stupendous. Her cane was hanging on the brass hook under the bar, but she'd been able to hoist herself up onto the tall stool.

Joe narrowed his eyes on him.

Jeremiah dropped his gaze to his beer label. "I... I know it's none of my business. But is it okay for him to be here?"

Loretta and Joe maintained a silence that was distinctly daunting coming from the effusive Torres clan. He glanced at Loretta.

She unabashedly examined him like a hawk watching a juicy field mouse. "If she told you why she was upset, then my granddaughter made it your business," she said.

Joe chuckled. "I knew it."

Before Jeremiah could do something childish like push Joe off his bar stool—perhaps he'd been in the cousins' company too often—Loretta tipped her cup at the blond man now carrying a tray of dirty glasses to the kitchen.

"Tucker is a writer. He stayed home with the girls while Mary worked at the bank. Sometimes he needed quiet, so he'd ask me to take Alejandra because he didn't want her to think she was being too loud. He didn't want her to think there was anything wrong with being an energetic, active girl who refused to take any crap from anybody." *Crap* out of Loretta's mouth was always startling, but she said it with a fond smile. "I'd bring her here with me. She was lively, funny, good with her hands, good at making people feel at home. People came to Loretta's just to see her. Sometimes she'd get into trouble, sure…"

Joe laughed quietly.

"But the kind of trouble that if a boy did it, it'd hardly be noticed." The colored-glass lamp lit the admiration for her granddaughter on her face. "She convinced all the kids to sneak out in the middle of the night to catch crawdads so we could have them for Sunday dinner."

"She never needed much sleep," Joe said, a smile in his voice. "Remember that time she got us to make that huge leaf pile on the side of Tía Josie's house?"

Loretta laughed. "Your mom," she said. "When she saw

you kids jumping out of that second-story window, she almost had a heart attack."

Alex had her back to them as she filled glasses with the dark orange mix churning in a slushy machine. Jeremiah eyed the soft hairs at her nape as she walked off with a tray of them.

"About the time she naturally needed a firmer hand—just being young and high-spirited and confident..." Loretta's voice had sobered. "Tucker started drinking. Alex was so confused. Her confusion comes out angry. The trouble she got into got worse. People usually called me instead of the police until...until they didn't." Loretta bent her head over her coffee. "I still wonder if there's anything I could have done differently not to lose her."

Joe drew little circles on the wood with his beer bottle.

They acted like Alex had died, like she was the entity haunting the Hugh Building and wasn't standing a few feet away from them joking with a customer. She was still lively, still funny. But what would she be like without that edge of caustic she applied to everything?

"Her father hurt her with his drinking and his absence," Loretta said. "She thinks Mary did, too, by not stopping it. She's been punishing them ever since. Punishing herself, too."

Jeremiah frowned. "If he's an alcoholic, should he be spending time in a bar?"

Although his own father's drinking had never been hindered by location. Regardless of which estate they were at, great quantities of high-end spirits were delivered by the truckful.

"He says he's in recovery," Loretta said. "Mary is trying to trust him again. Si Dios está con el."

Loretta crossed herself and Jeremiah hoped God was with the man as well.

In that whiplash way her family had of acknowledging

life's sorrow and joy in the same breath, Joe cleared his throat. "Sure nice of you to be keeping such a close eye on her."

Jeremiah ignored the heavy tone of teasing and took a deep drink. His expressions had never been stoic, and he didn't want her family reading on his face everything that had happened with Alex the night before.

He shifted slightly away from Alex's grandmother.

They'd agreed to wait until Sunday to check out the blueprint and search the building. Even their excitement that they might be sleeping on top of the second deed hadn't diminished the fact that they'd both needed a beat after this morning's armistice.

Jeremiah had gone over and over it like a child turning a snow globe: her chasing him down, apologizing, revealing her hurt about her dad, and her envy about his relationship with her family. It'd been startling to watch her expose herself. She'd been far more naked in the morning sunlight than the two times they'd had intercourse in the dark. Alex's pride was her armor and everyday outfit, but she'd taken it all off to make amends to him.

His mother had always told him that he was naïve, trusted too easily, and deserved whatever hurt he'd earned. But going over this morning's gift from Alex, he couldn't find how it benefitted her. When Joe had stopped by his room this afternoon to hand him the new key to the dead bolt he'd installed, Jeremiah had held it against his chest.

She was willing to try to believe him and his wild conspiracy theories.

He needed to stop pigeonholing her as the wild woman he found on the internet.

Loretta interrupted his thoughts when she bumped his shoulder.

"*Mira*, say hello," she said, turning on her bar stool. Jeremiah turned as well to find she'd stopped Tucker Armstead in his tracks. "Tucker, this is Dr. Jeremiah Post. He's our tenant."

"Mr. Armstead," Jeremiah said, holding out his hand with the tiniest bit of hesitation. He hoped Alex wasn't seeing this.

Tucker put the water pitcher he'd been carrying down on the bar then wiped his hands on a clean towel slung over the string of his apron.

"Good to meet you, Dr. Post." They shook hands. "Call me Tucker."

"Of course," Jeremiah said. Alex's father had a strong grip and great blue eyes. He also had Alex's sharp chin. Or rather, Alex had his chin. He realized he was searching and finding traces of her in all this Nordic blondness. Tucker had the kind of thick blond hair and moustache that must give other men his age fits. "And yes, it's Jeremiah."

In the space of the hand clasp, Jeremiah realized that he was being observed, too.

"Mary has talked about you," Tucker said, crossing his arms over his chest. "You've certainly made an impression on Freedom."

What an…interesting way to put it.

"It's a great town," Jeremiah said.

"I know Dupen College is glad to have you. Professor Williams and Professor Naima speak highly of you."

Mentioning the chairs of the English department lit a fuse in Jeremiah's brain that ignited a whole series of fireworks. At a faculty event at the dean's home a couple years after Jeremiah had moved to Freedom, Sierra Naima had mentioned a writer from town. Specifically, a piece the writer had published in the *New Yorker*. Jeremiah had read it and loved it. He'd even bought the man's novel. But the sheer number of books he regularly bought meant that he'd forgotten about it before he'd cracked the spine.

Right now, Tucker Armstead's book sat on a floor-to-ceiling bookshelf in Jeremiah's room that was stuffed strictly with his to-be-read pile.

"I have your book upstairs," Jeremiah said numbly. "Congrats on making the *New York Times*'s list."

Tucker thanked him with a nod. "The debut book was only on there for a week."

Loretta, who'd never, ever, ever mentioned that her son-in-law was a successful fiction writer, watched their interaction as if no new information was being shared.

This wild town.

Pulling castles from the air to write fiction took a tremendous work ethic. Jeremiah was beginning to understand what Tucker Armstead and his daughter had in common.

"Are you enjoying the tenant room?" Tucker asked, blue eyes focused.

As Jeremiah was about to nod, Tucker continued: "Quarters are tight. With only one bathroom and all."

Jeremiah halted his movement by wiping his chin on his shoulder. Perhaps he was learning another characteristic that Tucker and Alex had in common—they both had death-ray stares when they were feeling protective.

"Alex and I have different schedules," he said. "We try to stay out of each other's hair."

Why was he explaining anything to this man whose protective instinct should have kicked in years ago?

"Mary says you're good people," Tucker said. "But you're here alone every night with a beautiful young woman. You're not the kind of man to take advantage of that, are you, Dr. Post?"

Jeremiah wanted to squirm like he was picking up his prom date. "No, sir, I…" Did he just call him *sir*?

"Jeremiah." Alex's voice was tight and full of warning behind him. "Do you need another beer?"

Busted.

Tucker dropped his arms from his chest and hooked his thumbs casually over the string of his apron, but his resolve to keep those blue eyes on Jeremiah was clear.

Jeremiah turned on his stool to catch Alex giving him a matching glare.

"Just meeting your neighbor," Tucker said.

"Great," she answered. She didn't look at her father. "Well, time to get back to work."

Jeremiah didn't break eye contact with Alex. She wore a deep-red drapey sweatshirt and it was a gorgeous color against her skin, with her defined eyes and lush red lips and high twirl of her hair. He put his hand palm up on the bar. "Alex…"

He desperately wanted their truce to last longer than twelve hours.

"What the hell are those orange things everyone's drinking?" Joe asked. "That's why you made me fix that old slushy machine? So you can ruin perfectly good alcohol?"

She stayed silent, assessing Jeremiah in full view of her cousin and grandmother. Then she looked down at the wood, inhaled in then blew out, then met Jeremiah's eyes again.

She gave him "I'm sorry" and "you're forgiven" and "this is hard" and "whoops, I almost blew it, didn't I?" in one soul-piercing gaze.

"Don't knock it 'til you try it," she said. She moved to the antique-looking machine and half-filled three rocks glasses with the dark-orange brew.

She cautiously put a glass in front of her grandmother. Loretta was not a fan of experimentation.

She sat a glass in front of her cousin.

Then she sat the last cold glass right in the middle of Jeremiah's upraised palm. Using the glass as cover, she stroked four fingertips over the sensitive meat of his fingers.

"Gotta give everything a chance," she said. As she moved away, his fingers curled tight around the cool glass, trapping the warm sensation of her touch.

A couple of hours later, with the onslaught of the Saturday night crowd receded back and the nurse's phone number stored in his phone, Joe looked especially mellow nearing the bottom of his second Spring Sunrise, Alex's name for the orange slushy. His chin was in his hand and he'd stuck both umbrellas Alex decorated the drinks with into his dark, wavy hair. Jeremiah was feeling surprisingly mellow himself, although he'd only inhaled one of the drinks before he switched to water. He had tomorrow to look forward to.

Loretta had taken two slow sips of her drink—both under her granddaughter's watchful eyes—given a nod of approval, then returned to her coffee.

Tucker Armstead had slipped out when the crowd died down.

Jeremiah observed Alex break down the bar: cap the well liquor bottles, replenish the cocktail fixings for tomorrow, restock the glasses. He enjoyed her dance, understanding the rhythms, being familiar with what movement came next, even if he'd never been invited to participate.

"So, Joe," Alex said, draping a rubber mat she'd just washed off over the divider in the sink. "Tell me about these traqueros we're all supposed to be sprouted from."

Her lips showed no color but her own and her eyes had that softly smudged look that Jeremiah associated with Alex coming to bed.

Going upstairs.

Jeremiah straightened and shook his head as Joe flung out a hand.

"See?" Joe said, motioning to Jeremiah as if this was a topic they'd just been discussing. "She was raised here and she doesn't even know about traqueros."

Jeremiah nodded and bit back his smile. Joe's passion for this topic was always exhilarating.

Joe jabbed his finger toward his cousin. "Did you know that all the railroad tracks around here were built by Mexicans?"

She shook her head.

"After 1880 until the railroad started to die, two-thirds of all track labor was made up of Mexican immigrants." Joe stabbed the mahogany bar with a emphatic finger. "After farming, the railroad was the biggest employer of Mexicans. One million of us immigrated here, and we built and maintained tracks through the Southwest and Central Plains. But nobody knows that. Why? Because the image of the railroad stops being romantic when you've got a dark-skinned cholo building it."

Loretta harrumphed. "Mijo, don't say that word."

"Sorry," he said. He still had umbrellas in his hair. "But it's true."

Alex filled straw dispensers as Joe spoke, but she'd focused her shrewd absorption on her cousin. Jeremiah really enjoyed that look on her face. Her lovely, lovely face.

"I thought the railroad was built by Chinese people," she said.

"It was," Joe replied. "Until the Chinese Exclusion Act of 1882. It was a totally racist law that shut down Chinese immigration, so the railroad had to go looking for a quick source of cheap labor." He plucked an umbrella out of his hair and began twirling it.

"At first, the traqueros were just guys alone coming up for seasonal work. They'd work for six or seven months, pull ten-hour days for ten cents an hour, then go back to their wives in Mexico."

Joe leaned on the bar. Alex shot a glance and quick side smile at Jeremiah. She knew storytelling Joe, too.

"Then the railroad figured they could get more reliable workers if they invited whole families. So, a few guys coming from one village would send for their families, then those families would invite their compadres, and pretty soon, you've got chain migration connecting a little village in Guanajuato, where our family is from, to a growing Mexican immigrant community in Kansas. They all knew each other, they relied on each other, they were all compadres y commadres, sharing food, resources, childcare, and pride of culture."

Joe gave Alex that high-beam smile that made councilwomen blush. "The strong sense of community we have now was set up by the traqueros way back then. That's why we don't leave."

Alex set up four small jelly jars in front of her and began pouring a high-end tequila into them.

Joe's grin faded and he put the umbrella on the bar. "But now we've stayed so long we've forgotten how we got here. In our desire to assimilate, we've let everyone else forget, too. Some train lover will talk about the Old West, and the railroad, and the good ol' days, and deny until he's red-white-and-blue in the face that Mexicans are the reasons those tracks are there. Our grandparents built those tracks, and yet we've been denied the dignity and recognition that we built something foundational to this country. To our country."

Alex tipped a small amount of tequila into the shot glass beside the framed photo of her grandfather. Then she slid glasses filled with a finger's-worth of crystal-clear tequila in front of each of them. They raised the glasses to Loretta's husband, to each other, then clinked them together, and drank.

The tequila was as smooth as Alex's skin.

She rested her glass in her cleavage. "I feel like I should put my hand over my heart," she teased gently.

Joe snorted. "Shut up."

"Mijo, we have a bunch of those little Fourth of July flags in back," Loretta joined in. "We could organize a parade."

Jeremiah laughed. That was the thing about this family— they loved deeply and felt intensely and teased mercilessly.

"It is pretty wild I didn't know this," Alex said.

Joe finished off his drink.

"Granmo, did you know about this?"

Loretta was savoring her tequila. "We'd hear the tíos talk. But we were young Americans—we didn't care about the stories from the viejos. We wanted to go to the tiendas on Milagro, the dances at the community center, we wanted to sneak kisses going from the church to the rectory after mass. We didn't want to listen to old men talk about the old ways."

Jeremiah looked at the framed photo of her husband, a votive flickering beside it. He bet Salvador never stood a chance when he saw young Loretta León sparkling with life as she walked down Milagro Street.

"You had other spots, right?" Alex asked Joe. "Before you guys thought of installing the museum here. You had other spots in mind, right?"

Jeremiah made his eyes settle on the middle distance.

"We did." He could hear the caution in Joe's voice. "A pipe dream was to renovate the old train station. Why?"

"Just because I don't want you to put the museum here doesn't mean I don't think it's a good idea," she said, breaking his heart a little.

What could have come of them if they hadn't met as opponents on a battlefield? What if Joe had brought her to a historical society meeting? What if Jeremiah had wandered into her exclusive Chicago bar and ordered a drink?

What if cats flew and birds gave you condescending looks while licking themselves?

Joe motioned to the room. "You keep bringing in crowds like this, we're gonna have to find a new spot. The dartboard, the new music, these drunk slushies...you've made some good changes around here. Right, Granmo?"

Alex had given them something. Joe wanted to give her something back.

The smelly trash look on her face ruined his efforts. "Those aren't the changes I've got planned," she said. "That's just..." She waved her hand at the bar like she was shooing away flies. "...keeping the inmates occupied."

He thought he'd misjudged her, but he'd never misjudged Alex and her hard-core truthfulness. Jeremiah looked down at his clenched fingers.

"The top-to-bottom renovation I have planned is going to allow us to increase the price point and draw the type of customer from the college and beyond that will be educated and sophisticated enough to appreciate your museum. That's a win-win for all of us, right?"

She took their silence as tacit approval to launch into her renovation plans.

Unable to stand it, Jeremiah begged off and said goodnight. He wasn't the one she needed to convince. And he wanted to get in bed and asleep before he had to deal with the haunting sensation of Alex nestling up next to him on the other side of the wall.

He might like her. He might even want her with a desperation that he'd never had for anyone. But he was losing hope he'd ever understand her. Alex loved her family, but she'd changed from that girl who'd been good at making people feel at home.

Now she was insistent on making home hostile to the people who loved her most.

Chapter Seventeen

Alex made sure that all the outside doors were double-locked with the new dead bolts Joe had installed before she invited Jeremiah the next day to spread the Hugh Building blueprint on Loretta's clean desk. If Doody-meyer was going to spend his Sunday searching for the second deed, he'd have to look somewhere else.

She'd finally whipped Loretta's office into a state where a clean surface was possible, where terrifying bills weren't going to jump out of the endless stacks of paper and piles of old church announcements and used Bingo cards weren't going to drown anyone. Studying the blueprint in one of their bedrooms would have been a bad idea. She weighed down one corner of the blueprint with the heavy crystal rocks glass she received when she was named the best bartender in Chicago and another with a neat stack of notes and sketches for her future bar.

She tried not to be annoyed that Jeremiah seemed to be more interested in what she'd held the third corner down with: a jar of Loretta's hand cream. She should just gift wrap it and give it to him.

"This isn't the blueprint the builder used," she said, hands on her hips.

"No, it's not the original," Jeremiah confirmed, standing next to her, his arms crossed over his rust sweater vest as he looked at the drawing. With his glasses on and that soft plop of hair on his forehead, he was really projecting the hot professor vibe. "This is from the early sixties. The Freedom Historical Society nominated several local buildings to be added to the National Register of Historic Places. The Hugh Building was one of them. They paid to have the building assessed and the lost blueprint redrawn. The owner certainly wasn't going to pay for it; the Hughs had sold the building decades earlier and it passed from one harassed owner to another." He huffed. "They complained that the building was so troublesome it must be haunted."

He stopped and frowned at her. "How did you know this wasn't the original blueprint?"

Alex smiled. He wasn't the only smarty-pants in the room. "Because of what's missing."

"What's missing?"

She smiled wider. "Bring it. I'll show you."

At least he was gentle with her stack of bar plans as he moved them.

She led him into the hallway where she'd already put out buckets to catch the inevitable drips. Cold rain had settled in for the day. When she opened the door to the long storage closet next to her room, it sounded comforting plunking off the roof.

"When I was a kid and off from school, I used to come to the bar every few days with my Granmo," she said, flipping on the light. "When I got in trouble, which happened a decent amount, my Granmo made me come up here and reorganize the stock areas. She knew I hated being on my own."

The closet was a room's length long but narrow, and she motioned him in then led him past built-in wooden shelves filled with neatly stacked toilet paper rolls, cleaning supplies, and linens for the tenants. The larger storage room across the hall held the extra liquor, surplus condiments, plastic-encased jelly jars, paper rolls for the cash register and the rest of the raw goods that made running the bar possible. She'd wrestled both storage spaces into order just like the office. Loretta's "system" had involved cramming items onto the shelves like it was a game of Tetris.

Alex started pulling stacks of paper towels off the back case. "Help me clear this off."

Jeremiah emptied the higher shelves while she worked on the lower.

"One day, I was here because I'd 'accidentally' poured a bowl of hot soup on this guy who kept staring at Loretta's butt—I took care of it before my tíos could, they're not here just for free refills. That's when I discovered this."

On her knees, she reached to the bottom back corner of the bookcase and watched Jeremiah's face as the unit sprang forward a few inches on the right side. He looked as young and astonished as she'd been the first time she'd pulled open the bookcase to reveal the narrow landing and old wooden stairs behind it.

Alex quickly covered her nose. The odor of wet, dusty rot was drifting out of the secret passageway.

"If Wayland was going to hide something in the building, it'd be here," she said from behind her hand.

With the number of leaks the Hugh Building had sprung, she'd been prepared for this unused, unmaintained stairwell to be gross and had dressed for it: she wore old jeans, tall black work boots, an oversized ratty sweatshirt, and a canvas coat.

She looked at Jeremiah in his cashmere sweater vest, khakis and two-tone loafers. "Do you want to change?" she asked.

"Why?" He was already peering down the stairs.

She snorted as she grabbed two flashlights out of their

charging stations. After all the shit she'd given him, here she was feeling sorry for his fancy clothes.

They turned on their lights and Alex ducked gingerly through the doorway. The narrow landing of unstained wood creaked ominously beneath her. Steps descended down into the dark, squeezed between the brick of the outer building and the false wall that ran behind the stage, bathroom, and kitchen. She could hear water dripping. Her light lit up a thick cobweb blocking her way, declaring how long it'd been since people had used these stairs.

It smelled—unfortunately—like animals felt free to party here. As she shined her light around, she realized the thick drip of gray down the wall and covering the top steps was old bat guano. She quickly shined the light up into the rafters. Fortunately, there were no bloodsuckers perching there now.

Alex took one last breath of sweet, fresh air then batted the web away so she could step a few steps down. Jeremiah came in behind her and instantly sneezed.

"We should be wearing masks," he said.

"And hazmat suits." He was going to have to burn his fancy cashmere sweater when they were done. "I thought treasure hunting was supposed to be all cool and shit."

"What was this stairwell used for?" She heard him tapping the brick behind her.

Alex searched at step level for another button or lever. "Loretta doesn't know. We never use it. It exits out that far panel at the back of the building."

"I thought those wooden panels were purely decorative."

"The other two are."

"Fascinating."

Crumbling mortar skittered under her feet as she moved to the next step.

"Did you enjoy working here when you were young?" His

voice was quiet in the close-in space. She could hear the rain just beyond the cold brick wall.

"Yeah, I did."

She smiled when she thought of the little apron her grandmother had sewed for her. "You can never get too bored working in a bar." She slowly panned her flashlight over the brick. "There are beer cases to carry and saltshakers to fill and orders to take and heartbreaks to listen to and limes to cut and dine-and-dashers to chase, usually all at the same time. But if you can get it all synchronized—" She kicked an old nest of moldy paper shreds down the steps with a shudder. She was going to have to come back in here with a blowtorch. "A good bar feels like magic. People step in and feel right at home."

"Some kind of part-time work would have benefitted me in my youth. I would have been too shy for anything as extravagant as bar-backing, but maybe as a librarian's assistant."

Alex turned and flashed her light on him, immediately lowered it when he winced. "You never had a part-time job?"

A step above her, he was bigger and more loom-y than ever, but his face went cautious in that way she'd planned not to make happen again. "You must think I'm excessively precious."

"I think…we were born into very different lives."

The look on his face changed. If a librarian's assistant had ever looked at her like that, she would have found the sturdiest bookcase to shove him up against.

She turned away. After the evergreen scent of him, she was struck again by how truly disgusting the smell in here was.

He cleared his throat. "I recognize how fortunate I am. The poverty I see in Freedom is unfamiliar. It's unsettling at times."

As a kid growing up on the east side, Alex hadn't known

they were poor. She liked the vegetable gardens and tire swings in the ramshackle backyards, the screened-in porches stuffed with crap, the broken-down bikes that everyone shared, and the general open-door policy of "what do you need." The Hugh clan used their nominal wealth to torment those from the east side, enjoying their status of "haves" over "have nots." But there was some truth to the cursed state they thought they were trapped in: you could only be so rich in the little microcosm of Freedom, just like you could only be so poor.

In Chicago, she'd finally understood the true injustice of wealth disparity. Poverty was a tool imposed by the powerful so they could use their wealth for handbags and Cristal and second homes on beaches that still didn't fill their empty places.

She wondered how "fortunate" Jeremiah was.

Because she'd agreed not to ask until he trusted her and she trusted him, she asked the other question bouncing around her brain. "Why do you think Edward Hugh came back to Freedom? He'd been lucky enough to escape."

She swiped quickly at wet against her neck and saw that something had dripped on her. She was going to take a Silkwood shower when they were through.

"Maybe he hadn't wanted to leave," Jeremiah said, pointedly. "If he was apprenticing as an apothecary with his father, then he would have grown up here on Miracle Street. Looking out the front windows every day to see the close community of the colonia develop, I can imagine how beguiling it would have been.

"That's what Joe was talking about last night," he continued as Alex randomly pressed some bricks, feeling silly as she did it. "The compadrazgo. Technically, it means godparenthood. But what it represented in the colonia was the way Mexican immigrants turned their shared understanding of culture, food, societal rules, and religion into ties that bound them and made them feel safe in a foreign place. That 'family-hood' turned Miracle Street into Milagro Street. It created the unique, nurturing community that still exists today."

As Alex jiggled a cock-eyed brick with the toe of her boot, only to have it break instead of revealing a doorway to second deeds and riches, she thought about the close connection she'd felt to so many people when she was young. Although technically every Mexican-American in Freedom wasn't blood related—there would be some serious inbreeding if they were—they had a saying: "If you're brown and in town, you're family."

Growing up here, the ties that bound her to her family and community had felt as firm as the Hugh Building's cold, brick wall. That's what made it even more awful when, at sixteen, she discovered how easily they crumbled.

"That unique, nurturing community won't last long without Loretta's."

The way Jeremiah muttered it under his breath raised her hackles.

"Hey." She turned around to poke his ribs, two steps up from her. "The bar's not a soup kitchen or a shrine. Loretta's needs to take care of Loretta's."

The damp was making his hair curl up. "But it *is* the last physical remnant of that compadrazgo here in Freedom. It's too important to be swept away in whatever Dutimeyer has planned. Or..." He set his jaw and met her eyes. "Or to be so transformed that it's no longer welcoming to the people who find comfort and community here."

She'd worked really hard last night to keep the peace and not have her feelings hurt when Jeremiah had left right when Alex had started explaining her plans for the bar.

She stepped down to a landing that was slippery. "Weird you've got such a good sense of my big, bad transformation when you didn't stick around last night to hear any of the details."

He was pointing his flashlight at her feet. "I'm not the one you need to convince."

Her irritation meter headed into the red. "I really wish you would stop—"

"Why is there a landing there?"

"What?" She wanted to hash this out.

He frowned. "Alex, what's under the main stairs? Is there a storage closet?"

She slapped her hands against her thighs. "There's... I don't know." She tried to think through her frustration. "No, there's not a closet."

He turned around and took the slippery, creaking stairs back up two at a time. She watched as he leaned through the doorway and then came rushing back down with the blueprint in hand.

"Hold this," he said, handing her one side of the paper as he unfurled as much as he could in the narrow space. "The storage closet is above the stage and this would exit—yes—behind the kitchen. This false wall runs all the way down. That's why the stained-glass windows are inset. And our stairs, leading to the bedrooms, they make an L." He focused his flashlight on the blueprint's south wall, the wall their bedroom windows looked out of, that fronted Penn Street.

He looked up at Alex. "What's under the main stairs?"

Were there two false walls in a building she thought she knew like the back of her hand?

He rolled the blueprint back up then handed it and his flashlight to her. "Step down," he said.

She went down enough steps to make room for Jeremiah

to squat in front of the landing. She aimed the flashlight over his shoulder as he put his fingers beneath the two-by-two-foot wide square of old worn wood.

When he jerked his hand back and wiped it on his khaki pants, Alex grimaced in sympathy.

He grabbed hold again and when he pulled up, the landing gave a squeal as the wood lifted up on rusty hinges.

"I'll be damned," Alex breathed.

Jeremiah had found another set of narrow steps going the other direction.

It took some negotiating getting through the hatch and down the steps until they could stand again, especially for Jeremiah. This stairwell was no cleaner than the other one, but neither of them were worried about the filth or the smell as they passed under the enclosure for the stained glass windows and found, at the bottom of the stairs, a short door.

Jeremiah nodded at her with an eager expression, and she clasped the heavy metal ring and pushed the door open.

She didn't know what she expected when she stepped through and shined her flashlight around the midnight-dark space. Shiny chests of gold and a rolled-up scroll would have been nice. Instead, the long alley of brick and concrete that existed beneath their bedrooms was anticlimactically empty except for a small pile of metal and wood at the other end. The animals hadn't found a way in. Alex could at least be glad she wasn't breathing in scat dust as she slept. This space just smelled forgotten.

She was sweeping her flashlight around as she moved toward the back, still halfheartedly looking for a glint of jewels when Jeremiah said, "Alex, is that... Is that a still?"

She swung her flashlight on the junk pile where Jeremiah was pointing his light.

It was actually just one part of a still that would be used

to create alcohol: covered in the lime green of oxidation, the copper pot that would be filled with mash and heated stood against the back wall, its cap looking like a cylindrical robot head.

She hurried back and brushed her finger over the still's green, powdery surface. "Why would this be here?"

"Why would Wayland Hugh build a building with hidden rooms and secret exits?" Jeremiah answered.

"Holy shit." Alex put a hand to her forehead. "Wayland Hugh was a bootlegger?"

It seemed too impossible that the Hughs' high-and-mighty were built in part on a substance that was illegal in Kansas until 1948.

Her pulse sped up as her light slid over more evidence of Wayland Hugh's side hustle: rust-eaten coiled copper tubing; a small, stained barrel; a collection of brown glass jugs cloaked in spiderwebs. She aimed her flashlight high on the wall and saw that there were holes in the brick to vent the fumes that made bootlegging dangerous. If there were small, unmaintained chimneys running through the wall and venting up through the roof, that was probably the source of some of their leaks.

"But..." She was still trying to wrap her head around it. "Mother Hugh said Edward was the bootlegger. It's what got him kicked out of the family."

Jeremiah shook his head. She doubted there were many questions he couldn't answer. "Maybe he was just the one who got caught. Or the one who took the blame?"

"But if he was only doing what his dad taught him, why would he be disowned?"

Jeremiah just shook his head again.

Alex had a sudden pang for a rich kid she'd never met.

"What's that?" Jeremiah asked. His flashlight was aimed

at the wooden box of jugs. Beneath the cloud of webs, between the glass bottles, Alex could see the spine of a booklet.

She combed aside the webs and pulled the booklet out.

She brushed dust off the cover, then shivered. The book was over a hundred years old, but looked like it could have been printed yesterday.

Old Man Hugh had never helped them out, and she refused to believe he'd supernaturally preserved this piece of evidence for them now.

M. K. & T. Railway Personnel Record Summaries.

There was only one guy they were interested in reading about. On a hunch, she flipped to the *H*s and scanned down the page.

And shivered again. "Edward Tobias Hugh," she read out loud. Squinting her eyes at the small font, she read out loud: he'd been a switchman, was promoted to a yard conductor, then became Freedom's yardmaster.

"Yardmaster is the top position in the train yard," Jeremiah whispered. He must have been feeling the same *something* she was.

She huffed when she saw the asterisked note at the bottom of his record. "Well, he stayed rowdy." She read from the book. "Suspended ten days for union agitation."

Jeremiah's grin matched hers. "He was a railroad employee, a union organizer, *and* the son of a bootlegger."

"I think we found that dirty laundry," she said.

She had the sudden hair-raising awareness that they were two people in the dark, where no one could find them, in a room built by a man determined to hide his secrets. Jeremiah looked like he was feeling some hair raising, too.

But Old Man Hugh stayed surprisingly quiet.

Chapter Eighteen

If the second deed and treasure were hidden in the Hugh Building, then the building was bearing down to keep its secrets. For the next couple of hours, they tapped on every brick, probed every gap of loose mortar, and breathed in enough mold and desiccated animal feces to contract something fatal.

When they stumbled out of the storage closet, damp and barely able to stand their own smell, they quickly began to shed layers in the hallway, wanting to avoid bringing that smell, mold spores, or creepy-crawlies into their rooms.

Alex's filthy canvas coat hit the old boards with a *plop*. "If the second deed is in this building, Lance'll need a wrecking ball to find it." The coat was going in the burn pile.

Jeremiah pulled the poor, dirty cashmere over his head, and tossed it to the floor. "Perhaps that's his intention." His wet hair was tamped down in some spots, curled up in devil horns in others. He ran his hand through it. "He'll buy the building or steal it to get to what's in its walls."

"So we can't assume the second deed is safely hidden and he'll just go away?" Alex asked from inside the sweatshirt she was pulling off. She wore a plain black T-shirt beneath it.

Jeremiah didn't need to give her his "Are you serious?" look as he toed off his expensive shoes.

She leaned a hand against the wall to steady herself and

tried to do the same to her tall boots. What she knew from her lifelong association with Doody-meyer was that he never walked away from a chance to make other people miserable. Jeremiah pulled his white shirt out of his belted khakis and unbuttoned it from the bottom up. "We need to learn more about Edward to find the location of the second deed. Family legend has it that he jumped a railroad car and left town to avoid a woman he impregnated. But what if, since he could no longer do the apothecary work he'd been trained to do, he started a new profession on the bottom rung? What if he left town with the traqueros to maintain the rails?"

Not making any progress with her boots, Alex sat on the floorboards to tug at the left one. "With the Mexicans?" she grunted as she pulled. "That's tough work." She tugged again. "Doesn't seem like the kind of...work a boy born with a silver...spoon in his mouth would do."

The dirty boot wasn't budging.

"Neither does distilling moonshine or smuggling it out the back. What were his options when his family resources and profession were taken from him?" Jeremiah's wet shirt hung open, showing his damp muscle tee. "He would have grown up around the immigrant community. Been familiar with the work they do." He beckoned with his fingers. "Give me that."

Alex leaned back on her elbows to put her left heel in his hands. "Doesn't seem fair that Edward was rejected from his family for doing what his dad taught him. If I was Edward, I'd hang on to the deed and never use it just to spite the man."

Jeremiah's eyes widened brilliantly. He'd taken off his glasses and his lashes were thick and clumpy. "That is an excellent hypothesis. What if Edward gained possession of the second deed but never used it?"

He tugged gently and her boot slid off as slick as water.

She raised her right boot and looked at the booklet and blueprint against his bedroom door. "That still puts us at square one."

Jeremiah pulled that boot off then turned it over to knock out anything crawling.

She hurried to her feet.

Jeremiah unbuttoned the cuffs of his shirt with a thoughtful expression on his face. "The historical society has railroad personnel records stored inside the train depot. It's just minutiae former employees wanted to keep but we had no room for." He pulled the shirt off, exposing his bare shoulders and arms in his undershirt. "There might be more about him in them. I'll need to email the man who has a key."

Alex shucked the filthy jeans she'd worn over black leggings and kicked them aside. She opened the bathroom door and turned on the light.

"You're kind of like Edward," she said over her shoulder as he followed her in, grinning at him as he took off his Rolex. "The rich guero working with all the Mexicanos." She turned the tap on the pedestal sink to full hot. "Your college friends must wonder what you're doing, shacking up with the poor townies."

As she waited for the water to heat up, she'd never been more excited to wash her hands.

When she glanced at his reflection in the mirror, she saw that he'd dropped his pants from beneath the navy-blue bathrobe he'd put on and tied. That robe hung close to hers on the hooks by the tub, and she might have touched it more than once. Might have smelled it, too.

He kicked the pants out into the hall and tossed his socks out, too.

When he met her eyes, she was surprised by the high color in his cheeks. "I know you're teasing," he said slowly, those crinkles around his eyes narrowed to consternation. "I know you speak without a filter. But sometimes you have to consider how off-putting the things you say are."

Steam was billowing up from the sink. She bent to it, pumped her palm full of hand cleanser, and put her service-hardy hands under the steaming tap.

As she carefully washed between her fingers and under the nail beds and up her wrists, she thought about what she'd popped off as a joke. Calling her and her family *poor townies* was a protective tactic she'd learned early. Make fun of yourself before someone else can. With Jeremiah however, she repeatedly ducked behind that wall then laughed at him because he stood outside it.

They'd agreed they'd misjudged each other, but Alex kept highlighting the differences between them, while Jeremiah—rich, educated, with the kind of job you could bring home to mama—never did.

It was a weird thing to do for a person who was so annoyed by the other-ism she'd been subjected to for much of her life.

"Sorry," she said, stepping aside to let him have a turn at the sink. He stepped in next to her. He had to stoop over to get his hands in the little pedestal bowl. "I caught a bad habit with you that it's time I break." He had nice hands. Long fingers. Wide nail beds and pretty moons. "I'm sorry to make you feel like you don't belong."

"Thank you," he said without looking at her.

She reached for her hand cream and unscrewed the lid. She thought, maybe, she knew one reason she kept zapping him with her cattle prod.

"Why did you leave when you did last night?" she said, scooping up a thick dollop of the cream then putting the jar down. The soft rose smell was a relief to her poor nose.

He glanced at her hands, then turned off the tap. "It was late," he said, straightening and grabbing the towel.

She slathered the front and back of her hands.

"Too late to stay ten minutes to listen to what I had to say?" She slowly rubbed the cream in.

He was drying his hands like he was about to go into surgery.

"I'm not the one you have to convince that—"

"You gotta stop saying that."

She faced the '70s-era gold-framed mirror. She didn't want to fight with him. She reached to begin pulling out all the studs and hoops in her ear. The toxic waste from the stairwell could be hiding anywhere and she needed to dunk the lot in alcohol.

As her fingers slipped off the first fastener, she realized she should have done this before she moisturized.

"You say that I don't have to convince you about the bar, but that's not true." She tried to twist the stud to pry it free. "If we're going to keep..." He threw the hand towel out in the hallway then watched her warily in the mirror. "...keep treasure hunting together, if we're going to protect Loretta, then we probably should have some mutual respect for each other's plans. You want me to stop making fun of you and my family, and you're right. I want you to stop behaving like your plan is morally superior to mine."

He drew himself up. His shoulders in his blue robe looked a mile wide. "I've never—"

"Yeah, you have." Dammit. Her fingers kept slipping off. "I haven't sat for the play-by-play, but I have listened to and learned about your plan and why y'all think it's important. Can you say you've done the same for me?"

She watched his firm lips stutter open then close in the

mirror. "What are you doing to your ear?" he finally asked with exasperation.

"I can't get ahold of the backs."

"Here, let me..." He turned her around to face him. She tilted her head down and to the side, and he stroked her hair out of the way.

She felt his finger run over the back of her lobe. "Leaving last night wasn't because I think your vision for the bar is beneath my notice. I'm sorry if I gave you that impression. In truth, it's the complete opposite." She could feel the hot bursts of his breath against her jaw as the earrings began to give way. "I'm afraid your plans will be wildly effective. It's difficult to swallow that Loretta's will be guided by someone who says things like you're 'keeping the inmates occupied'."

She stared at the tie of his robe as he worked his way up to the hoops near the top. "That's just the way I talk."

"Really?" He was surprisingly gentle when he was all heated up. "You don't intend on changing the establishment so much that your family no longer feels welcome?"

He pulled out the final stud, and she raised her head to find him holding a palmful of earrings out to her. They looked like pebbles in the center of his big hand.

"No," she scowled, scooping the earrings up and casting them on top of the toilet. That had never been her goal.

Had it?

Sure, she'd avoided coming back to Freedom very often, and when she had arrived on that thunder-stormy night, she'd been in a pretty bad mood that had just gotten worse when Loretta told her that the guarantee of owning the bar was anything but. Sure, she might have wanted to take out some of her bad mood on her family by raising the prices and throwing out the furniture and altering everything about Loretta's that they loved.

But so many of those plans had changed, kind of without her realizing it. She really thought she could leave something good here, something good for family *and* townies *and* new money that would thrive under her sisters' care after she left.

If she could get her sisters involved again.

She put her hands on her hips and faced him. "Jeremiah, do you honestly think Loretta's can survive without some kind of evolution? You're an optimist and I'm a pessimist but, real talk, this is a business and its owner is deeply in debt, it's on a street with no other draw..." She counted out the issues on her fingers. "...in a neighborhood that half of the town believes is sketchy, in a town with a declining population, in a state that a good portion of the country believes is best flown over. Think like a business owner and not just a person with good intentions.

"If Loretta's is going to stay a bar, what is going to keep it alive? Because it isn't charity or wishful thinking for the good ol' days."

He had that look that he could get sometimes, that look of almost kidlike awe when he was working on a piece of information he hadn't already known. He was such a smart guy that she imagined little surprised him.

"You said that before. Your grandmother is behind on her taxes?"

"Yeah. By a lot."

"She never said—"

"She wouldn't. She doesn't talk money with anyone, not even family. Sometimes all she's had to rely on is her backbone, but her pride can also be a tremendous pain in the ass." She gripped her fingers into her hips. "It's probably why she was considering Doody-meyer's offer in the first place. There's no other reason she'd consider selling to him."

Alex could see the gears to help, solve, and protect spinning in Jeremiah's multicolored eyes, in the muscles in his jaw, in the press of his fine, pink lips.

Suddenly, she realized the movement in his hair wasn't just from his brain waves.

He noticed the expression on her face. "What?"

She pointed. "You've got…oh, God, sit, sit."

She grabbed the lapel of his robe, dragged him to the toilet, then pushed him down onto the seat.

"Something's moving in your hair," she said as she shoved her fingers into the lusciously thick head of it.

She swallowed her shudder when she closed her fingers around something big and hard-shelled. She threw it in the sink then turned on the faucet to wash it down.

She combed both of her hands through his hair, spreading the length and separating the strands. "Let's make sure nothing else is hiding in there."

Jeremiah's wide shoulders gave a shiver.

As Alex stood between his muscled naked legs, the robe covering his lap, she pushed his damp hair back from his forehead. She tried to do it perfunctorily. Like he was one of her sisters.

Her short nails accidentally raked his scalp and he shivered again. Even dirty and wet, his hair felt like some silky animal pelt. Dry, she bet it would cling to her wrists.

"Alex."

She traced her fingers through the hair over his ear, then combed through the hair at his nape. The heel of her hand brushed the lapel of his robe. Through it, she could feel the heat of his strong neck.

She settled her hand there. The other fingered the ends of his hair.

He shifted, making the toilet creak, then captured her waist in his big, hot hands. "Alex."

"Doesn't look like anything else is living in there." She stepped closer, tugging his hair and tilting his jaw up. He was so warm.

He squeezed her waist and he was so strong.

"Alex... Alex, stop."

She slid her hands to his shoulders and dropped her head to look down at her feet. She was in her black-striped tube socks, tight black leggings, and a tissue-thin T-shirt. There was only the barest layer between their skin. He was in a robe and undershirt. Probably boxers. Hopefully boxers.

With a huff of surrender, Jeremiah tilted forward and pressed his forehead against her breasts.

They'd gotten undressed together, helped each other undress, and it had been like they'd been lovers for ages, like the easiest, most comfortable thing in the world was getting undressed and falling into a shower together. She'd never craved to wash a man's hair before.

"Sorry," she whispered into the warm, thick waves of it, restlessly squeezing his strong shoulders.

"I'm going to take my hands off you now," he said, muffled and slow as he gripped her. She could feel the heat of his breath and the movement of his lips through her T-shirt. "If I don't, I won't be able to take my hands off you."

She wondered if he felt her stomach clench before he let go.

He didn't move his head.

Remembering their promise—no sex until they found the second deed, until they trusted each other—she dropped her hands to her sides and began to step back.

"Don't," he said, a low sharp command against her body. "Please. Stay there. Let me... If I can't touch you, let me feel you."

He turned his head and nuzzled the heft of her right boob.

She gave a helpless sound and looked blindly up to the ceiling. He rubbed his cheek against her peaked nipple.

She could feel it in her curled toes. The memory of the restrained man who'd let loose, picked her up, and slammed her against a wall played through her mind like a fever dream.

Distract, distraction, she needed...they'd been talking about something incredibly important.

"Let me explain what I have in mind," she breathed out into their little bathroom as he skimmed his lips over her breast without opening his mouth. "Why some pretty radical changes are necessary if Loretta's is going to stay a bar. I'm... I'm not trying to change things just because I'm a bad person."

That finally got him to lift his face from her now-throbbing body. "Hey."

She met his multicolored eyes.

"I never thought you were a bad person."

She tested her own fortitude by not stepping away. "Maybe not bad. But selfish."

"I was wrong."

It actually hurt not to kiss him.

"I was wrong, too." There was one thing that the major hard-on she had for this guy couldn't distract her from. "You still stink."

He smiled and she wanted to settle her thumbs into his grin crinkles. "So do you."

She stepped back so he could stand, and he offered her the first shower.

As she was about to close and lock the bathroom door for both their sakes, he poked his head back in from the hallway. "I'd be honored if you'd tell me about your bar, Alex," he said.

Instead of bouncing up on her toes to kiss him, she put her hand on his forehead and shoved him out.

When she saw her grin in the mirror, she rolled her eyes. Then started planning.

She wasn't a bad person, but she had shown up angry. Her anger probably had something to do with her sisters' silence, Loretta's resistance, even her mother's maybe valid distrust.

They weren't as easy to please as her continuing-to-explode social media audience.

But she couldn't transform Loretta's in a way that won her grandmother's approval, protected her grandmother from Doody-meyer, and got the exposure she needed for her ticket out of town all by herself.

Her sisters' absence made it easy to forget that she had partners in this gig, just like Jeremiah had Joe and the historical society. Their silence fogged over the three weeks of excited chatter before Alex returned to Freedom. But it didn't make it disappear.

Jeremiah had his committee. She needed hers, too.

She had to get her sisters back onboard.

Chapter Nineteen

Jeremiah hadn't intended to be alone on a lazy weekday afternoon with Alex.

If anything, he was actively working against being alone with her. Every night, he would lock himself in his room before she came upstairs, take melatonin, and sleep with his earbuds to counteract the wall's ability to transfer her mattress movements into his. They could get to know each other in front of her family, at the bar, or while they were searching for the second deed. He was still waiting to hear back from the historical society member with the train depot key.

He'd proven in the bathroom he couldn't be trusted when he had all of her interested, challenging, caring, exhilarating attention to himself.

But he'd left a grant application for seed funding for the museum in his room, and since he was up against the postmarked-by deadline, he'd decided to sit at the bar to complete it. Alex's mother had given him a bright hello and her grandmother and tíos had tried to wrangle him into the latest gossip.

Then Loretta left for physical therapy, Mary went to run errands, and the tíos finally had their fill of coffee.

Now he was alone with Alex who—for once—seemed to have no idea how gorgeous and tempting she was as she leaned on the bar with her arms crossed, those bright flowers he wanted to trace with his tongue right in front of him, reading his application upside down and asking about the American Alliance of Museums and where he thought he would go for dollar-for-dollar private matches.

If she asked one more curious question or gave him one more of those thoughtful gazes through her long lashes, he was going to yank her over the mahogany and unleash himself on that unpainted mouth.

When he heard the clang of the cowbell and turned around and saw Joe, he was as disappointed as he was relieved.

"Jeremiah, good, you're here." Joe had a look on his face that Jeremiah hadn't seen since the waiting room of the ER all those weeks ago. "Alex, I just heard from Gillian. Is anyone else here?"

Alex looked mystified at her cousin; Joe was usually the epitome of ease. "Just Danny." Loud Tejano music came from the kitchen. "He's reviewing flash cards."

"Okay." Joe put his phone on the bar surface and pressed a button. The phone began to ring.

"Why's my sister calling you and not answering my emails?"

The phone clicked on. "Joe, did you find Alex?" Alex's older sister asked through the speaker.

"Why're you calling Joe and not answering my emails?"

"I…uh…" Gillian stuttered. "Your email worried me."

Alex scowled at the device. "Why?"

"What it said, about a second deed and Lance Dutimeyer's plan and finding a secret room behind the walls… It all sounded a little…conspiratorial. I was afraid the professor had…"

Gillian's voice meandered off as Jeremiah's eyes widened. Alex pinched back a smile. "The professor had what?"

"I don't know," Gillian said. "He's very attractive. And a bit intense. I thought he'd...gotten into your head."

"By getting into my pants?" Alex's smile stretched from ear to ear as she looked at Jeremiah. She was shameless.

"Maybe? He's very attractive," Gillian repeated. Jeremiah had never been described as a sexual Svengali before. "Although he's more my type than yours."

"No, he's not," Alex shot back.

Now it was Jeremiah's opportunity to grin. He kept his eyes on Alex's flustered face as he leaned over to speak directly into the speaker.

"It's nice to hear from you, Gillian."

There was a long pause. "You are all dead to me," she finally answered.

Alex shoved him back down onto his stool. "I guess I should be glad you were worried about me. I was afraid you'd fallen into a well or something."

"Sorry I've been out of touch," Gillian answered stiffly. "I'm the event matron for the kids' Montessori school and planning for the Spring Equinox gala fundraiser is always hectic. And Tom's firm has asked me to chair the wives' golf tournament, so I've been..."

Joe was obviously frustrated—he'd rushed here for a reason—as Gillian droned on about all the wealthy, East Coast reasons she'd left her sister in the lurch after they'd presented their plan to Loretta as a joint endeavor.

Jeremiah had grown up around this kind of person who listed their résumé—college, career, and positions on the board of charities—at first introduction, flashing the price tags they felt displayed their worth. The surname on his birth certificate had carried all his value, and his mother had used it all her married life to become powerful, venerated, and feared.

It was unfair to compare Juliana-turned-Gillian, a woman

he barely knew, with a woman he actively avoided. But he had a violent distaste for those who judged others as not being up to snuff after a childhood of being victimized by it.

Stop behaving like your plan is morally superior to mine.

He shifted uncomfortably on the stool.

Alex had yet to share her plans for the bar with him—they'd both been busy—but he'd mulled over her accusation. He'd thought of his plan to build a museum in the shell of Loretta's as a way to save a family, community, and little-known but important piece of history. He'd thought of her plan to update Loretta's as a way to save herself. But his idea to build a museum with a small coffee shop where the family could still gather no more maintained the status quo than her bolder, flashier, beer-garden-and-kick-out-the-tenants concept.

He'd been so focused on her plan being "wrong" that he hadn't considered what her alternatives were. If she and her sisters took over Loretta's, should they be expected to maintain it as a profitless dive bar?

Gillian assumed her East Coast activities were more important than Alex's fight, and Jeremiah assumed his museum was a better solution than Alex's updates.

Who was on Alex's side?

"That's not why I'm calling," Gillian said abruptly. "After I talked to Joe, I called Cynthia."

They'd shared with Joe everything they'd discovered. He'd agreed to keep his ear to the ground while keeping a low profile—they didn't want to shake the wasp's nest of the Hughs—but he'd shared Alex's skepticism that Freedom Rings Development could use the deed to claim a large swath of the east side. Jeremiah only knew of one Cynthia and it was Cynthia Madsen, the heir and owner of Liberty Manufacturing, a struggling after-market auto parts maker that was Freedom's last stand against a sea of minimum-wage jobs.

She had one devotion—Liberty Manufacturing—and kept herself above the fray of Freedom's politics and squabbles as long as the company her grandfather had established was left alone.

"Cynthia is friends with the city attorney," Gillian said. "He told her that he's been worried about what Mayor Mayfield is up to." The city had been ordered by the state to hire out-of-town counsel after a Hugh-related city attorney had been caught using city coffers to fund a lavish Las Vegas lifestyle. "The mayor has been having him research eminent domains."

Jeremiah frowned. Eminent domain allowed cities to seize private property for public use. Throughout the US, it had been used to build highways through predominantly black neighborhoods under the auspices of "urban renewal." The traffic, noise, and overpass structures had destroyed once-thriving black communities.

Gillian went on. "There aren't a lot of restrictions on it. If a city can show there's an economic advantage, they can seize private land and say it's for the public good. If Freedom Rings Development owns parcels on the east side and is in possession of a document that allows them to legally claim more, that might give Mayor Mayfield and Dutimeyer enough clout to claim the east side, sell it to someone promising to create jobs, and line their own pockets."

The normally relaxed Joe bobbed his knee. Alex frowned fiercely.

The curses and secret rooms and long, lost sons had given their second deed search the soft edge of myth. Gillian's revelation made it very, very real.

"So what do we do now?" Gillian asked.

Alex sucked on her bottom lip before she asked, "Are we a we, Juli?"

Jeremiah empathized with the ache of a younger sibling wanting the acknowledgment of the older.

"Yes, always Ali. I... I've been feeling guilty that me and Cici encouraged you to go back there without really considering what we were asking of you. With what happened, when you had to leave Freedom, I wish I'd done more to take care of you. I wish you hadn't felt so alone."

In the quiet, Jeremiah kept his eyes on his crossed hands.

"That was a long time ago, Juli," Alex said.

"I know. Look what you did in that time. You built an amazing life and career for yourself all on your own, with no full ride and seeking no one's approval. I admire you so much. I wish I had one-tenth of your courage. Are you sure you want to waste all that on Freedom?"

The sisters shared a habit of maligning his adopted home. They also loved each other fiercely.

"Loretta needs us," Alex said. "It sounds like they all do. But *I* need you and Cici to get involved again. To get...excited again. If we're going to keep and claim this place, I need your help."

It was a measure of how much their relationship had evolved that Alex was willing to have this vulnerable conversation in front of him.

Jeremiah had needed his mother when the impending storm of his brother's popularity had first rumbled. Home from boarding school for his one-weekend-a-month visit, he'd gone to her, confused and upset by the internet messages from strangers. She'd told him to grow up.

"If you could learn to finally carry yourself like a Harrington," she'd said, "you'll find you'll be far less desperate and needy for the approval of others. It will lessen the sting when you're inevitably compared unfavorably with your brother."

He'd been eleven.

"Okay," Gillian said, interrupting his thoughts. "Okay, Ali. I'm in."

It was a vow in four words.

"God, good," Alex said. Her relief was palpable. She picked up the phone and walked out the pass-through. "Great. I've been thinking about what we could do with that hidden room and..."

She headed up the stairs.

Joe pointed and sighed. "She took my phone."

Then he frowned at Jeremiah who was staring back as an idea blossomed.

Alex was not a woman who asked for or accepted help, yet she'd repeatedly put her pride on the line to reach out to her unresponsive sisters.

As unpleasant as the memory of his own family was, it reminded him that he, too, had resources.

Perhaps he could do more to protect the east side.

While he couldn't imagine sharing this adventure with his sibling the way Alex had—frankly, his brother wouldn't care—he was still connected to his family. Even with the name change to his great-grandmother's Post away from the familial Harrington, he still had resources beyond his trust fund.

You had other spots in mind, right? Alex had asked. *Just because I don't want you to put the museum here doesn't mean I don't think it's a good idea.*

The museum could go anywhere on Milagro Street. If they were able to protect the east side, then a museum somewhere else on the block could feed Loretta's. Loretta's could feed the museum.

Jeremiah could keep his connection to Loretta's family.

He could keep his connection to Alex.

They wouldn't be adversaries, or the victor over the defeated. They could be friends. They could be partners.

They could, perhaps, be something more.

Chapter Twenty

"Hoist me up," Alex commanded several nights later as they stood in front of one of the boarded-up windows of the Freedom train depot. They were on the side that faced the weed-strewn tracks, not the street, but the bright full moon still made Jeremiah too visible for whatever Alex had planned. He'd agreed that, after what they'd learned from Gillian, they couldn't wait to search for more information about Edward Hugh until the historical society member with the key returned from his vacation in Boca Raton.

He was also eager for his own reasons to get a look at the insides. That still didn't make him comfortable with breaking and entering.

With her hair covered by a droopy black beanie and her eyes with that smudged-makeup look she got at the end of a shift, she looked like a sleepy panther. She motioned to him impatiently. "C'mon, big guy. You want to find this deed or not?"

"Yes," he said, exasperated at how easily managed he was by her hissing prettiness. He made his hands into a cradle and bent over. "I would also like to avoid getting arrested while looking for it."

She put her black, high-top Converse into his connected fingers and her hands on his shoulders. With a "Hup" from him, she had a foot on the jutting brick of the train depot and then a sneaker—"Hey there!"—on Jeremiah's shoulder.

"I didn't say you could climb me," he protested as she got both feet up on Jeremiah's shoulders as he straightened and he grabbed her calves to steady her. They were thick and firm. She was in slim black sweatpants and a black zip-up sweatshirt. She was the hottest hooligan he'd ever met.

"Your brains are…no good to me…out here," she grunted, working at something. Jeremiah braced himself as she wiggled. "Just need you for your brawn."

He heard a loud squeal above him and scanned the tracks for witnesses. Nothing but moonlight and the empty yard.

"Okay," she said, panting. "Gimme a boost."

Still holding her calves, he carefully lowered into a squat, counted out a "1-2-3," then helped her launch off his shoulders. With a soft grunt, her feet lifted away. He turned around, stepped back, and looked up to see her gorgeous butt then shapely legs disappear into a high, rectangular window, one of two over the bright white letters spelling out FREEDOM. He thought those windows were purely decorative.

She stuck her head out. "I just discovered something."

"What?"

"How easily you lifted me up here was totally hot." She held out her phone and took a picture of him.

She ducked back inside. "Not a tease," she called out from inside the depot. "A straight-ass truth."

"Deniability of this break-in will be easier without photographic evidence," he called back.

He smiled to himself as he turned around, leaned back against the century-old bricks, and waited for her to make her way through the building. He hoped she didn't twist an ankle. Or maybe hoped that she did. It would give him an excuse to carry her again.

The M. K. & T. Railway had once proclaimed the Freedom train station its loveliest depot north of Texas with its beveled glass windows, roof of red clay tiles, broad eaves, large archways, and elegant brick pass-throughs to protect "carriages." Passenger service through Freedom had been suspended in the '70s and the last train had ridden over these tracks in the early '00s. A few die-hard train lovers in Freedom maintained the building's exterior—cleaning the gutters, keeping the Freedom signage a bright white and the doors, window trim, and eaves a nice mossy green, replacing the boards over the glass windows whenever a kid got artistic with a spray can.

But the interior was an abandoned mess. The Herculean task of making it tenable was why the city ignored it and the historical society had done nothing more with the building than store documents without historical value from well-meaning residents.

Arms crossed, he turned his head to watch her round the corner.

Funny. He'd looked in that direction just knowing she would be there.

He followed her in through a propped-open lobby door. When she pulled it closed, it was cocoon dark. Jeremiah clicked on his flashlight and slowly scanned it over the main lobby, struck once again by the building's potential. The middle waiting area was a two-story square with a termite-eaten but still-lovely balcony ringing the interior. The black-and-white-arabesque floors had been destroyed by various leaks. One-story wings bookended the building: the ticket-taker's booth and offices were on one side, and the glassed-in offices of the station manager and superintendent were on the other. The city was fortunate the roof's curved tiles still balanced on the mush of the support beams.

He pointed in the direction of the executive offices. They

made their way carefully through the detritus of overturned benches, stacked railroad ties, murky puddles, and an unlikely mess of Styrofoam cups spilling out of rodent-chewed boxes.

Alex stopped and shined her light on a mounted framed poster. "Huh."

It was a visitor's map of Freedom, circa 1960s. Clearly marked were the then-thriving businesses along Main Street and Penn Avenue—the furniture store, the ice cream parlor, the theater, a JCPenney's that had pride of place at the intersection of the two thoroughfares. Freedom's hospital, bank, golf course, park, city hall, and several hotels and motels were labeled. But beyond marking the depot, naming Milagro Street, and filling in the portion of Penn Avenue that led away from it, the east side was blank.

Loretta could attest that Milagro Street in the 1960s had been thriving. But this map dismissed the bustling businesses that had served a vibrant community. Instead, someone had scratched "Boxcar Barrio" on the glass over the blank space.

"Boxcar barrio?" Alex asked, looking over her shoulder at Jeremiah.

She had a right to the sharp, pugnacious jut of her chin.

"Remember how Joe mentioned that the railroad wanted to attract families rather than solo traqueros because it allowed them to have more dependable workers?" He nodded at the glass. "That's how they attracted them. They offered them free 'rolling housing.'"

Alex's full lower lip dropped open. "They lived in boxcars?"

Jeremiah nodded. "The railroad provided a woodstove, a stovepipe, a wood floor, and a partition with the expectation that two families would live in each of them. They'd keep the boxcars on the tracks to use them as a mobile village, or—like in Freedom—they'd establish permanent settlements by moving the cars off the tracks and setting them in the periphery of the yards."

"They lived in boxcars," Alex said again, as if needing to verify.

"The families were so successful at turning the cars into homes that railroad officials believed they were thrilled to have the cheapest nod to housing when, in reality, the Mexican families were just making the best of what was given to them." Her eyes were thrillingly furious and focused beneath her beanie. "They would create furniture from old crates and scrap lumber, decorate the insides of the boxcars with wallpaper, set up chicken coops. Apparently, they were very prideful of their flower and vegetable gardens. One railroad tried to hire a 'matron' to teach the Mexicanas a US style of cooking. You can imagine how well that went."

She huffed through her nose and gave him a begrudging smile.

"Freedom's boxcar community allowed families to retain and reinforce their language and cultural identity. Some would say it inhibited assimilation but—"

Alex scoffed. "Our skin tone does that better than a tincan house does."

"Yes," Jeremiah said. "Families made the boxcar community into their neighborhood and lived there until they migrated into inexpensive housing on the east side. Boxcar housing was gone by the time this map was made, but the slur remained."

She took out her phone, took a picture of the map, then—too his surprise—put a many-ringed hand on top of her beanie and began to laugh.

"What?"

"You know what everyone is using as a green building material in Chicago? Shipping containers!" Her eyes were bright with the irony. "They're using them for restaurants, bars, guesthouses, backyard offices. I knew this one tech couple that stacked a bunch of them together and turned them into a mansion that looked out over the lake."

She turned to him, her humor brighter than the flashlight, and put a hand to her chest. "We were the original hipsters."

He'd seen the shipping container fad in *Architectural Digest*, but hadn't made the connection to the traqueros' boxcar homes. Alex had. She and her family had a perspective that, for all of his training and best intentions, he never would. What a fascinating exhibit that would make, comparing the fashionable shipping container structures of modern-day elites with the shunned boxcar homes of Mexican immigrants doing the best they can.

He resisted—as was becoming the norm—the urge to kiss her.

"Maybe I'll turn a boxcar into an outdoor bar on the side of Loretta's," she said, grinning. "Give a shout to the original neighborhood."

"That's a great idea," he said, meaning it.

She sobered. He nodded toward one of the offices.

Inside the superintendent's office, which had been cleared of everything but document storage, Jeremiah scanned his light over a depressing number of old filing cabinets, aged trunks, large plastic tubs, and cardboard boxes.

"Man," Alex sighed. "What a needle in a haystack."

A local railroad enthusiast had made their needle search a little simpler by labeling the plastic bins holding the railroad employment records with dates. But the bins were numerous. Jeremiah hauled a few into an open area of the room. Alex stood her wide flashlight down on its end, and it shined like a lantern. They popped lids off two boxes and settled on the dirty floor to begin slowly rifling through papers.

"That's the first time you've said something nice about my ideas for the bar," Alex said without moving her eyes off a paper she was scanning.

"Yes," he said, watching her. "I'd like to hear more about your plans."

She did raise her eyes then, and he felt the weight of her dark-eyed assessment.

She held the paper out to him and pointed at it. "Do you think that says Hugh or Pugh?"

Hiding his disappointment, he looked down. It was a schedule roster. "That might be an *H*," he said.

She set it to the side.

"I talked to Joe and he thinks it'd be possible to open up the east wall of the building without running into anything load-bearing," she said, launching in without fanfare. "Taking advantage of the parking lot would double our space and attract..."

As they slowly worked their way through the boxes and incrementally added papers to the pile that might mention Pugh, Hugh, or Mugh, she told Jeremiah her plans for an outdoor beer garden, now anchored by a boxcar bar at one end. She told him about her plans to entirely rehaul the kitchen and update the speaker system to showcase local and regional live music acts.

She told him about her hopes to get her little sister Sissy truly committed to the project. While Sissy—a well-regarded sous-chef working in Kansas City—had offered to hire and train a cook to improve the food at Loretta's, Alex thought she deserved a chance to have her own kitchen. She hoped that Sissy could finally get Loretta to okay using some of their popular family recipes and improve Loretta's draw as a dining destination.

Jeremiah put down a stack of salary receipts he'd been flipping through. "I've always wondered about that," he said. "Your grandmother is an incredible cook. Why does she serve subpar food at the bar rather than her own?"

"Tell me about it!" Alex rolled her eyes in exasperation. With the beanie holding back her hair, he could focus on the velvety skin of her forehead. "Granmo says she cooks for pleasure. She doesn't want to do at her job what she does out of love. I think she just doesn't want people stealing her recipes. Her cooking has always been her superpower."

"Did she teach the recipes to Sissy?"

"I think so. But then they stopped cooking together. I don't know why."

Their harmony over the need for a better menu went out the window when Alex talked about turning the tenant rooms into private event space.

"Jeremiah!" She shoved a box to the side and dragged another one closer. "Do you honestly think it's a good idea to give strangers free range of our family's business? Because that's what we're doing—pay rent and you and whoever else you let in after hours can grab yourself a bottle of Jack and go...flambé yourselves on our industrial grill. If we don't get sued because of the million liability issues, we're definitely going to get robbed."

He didn't want to give in to her reasonable argument. "There are still trustworthy people out there who appreciate the camaraderie of being in the thick of things." He could feel his irritation in his ears. "Who need it."

He didn't expect her soft smile as she rested back on her bottom. "You know you're not getting rid of the family," she said. "They're like fleas. Just because you don't live upstairs doesn't mean you're going to be able to scratch them loose."

Jeremiah cleared his throat and pretended he was reacting to the dust.

With only a few boxes left to search, they'd found pitiably few documents with Edward Hugh's name. If they found no new leads, he didn't know where they would look next. He wondered how Dutimeyer's search was going.

"We're gonna adjust the prices to modern-day standards," Alex said. "We're going to need to attract new clientele to pay those prices."

She held up a staying hand up before he could say anything. "I'm not doing it to chase away family. But we've got to. It's the only way Loretta's is going to survive. We'll have daily specials. Two-for-one deals for locals. Punch cards for repeat customers. But if we don't change, Loretta's is over. Whether it dies quick because Doody-meyer demolishes it or dies slow because our ten-year-old pricing doesn't allow us to keep up with natural food and beverage inflation, both have the same end results: this gathering place goes away."

Jeremiah had planned for a coffee shop on the side of the museum run by Loretta and Mary and an office upstairs instead of a bedroom. But the historical society's plan also fundamentally changed Loretta's, also out of necessity and not choice.

"What you've described doesn't…match your social media presence," he said, pulling the two remaining boxes closer. Her renovation plans confirmed what he'd already discovered in the weeks of watching her work: she wasn't anarchic, cruel, or even particularly outlandish. The woman he'd seen had patiently listened to long-winded stories from her tíos, soothed petty squabbles between the staff, given a smile and a free drink to a lonely face at the bar, handled the chaos of a rush with a ballerina's poise, and taken in her grandmother's wisdom with serious, absorbing eyes.

He didn't understand how "the best bitch in bartending" and the Alex Torres he'd gotten to know intersected.

"You've been looking at my social media?"

"I…" He'd never been good at hiding his fascination with her. He shrugged. "Yes."

Her velvety cheeks curved up into smug balls. "Did you get one of your students to help you figure out Instagram?" She pulled what looked like a stack of thin magazines out of her box. "Did they explain hash-tagging to you? Don't go on TikTok; your heart couldn't take it."

Actually, what his heart had been having a hard time taking was the photos she'd posted since she'd arrived in Freedom. What began as pithy or dismissive statements attached to an image of a leaky window at Loretta's or a farm with a row of old toilets stacked on its outskirts had quieted to pictures of Freedom enjoying its spring awakening. The buds on the oak trees, a fan of peacock feathers, a birdbath gleaming in the morning light, and the orange rays of sundown reflecting in Loretta's front window… He wondered if she knew how beautifully she'd been capturing her hometown.

She put the stack of magazines on the floor and began to flip through the top one.

"What do you want me to tell you, Jeremiah?" she said without raising her eyes. "You think a woman who looks like me makes a name for herself by being polite? I'm naturally snarly, but when you pair it with my skin tone, my hair, my body…people would hoot and call me 'sassy.' Which is just another way to demean and dismiss a grown-ass woman who's telling you clearly what's what."

Her long lashes shadowed her cheeks as she continued turning pages. "So I could huff around being mad or I could double down on their stereotype and use it to my advantage. If someone came to my bar wanting to harass me or my co-workers, treat us like they thought serving them meant we were servants to them, then the character I played was a stone-cold bitch."

Her tone was straightforward, not defensive but also not asking for permission. "I used it against them to benefit me, and it worked."

She flipped another page and traced over it with her finger.

When he'd initially researched her, her antagonistic social media presence had been a detraction from the numerous industry articles that said that she was skilled, adept, and innovative at her job. But she was right; it had worked. The "best bitch in bartending" was a construct she'd ridden all the way to an *Esquire* profile. The last thing she needed was his—or anyone's—permission.

The internet and Jeremiah's dubious fame-by-proxy had contributed to some of the most distasteful moments of his life, but he needed to detangle his emotions about the online world from his emotions about her.

"Alex, feel free to tell me it's none of my business. But that last video in Chicago. What happened?"

The yelling, the wild eyes, the humiliation of her former boss...that woman was still a stranger to him.

She put down the magazine and picked up another. *Freedom Railroad Yard Quarterly,* it said on the cover. "My friend Joanie was pregnant." She began to slowly flip pages. "Working as a server at the Fantasy Box was great money and she wanted to keep her job after the baby was born. But we all knew, once you got pregnant, management was going to come up with a transparent reason to fire you. So, I hosted a meeting at my apartment. I'd Googled how to organize restaurant employees and figured, with my clout and if all the female staff banded together, that we could put our foot down. Make some demands. Me and my sisters were already talking about Loretta's, and I didn't want to leave Joanie and the others in the lurch."

She continued flipping but Jeremiah wondered if she was seeing the pages. He'd certainly given up all pretense of looking through his box. His full attention was on her in the soft glow.

"Joanie didn't show up for her shift that night. When I told Randy that I was going to give her a call, he told me not to bother. They'd already fired her with some made-up bullshit. But really it was because they'd found out about the meeting, that she'd been the inspiration. They told the rest of the women that if they tried to organize again, they'd all be let go. Fucking Randy...he waited to tell me until he could do in front of everyone, right out in the open. You should have seen the look on his face; it was the happiest I'd ever seen him. I knew if I hadn't had that meeting, Joanie could have worked a couple more months before she started showing. Built up a nest egg."

Alex chewed on her lower lip. "I kinda lost it. Then I made a show of it. Told myself that I needed to go out with a bang to get my followers to follow me to Kansas." She shrugged. "Humiliating him and making an ass of myself was better than punching him and getting arrested. So that's what I did. End of story."

She carefully put the magazine down and picked up another.

The railroad office was silent. Not even a dust mote moved.

All Jeremiah could hear was his heart pounding. It was the loudest, most life-shattering gong he'd ever heard. "How's Joanie doing?" he asked. He was one hundred percent certain that Alex knew.

"She's moved in with her parents. I told her that if I can

make this work, she's always got a job in southeast Kansas. Who knows, she might take me up on it?"

Alex Alejandra Torres-Armstead had graffitied the mayor's house to stand up for her cousin. The best bitch in bartending had tried to unionize in order to support her friend. She'd aimed that sharp, fighter's chin at Jeremiah when she thought he was using her family's legacy to enhance his white, male elitism. And she'd engaged in a treasure hunt with the enemy in order to protect her grandmother.

She wasn't a hooligan. She was an avenging angel of justice.

As the understanding of who Alex was roared through his veins and scorched away his misconceptions, he wrapped his fingers around the edge of the plastic crate to keep himself from launching forward and mainlining her.

She tipped the magazine toward the light.

Then her eyes went wide. "Woah! Look at this," she demanded, scooting closer.

Jeremiah clung to his promise—*no sex while we're searching for the deed*—as he sat a hair's breadth from her dusty, curvy, baby powdery soft body. He looked down at the magazine rather than covering her so that her truth and passion and willingness to wage war for fair play could burn him clean.

She was pointing at a picture. "I flipped through a couple of these and just realized that I was seeing some brown faces. Look!"

Jeremiah followed her finger across the small print below the image.

The first-place winner of the largest watermelon contest was Mr. Edward Hugh. Here he stands with his wife Rosalinda as they present their whopper at 34 pounds.

Wife. Rosalinda.

Jeremiah's eyes shot to the photo. Edward Hugh had the formal mien of a gentleman wearing his Sunday best for a photo. He was handsome, with a high-standing collar and a flat-brimmed hat tucked under his arm. There was a definite twinkle in his eye. And next to him was a pretty young woman, her dark hair in pin curls around the side of her round face, in a floral, dropped-waist dress. She didn't smile. But her chin was raised as her left hand was spread on the watermelon that was indeed a whopper. Jeremiah wondered who truly was responsible for raising the thing.

On her ring finger was a band. Rosalinda. Edward Hugh's wife. She was unmistakably Latina.

Jeremiah looked at Alex. She looked back at Jeremiah just as stunned.

"Edward Hugh's wife was Mexican," he said. "So his descendants…"

Alex grinned. "Doody-meyer is going to shit himself."

"Who published that?" he asked. "It should be on the back cover."

Alex flipped it over. *Printed by Peridiodicos de Independencia*, it read.

"That was the publisher of the Spanish-language newspaper here in the colonia," Jeremiah said. "They had an office up the street. Your aunt Ofelia has a collection of the newspapers and knows them front to back. She knows more about the Mexican immigrants of the colonia than anyone else in town. We need to ask her about Rosalinda Hugh."

Jeremiah's smile grew with a confidence that would have been misplaced if he wasn't so certain. "We find Rosalinda, we find the next place to search."

Chapter Twenty-One

Alex didn't need much sleep.

But she did need more than the zero hours she was going to get if the big guy didn't stop tossing and turning. If he didn't stop reminding her that his huge, muscular, overwarm body was there, just there, a foot away in a dark room. Going to bed had become a reliable torture, the wall between them like a tuning fork humming his presence into her mattress and over her skin every night. But tonight, the wall felt as diaphanous as the gauzy curtain that let hazy blue-white moonlight into her bedroom.

She felt like she could reach through it and pull him close.

She flung off the pillow she'd put over her face and pounded her fist on the wallpaper-covered plaster. "Go to sleep," she yelled.

For a moment, only silence answered her. Then he said, "Can't."

He sounded like he was next to her on the pillow. Maybe a grate was open?

"You want tea or drugs? I've got both. Come on over."

"No, I...shouldn't..."

Shouldn't.

Not *I don't want to.* Not *can't.* Not *won't.*

She flattened her fisted hand against the wall.

Her hand reminded her of Rosalinda's, claiming that watermelon.

"Do you think Rosalinda is the reason Edward was disowned?" she asked, looking at the brown of her skin. She ran it slowly over the embossed gold and white of the old-fashioned wallpaper, imagining it was his paler skin she was gliding it across.

"That would make sense," he said. His voice was deep and slow and musing, as soft and luxurious as the plushest down pillow. She wanted to wrap it around her as she fell asleep. "It was well-documented how angry Wayland Hugh was about the number of Mexicans settling around Miracle Street. I can only imagine how much angrier he got when he discovered that his firstborn and heir had fallen in love with one."

Him saying *fallen in love* in that late-night voice made her stomach swoop stupidly.

When they'd made it back to Loretta's, Alex had hurried into the shower then locked herself in her room. Now she was underneath the sheets in a black tank top and panties while he was restless on the other side of the wall. What had he worn to bed?

She imagined the cool solidity beneath the wallpaper was the broad muscles of his back. But he would be so warm. "Maybe she was the woman who got pregnant?"

"Yes," he said, low. Could he hear her hand caressing the plaster? "It would explain why he came back."

This was the first time they'd talked while in bed, and it was like they were sharing a pillow while they murmured the same fairy tale to each other. The story of Edward and Rosalinda falling in love. Edward risking his family and fortune to have her. Turning to the lowest rungs of a backbreaking industry to support her. Standing up to his father to keep her. It was all stomach-clenchingly romantic.

She was such a sap.

"It was stupid that they stayed in Freedom." She pulled her hand from the wall and ran it through the curls her hair had air-dried into. Tried to comb out some of the nonsense. "What was the point if he was never gonna accept the inheritance his dad tried to give back to him? They could've lived anywhere. He didn't have to work across the street from his dad."

"Hmm..." Jeremiah shifted on the other side of the wall. Had he turned to face her? If she looked hard enough, could she see the gold flickering in his eyes?

"Freedom is unique now," he said, soothing soft, like those academic fingers were joining hers in her hair. It was irritating that he wasn't irritated. "You've mentioned how weird it is. It was unique then. Maybe they refused to be driven from a home they both thought was special."

She really needed to get some sleep. "Or maybe he just liked sticking it to his dad."

She rolled away from the wall.

"Alex?"

She didn't say anything.

"Are you free Sunday? We could talk to Ofelia then."

She tilted her head back over her shoulder. "I'm gonna be a little busy on Sunday. Aren't you?"

"No." She could hear the disappointment in his voice. "I'll just be grading papers. It's fine, I'll just..."

"That's what you're doing for Easter?"

"Sunday is Easter?"

Her absentminded professor.

Few people kept up the rites leading to Easter like her family did. Her tíos gave up their occasional light beers during Lent, and the tías came in with blessings of the cross on their foreheads on Ash Wednesday. Loretta's even served fish sticks for lunch on Fridays, while her Tía Elena served tiny breaded perch to the rest of the family who showed up at her home for the huge Friday luncheons.

"You should just come to Granmo's with me," she said. It was nothing to invite a guest to Sunday dinner. "We can talk to Tía Ofelia there. You'll have to go to Mass, or someone will narc on you, but the spread at Easter is totally worth it. Granmo will have pineapple tamales. And Tía Elena will make her world-famous fried chicken. Granmo might be the best cook in the family, but Tía is breathing down her neck."

Her family invited people to Sunday dinner all the time. It gave them the opportunity to watch their guests' eyes bug out over the enormous amount of food, the sheer number of desserts, and the astounding scene of so many Chicanos crammed into one little house in Kansas.

As Jeremiah stayed silent, she avoided thinking about how it was *something* to invite him to Easter dinner. To Easter dinner and Mass. With her.

Maybe she'd meant it to be *something*.

"Now I'm *really* not going to be able to sleep," he said.

She laughed and turned toward the wall, felt the cool sheets slide over her bare legs, and tucked her hands under her cheek. "Keyed up for treasure hunting and Easter. You're such a kid."

He didn't answer. The silence stretched. Had she offended him? After all the times she'd aimed for offensive, this was the one time she hadn't meant...

"That's not all that's keeping me awake, angel."

His voice reached between her legs and rubbed. Her thighs clenched around the sensation.

"Alex?"

Tonight had been awesome. Just plain awesome. He was fun and funny and just reckless enough. She was so into his stories, could listen to him with her chin in her hand for days.

He told her about her community in a way that never con-descended, that was like a tequila maker eager to show her the heart of his agave plants. He'd listened closely as she'd explained her plans for the bar, he'd pushed back and not just rolled over, and he'd even given a good suggestion or two. The way he'd asked about what had happened with Joanie—he really was trying to understand her better.

The lust they'd shared in the beginning had made them crash together and left damage. She didn't want it wrench-ing them apart now after their awesome night.

"You said it wasn't good for us," she blurted out. "You said we'd wait 'til…'til after we found the deed."

"I know what I said." She could hear the groan of his de-sire like toothache. "It's hard to remember why when I want you this much."

God.

"When I go to bed *every night* wanting you this much."

He was an oncoming train.

"I can feel you in bed with me. I can smell you on my sheets. I'm close to clawing through the wall to get to you."

It was like she'd broken the dam of his words and now she was drowning in them. She flung herself to her back and grabbed her breasts. Tried to restrain her heart from banging so hard behind them. "Your mouth…" She cursed.

"Do you like it?"

She buried the heel of her hands in her eye sockets. "You know I do."

One of her survival skills was knowing how to read people. But she never could have imagined, that first night when she had him, what a craving this man could create in her.

"Would you touch yourself, Alex?" he panted. "For me?"

She wanted to remember his voice, the exact words, the command in the request, the blue-white glow of the night, the ache of temptation, and the smoothness of the sheets against her skin for the rest of her life. When she was lonely, when she had to be hard and mean again, she would remember that she was once adored.

She lifted her hands from her face and spread her thighs.

"Wait," he said. "Wait. Put your hands...put them on your ribs. Just under your breasts."

"I'm wearing a tank top."

"Take it off, Alex. Yes. Take it all off. Get naked for me."

Her iron frame squeaked and the springs twanged as she whipped her tank top off then wiggled out of her panties. The squeal of her bed broadcasting her eagerness would have been embarrassing if she wasn't so eager.

The silence settled around them both as she put her hands to her ribs. Her skin was so warm.

Could he tell?

"Alex...sweetie...rub the undersides of your breasts with just your index fingers. Light, make sure to make it light. I want it to tickle. Can you do that for me?"

She'd lost possession of her hands. It was his fingers, long and thick, touching her, back and forth, where she was so sensitive. Teasing her. Making her squirm. She tossed her head to the side and spread her thighs under the sheets to release the pressure.

"I love your body," he sighed like he was above her, touching and watching.

She arched into the feeling. Into him.

"Hold your nipples, honey. Stroke them with your thumbs...yeah...yeah. Now pinch. Hard."

She bit her lip in pleasure and humped up her hips. She loved his body, too.

"Would you run your hand over your bicep?" she said, her eyes still closed, her hands squeezing and pinching. "That big, gorgeous bicep. Over those shoulders I want to sink my teeth into? How's that feel?"

"Good," he said. She could hear her tremble in his voice. "Amazing. Rub your hands down your stomach."

She winced against the surge of want. "Yeah, you too," she panted as her hands as his hands slid off her hard nipples and big breasts and over hot skin and round belly and...

"To your thighs, Alex," he shot out. "Just to those sweet, honey thighs. Not between them."

Asshole! She rubbed her palms over the soft grippable flesh there just like she knew he wanted to.

"Grab your cock," she said, dark and dirty. "Start working it. I know you gotta use two hands, big boy."

He groaned and she was cruelly glad for it.

"Tip...tip to your side," he panted. "Grab a handful of that bottom. Stroke it." She did as he asked so she could bury her whimper in her pillow.

"You stroke, too," she gasped. "Hard."

She wanted to hear the *thwack* of his dick in his hands.

"Do you have any...any idea how often you bend over in your job? Do you know how many debil—debilitating fantasies I've had of your bottom while one of your family members is sitting next to me? That beautiful...luscious...*unh*... heart-shaped rear makes me into a monster. I'm going kneel behind you and eat you up."

Oh God. He'd just given her her own debilitating fantasy.

"Yes, yes," he said like he could feel the gooseflesh rising over her skin. "Rub that soft, soft cheek for me."

She did. For him. Then she smacked it, loud and sharp, enough to sting.

She felt the vibration of his deep, pained groan through the wall and into her bed frame.

"You...you keep that stroke on your dick nice and steady," she gasped. "Do you get wet at the tip?"

"Yes." She could hear his strokes in his breathing. "A little."

"Rub it over the head." She wanted to hear the moisture as he jerked himself. "Do you like playing with your balls?"

"I'm not telling you that," he growled.

She chuckled with both hands full of her ass. "Shy boy."

"Not shy...*guh*..." Had she inspired him? "Not shy. But I'm not telling you everything. You have to find out when you touch me."

Not *if*. When.

She clamped her thighs together and squirmed. "Now?"

"Not now. Roll to your back. Spread those gorgeous thighs like you're making room for me."

Oh God. The sharp command of his voice was almost as good as his huge dick, his long fingers. His dirty agile tongue.

"Jeremiah!" she called, beyond frustrated as her hips rolled fitfully on the sheets with her feet planted, her knees bent, and her thighs spread wide.

"Trail your nails down the inside of your thighs." She did. With one hand. With the other hand, she began to stroke into her pubic hair.

"Alex!"

"What?"

"No cheating."

"How could you know that?"

"Just knew."

Just like he knew when she was walking around the side of the depot when she had every intention of scaring the beje-sus out of him.

She stomped the mattress with her bare foot. "Then get on with it."

He went silent.

Goose bumps lit up her skin.

"Oh...sweetheart," he finally cooed, low and deep. She felt a tiny, teary drop drip out of her. "Are—are you—impatient?" He was making sure she could hear the exertion of him beating off. "Because I feel...*ungh*...my hands...my penis...the veins. I feel great."

She couldn't reply because, with her hands gripping into the soft flesh on the inside of her thighs and chin up, she was absolutely panting for it.

"I've done this...*yeah*... I've done this to myself so—so many times fantasizing that I was sliding up inside of you again."

Her thighs were shivering.

"Sometimes...sometimes... I'll just rub against the sheets. Pretend that luscious bottom is in my hands...your soft thighs around my ears and I'm just...just gorging on you..."

She didn't know when she started whispering *please*.

"I'm tasting you, eating you, orgasming into the sheet as I do it."

Her cunt spasmed wetly on empty air.

"Sweetheart...are you ready? Can you spread that pussy for me? Let me see."

She felt stripped of everything but raw want, as tender as a bared nerve.

"Darling...angel... I'm at the end of your bed. I'm at your feet. Can I see?" She v'ed her pussy lips apart. Felt the room's warm air touch her wetness. "Can I watch? Can I touch? Wet your fingers for me, sweetheart, get them nice and wet." She did, licked her own fingertips. "Good, good darling. Now touch that eager little clitoris. Be sweet to it just like I would be..."

She groaned as she dabbed at her wet, hard bud.

"Yes. Yes. Your sexy, powerful body, what a gift you are.

Please." She arched her back into his begging, slid her free hand down to push his words between her legs. "Show me. Teach me. Let me learn how to please you. How to pleasure you. Show me how I can keep you."

She grit her teeth against a sob.

"I can hear you, sweetheart. You're so wet. Two fingers?"

"Three."

"Fast."

"And hard... I need it... Jeremiah."

"Yes, sweetie. Hard. I'll remember. Give it to you hard. Thank you. And your sweet, round clitoris?"

"Circles. Jeremiah. Circles. Tongue. Fuck."

She heard him grunt. "Yes, tongue, sweetheart. Brave, delicious angel. I'll kneel between your legs and lick it, suck it, love it 'til you're done with me."

She began to pump her hips up to meet her hands, his face, his soul-destroying words. The bed was creaking with her movements. She'd never been worshipped so thoroughly.

"Jeremiah," she pleaded.

"As long as you want, as much as you want, darling, I'll watch you, I'll lick you, I'll finger you, I'll fuck you—" He bit off his words with a grunt and deep groan. "As long as you'll have me, sweetheart. Everything you want." She heard him suck in a shocked gasp of air. "God." He groaned. "Alex."

She clenched her teeth against a scream as her body went up in flames from neck to knees. The bed rocked beneath her as she rolled and spasmed, as she heard him beg her name through the wall. She imagined him coming all over his chest and abs and it incinerated the bits of her that were left.

It was many minutes before the chill of the room against her sweat-soaked body roused her enough to pull her hands from between her trembling thighs.

"Ow," she complained.

"What?" His voice, gravel rough, was still as clear as a bell.

"My..." She began to chuckle and her voice sounded wrecked. "My hands are cramped."

He was silent for a second before he said, "So are mine."

That made her laugh harder—this was so stupid—and she heard him join in on the other side of the wall.

"We weren't even doing it for that long," she groaned.

He sounded like he was laughing on his back, his big arms splayed wide. "At least this time you can't make fun of me for my staying power."

She flexed her aching knuckles. "I'm going to need a brace for my hands."

"That's not the only thing I'm going to need a brace for."

It was so stupid and juvenile and they both started to howl with laughter.

Anyone walking by at 4:00 a.m. would assume the hauntings had gone official at Loretta's. Their laughter made them sound as loony as chain-rattling ghosts.

Their laughter sounded like freedom.

Chapter Twenty-Two

When Alex finally answered her phone Friday evening, her voice was sharp and deadly.

"I don't recognize this number so if you ring me one more time I'm gonna—"

"Alex," Jeremiah interrupted, keeping his hands at two and ten as he leaned closer to the mobile phone he'd mounted with a clip onto an air vent. "It's me. It's Jeremiah."

"Jeremiah?"

He realized his hunched state, his distraction, and straightened, quickly scanning this stretch of two-lane highway that connected Dupen College and Freedom. These devices were deadly. Fortunately, all he saw in the pale light before sundown was empty road, a line of barbed-wire fencing, and the water tower in the distance that signaled city limits.

"Yes, it's me. Sorry I kept calling. I just—"

"When'd you get a phone?"

"Oh…uh. Earlier this week."

"Wanted to keep up on your social media stalking?" He could hear the clink, clatter, and chatter of the Friday happy-hour crowd at Loretta's. She still found time to tease him.

He'd repeatedly missed calls from Allen Winstead, his family's attorney, whose exasperation at having to leave voice mails on Jeremiah's office phone had reached a zenith. Additionally, there were a multitude of forms that needed to be downloaded, reviewed, signed, and returned, and Allen's assistant had convinced him that her job would be easier, her boss would be happier, and Jeremiah would get what he desired quicker if he bent to her will and used an app.

He'd been…surprised when the family attorney had called after he'd emailed his mother. He'd assumed there would be some negotiation. Some pleading. Certainly groveling. All on his part, of course.

Perhaps, foolishly, he'd anticipated an argument about coming back into the family fold or—at the very least—a politeness-sake inquiry into why Jeremiah had made his request.

But no. Just a cell phone conversation with a man connected to Jeremiah only because he'd been paid. In fact, when Jeremiah had offered this morning to send a one-page prospectus for his mother's perusal—what he would send to any investor—Allen had said it wouldn't be necessary.

The lawyer had explained uncomfortably that Jeremiah's mother had asked that all future communications from Jeremiah go directly to him. Allen was to be "first contact."

In other words, his mother didn't want to see Jeremiah in her inbox.

He was a blown-off dandelion seed.

"Why're you harassing me, stalker?" she said with lazy, soft affection.

"Yes, sorry about that." He'd been panicking the first four times her phone had gone to voice mail. "I wanted to let you know before they showed up. I invited some colleagues to the bar."

"What?" she said, alarmed. "Who?"

The second the invitation had fallen out of Jeremiah's mouth, he'd worried he'd misstepped. "We have a visiting professor from Denver with us for a month. He wanted to go someplace off-campus. I suggested Loretta's."

He grimaced at the windshield.

When the co-chair of his department hooted at the suggestion then launched into his favorite characterization of Jeremiah as an academic eccentric who lived above a townie bar, Jeremiah realized that his grab to give Alex an opportunity to make inroads with the college crowd might have been a horrible impulse. For all of her fireworks, she was methodical about how she did things. He might have introduced the specimens into the petri dish before she was ready.

He was too eager. Too needy.

"I'm sorry, Alex. I should have asked first. If you'd like, I can—"

"No, no, it's cool," she said, surprising him. "I was just checking through some of the drink ingredients… Yeah. Yeah, okay. What time are they getting here?"

"In the next hour or two."

"Okay…okay. Thanks for the heads-up. See you soon."

She hung up, which allowed Jeremiah to concentrate on his driving as he passed the once-cheery water tower painted with sunflowers and a Welcome to Freedom message. The paint had long ago chipped, faded and bubbled, and the sunflowers made the tower look like it had ringworm.

Sunflowers were invasive, according to the many gardeners in the historical society. Some still appreciated their sunny faces in the Sunflower State. But most thought they were something to dig up—roots and all—and throw away.

When Jeremiah came downstairs to the busy restaurant after freshening up and changing into dark khakis and a cable-knit sweater, he was surprised to see Alex's baby sister behind the bar. He was more surprised when she made a beeline toward him as he took a seat at the corner where the Hugh plaque was carved.

With practiced regularity, the faux-Tiffany lamp gave a spark and flicked off.

"Your family needs to get rid of this lamp," he said. "It has to be a fire hazard."

"They've tried that." Cecilia "Sissy" Armstead smiled gently, her delicate fingers spread to hold an impressive number of limes. "They've thrown away lamps, switched out lamps, looked at the wiring for the plug." She shook her head, swishing her thick medium-brown ponytail. Her hair pulled back emphasized her heart-shaped face, big eyes without makeup, and cupid's bow of a mouth. She was a beauty, even in nothing more evocative than a gray sweatshirt and jeans. "Nothing takes."

"Then why have a lamp here at all?" he asked.

She grinned wider and tapped the limes against her chest. "I'm the easygoing sister and even I'm not going to give Old Man Hugh the satisfaction of winning. Why do you think he only extinguishes the lamp above his plaque?"

Wayland Hugh rejected his son because of the Mexican woman he married. It made sense that his petulant ghost would work to hide his name from the sanctuary these Mexicans had created.

Sissy motioned to the other side of the bar. "Ali wants you to sit on that side anyway."

He moved to the empty corner as Sissy followed him. "When your friends arrive, don't let them look at the menu. I'll bring you food."

"O-kay," he said, settling onto the stool. "Why?"

"Ali wants me to—"

"Good, you're here!" Alex lifted the pass-through and hustled toward them. "Look, when your buddies get here, don't give 'em a menu. Cici's gonna—"

"Yes, she told me," Jeremiah said. "What's going on?"

Sissy was a beauty but Alex was... Alex was blinding. Her hair was a mass of abundant black curls, all styled high to show off the sleek shave of one side of her head, then dripping down the other side. A curl bobbed around her smoky painted eyes and long lashes. Her lips were painted a sharp, matte red and she was wearing a white V-neck T-shirt, tied at the waist and showcasing her astounding cleavage, and a flouncy black skirt over black bike shorts.

She crackled with power.

When she shot two finger guns at him, the brightness of her flower tattoos pierced his heart.

"My chef sister is in town. If this is my first chance to impress the folks from Dupen College, I'm not serving them frozen mozzarella sticks."

"I'm sorry," he said with a grimace. "I didn't mean to make you go to any trouble."

"Trouble!" Alex exclaimed. He'd never seen in her in such high spirits. "This isn't trouble. This is the industry, my dude. Think quick, act on your feet." She snapped her fingers like a card shark, then threw an arm around her sister's shoulder. "Right, Cici? The Armstead girls are cooking with gas!"

Sissy smiled at Jeremiah under her sister's tight squeeze. "I'm just glad I can help. I've been getting an earful from Juli; this will give me a chance to experiment with a menu."

They slouched on the same hip. They were two towers leaning together. Whatever reconciliation needed to happen between the sisters had begun.

Jeremiah was happy for them.

"That's right," Alex said. She shifted away from her sister as she shot a single, slower gun at Jeremiah. "Someone's gotta prove to this one that Loretta's is better off as a bar and not a museum."

He never imagined a pointed finger looking so provocative. He leaned forward and met her slopey, sexy eyes. "I'm not the one you have to convince."

She put both hands on the shining mahogany. "'Cause you're already seeing things my way."

He grinned slowly. "You think so?"

She shrugged with a pert expression. "Why else would you be bringing your friends to my bar?"

"Maybe it's my dastardly plan." He put his hand on the wood and slowly slid it toward hers. "Maybe I'll tell them to try the burritos."

Continuing to offer those frozen monstrosities was her grandmother's worst crime.

"Be careful, professor," she purred, leaning forward, tickling his nose with her roses and spice. She knew exactly what she was doing, propping her breasts on her forearms, offering herself up, tempting him after he'd made it clear how little restraint he had left. "I know where you sleep."

His fingertips brushed the side of her hand, sending an electric charge up his arm as he stared into her eyes. It was the first time he'd really touched her since he'd boosted her into the train station. But he could still recall the phantom sensation of running his palms over her skin, having free range of her body as he spoke his fantasy out loud, and feeling her own sweet ghostly grip as she squeezed and stroked and fondled his…

An exaggerated clearing of a throat behind him had Alex lurching straight up as her eyes went wide. Jeremiah closed his. Imagined dead puppies and an empty student roster on his first day of class.

Then he looked over his shoulder to see Alex's father and

mother. They were in light coats and carried reusable bags filled with groceries.

"Your mother said you needed these oranges," Tucker Armstead said with dry humor, keeping his eyes on Jeremiah as he handed the bag over the bar to his daughter. "Make Dr. Post a drink first. He's lookin' mighty...thirsty."

Both girls swung matching horrified expressions on their father but only Sissy said, "Dad!"

"Stop it," Mary said, stepping up to nudge Tucker with a bag of groceries. She frowned at Jeremiah before she addressed her daughter. "What else do you need?"

"Cinnamon?" Alex said with a quick, wary glance at her dad while her mom looked through the sacks. "Then if you... two could help Gina and Matthew." She motioned to the bartender and server on the other side of the bar. "Help them keep up with Friday night. Thanks for coming in on your night off, Mom; it's a big help."

She didn't say anything to her father, but she gave him an uncomfortable nod.

As Sissy corralled Mary and Tucker back to the kitchen, Jeremiah could feel the bright, fire-engine red of his ears.

Alex began to slice oranges. "How does he know the word *thirsty*?" she muttered.

From context clues, Jeremiah gathered that it had something to do with being...lustful. Randy.

Horny.

If he continued living upstairs, he realized uncomfortably, he'd always be under her family's watchful eye. He wouldn't be able to make love to her naked and spread out in daylight. He'd have to cover her mouth instead of making her scream. And with the age of the furniture—and the fact that it belonged to her grandmother—there was nothing to tie her to.

He didn't want restraint. He wanted to show this powerful woman how powerfully he could please her. As soon as they found the deed, he'd wanted to take her as much as she wanted, for as long as she let him.

Half an hour later, Jeremiah got his head out of the gutter to greet his colleagues as they came through the saloon doors, sending the cowbells that hadn't gotten a rest all evening clanging, and then herded them back to where he and Alex had saved four stools, two on each side of the corner.

There were three of them. Hoang Nguyen from the anthropology department was more friend than colleague, always more focused on life's pleasures than in moving from assistant professor to associate professor. He'd been politely interested in Jeremiah's work on the historical society, if only out of an amused curiosity.

Bart Simon thought it was a waste of Jeremiah's potential. As co-chair of the history department and a man that Jeremiah would have to impress when he came up for full professorship, his grousing could have been disastrous. But at the end of the day, the burly man was a friend, and Jeremiah was on his way to being the most-published professor in the department. The two enjoyed what the contrasts in their personalities—the hermetic eccentric and the palm-slapping administrator—brought out in each other.

Stephen Kanowitz from the University of Denver was a little slick for Jeremiah's tastes. In his late fifties, he looked ten years younger with his lean build, full head of gray-blond hair, and proclivity to wear oversized scarves and extremely tight jeans. He sought to be twenty years younger. Kanowitz fashioned himself the kind of person who populated Alex's social media feeds, and his inclination to name-drop and talk ad nauseum about his hard-to-find preferences were why Jeremiah had suggested he come to Loretta's.

Alex could impress even the most bullheaded fool.

They all took their bar stools at the corner—Jeremiah and Nguyen on one edge, Bart and Stephen on the other—and Jeremiah pointed to the chalkboard hanging from the ceiling. The colorfully-chalked boards were another Alex addition, hanging from each side of the four-sided bar and listing constantly changing drink specials and specialty beers.

He doubted his colleagues would notice that the chalkboard facing their direction listed different drinks than the other three.

"Is that accurate?" Kanowitz said, narrowing his eyes at the chalkboard through square glasses with chunky black frames. "They have Devil's Prayer IPA?"

"Is it good?" Nguyen asked, smiling. He greeted life with amusement. When he'd entered the bar, he grabbed a saloon door and swung it back and forth repeatedly like it was one of the world's marvels. Jeremiah envied Nguyen's ease with everything.

"It received a gold two—no, three years ago." Kanowitz gave a nod to acknowledge his vast beer knowledge. "Afficionados stand in line for it."

Jeremiah pushed his decidedly unfashionable glasses up on his nose.

"Barkeep." Kanowitz's double thump on the wood had Jeremiah swiveling to see him calling to Tucker, who was filling the under-the-bar cooler with Bud Light bottles. "I'd like a Rittenhouse Rye Old-Fashioned. Just this side of chilled, with a big cube and a Luxardo cherry if you've got it."

Alex, who'd been standing in earshot with a pleased expression on her face, hustled over. "Sorry," she said. "Didn't want to rush you. You'd like an Old-Fashioned?"

"Um…" Kanowitz stared at Alex. Then he looked forlornly at Alex's dad.

Tucker Armstead, a white guy with fit forearms and a thick

moustache, looked like he could have been on the cover of *Hipster Bartender* monthly. While Alex was a young, voluptuous, brown woman. A shorn-haired and tattooed badass. But a Chicana, nonetheless.

Jeremiah had brought this man here, set him up as judge of Alex's efforts, and instantly knew it was the worst idea he'd ever had.

But Alex tilted a smile at Kanowitz. "Old-Fashioned?" she said gently. "Rittenhouse Rye. Big rock. Luxardo cherry."

"Sure," he said slowly. "Are you comfortable making one?"

Jeremiah wanted to cover his eyes, but he couldn't as Alex's cheek went rounder and she tilted her full, glorious hip. "Let's just say that I know how to work a long, hard muddler."

Bart and Nguyen laughed as Kanowitz smiled nervously. He should be nervous. He was lucky Alex hadn't crushed his oranges.

"What'll you two have?" she asked Bart and Nguyen.

"Got any recommendations?" Nguyen asked. The way he said it, putting his chin in his hand, wasn't flirty. But it wasn't *not* flirty. He had black eyes and straight black hair he wore a little long; he was handsome and an equal opportunity lover.

"Sure," Alex said. "Do you like mezcal?"

"I do if you do."

That was definitely flirty.

Alex explained that one of the drinks listed—Sundown in the Barrio—was smoky and sweet with mezcal, orange, cinnamon, and a tiny kick of Ancho Reyes liqueur.

"Mezcal with fruit is a great way to try the spirit," she said. She had a way of making the drink experience inclusive, so different than Kanowitz's excluding superiority or the many sommeliers who made Jeremiah feel his palate wasn't worthy.

Nguyen looked one dreamy second from proposing. "Cool. Yeah. I'll try that." He lifted his chin. "What's your name?"

Bart laughed over him. "Yes, please. I'd like one, too."

Jeremiah put up three fingers.

He and Alex had already agreed how to handle the food ordering, so he jumped in and said it was his treat, then ordered what Sissy had coached him on. When Alex put their drinks in front of them minutes later, Sundown in the Barrio was exactly as she described it: light, refreshing even, with a smoky bite that made it feel like a mature drink.

She'd wrenched the barrio out of the "boxcar barrio" slur and made it sophisticated and fashionable.

They all ignored Kanowitz as he sniffed, studied, and stirred his Old-Fashioned like he was analyzing it for toxins, then finished it before they were halfway through their drinks. When he ordered the next drink from Alex, at least he did it with reverence.

Nguyen lost all interest in their rousing conversation about whether historians' perspectives were desperately needed in current policy discussions—Jeremiah felt fortunate when an annual AHA meeting tackled anything after the 1940s—when Sissy brought out a tray of food. While Jeremiah, Kanowitz, and Bart fell on the Cubano sliders, grilled cauliflower tacos with tomatillo salsa, and individual mugs of chicken posole like men home from the mine, Nguyen tried to smile repeatedly at Sissy, who was ignoring him but lurking to catch the men's thoughts on the food.

Kanowitz waxed tiresomely rhapsodic over every bite—how was a "foodie" different from someone who liked good food?—but the licked-clean status of their plates was all Sissy needed to know as she gathered them up with a pleased smile and immediately disappeared.

Bart ordered another round of drinks and dragged them all to the dartboard to put Nguyen out of his misery. He'd had to nudge Jeremiah a couple of times, too.

Alex's beautiful, beaming face could have powered the Space Station.

As the drinks flowed and Bart Simon revealed himself to be a ringer who would have certainly cleaned out their wallets if they'd been betting men, Jeremiah occasionally straightened to take a bad shot. He spent the rest of his time leaning against the wall, sipping his beer, watching his colleagues laugh and enjoy themselves, and bidding *adieu* to his dream of opening a museum in Loretta's.

Milagro Street's vacant buildings brimmed with potential. The train station across the street pulsed with unexplored possibility. He would throw a kiss and wave a fond farewell to his tenant bedroom.

As he watched Bart discuss the Jayhawks' tournament run with a big-bellied man in a dirty T-shirt and suspenders, he saw how much good could be accomplished by a gathering place that attracted all kinds. As he watched Nguyen scootch his bar stool a touch closer to Owen Torres, one of Alex's handsome first cousins, he felt the thrum of embryonic excitement in the air.

Even as a disciple of this town, he knew how rare that thrum was.

As he watched Kanowitz…

Where was Kanowitz?

A warning prickle had him looking quickly toward the bar.

Kanowitz was sitting on a stool staring at Alex's bottom as she turned to get a liquor bottle. Jeremiah shoved off the wall and began pushing through the crowd. He watched Kanowitz—who was handsome and despicable and easily thirty years older than her—raise his eyes to Alex's face an instant before she turned and sat the liquor bottle and a cut-crystal carafe near him to make his drink.

The levity of the Friday night revelers made Kanowitz raise his voice loud enough for Jeremiah to hear him.

"¿Hablas español?" the man asked in an irritatingly flawless accent.

"A little," Alex said, looking down as she poured liquor into the carafe. "Not much."

"Where are you from?" he asked.

Alex poured another something in. "Kansas."

"No," Kanowitz said. He put his hand out and, for an instant, Jeremiah thought he was going to touch her. To grab her.

For an instant, Jeremiah saw nothing but red.

But Kanowitz put his hand down on the bar, close to the mat where the carafe sat. He demanded her full attention.

Her beautiful brown eyes met Kanowitz's through his expensive frames.

"Where are you *originally* from?" Kanowitz asked like a summons, demanding her secrets although his smile said he already knew them.

Jeremiah stopped moving through the crowd and watched. If Alex needed him, he would be there in an instant. If Kanowitz needed a hand...well, Jeremiah had a beer over by the dartboard he didn't want growing warm.

Alex crossed both forearms on the bar, leaned against them—she'd used that trick on Jeremiah earlier—then stared into Kanowitz's eyes with a glare that dared him to look down.

"I'm...from... Kaaannnsssaaassssssssssssssssss."

She said it slowly, enunciating every letter, letting him read the words on her magnificent lips if he was too thick to hear them with his ears.

She drew out the final *sss* like a prairie dog rattlesnake.

Kanowitz straightened like he'd been bitten. "Oh...okay."

Alex straightened, too, and went back to squeezing a lemon into the carafe as if nothing had happened. "And where are you from?" she asked brightly.

Jeremiah let Kanowitz stumble through a painful description of French-Polish grandparents coming to Indiana before he figured he'd go save him from himself. Alex was stirring his drink in the carafe and giving him a blank smile and wide-eyed stare that said, without question, she wasn't listening to one word.

"Stephen," he said sharply as he approached them, glorying that he made the man jump. "It's your turn at darts. I'll bring your drink."

Kanowitz shot out of his seat and disappeared into the crowd.

Alex looked into the carafe as she stirred. "Like the show?"

He rested his hands on the bar. "Yes."

"You know a guy as big as you is no good at sneaking through a crowd." She smirked as she emptied the ice from a chilling coupe glass into the sink.

"He was staring at your bottom," he said.

"You stare at my bottom."

"That's different."

She poured Kanowitz's drink into the glass. "How?"

"You like it."

His answer made her eyes flash, made that smirky mouth go soft. She looked to the side, away, but with a helpless smile.

"He's not so bad," she said, picking up the glass to hand it saucily to Jeremiah. "He likes my drinks."

"Yes, he does." Without a drop of compunction, Jeremiah took a sip. It was silky and vodka based. "Everyone I've brought tonight enjoys what you've done with Loretta's."

"This is just the beginning," she murmured, leaning against the bar, lifting her face to meet his eyes.

He wished she was leaning against his chest.

"I know," he said. He took another long drink without breaking their gaze and then put the glass down. "I'm not going to rescind my offer to your grandmother; it's still her choice and I don't want her to feel that's been taken from her. But I will tell her—as the head of the historical society—that I believe selling this building to you and your sisters is the best course of action."

Alex's lush, red lips stuttered open before she firmed them.

"I believe Loretta's continuing as a bar under your guidance is the best future for this building, your family, and this town. You have my full support, Alex."

Tonight, he'd seen the best bitch in bartending in action. And she was magnificent. At last, he understood who that woman was and why she was so fascinating to so many. She was good at her job. And she showed everyone what she had to do to be successful at it. People didn't adore her because they liked to be flogged; they admired her because she gave an inspiring example of a way to be. Proud. Uncompromising. Unwilling to accept anyone's crap.

Alex's flaming sword would help protect Milagro Street's limitless potential.

The museum would benefit Loretta's and Loretta's would benefit the museum and what a team they would make. With his know-how and her fight, they would stop Dutimeyer and Mayor Mayfield and any Hugh who thought they could ruin their home.

His home. Her home. Their home.

Jeremiah should have told her some of this. Perhaps fleshed out *why* she suddenly had his full support.

But he had to turn away. He had to shove through the people and get back to his dart game. Kanowitz complained about his drink and Jeremiah ordered another round from

Matthew, put a fifty percent tip on it, and put the whole bill on his credit card.

He couldn't go back to the bar. Not tonight. If he did, he'd drag Alex upstairs with him. Or down to the dirty mat on the bar floor. He didn't care if her parents saw. He didn't care if her family and his colleagues and the entire town saw.

He certainly didn't care about waiting until the end of a treasure hunt.

When he saw Alex's eyes filling with shining, hopeful tears at his words—at his support—he didn't care about anything but pulling her into his arms and claiming her as his.

Chapter Twenty-Three

As miraculous as Christ rising from the grave, a groveling apology and a plea for her to come back to the Fantasy Box appeared in Alex's inbox after Easter Mass. She changed out of the long skirt she'd worn to church in favor of the leggings with the stretchy waist while she read through the email, amazed but not surprised.

Randy had proven himself to be as big of an asshole as every staffer had predicted.

Indeed, he had risen while Fantasy Box's revenues had fallen, along with their once-glorious Yelp rating. Alex would have carte blanche if she returned: Randy's management position, hiring decisions for front-of-house, and oversight of the drink program. Because while Alex had yet to connect her name to Loretta's on her own social media, she hadn't needed to. Even in Freedom, Kansas, people took pictures of their attractive drinks, of friends having a good time, of interesting bar aesthetics like liquor altars strung with rosary beads and Tiffany-lamplight falling over artfully carved chairs. Internet sleuths had gotten to sleuthing and suddenly #bestbitchinKansas was a hashtag popping up in her mentions.

She'd let the owners sweat a few days before she told them no.

Speaking of sweating... She put her hand on Jeremiah's thumping knee after she pulled up and parked across the street from her grandmother's house. "You don't have to wear that bow tie if it's uncomfortable."

There was a shine in the hollow above his blue bow tie, a blue as rich as the perfect spring sky out her car window.

"Um…" He was going to destroy whatever he had in that expensive-looking bakery box on his lap with his knee jiggling. "I want your family to know how honored I am to be invited."

She'd found the time yesterday to bake an apple pie in the bar's kitchen. According to the gold scroll on the outside of the box, Jeremiah had driven the four-hour drive to Tulsa and back to pick up the offering she'd told him he hadn't needed to bring.

She slid her hand a little higher up his leg. That got his attention. "They know, Jeremiah."

At least he'd taken off the jacket of the light tweed, three-piece suit he'd been fucking gorgeous in at Mass. She'd let her family admire him and ignored the rest of their smiling, questioning, speculative looks. He looked at her now through his glasses like he didn't realize how perfectly wrapped he was. He was the best gift the Easter Bunny had ever left her.

She was relieved—and saw him breathe a little easier—when he finally took off the tie.

With the top button of his white shirt open and his mammoth body gorgeously defined in a fitted vest and trousers, he stepped out of her little car carrying his box and surveyed everything in wonder as they crossed the quiet, residential street past cars parked bumper-to-bumper, went through the front gate past the Virgen de Guadalupe birdbath, and around the pink-and-purple petunias planted in the brick-bordered beds.

He reached for the front door.

"You could go in that way," she said. "But you'd be doing it wrong." She'd set him up for this. She tilted her head. "Family always enters through the back."

He looked at her like she'd told him she was pregnant. Like he was *excited* about her being pregnant.

At the bottom of the back porch stairs, they were mobbed by little cousins who made Jeremiah promise he'd lift them up to search the hard-to-reach places during the Easter egg hunt. Then they went through the screen door to wade into a sea of Torreses heating up food in the narrow kitchen. She and Jeremiah pushed through, returning hugs and kisses as they went, until they reached the elders sitting in a circle around her grandmother's small breakfast table.

The rapid Spanish cut off when Alex leaned over to kiss Loretta and saw her eyes leap with pleasure when she saw Jeremiah. For once, Alex didn't mind.

"Jeremiah!" Loretta exclaimed as Alex scooted aside so he could squeeze in to kiss her grandmother's upraised cheek. "What a nice surprise."

Her grandmother went to Saturday evening Mass, even on Easter, so she'd missed Jeremiah at church. She looked as vibrant as the sunrise, with coral-painted lips and a white orchid corsage pinned to her blouse.

"Thank you for having me," he said shyly.

"Of course, mijo." Loretta patted his hand, her hair a salt-and-pepper halo around her face. "You're always welcome. Come back next Sunday."

Alex grabbed his box and left him to chat with Loretta and her gray-haired tíos and tías while she found a place for their dishes among the already groaning serving tables. She also needed a minute after seeing the look on his face after her grandmother called him mijo.

If she'd seen that look on his face in the beginning—if she'd been capable of seeing that look on him—she never would have wondered why he clung to her family and his room above the bar so fiercely. She didn't know how such a nice, fun, considerate, smart, hot-like-fucking-fire guy could have been denied the comfort of family and the warmth of home.

What the fuck had his family done to him? She was starting to hate people she didn't even know.

Her great-aunt announced it was time for grace. Alex took Jeremiah's firm hand in hers while her eight-year-old cousin on the other side of him impatiently waved her hand in his face. When he gently clasped it, then took in the fact that he was connected in a big, ring-around-the-rosie with the entire Torres clan as sixty people began praying "Blessed oh lord and these thy gifts which we are about to receive…" Alex almost had to take another break.

His amazement when he saw the dinner spread was expected.

Her grandmother's house was set up shotgun style—kitchen then dining room then living room then front room, with four bedrooms off the main rooms, two on each side of the house. Stretching through the dining room and half into the living room were shoved-together tables covered edge-to-edge with food: pre-sliced hams, baskets of fried chicken, green bean casserole, nopales with bits of scrambled egg and onion, scalloped potatoes, soupy sopa with vermicelli noodles, fried okra, a fruit salad with lettuce in it, macaroni and cheese, and several cloth-covered baskets of warm tortillas. She'd warned him when they got into the long line that snaked out the back door: Don't take too much of any one dish. You can come back for seconds. And thirds.

But his plate was already three-quarters full from when they'd stood at the stove to get tamales, frijoles, and sopa and it was swimming in the dark red-brown molé—a treat for the holidays—that her grandmother was ladling out.

He'd learn for next time.

The gorgeous quiche she'd unpacked from his bakery box with the golden, braided crust and sage leaves artfully decorating the top sat untouched. "I... Our chef would always make that for Easter..." Embarrassed heat radiated off of him. "But it's too much—"

So, there'd been a chef.

She leaned over, cut a slice, slapped it on top of her pyramid-like pile of food—it'd been awhile since she'd had a holiday at her Granmo's—then picked up a chunk with her fingers and popped it into her mouth.

"Ooooh, that's good," she moaned. She didn't have to play it up, it really was buttery and creamy and bacon-y. "Try this pie, everybody. Jeremiah brought it."

He looked at her with that dark wave hanging above his eye and his neck strong and his vaulted chest defined in tweed and mouthed *Thank you* with the world's softest, shiniest look in his eyes.

She put a piece of her tía's fried chicken on his plate. "C'mon, you big baby," she murmured. In lieu of sticking her tongue in his mouth.

Puffy white clouds now decorated the blue sky when they found a place at the table under the pecan tree with Sissy and Joe. It was still a few months before the birds made sitting here gross or dangerous.

"Jeremiah?"

Alex looked up from her scoop of rice and molé to see her mom walking cautiously toward them with her plate and iced tea. Her mom went to Saturday mass, too.

"Dad," she exclaimed.

Carrying his plate, Tucker nodded at her solemnly. "Alex. Sissy. Happy Easter, girls. Jeremiah."

Jeremiah glanced at her then stood and said, "Happy Easter." He leaned across to kiss Mary's cheek, nodded at Tucker, then sat again as Sissy nervously drank her iced tea.

At the end of the table, Joe drawled, "Now that we've all been introduced…"

His shin was just close enough to kick.

Mary and Tucker stood behind the empty folding chairs. "Do you mind if we eat here?" her mom asked softly. Her black hair fell over her pale green sweater set and brushed an orchid pinned to her cardigan. Had he bought her that? Her dad was wearing a pale blue shirt that brought out his bright blue eyes and the slight shine in his hair showed he'd taken extra trouble with it.

There'd been a time when she'd thought her parents were the most beautiful couple in the world.

Alex looked down at her plate. "I don't mind."

Her mother no more needed her permission to invite her dad to Easter dinner than Alex needed permission to invite Jeremiah. As long as it was just this, just the occasional forced meal during the occasional holiday, Alex could do this.

For several awkward minutes filled with food inhalation, they were the only spot of quiet on the entire Torres compound.

"Danny stopped by the house before dinner," Mary said, breaking the silence as she picked apart her fried chicken with her fork. "He said if he didn't get some help and more time for classwork at Loretta's, he was going to have to quit."

"Actually, Cici and I were talking." Sissy was currently staring down at the plate and not helping at all. "Barbara can learn Cici's recipes. But Danny—I think we're going to have to let him go."

Her mother raised one eyebrow.

In any other situation, Alex would have argued that they didn't need to retain an employee who threatened to quit if he didn't get more free time. But Danny was family. She got that now.

"I wasn't going to do anything until I talked to you," she said. "In fact, I want to sit down with you and get your input on some of the changes I've been thinking about."

Now both eyebrows went up.

Alex's small changes—chalkboards, better drinks, a bunch of '60s soul and '80s pop cassettes she found at the used bookstore that let her switch out the music—had had a big impact. But if she was going to pull Loretta and Loretta's out of the debt they were in and make the bar thrive, she needed to take advantage of what the place already had, something no amount of money could purchase, and something she hadn't been able to see through thirteen years of being good-and-pissed back in Chicago.

Loretta's had a story.

With its stained glass and original-to-the-building mahogany bar, heavy chairs carved in Mexico and pretend Tiffany lamps, coffee-guzzling regulars and endless family, legend of a ghost and reality of secret rooms and a bootlegging past, Loretta's had the kind of authenticity that urban speakeasies, craft breweries, and every bourbon marketer from here to the Atlantic would kill for. She knew from past experience how its unique purveyors—three generations of Mexican-American women—could attract press. Paying attention to their customers and absorbing a little of the wonder Jeremiah had about Loretta's people, place, and story made her realize she needed to build on that authenticity, not renovate over it.

Mary could help her figure out how to keep the hometown crowd happy while still making the changes that would draw the higher-earning Dupen gang and out-of-towners and road-traveling hipsters.

Her mom took a drink of tea. "Let's give Danny plenty of

notice, but I think he'll be glad for the excuse to find something else. Who will take his place?"

Alex shrugged exaggeratedly. "I don't know. Maybe we know a talented chef in Kansas City who should step out of other chefs' shadows and establish her own kitchen?"

"Hey," Sissy said, coughing on her drink before she put it down. "I'll be in charge of the menu and training. But…" She smiled and gave Alex a sad shake of her head. She hadn't done anything with her hair, so it was annoying how thick and bouncy it was. "I don't see myself moving back for good. I like working for other people."

"But Sis," Alex wheedled. "Think about our family." That was Sissy's kryptonite. "When Granmo is fishing with Granpo in that fully-stocked pond in the sky, we don't want to lose her food, too."

Sissy rolled her eyes. "She doesn't want us to use her recipes at the bar."

"You can change her mind."

"No one can change her mind."

Sissy had given up Saturday morning cartoons, slumber parties, and Little League games to be at Loretta's side, helping her cook the food for the Sunday dinner. Alex had been neck-deep in boys and trouble when Sissy stopped cooking with their grandmother.

She'd asked a couple of times why. Sissy never had given her a good answer.

Another silence fell over the table and Joe, the lucky sonofabitch, got up to refill his plate.

Jeremiah cleared his throat. "Tucker, I've signed up for the college's Writers on the Plains symposium," he said. He'd rolled up his cuffs when they'd sat down and she'd been very aware of his strong forearms, the few freckles, and the light dusting of medium-brown hair. His vintage Rolex was wrapped around a very nice wrist.

He cleared his throat again. "I'm looking forward to your lecture."

Her dad gave Jeremiah a smile and a nod, then looked down at his plate.

In the shade of the pecan tree, Alex looked at her sister. Sissy shrugged.

"Dad? Are you teaching at the college?" Sissy asked.

Their dad "wrote," but Dupen College was a very prestigious school.

Tucker played with his nopales. "After I hit the *New York Times* list, I was the writer in residence at Dupen for a year. They still invite me back every now and then."

Her dad hadn't changed his look in the twenty-nine years she'd known him, but right now it was like he'd sprouted bunny ears.

"You published a book?" she got out.

Tucker nodded slowly, chewing on a corner of his thick, blond moustache. "Books," he replied.

Alex met her sister's eyes at the same moment, two magnets coming together. "You didn't know?" she asked her. "You see him all the time."

Sissy gave a huff. "We have a cup of coffee at the Waffle House." She studied her father. "We mostly talk about me."

The Waffle House was the destination for most divorced weekend dads in Freedom. There'd been times—most of the time—over the last thirteen years that she'd been angry at Sissy for straddling the fence, for not siding with the older sister who'd always stood up for her. It was something to know that their conversations had been awkward catch-ups over a lousy cup of coffee.

They both looked at their mother, a famously slow eater

whose plate was still half full. She was cutting a piece of chicken. Without looking up, she said, "How do you think the conversation would have gone if I'd started listing your father's accomplishments?"

She slid the bite into her mouth and smiled.

"I am so sorry," Jeremiah said. His ears were red-hot; she wished she could lean over and blow on them. "I had no idea—"

"Son, you didn't do anything wrong," Tucker said. He wiped his mouth with his napkin and put it on his plate. "It wasn't a secret I was keeping from you girls. There are a lot of sorries I need to say before I can start talking about a good day I'm having. You girls had to live through all the bad ones."

As her father's blue eyes met hers, Alex felt a squeeze in her chest, just under her ribs. Heartburn.

"I'm happy for you, Dad." Sissy was blinking fast and hard. "Congratulations."

"Me too," Alex said. Then she nudged Jeremiah and reminded him of the number of dishes he hadn't tried yet. They both grabbed their plates and stood.

She could do this. She and Tucker could be polite when they had to interact. She didn't have to trust him to be in the same room with him. Her mom could have the occasional meal with him, he could help out around the bar when necessary.

Her father could be like a cheap plastic tool from the Dollar Store—a useful accessory that she never relied on because she expected it to break.

By the time they wrapped up the Easter Egg hunt—Jeremiah had never hidden eggs before and had strategized like a pirate burying his booty—clouds with a distinct tinge of gray dominated the sky.

The adults went back inside and found places to chat or relax into food comas. Alex and Jeremiah got coffees and a shared plate loaded with desserts and found Tía Ofelia enjoying her own coffee and dessert at the corner of the long table in the living room.

Alex's favorite aunt got up to hug and greet them.

"It's nice to see you home," she said, holding Alex's face in her hands and staring at her through her round, hot-pink glasses, her thick waves blunt at her chin. "You look happy." She lifted Alex's chin and narrowed her eyes. "Why do you look so happy?"

When five-year-old Alex had asked where babies come from, Tía Ofelia had sat down with her and a friendly book filled with drawings of smiley-faced sperm. Her mom had been furious at her youngest sister when all three girls announced that evening that they had "vaginas." But that was just Ofelia's way. You could trust her to tell you what you needed to hear. It was why she was such a popular English teacher at the high school.

Her brilliant, perceptive, loving aunt seldom talked about herself. Although Ofelia had visited her several times in Chicago, Alex had known nothing about her aunt's passion for their family history or her work on the historical society.

Right now, she didn't want her brilliant, perceptive, and loving aunt looking too hard when Jeremiah was close.

Alex shrugged out of her hold, laughing. "Stop. God."

Ofelia hugged Jeremiah, too, then they all sat and Alex dug into a slice of apple pie as they caught up.

When Jeremiah asked if Ofelia had learned anything from the Spanish-language newspapers about Edward Hugh's wife, Rosalinda, Ofelia reached into a leather satchel.

"Well, if it's the same Rosalinda..." She smacked a file folder down on the table. "I already knew a ton."

Because of course she did.

Jeremiah grinned his crinkly grin, a smear of Cool Whip on his lip. It took everything in Alex not to lean over and lick it off.

Ofelia opened the folder. "I know her as Rosalinda Padilla. But she was married to a man named Edward." She shuffled through a few pieces of paper, then held out a newspaper clipping in a plastic sleeve.

"Yep," Alex said, nodding. "That's her."

She was older in the aged newspaper clipping, regal with a not-fucking-around expression, wearing a silk dress, a long strand of pearls, gloves, and a low-brimmed hat with flowers over her dark curls. The caption read: Rosalinda Padilla, la presidente del Sociedad de Mexicana Señoras y Señoritas, explice...

Ofelia shook her head. "I can't believe she was married to a Hugh."

"The first Hugh," Jeremiah said. "Wayland's firstborn."

Ofelia tapped her nail on the papers. "Rosalinda Padilla was the reason Milagro Street became a thriving business district for Mexicans. I've been working on a proposal for an exhibit on her."

"What'd she do?" Alex asked.

"Rosalinda started a woman's organization, an auxiliarie, called the Sociedad de Mexicana Señoras y Señoritas. The thing about the colonia was that the men, the traqueros, were gone a lot to work the rails. So women had to take over the leadership roles in the families and the communities. These traditionally machismo communities leaned on powerful matriarchs here in the US and that inclination still exists today. Think about it, Alejandra—we trace our lineage through the grandmothers, not the grandfathers. We focus our gatherings around Big Granmo, not the Granpo."

Alex had never considered it before, but her aunt was right. Sunday dinner used to be at her great-grandmother's house before she passed away. Alex had never gotten comfortable calling Loretta "Big Granmo" like her younger cousins did. And she knew little about her Granpo Salvador's parents.

"Rosalinda was born in Mexico but grew up on Miracle Street. She helped her father who sold food to the traqueros. He'd set up a sidewalk stand right across the street from the Hugh Building every morning and evening."

Alex huffed. "That must have thrilled Old Man Hugh."

"Edward would have seen her every day," Jeremiah said. He looked at Alex. "That's how they met. That's how they fell in love."

The day was getting darker outside and someone had turned on a lamp. The soft light made Jeremiah's expression all warm and amazed. Alex's stone-cold heart gave a silly flutter.

When Alex returned her attention to Tía Ofelia, she ignored her aunt's delighted smile.

"When Miracle Street's shop owners abandoned it, Rosalinda and the Sociedad began providing microloans so Mexicans could rent the buildings and set up their own businesses," Ofelia said. "Without her, Miracle Street would never have become Milagro."

"Where did she get the funding to provide microloans?" Jeremiah asked.

"No one knows." Ofelia shrugged. "But there were rumors. Some said Rosalinda's family was descended from Spanish royalty, others said her grandfather had been hung for cattle rustling but the family had escaped Mexico with his ill-gotten gains. And then there's my favorite: Rosalinda was a bruja who created treasure out of graveyard dirt and chicken bones."

Treasure. Alex knocked her knee against Jeremiah's.

Her tía leaned back in her chair and scrunched her curls. "I still can't believe she was married to a Hugh. Not using his last name probably kept Wayland Hugh off her back."

Alex stabbed her last bite of pie. "He rejected his son, prevented his daughter-in-law from using her husband's name, and wrote off his grandchildren. I'm not surprised Edward refused to accept the second deed after his dad died. I'd let that old man stew in hell, too."

"But did Edward refusing to forgive his father help anyone?" Ofelia asked in that way she had of couching a point in a question. "We're stuck with a ghost that haunts the building and a deed that, if it's found by the wrong person, could destroy the east side." Jeremiah had shared with Ofelia everything they'd learned when he called her. "Edward and Rosalinda's daughters might have put the Hugh inheritance to better use than the rest of the family did."

"Daughters?" Jeremiah asked. He sounded like someone had shot his puppy.

Ofelia nodded. "Rosalinda and Edward had five girls."

"Why is that a problem?" Alex asked.

"Women are harder to trace genealogically because they assume their husband's last name," she said.

"Have you found a connection to Dutimeyer?" Jeremiah asked.

"Nothing to prove or disprove it." She tilted her head. "Although I do have a suggestion for where you could look next."

There was a gleam behind her tía's pink glasses. She'd been holding on to this nugget their entire conversation.

Ofelia leaned closer. "Rosalinda and Edward bought a family farm."

A rumble of thunder sounded in the distance.

"And while the *rest* of the sisters have been difficult to

track, descendants of the second-to-oldest daughter still live there." She was loving this. "Doing my research, I've become friendly with them. The great-grandson is a wonderful man. He would never use a second deed to claim something he hadn't worked for. So I called him. Told him about his connection to the Hugh family and what Lance Dutimeyer was trying to do. He said he'd be happy to let you look around."

Rain began to patter on the roof.

Her tía had taken a big risk, telling someone who could benefit from the second deed that he might be sleeping on top of it. But Ofelia's judgment of people was rock-solid. Jeremiah must have trusted her, too.

In full view of her aunt, he covered Alex's hand over the plastic lace tablecloth. She turned her hand over, tangled her fingers with his, and squeezed. They'd found Edward and Rosalinda's home. They were so close to finding the second deed she almost could feel it between their crushed palms.

Not only would she finally—finally—be able to stop Dutimeyer from wreaking havoc on her people, she'd be able to make sure no Hugh descendant would ever be able to threaten the bar or the east side after Alex was gone.

Alex would make Loretta's great again.

And then, as planned, she would parlay that greatness into a beverage director position at a top restaurant or bar. She would have her pick of locations: Vegas? San Francisco? New York City?

That's what she would tell the owners of the Fantasy Box after they stewed for a bit: Why would she go back? Why would she ever trust them again?

She would train Mary or Gina or Matthew to oversee the day-to-day and, like Gillian and Sissy, she would oversee their investment from afar.

Loretta's would flourish. Loretta could finally go fishing. Her parents would do whatever they were doing.

And Jeremiah—sweet, handsome, hot, down-to-clown-when-she-was-in-town Jeremiah—would build his museum. She would think of them all fondly when she was gone.

Chapter Twenty-Four

The Easter that began as postcard-perfect as a fantasy ended in a torrential downpour that pummeled Alex's poor beautiful car, the tires skittering all over the pavement as they drove home, then nearly drowned them as Jeremiah and Alex raced up the back stairs. By the time they shoved open the door and stumbled into the hallway, they were soaked to the skin.

Jeremiah took one look at Alex—her long sweater clinging to the outline of her breasts and waist and hips—and dropped his eyes to his own dripping clothes. Thinking to shed the most-soaked layer out in the hall, he kicked off his shoes then began to unbutton his wool vest. The white shirt beneath it was soaked transparent.

His head startled up when the bathroom door slammed.

"First dibs on shower," Alex called in a hoarse voice from behind it.

He didn't hear the click of the lock.

Jeremiah closed his eyes, resisted palming himself by digging his fingers into the wet wool at his thighs, then turned and shoved open his bedroom door.

He fell back against it and listened to the little milagro—two hearts pierced with the same sword—plink against the wood.

Each time he thought he'd reached the zenith of wanting Alex, the clouds cleared and he discovered there was a new peak.

That first night weeks ago, he'd wanted her because she'd been a voluptuous woman who'd looked at him with hungry eyes. She'd wanted to fuck him without knowing a thing about him, including who his brother was.

Now, she knew so much. She knew he got misty-eyed at family prayers. He was awkward and brought inappropriate quiches. She knew he flushed red like a warning beacon for every emotion. He got pedantic when he was angry, and too exuberant when he was happy.

She knew he had a filthy mouth and craved to ride her until she broke.

All of that knowing seemed to make her like him and want him and enjoy his company more and more. Seemed to make her value him more.

He now knew exactly who she was.

She was the best bitch in bartending. Who she inherently was—concerned for people, generous with her time and energy to make lives better, funny, quick-witted, clever, confident in her ability to bring pleasure, assured in her power to strike down injustice and balance it with fair play—made her a great bartender. Made her the kind of bartender and coworker and family member and friend that people craved to be around.

Her family adored her and he saw it today when, to a person, their eyes lit up when Alex walked into a room. That, truly, was what had sparked Loretta's popularity. He'd accused Alex of wanting to destroy Loretta's. Instead, she was the bolt of lightning that brought it back to life.

Her father hurt her with his drinking and his absence, Loretta had said. *She's been punishing them ever since. Punishing herself, too.*

Her sister had wished Alex hadn't felt so alone.

He wanted to charge into the bathroom, snatch her into his arms, and press her against him until she absorbed what he knew: They all admired her. They all loved her. She wasn't alone.

She never had to be alone again.

But it wasn't time and Jeremiah was desperate and needy and there was still so much she didn't know about him and so much he hadn't told her about what he was planning with Joe. He and Alex had put a glass box around what they wouldn't do and said it could only be broken in case of trust. Did he trust her? More importantly, did she trust him?

Did she trust him enough to lay down her sword?

He stiffened when he heard the bathroom door open. He was still in his soaked clothes, still desperate against his door.

Please, please, please, please, please let her come tapping at it.

"Holy crap!" she yelled.

He threw his door open, lurched forward...

Stopped dead.

Alex was standing in the hallway wrapped in the blue-sapphire dragon robe of his lust-filled dreams. With her black hair slicked back and her face washed clean, she stared astonished into her room. Jeremiah's eyes wandered helplessly. The blue silk slid over her body like water while the dragon flicked its fire over one heavy breast, wound around her waist with the tie, then curled its tail over her full hip. The robe stopped at midthigh, revealing glistening brown skin stretched over thick muscle and knee and calf and bare feet.

Under the bare bulb of the hallway light, Alex Torres was silken and naked and wet and Jeremiah almost fell to his knees.

"What?" he croaked, not daring to move closer.

Alex just motioned through her doorway. Jeremiah could hear a waterfall in her room.

He breathed through his mouth as he approached her and looked over her shoulder.

Rain sprinkled down from the ceiling, onto her bed, and into a laundry basket of folded clothes. Water ran from the holes of the basket like it poured from a pitcher.

Alex flapped at the mess. "My bed. That's…all my clothes. Granmo would put me up for the night but I can't drive back there in this." A window-shuddering blast of thunder agreed. "Or in this."

She put a hand on her robe and Jeremiah focused on the ceiling.

"Let me…" He cleared his throat. "I'll get a bucket."

He ran to the kitchen to grab a metal tub and inhaled big breaths of rose-free air.

The next minutes were busy: Jeremiah helped Alex move the bed and all her belongings away from the indoor shower and soaked up what they could with the storeroom's stack of old towels. He positioned the tub to catch the still-falling rainwater.

"I'll check on it later," he said, straightening.

Alex shivered as she clutched herself and looked around at the mess. The cuffs and hem of her robe were wet. She'd taken off all her rings and most of her earrings. Her eyes, eyes he almost always saw boldly defined in warrior paint, were bare and wide and searching for a solution.

He surrounded her silk-covered elbow with his palm.

Without a word, he steered her out of her room and into his, leaving the maddening plonk of the rain hitting the tub. He spun his leather desk chair away from his desk and pushed her into it, shook out the gray blanket from the end of his bed and placed it over her lap, then turned on his small space heater and pushed it closer to her feet.

He pulled his pajamas from the armoire. "I'll just…"

With her black hair starting to dry into curls and her eyes wide, she blinked up at him as if he'd twirled her into a dance she didn't know.

He escaped to the bathroom.

Once he'd showered and changed into his gray flannel pajamas, he leaned on the pedestal sink and stared at himself in the mirror.

He, Jeremiah Post, formerly Harrington, could do this. Rather than some extreme maneuver—sleeping on the bare floor of the bathroom, driving through a dangerous spring thunderstorm to find her a bed, jumping back into the shower to stroke one out—he could calm his lust for the one woman he wanted more than any other. He was an adult, a man of letters, and he'd been self-pleasuring twice a day for weeks. He could do this.

He could take care of this woman who took care of everyone else.

Resolved, he went to his bedroom. When he closed the door behind him, he saw that she'd pulled her feet up into the seat of the chair and tucked the blanket under her chin. Her cheek was soft and round in the lamplight as she leaned her head against the wing of the leather chair.

He could do this easier if he wasn't looking at her.

He walked to his bed and pushed the space heater closer to her with the toe of his slipper. He sat on the edge of his mattress; the frame gave its normal protest.

"That sound is just as clear in my room," she murmured. "I don't know how this place stayed standing for so long when it's made of tissue paper."

Jeremiah put his elbows on his knees, entwined his fingers,

and looked at the Aubusson rug covering his floor. "Can your grandmother afford to fix the roof?" he asked.

"My grandmother can't afford the next beer shipment," she said. Then sighed. "This place started getting away from her financially a couple of years ago. Instead of asking for help, she began going to Kansas City and trying to win what she needed playing the slots. That put her deeper in debt."

"Your poor grandmother."

"No," Alex said, the chair squeaking beneath her. "Don't pity her. She wouldn't want it any more than I would. It's a problem and we'll fix it. Joe can patch the roof; that'll hold until we renovate. Maybe..." Her voice softened then. "Maybe the head of the historical society can help me find a grant to save the roof of a historical building."

It's a problem and we'll fix it. When she said *we,* she was including him.

"Thank you." He straightened and crossed his arms over his chest, aimed all of his adoration at the navy blue curtain covering his window. The velvet muffled the storm outside. "Thank you for telling me about her debt. Thank you for... trusting me."

She shifted and he could hear the soft slide of her robe.

"I'm tired," he said. "I'm sure you're tired. And we both have work tomorrow."

He clutched his biceps.

"The bed is big enough for both of us."

The chair lurched as if she was trying to burrow into the leather. "I'm good here." Her voice was unnaturally tight. "I'm fine with—"

"Alex."

He could do this. He could take care of her.

He aimed his eyes at her curls. "You won't be able to sleep

there. With the thinness of the wall, we've already been... bunkmates. This won't be any different."

He knew how foolish he sounded, how naive and delusional. If foolishness was what was necessary for her to relax and get a good night's sleep, for him to take care of her, then he'd play that part.

She turned her head. He'd been looking for fortitude and salvation around his room, too, but had yet to find it.

"Is that one of my dad's books?"

He shot up and crossed the room to one of his floor-to-ceiling bookshelves. "Yes, excellent." He picked up the paperback with Tucker's name boldly printed on the spine. "We'll get into bed and read your father's books." He tossed it across the room onto his queen-sized mattress then turned to face the bookcase again. "Make yourself comfortable. I'll find the other one."

If Alex ever had a reason to laugh at him, it was now, when he was behaving like a loony librarian intent on using her father's books as a ward against touching her. She didn't laugh. Instead, he heard the slither of the wool blanket as she draped it on the leather chair, the creak of the wood boards as she crossed to his bed, the infamous squeal of the springs she was now getting to experience live and in person, the slide of her silk robe against his high-thread-count sheets, and the shuffle of goose-down duvet and her grandmother's homemade quilt as she covered herself.

Jeremiah reached for his copy of Tucker Armstead's third book. He'd known exactly where it was. With a deep expansion of breath into his jogger's lungs, he turned around.

He didn't want even his breathing to disturb this moment.

She was on her side, facing the wall, almost as close to it as she could get. All he could see of her, beside her hill-and-dale curves under his blankets, were black curls, a delicate shell of a lobe, and the cover of her father's book.

After imagining her in his bed every night since he'd met her, Alex Torres was finally here. Tomorrow, when she left it, his sheets would smell like rosebuds.

Tonight, he would take care of her.

He turned off the overhead light but left on his bedside lamp. The hum of the rain made it sound like they were inside a seashell.

He tried not to jostle her as he got into bed, on top of the covers, his knees hanging off the mattress as he lay on his side away from her. He put his glasses on the bedside table and opened the book. Then he listened to her breathe, felt the warmth of her behind him, sensed her in the curve of the mattress. He could smell her like she was tucked into the bend of his body.

"Are his books any good?" she asked quietly.

"Very good." After he'd finally gotten around to reading Tucker's debut book, he'd devoured the next two. "Very entertaining. They're about a group of female vigilantes and the man who's their sidekick. He's their Watson. It's a modern-day feminist western, very high-brow pulp."

Jeremiah could imagine where Tucker got his inspiration from.

"It's all he ever wanted," she whispered. "I should cover this book in lighter fluid and strike a match." Her voice cracked like a heartbreak. "But when I was young…this is all I wanted for him, too."

The thick paperback creaked under the grip of his fingers.

"Alex…" He bit out her name. "We can't…talk about this. Not tonight."

"Yeah. Of course, it's late. Sorry. That was dumb. I…"

He was supposed to be taking care of her. He was supposed to be reassuring her that she wasn't on her own, that she had support.

He put his book on the bedside table then turned over to face her, conscious of her feeling his weight and movement and intent in the mattress.

"Look at me," he said. She didn't move. "Alex, would you look at me?"

She slowly turned over to face him. She shifted under the covers and Jeremiah realized she was straightening the robe. Then she tucked her hands under her soft cheek and stared at him, her dark eyes luminous in the lamplight.

She was in his bed. Her silk-wrapped body was right there. He'd barely have to extend his elbow to caress her.

He raised his eyes to study her hairline.

"*I'm* sorry," he said. She had a little chicken pox scar, at the top of her forehead, and he wanted to taste it with the tip of his tongue. He was on the edge of his bed, as far from her as the mattress would allow. "I want to hear everything you have to tell me. I admire you deeply and I want to know everything about you. But I can't...tonight—I can't take care of you if—"

"Take care of me? You don't have to—"

"Yes, I do." Light shined in the black curls lolling on his pillow. "You take care of everyone else, all the time. You point people to the most edible thing on the menu, you know before they do what they want to drink, you tease them until they forget about their lousy day. You avenge your cousins and stand up for your coworkers and protect your family's bar. You save me from the embarrassment of my quiche."

She huffed and he smiled at her forehead. "You're a badass angel who uses her flaming sword and her talent with a muddler to take care of people. Tonight, let me return the favor."

He'd explained himself. She could close her eyes and relax

into sleep and Jeremiah would keep watch. No ghosts or haunting memories or horny professors would bother her tonight.

"Then…" She swallowed. "Then why won't you look at me? You've barely looked at me since we got home."

Her confusion made her vulnerable, and Jeremiah knew from experience that this warrior woman put her knife to the testicles of any other man who made her feel that way. She was willing to be vulnerable with him, willing to ask instead of stab.

Home.

He was cracking.

He closed his eyes and made one last pitiful attempt to shore up his resolve. "I can't look at you."

"Why?"

The quiver in her normally confident, caustic, furious voice shattered him free.

"Because of this."

He reached for her. Instead of finally, finally touching and claiming, he hooked his fingers into the top of the covers and slowly, so slowly, pulled them out of her hands. If she'd resisted, he would have stopped. She didn't resist. He pulled the blankets down, centimeter by centimeter, and allowed his eyes to wallow in what he uncovered: the velvet skin of her neck, the delicate hollow and pulse, and—finally—the luscious blue at her collar.

"This horrible bathrobe has haunted me since the day you moved in."

He held the sheets away so he didn't touch her body, but his eyes stroked over her mouthwatering cleavage framed in blue, the dragon's flame touching one breast. "Every day I resist fondling it like the worst of perverts." He could clearly see her pebbled nipple through the material. Would she like it if he rubbed the robe over that aroused bit of her? Would she like it if he made the silk move with his hands, made it a conduit for her pleasure by stroking down her waist, over her bottom, and gently sliding the silk over her hard, sensitive clitoris?

"I wanted you when I didn't know you." The robe was twisted around her waist and hips like the dragon had coiled closer. "I wanted you worse when I hated you." She gave a breathy gasp when his knuckle accidentally brushed her thigh as he pushed the blankets down. "And I wanted you like a fever when you were a friend falling asleep next to me every night."

He'd revealed as much as his long arm would allow.

"But now, I see you clearly. Tonight, when I've never wanted you more, you appear in front of me like a vision, like my obsessive fantasy in this horrible robe."

He heard her shaky exhale.

"How can I look at you and still hold to our agreement? How can I take care of you instead of just taking you? How can I want anything but to be inside you?"

She slid her thighs against each other under sapphire silk, and he watched as she did it.

"Jeremiah…" Her voice was trembling. "We've as good as found the deed."

He bit back a grunt as he felt the kick of her words.

"And Jeremiah…"

"Uh-hmm."

His grip was going white-knuckled on the covers he still held.

"I trust you."

His eyes raced up her body to meet hers. Her deep brown eyes were open and unwavering and, as always, so painfully honest. This was why he hadn't looked at her.

They both could see too clearly what the other one hid.

She trusted him. She trusted him enough to let him see her furious, hardworking body and brave, curious brain and huge, garrisoned heart.

He trusted her enough to be needy with her. Desperate for her.

He trusted Alex Torres.

He was in love with Alex Torres.

He was going to rail her through the mattress.

"I trust you, too," he said.

Then he pounced.

Chapter Twenty-Five

If her head wasn't already spinning from all he'd said to her, from his big info dump of how much he admired her and desired her and how he wanted to take care of her—her—because he thought she took care of everyone else, then it would have been spinning from how quickly he grabbed her, dragged her to the middle of the bed, and dominated her mouth.

She felt him toss her dad's paperback across the room.

Light-headed, she started to giggle.

He bit her lip with a growl. Then he sucked. Tickled. Probed deep to taste. She'd kissed her fair share of people, but Jeremiah's kisses—after nights of lying in the bed next door thinking about them—were like his stories. Fascinating. Unique. She could fall into them and be captivated for hours.

She could easily be convinced that no one could deliver them better.

He tipped her jaw up and arched her head back. Her hands twitched helpless against the sheets. She surrendered to him, her limbs sprawled as he loomed over her and ate at her mouth.

"Jeremiah," she groaned, wrenching up her hands to dig them into his light-blocking shoulders. She needed him closer. "More. I need…"

He said he would take care of her. It was as rare as someone making her a drink.

"Wait," he muttered against her mouth, and he yanked hard at the bow of her tie, making her jerk as he freed it, as he nudged up her chin so he could suck on her earlobe—a deep fervent suck she felt between her legs—then moved his mouth down her neck, licking and testing the thin skin with his teeth. He nuzzled at the collar of her robe, and it was an endearingly sweet gesture from a huge man who was tearing her apart. His lips slid over the silk, over the mound of her breast, down to the underside and around, creating a slow-building buzz as he shoved the other half of her robe aside. She looked down to find him staring at her exposed boob as he took her covered nipple between his teeth. He dragged her robe under her breast, framed her dark skin in shiny blue, and stared as he sucked on her nipple through the wet silk, hollowing his cheeks.

He was acting out one of his pervy fantasies and it made her toes curl.

I wanted you when I didn't know you. Now, I see you clearly. I've never wanted you more.

Her.

She dug her fingers into his thick, silky hair and yanked. "Jeremiah, stop…fucking around. I've waited so long. Take your clothes off."

He levered up on one strong arm, reached behind his head with the other, and pulled the flannel over his head, a move that revealed so much startling, straining muscle planking above her that she made some kind of babbling gasp as her eyes wandered down him—the tight pink nipples, the mounds of his pecs, the hard abs bisected with a happy trail.

The crotch of his pajama pants pointed at her.

"Do you want me to take it out?"

Her eyes zoomed up to his face and he was grinning at her, the crinkly-eyed, slash-in-his-cheeks grin while the lamp caught the gold in his eyes.

She bit her lip and nodded.

"Do you want me to put it in your mouth?" She pressed her lips against a whimper. How could he be grinning when his dick was about to split seams? "Do you want me to let you get it wet for me? Let you get it soaking so I can slide it into your hot, tight vagina?"

He said *vagina*. How in the world was that hot? "Yes. Yes, yes, yes, yes, yes—"

"Too bad."

Sonofabitch.

He swooped down, rubbing his lips over her silk-covered tummy, and she struggled because he might owe her a tease or two but she was a sex goddess and he was muscling her legs apart with his thick shoulders and she was going to strangle him with her thick thighs and then he was laughing as he ripped her robe fully open and she was covering her pussy with her hand and he was licking between her fingers and she was thinking, "What the hell am I doing?"

She lifted her hand and he went still, looking up at her from between her legs.

Jeremiah Post's flushed face was between her legs. His grin crinkles smoothed out. He looked over every inch of her torso as if she were the Hugh treasure.

He met her eyes. "I'm looking at you now, sweetheart." He tilted his head and kissed the inside of her thigh. "Will you let me see?"

It's what he'd asked her when he'd been a phantom in her bed, haunting her from the other side of the wall. *Can I see? Show me how I can keep you.* She'd dismissed his words as a spell said in the heat of the moment. Now, he and his demand were as real as his plush, high-end mattress cushioning her back and his silky white sheets tickling her skin.

He'd wanted her when he hated her. Now, he said he admired her. He supported her. He trusted her. Now, he wanted her more than ever.

She couldn't deny him this when he was a fantasy. She definitely couldn't say no now that he was a flesh-and-blood man. A flesh-and-blood man she trusted.

She v'ed her pussy lips apart—just like she had that night—but this time he was there to look and smile and lick his lips. He stared hungrily at her pussy, and it was the hottest fucking thing she'd ever seen in her life.

He lowered his head.

She watched him as he lapped out with his tongue. Pulled back and closed his eyes, swallowed like he was savoring. Then he leaned in for a kiss. A sweet, slow kiss then a long, pussy-dragging taste with his eyes closed, his hair brushing her thighs. He kissed, turned his head, and kissed again, so many soft, slow, wet kisses, then he dragged his tongue over her crease until he touched her clit and made his tongue flutter.

She was still watching him as she held her pussy lips apart, as her heart pounded and she controlled her breathing, but when he looked up at her and smiled as his tongue fondled her clit, when he got those grin creases as his wet, pink tongue worked her, and the lamplight showed all the dazzling colors in his eyes, she had to look up at the ceiling. She had to think about the rain flooding her room.

When he dipped down and buried his tongue into her cunt, sunk it deep into her "vagina," she had to kick him away by his shoulders.

"Inside me," she gasped. "Get fucking...inside..."

She wasn't a dude. She could come multiple times in a

night. It was so dumb to want to wait to orgasm until he was inside her.

But the man who liked to argue with her didn't now as he lunged up over her body, grabbed a condom out of his bed-side table, then shoved down his pajama bottoms to slide it on. She was helping, rubbing her hands over the hard bands at his hips, over his spectacular ass, hooking her toes into the flannel to push it down his muscular legs, to get him naked, naked, naked, the best fucking blanket in the entire...

With a growl, he shoved up her knee and pushed inside.

She wrenched her head back. The heat was spectacular. She was soaking.

Jeremiah hissed like her pussy was lava and he was burying himself deep. Then he wrapped those muscular arms around her and flipped them both, using his huge hands to settle her hips on top of him. Her robe trailed off her shoulders and over their bodies.

"Ride me," he demanded, the professor snapping his ruler. She was a good student, he was straight up inside her and she was already arching and rolling and squeezing.

All of his worship for her robe went out the window. He ripped it down her arms like it pissed him off. She laughed as he yanked it over her hands and threw it, then stopped laughing when he rubbed his hands over her thighs, over her round hips and up her waist, up over her boobs, stroking but not stopping there although she knew he was obsessed with them, continuing to touch and squeeze while she rolled nice and easy on top of his big dick and watched his eyes follow his hands, over her shoulders, down her arms, until he caught her hands, entwined their fingers and mashed their palms together.

She bit her lip. She'd never felt so vital and needed and

glorious. She squeezed his hands as she squeezed him inside her and looked into his eyes.

How much was she going to let him see?

He moaned and clenched up, and she moaned when she felt the kick of him, but he let go of her hand and jolted her halfway off his cock so he could grab his base and balls.

"Dammit," he growled. He breathed, slow and heavy, pretty eyes shut against her, as she hovered there, up on her knees and half on his dick.

He gave a huff then opened his eyes to look at her. "You're the only one who makes me need to orgasm before I'm ready."

He'd called her brave, but she couldn't hold a candle to him. He lived above a bar, even though his colleagues thought it was weird. He loved a poor town, even though he could afford to love someplace much better. He waded into strangers—with his quiches and foreign ways and valid fear of rejection—and asked if he could take a seat.

He exposed his underbelly to her, no matter how many times she kicked it, and told her repeatedly that he wanted her more than he could control.

She leaned over and took his face in her hands. She settled her thumbs into the place where his face dimpled and settled her wet cunt against his hand.

"I'm sorry I was mean to you about that," she said, staring into his gorgeous mood-ring eyes. "You desperate like that, losing it like that because of *me*, it's a total turn-on. It was hot even that night." She hugged him tight inside her to let him know she meant it. "What I said was mean and spiteful, focusing on things I don't even believe, like a man is measured by his stamina and a hard cock is responsible for orgasms. I mean, look how many times you've made me come without your cock!"

"Three times?" he asked, a smile growing on his face.

"Oh, you've made me come a lot more than that. You just didn't know it."

His eyes glowed like sunshine. She was struck by the fact that she could make him happy.

"I'm sorry I made you worry about your…" She blinked, looking for the word.

"Exuberance?" he asked.

"Yeah," she said, grinning. "Exuberance. I like that. You're exuberant. Don't take shit about it, not from me or anyone." She wobbled his head in her hands. "You're…really…the hottest, most original, interesting, nicest guy I've ever known. Don't let anyone change you. Or make you less exuberant." Her words had to sink in. "You're perfect just the way you are."

He needed to remember that after she was gone.

Suddenly, she was on her back again. He looked at her like she was where X marked the spot.

"Well, sweetheart," he murmured against her mouth as he pushed in hard. "I'm sorry to subscribe to…" He lunged. "…heteronormative constructs…" He thrust. "…but I have to be…" He kissed her. "…on top of you…"

The bed was squealing beneath them.

"I have to be over you…and inside you…and seeing…all of you."

He was pounding into her and shaking her to her core.

She was a big woman that no one pushed around, but she loved being manhandled by him. She grabbed onto his lats and hung on. Squeezed onto his hips to take his driving, flashing penis.

Fire was traveling into her stomach. She wrenched her mouth to the side and gasped, "Oh God."

"Yes," he grunted above her. "Let me see you." He shifted

up to grab her knee, pushed it forward and opened her up so he could hit a new angle.

"Oh… Jesus. Jeremiah!" She lurched up to grab the rungs of the old bed frame and he groaned, wrapped his hand around one of hers to trap her there while the pleasure lanced through her and he stared into her eyes to watch it happen.

Tied up in Jeremiah's room with his bed cushioning her. Him seeing her insides and liking it. Doing this to her for hours. Days. Years.

His exuberance took her.

She arched up her hips, yelling, coming, and he slid both hands to her waist to hold her up and keep her high as she gyrated against him and he pounded into her, the wetness between them audible.

But he wasn't slowing down. He wasn't stopping. She looked at him over the mound of her breasts and stomach and saw him glaring down at her, intent, terrifying, his chest and arm muscles straining and his entire torso flushed pink, but he was still hammering.

"Let me see."

She opened her mouth—to scream? To beg?—but she lurched and came again, clamping, clamping, clamping down on him.

He lowered her hips to the bed. Shuffled closer to sprawl her trembling thighs over his powerful ones. Surged gently in.

Her eyelids felt weighted, but she still managed to look at him in amazement. "You didn't come?" she croaked.

Sweat shined on his forehead as he shook his head. "Not yet." The slide of his cock inside her was slow, but the focused way he stared into her, how he surrounded her waist with his big hands and moved until…

She sucked in a breath when he hit her g-spot. His eyes narrowed and he rotated that big dick to hit that spot again.

He was a doctor. He was a professor. He knew how to study and research and become an expert in his field.

"Jeremiah, no," she gasped.

He grit his teeth. "Yes." He began to flash his hips faster to rub against that spot.

She began to pull her up feet to shove him off. "I can't."

"Yes, darling, you can." He grabbed her knees and held them apart, held her cunt up for his use. But he stopped and looked at her with the sweetest eyes. "I'll stop. Tell me to stop and I'll stop. But I thought I might see if I could make you come when I come. I've never felt that. Have you?"

Helpless, she shook her head.

"It would feel nice. Don't you think? Don't you think it would be nice if we saw each other that way?"

Nice? He was tearing the skin off her bones and she'd have nowhere to hide. He wanted to make Freedom home and it was the one place she could never call that. How naked did he expect her to get for him?

But all she could do was nod.

He began to move and he was just so...so Jeremiah. She reached for him and he let go of her knees so she could pull him close and he kissed her hard and she held him in her arms and then he moved, deep circles, pushing inside, as close as he could get, and she squeezed him between her strong thighs and stroked him with her mighty hands, and he pushed up on his elbows and looked and she let him see.

Her professor was right. When she came, looking into his eyes, and he came, looking into hers, it was very nice. It was the nicest thing she ever felt.

The rain had stopped by the time they remembered the metal tub. Jeremiah told her "Stay," like he thought he was in charge as he pulled up his pajama pants, so to punish him—okay, maybe to reward him—she had her thighs spread and her fingers working between them when he came back to his room.

"The tub was only about halfway full so…" Whatever he was going to say gibbered into silence as he saw what she was doing in his bed. He flushed a quick, very pretty rose up his chest and cheeks. It made him look so young.

He didn't sound young when he growled, "I can't leave you alone for a second." He stalked to the bed, grabbed her by her thighs, and dragged her to the edge before dropping to his knees. She fake fought him and he fake held her down and then both of them stopped faking anything and he buried his face in her pussy and she rode his face with his hair as her reins.

When she was gasping with release and he'd wiped his face on the blankets, she heard him take out his cock and begin to stroke it. "Can you play with yourself again, honey?" he asked. So sweet.

She pulled a pillow under her head and just traced where she was so sensitive and wet and tingly. Let him look. Their time together had an end date, but until then, she would let him see. She began to stroke more intently and he did nothing but watch. He was so gorgeous as he watched her stroke. As he studied.

Then he began to help. First with a finger. Then with his tongue. Then he asked what she had in her room, and she told him, and he retrieved it and he helped with finger and tongue and toy.

She was in the middle of another orgasm when her professor reared up, leaned over her, and came all over her stomach.

Sex in the clawfoot tub was slippery and athletic and experimental. Alex was glad she'd brought the waterproof lube. He liked her wet soapy boobs and she liked his wet soapy ass but finally, finally, they stopped stroking and licking and fingering and fondling each other's parts long enough to actually get clean.

In Loretta's kitchen, with Alex wearing his flannel top and a pair of his boxers but no pants and with Jeremiah wearing his flannel pants but no shirt, they shared a burger, an apple, and a slice of cheesecake. Jeremiah moaned and swore that she must have a sorcerer's control over the kitchen because it was the juiciest burger, the crispest apple, and the tangiest cheesecake he'd ever had. He tried to include her bottom in his oratory pleasures right there in the kitchen, but Alex did have her limits.

"Health codes," she said, and her eyes told him she was not fooling around.

But on the stairs up to their hallway… Jeremiah bent her over and she let him have his filthy way with her as she crossed her arms on the worn tread and came and came and came.

He'd flipped on the radio and she discovered that the AM station that was Masterpiece-Theater-boring the rest of the time was actually pretty good in the middle of the night when her sweaty self was sprawled back against Jeremiah's naked body as he absently stroked her hip and palmed her breast. The music was all slow piano and soft horns and added some moody class to this softly lit room that smelled of books and roses and relentless fucking.

"My brother is famous," Jeremiah said out of nowhere.

"And your family is rich," she answered, eyes closed.

They sounded like the chorus of "Summertime."

Your daddy is rich. And your ma is good lookin'.

"Yes," he said against her damp temple, brushing his lips against it. "You sized up my wealth quickly, didn't you?"

"Hazard of the trade." She angled her head to look at him.

Sweat made that hank of his hair she loved curl up into a ring-let. "Sometimes I size up people too quickly."

He gave a gentle kiss to the corner of her eye. "I'm never really going to be a person that blends in."

"Thank God for that." She snuggled back against his chest. She'd steamroll right over a blending-in kind of man. "Tell me about your famous brother."

He ran his thumb over the breast he was holding. It could be his security blanket.

For now.

"He's Prince Harrington."

She smacked his thigh in surprise. "No fucking way."

"Yes. And ow!"

Her palm was stinging. She hadn't meant to hit him as hard as she did. "Sissy *loves* him," she said, rubbing the mark she'd left. "I think she met him at a fan convention. She had a whole plan—she was going to become a famous actress then lose her virginity to him when she was eighteen and then marry him when she was twenty-one."

"Wonderful." It was a silly trivia fact, not something to put that much seriousness in his voice. "You can see why I changed my name."

She didn't care who his brother was.

She pushed off his chest and twisted around to look at him. "Is that his real name? *Prince Harrington.*"

"Yes," he said. She could see him trying to smile. "My family had high expectations of the first son."

"And of the second son?"

This massive, gorgeous, exuberant, genius man dropped his eyes to the sheets. "Oh, those were high, too. Unfortunately, I didn't meet them."

She wanted this conversation. She wanted to defy what put that doubt in his eyes. She told herself that she wanted to help him when he told this story to another woman in a year or two, the right woman. She wanted him to already believe that the story didn't define the amazing person he was.

She put her hand on his chest. "Tell me about your family. Although I might want to fight them after you do. I can't stand people with their heads up their asses and your family sounds like their heads are jammed pretty far up there."

He snagged her by the back of the neck and spent the next several minutes making her mouth feel like the cup of life offered to a dying man.

He snuggled them under the covers and curled up behind her, his mouth at her ear, his legs tucked up under her ass, his big hand once again holding her breast.

He told her of a family, the Harringtons, that had a family business and a multigenerational story in a specific place like her family did, but his place—on Connecticut's Gold Coast, overlooking the Long Island Sound—sounded like it could have come out of the Great Gatsby movie and his family business was real estate, new money invested long ago in Manhattan and early suburbs along the commuter line that now had become old money, so much money that acquiring more was just adding tears to an Olympic-sized pool.

He told her of his brother.

Prince Matthias Harrington was the sleek, golden-haired, icy-eyed boy you aspired to be if you didn't have to live in the same mansion with him: handsome, charming, clever, good at sports, girls, and parents. He was an okay brother, but he didn't really know what to do with Jeremiah James Harrington, the ugly duckling who emerged from the womb three years after he did, awkward and bawling, too chubby, too "exuberant," prone to crying at sunsets or making his tutors uncomfortable by knowing the answer before they did.

Jeremiah had tried to hide behind the Apollo-like glow of

his brother, but instead of letting Jeremiah pursue his geeky interests, feel his over-amped emotions, and live his best life in the shadows of their library, his very bitchy mother had constantly dragged him out to declare what a glaring disappointment he was in comparison.

It was because of this that young Jeremiah had been filled with malicious glee when he'd watched thirteen-year-old Prince hop the fence of their Connecticut boarding school to audition for his first acting job. Prince was finally going to get it. He got it indeed. Prince got the starring role for the pilot and with it, landed his first Emmy. He won his first Oscar when he was twenty.

For the first ten years of Jeremiah's life, his family had weighed him against his brother and found him wanting. For the next ten years, classmates, random acquaintances, strangers who were friends of strangers, and his brother's legion of internet fans got to join in as well.

"They took one look at oversized, lumbering, academic, very unhip me and were awestruck that Prince and I came from the same parents." He was telling this story into her hair. Alex had turned over to wrap her arms around him. "They pitied me. And that was the kind reaction."

She tugged him closer.

"His fame, his beauty, it followed me like a funhouse mirror—his was the reflection that warped my image. The few academic friends I could have made didn't want the infamy of hanging out with Prince Harrington's brother. Strangers sent me messages online to insult me. That's when they weren't sending me sexually explicit photos or offers to do horrible things to my body if I'd introduce them to him. I was a child. Eleven, twelve when they started. Then in high school, college, people approached me—my classmates, acquaintances of classmates, even fans who'd find me. They offered a lonely, unattractive, starved-for-affection kid their sexual scraps if I'd give them my brother's number."

She gave slow, light kisses to his chest and blinked quickly to get rid of her tears.

"What's funny was that I liked myself. I never felt worthless, although everyone except the random teacher or professor thought I was. Sex was fraught for me; I didn't lose my virginity until grad school. What's funnier is... I never had my brother's number. Nobody ever gave it to me."

Alex squeezed his strong body as tight as she could and pressed her lips together.

"When it was time to apply to grad schools, I knew that if I didn't break from my family, I might not make it. I changed my last name to that of my maternal great-grandmother, changed my look to fool anyone who stumbled onto me, buried myself in academic circles. My mother pretended she was insulted. My father didn't seem to notice. I receive a terse email and a direct deposit once a year. Prince and I exchange birthday cards, although I'm relatively sure his are signed by his assistant."

Any jokiness was erased by the way he buried his face in her neck. "They've shown in every way they can that they're glad to be done with me, and yet I would still forgive them if they asked. I've never understood why I inspire so much disdain in the people I call family."

Alex slung her thigh over his hip, covered him in as much defensive flesh as she could. "They're gonna be so sorry," she said against his ear. "They're gonna be so fucked when they realize what an incredible man they missed out on loving."

Tomorrow, she'd get her head right. Tomorrow, she'd tell him that she was happy to keep doing this with him, treasure hunting with him, trusting him, and letting him see. Tomorrow, she'd tell him why she left town thirteen years ago and why she'd eventually leave again.

But right now, she would kiss him and roll him over and climb on top of him. Starting now, she was going to spend the rest of the night showing him how valuable he was.

Chapter Twenty-Six

As they drove past waist-high fields of corn and sorghum on the way to Edward and Rosalinda's family farm several days later, the top of Jeremiah's two-seater down and the dewy spring morning whipping at the bow of Alex's adorable skulls-and-crossbones kerchief, Jeremiah wondered when would be the most appropriate time to ask her to marry him. Would she appreciate the spontaneity of him asking the instant they found the second deed, of him going down on one knee in the dust of whatever shed or basement they found themselves in and presenting his plans for the train depot and their shared future like an engagement ring? Or would she prefer a more traditional approach—him having an actual ring (something to complement the other behemoths she wore) and a romantic setting and a heartfelt, social-media worthy scenario after asking Loretta for her permission to marry her granddaughter?

Despite the détente Alex had established with her parents, he felt that the go-ahead from her grandmother would be the one she'd value most. He'd almost asked for the woman's blessing two evenings ago, when he'd gone to her home—feeling a burst of gladness when he entered through the back door—to thank her for the Easter meal and to let her know that the historical society had voted to begin scouting new locations for their museum, in anticipation of Loretta turning down their offer.

She'd given him that smile that warmed him to his bones just like her granddaughter's smile did.

But undecided about his proposal approach and still needing to tell Alex about what he'd been working on with Joe, he'd decided to wait to ask for Loretta's blessing.

When he told Alex the secrets he'd spent years protecting, the secrets he'd relentlessly guarded from *her*, she'd been supremely unimpressed that he was connected to a large-ish East Coast real estate fortune and the reigning king of Hollywood. She'd reacted much more passionately to the less glamorous details of his story. He'd had no doubts about his love for her when he'd first reached for her on that endless, incredible night. But when she'd pushed him onto his back after he revealed to her what he'd hidden from everyone else, when she'd taken him into her mouth and arms and body like he was precious and she was never going to let him go, she'd obliterated any doubts about her love for him. She'd pulled the For Sale sign from the parched dirt of his heart, and he'd let her have it for next to nothing because she made him feel so valuable. His mother's abuse, his father's dismissal, his brother's absence—Alex's bold claim that he was the *hottest, most original, interesting,* and *nicest guy* she'd ever known built something solid over all those empty places. She created the home he'd always sought, and he never wanted to leave.

He was certain she loved him back even though the word hadn't crossed their lips yet.

There'd been a lot of talking over the last several nights together, but most of that had been of the *let me touch* and *put your mouth* and *harder* and *more* and *again* variety. She hadn't returned to her bed—even though the roof was patched, the clothes were cleaned, and the mattress was replaced—and that had to mean something.

They'd been strangers then enemies then compatriots and now…

She let him see her. She let him see the tender, lonely, loving parts she hid behind a colorful and caustic exterior.

He let her see the rejected boy he hid behind the new name and training regimen. They'd both been hiding, and they'd both distanced themselves from the people that had hurt them.

She hadn't yet shared her story why. He still didn't know what had happened with Lance Dutimeyer or why she was so angry with her father. She hadn't yet explained what drove her from Freedom all those years ago.

He felt it hovering sometimes over their quiet moments. What she waited to tell, what he wanted to hear, fluttered like a moth as they rested against each other, panting, letting the sweat on their bodies cool. Then she'd reach for him again and or he'd reach for her and the opportunity was lost in the way they consumed each other.

If there was a hint of desperation to the way they grabbed and held, it was only because it was so new. So addictive.

He still hadn't told her about the property he'd purchased. It was hard to let go of the echo of those earliest accusations that he was *playing Lord and Savior to a bunch of dirt-poor Mexican-Americans.*

He trusted her, but he was dragging his feet. He didn't want to mar the exhilaration of what he was feeling—of what they were both feeling—with her suspicion.

Once they found the second deed, once they laid to rest the preposterous ideas of treasures and curses and century-old documents that gave a greedy white man a right to claim people's homes and community, Alex would have to see that she wasn't alone anymore. She would have to see that his plan ensured no one could ever threaten her home—their home—again.

They could be minutes from finding it.

When she tapped his shoulder and he slowed down to turn onto a long, gravel driveway, he checked his mirror on the empty country road, put the car in park, then pulled her close to kiss her hard.

"What was that for?" she gasped against his mouth.

"Waiting to kiss you was awful," he said. "I never want to wait again."

She shoved his forehead. "Perv. They're not gonna let us search their house if we're doing it in their driveway."

If her cheeks beneath her oversized sunglasses didn't curve up as much as he'd hoped, he wasn't going to point it out.

The Victorian farm home they pulled up to was tall and lovely, painted a stately Colonial blue with white trim and a white, wraparound porch. A cove of trees that helped shade the home from the hot Kansas summers had been maintained around it, and tulips bobbed around the front steps.

That Edward and Rosalinda's home was so pleasant warmed something in Jeremiah's chest. There was peace in the image of the two of them sitting on their large porch at the end of their adventures, comfortable in their home and proud of their lives and firm in their love. They'd defied so much to have it.

He was glad to see these descendants had beautifully maintained the home. Left to Dutimeyer and his ilk, the place would have been sold off and its fields cattled over long ago.

As they got out of the Mercedes, a screen door squealed as a fiftyish-year-old man in jeans, a short-sleeved shirt buttoned over the drum of his belly, and a baseball cap stepped out onto the front porch.

"If I'd known y'all were going to be so fancy, I would've worn my good shitkickers," he called with a friendly smile from the porch.

Ofelia hadn't mentioned that Walt Cunningham looked

like his great-grandmother's child: he had Rosalinda's skin and dark hair. He looked like one of Alex's tíos.

They met him in the dappled shade of his front sidewalk and introduced themselves, shaking hands.

"It was a real kick in the pants when Ofelia told us that Great-Grandpa Edward was one of *those* Hughs," he said. "As far as I knew, we'd always been farmers." He squinted as looked around. Just past the copse of trees, fields stretched out in all directions. "Until the last few years, the land's been pretty good to us."

He shook off wherever his mind went. "The wife put out a couple of scrapbooks that your aunt has already looked at. There's a little bit about the family and the house. We've never seen a deed to anything. But y'all are welcome to look around. You find it, we'll burn it right here. Make sure no one else can get up to any mischief with it."

"Thank you," Alex said. "Your generosity means a lot to me and my family."

If the second deed was found, Walt and his son would have a right to use it. But the man had reassured Ofelia that he wouldn't.

He chuckled now. "What would I do with the Hugh building?" he said. "The wife and I don't drink, but I got a few friends who'd have words with me if I tried to mess up Loretta's. What Lance Dutimeyer is tryin' to do ain't right. What kind of decent person would steal people's homes and businesses right out from underneath 'em?"

He scratched his dark hair under his worn KU cap as he looked at Jeremiah and Alex. Then he straightened it and put his hands on his belt.

"I've been thinking there's something I should show y'all," he said. "It's kind of a family secret, so I'd ask you to keep what you see to yourself. But, Alex, it might be of special interest to you."

She looked at him with surprise. She'd taken off the kerchief, and her hair was a soft mass of waves that she tucked behind an ear.

Jeremiah and Alex followed Walt around the side of his home, out of the shade of the trees, and into the dust-and-gravel yard. Behind the home was a large barn, a smaller shed for vehicles, and a squat grain silo. Walt grabbed a toolbox out of the back of his truck then led them through the morning sunlight toward a door submerged into a hillock of land.

It was a storage cellar that looked as old as the house. Walt heaved open the heavy wooden door and Alex—after giving Jeremiah a quick, mystified look—followed the man down the stairs. Jeremiah brought up the rear.

He was going to be very upset if this seemingly nice man was taking them down to his murder room.

The temperature dropped ten degrees by the time Jeremiah's loafers hit the dirt floor. Walt flipped a switch and clicked on a string of bulbs that lit the center of the room. "Like I said, the wife and I don't imbibe," he said, motioning them to follow him as he led them through the narrow but surprisingly long cellar past wood plank shelves filled with canned, preserved, and pickled everything. The floor gently sloped down into the earth, and the temperature declined with it. "I believe live and let live, but my parents were strict Christians. And what's down here has the whiff of family scandal to it, so we've just kept it underground."

The narrow cellar dead-ended at a medium-sized semicircular room carved out of limestone. Here it was twenty degrees cooler than the outside temperature; the smell of minerality and soil tingled Jeremiah's nose. Old burlap covered what was stored against the wall up to the room's beamed ceiling.

"I never expected a bartender to come by," Walt said, his hand on the burlap. "Seems fittin' for some reason, Alex. Loretta and your granddad—God rest his soul—they're good people. Even if what y'all are looking for isn't here, maybe you can do something with this to help y'all out."

He pulled down one of the burlap coverings, revealing ancient lidded crates stacked eight high. "Gimme a hand," he told Jeremiah, and together, they pulled off the top crate and put it on the packed dirt floor. The crate was heavy.

Under the single bulb, Walt dropped to a knee, pulled out a prybar from his toolbox, and went to work on the nailed-shut lid. He popped up one side, then the other.

Alex had crossed her arms over herself in the cool room. Jeremiah would have pulled her close to keep her warm, but he didn't want to disturb her laser-eyed focus as she watched Walt work.

Walt pulled off the lid. In the box were bread-loaf-long packages bundled in straw and tied. He lifted one and held it up to Alex.

"Walt?" She rubbed her hands over her arms. "Are you sure?"

Jeremiah felt it, too. This could change everything.

Walt nodded.

Alex took the weighty package and carefully pulled off the old, dry straw, uncovering gingham-patterned paper wrapped around a bottle. The paper was sealed with a drip of red wax imprinted with two hearts pressed against each other and flaming. The wax seal reminded Jeremiah of the milagros that decorated the hallway doors. Alex carefully thumbed under the seal to break it then unwrapped the paper.

The bottle was tall and green. A golden fluid was inside

it, up to the cork. She turned the bottle so she could read the label.

Her high astonished laugh made Jeremiah jump in the tense silence.

She turned the label so he could read it. But he couldn't look away from her eyes. Her sparkling, glorious, tear-filled eyes.

"Poor Eddie's Treasure," she said, her skeptic's voice full of wonder, her smile huge. "That's what they named their whisky. Poor Eddie's Treasure."

He finally ripped his eyes off her beautiful glowing face to read the label.

Poor Eddie's Treasure. Kansas Corn Whisky. Padugh Bonding and Bottling Co. Limited. Freedom, Kansas.

Jeremiah stared at the bottle, stunned. "This was the treasure the family's been whispering about all this time."

Alex stabbed at the label. "Do you see the name of the bottling company?"

He did. Padugh Bonding and Bottling. He looked at her and shrugged.

She shook the bottle in front of his face, her eyes gigantic. "Padugh! *Pad*illa and *Hugh*. I bet you this is what funded Milagro Street." The glee was priceless on her face. "This where Rosalinda and Edward got the money to offer microloans to Mexicans who wanted to start businesses. They took what Wayland had taught Edward, all the stuff that Wayland was ashamed of, and they turned it into…" She waved her free hand around, encompassing the cellar and the house and the farm and her family and her people and the entire east side of Freedom. "They turned it into all of this."

She spun to Walt, who was standing back with his arms crossed over his belly watching with amusement. "Mr. Cunningham, we can't take this from you."

Jeremiah looked at her, shocked. She was already holding the bottle against her heart.

"Why?" Walt drawled.

"This is Prohibition-era whisky." She enunciated each syllable. "Even if it's degraded and been stored in a boiling-hot attic, an unopened bottle of this goes for five hundred to a thousand dollars at auction." She pressed it between her breasts. "This still has its tax seal—they must have gotten approval to sell medicinal whisky at some point—and it's been stored in ideal conditions. If it's as good as I suspect it is…" She flapped a hand against her thigh. "Then it's skies the limit."

Jeremiah's ears rung with her words. A thousand dollars a bottle. And there were…countless crates down here. All of Loretta's debts. All of Alex's dreams.

One could be cleared and the other provided with this unexpected treasure from Old Man Hugh's son and daughter-in-law.

Walt was shaking his head. "Alex, you're a good girl. But my conscience won't let me make a fortune off a vice I've shunned my whole life. Whisky auctions? I wouldn't even know where to start."

"I can help you." In her dedication to fair play, she was going to give this windfall away. "I can show you…"

"Look," Walt said, raising his hardworking farmer hands. "I can see you're as stubborn as my son. He's got some ideas about heirloom corn and new methods of growing…" He shook off whatever he was going to say. "I'm not gonna cut off my nose to spite my face. If you figure out a way to make money with this stuff, I'll take…ten percent."

"Fifty percent," Alex countered.

"Twenty-five," Walt said, head shaking. "That's as much as me and my God can make peace with. We'll call it a storage fee."

Jeremiah stuck out his hand before Alex could force the man into taking half of the bar and their firstborn child. "Deal," he said.

They shook hands and Alex put her hand on Jeremiah's shoulder, sealing the pact.

She then slipped her hand down Jeremiah's arm and curled her fingers through his.

Jeremiah worked to hide his tremor that she was declaring herself this way. There'd been no such displays around her family, although they'd all been giving them curious looks.

"Walt, this kind of changes everything," she said. "Dutimeyer was trying to force my grandmother's hand. This means he has no leverage over her anymore. And we were just trying to find the second deed to prevent Freedom Rings from using it. If you don't allow Freedom Rings to search your property, then we don't need to search either. What are the chances we're going to find a piece of paper you've never seen?"

"If that deed is in one of these boxes, then it's yours," Walt said. "If Grandpa Edward buried it somewhere else on this property, it's gonna stay buried. No way I'm lettin' Lance Dutimeyer step a foot on my land to look for it. He and his daddy are big flaming buttholes, excuse my French. The only downside of this whole thing is learnin' I'm related to 'em."

Alex laughed and the sound was as light and pretty as spring flowers.

"Okay," she said. She exhaled a big breath. Then she squeezed Jeremiah's fingers and looked at him. "Okay."

Was that it? Was their search over?

Had they been looking for a document and found treasure and a happily-ever-after instead?

Suspended in this astonishing moment and Alex's beautiful eyes, he reached up and caught a single fat tear rolling down her cheek.

Extravagant and unashamed emotions would fill their home like fireworks.

She gave a watery laugh and let go of him to wipe her face with both hands.

"Sorry," she said. Walt was beaming at her. "I guess...we'll be in touch. We'll figure out how to haul all this whisky out of here. I'll probably want to video it so no one can question the authenticity. I promise to keep your name and location out of it. But whisky afficionados are going to lose. Their. Minds."

Alex and her savvy savviness. She was going to wring each bottle for every penny.

"Right now..." Her grin looked like it was going to explode off her face. "I'm gonna go tell my Granmo that we've saved the bar."

The way she looked as they drove back to Freedom, the sun adding a golden sheen to her joy and the wind whipping it off of her and sprinkling it all over Jeremiah, made it nearly impossible to drive. It made it even harder for him to resist turning off onto an empty country lane, taking her immediately and hard, then begging her to marry him.

He should have heeded the impulse.

Because when Alex answered her phone and he watched the blood drain from her face, he had a stabbing premonition that he might have lost his chance.

Chapter Twenty-Seven

Alex put her foot on the top of the door frame and leapt out of the car before Jeremiah came to a full stop in front of the Freedom police station.

"Alex!" he shouted. But she was already running. Just as she grabbed the handle to the front door of the brown squat building, Mary came from around the corner.

Tucker was right behind her.

Alex ignored him as she opened the door for her mom. "What happened?" she hissed as they hustled to the attendant's desk.

The lobby smelled like Christmas tree car fresheners and century-old coffee. Alex hadn't been in this building in thirteen years and had hoped to never be in it again.

"I don't know anything more than what I already told you on the phone," her mom said, looking around. The front office was empty. "Your cousin Zekie called me. Said they'd brought Loretta in."

Alex banged her hand against the desk. "Hey! We need some help up here."

A doughy-looking guy looked out from a side office as her father said "Alex" warningly behind her.

She shot him a glare. Jeremiah had just jogged in and was standing next to him.

"What's he doing here?" she said. Tucker had been here, too, the last time she'd been in this building.

"Not now," Mary whispered.

Zekie came rushing through a side door.

"God, Alex," Zekie said in her police uniform, her dark hair pulled back into a long ponytail. Alex would never forgive her cousin for thinking she could change the system from the inside. "I could hear you from the other end of the building." Zekie hugged her and gave Mary a kiss, then ushered them all back through the door she'd come out of.

"Zeke, how could you let them arrest Granmo—"

"She's not arrested," Zekie hushed as they walked down the hall through shadows and glaring shafts of fluorescent light. You'd never know it was a nice spring morning outside. "There was a concern about her state. There was a request to bring her in so she could cool down."

"Cool down?" Alex asked. "What happened?"

"She pulled a rifle on someone."

"What?!" Alex wasn't shocked Loretta had pulled a gun. She was furious that her grandmother was here. If her Granmo had pointed a rifle, she had a good reason. "Where was she?"

"At home. When the police arrived on scene, she had her weapon out and— Look, the fact that they were in her front yard is the only reason we're not pressing charges."

"She was at home? What the fuck, Zekie, you know Granmo wouldn't—"

Her cousin grabbed her arm with a grip stronger than she had when they were kids. "Calm down. If you don't get your shit together, I'm not letting you in there with her. You acting like this doesn't do her any favors."

Alex tried to focus on her cousin's no-nonsense eyes. But her chest was tight and her palms were sweaty. This place made her crazy. It didn't help that her dad was lurking somewhere behind her.

Then she felt Jeremiah's warm hand curl over her shoulder.

She hadn't told him, yet, what had happened here. Why she left was too tied up in why she couldn't stay. The last few days had just been so nice. She'd been letting him see a lot, but she'd been hiding this last little bit and trying not to feel guilty about it.

She couldn't even look at him now. He said he wanted to take care of her, but that was something she couldn't let herself get used to.

Still, she felt her racing heart slow down at the warm, silent squeeze of his big hand.

"Okay," she said. "Okay, sorry, I'll chill out."

"Good," Zekie said. Jeremiah's hand slipped away as they approached the glass window of the interview room. She'd experienced the worst moment of her life in this room. As she saw her grandmother through the glass, she had the out-of-body thought that the next moments might top it. "Because this is going to be a big—"

Alex pushed the door handle and rushed into that room with its fluorescent glare, her cousin cursing behind her.

Loretta immediately started to cry. "Mija."

Alex came around the beaten-up table and knelt on the dirty linoleum at her side.

Her Granmo, her dignified, proud, strong grandmother, was in her housecoat—the powder-blue one with the snaps—in the Freedom police station's interview room. Her salt-and-pepper hair had that bedhead look of pressed-down clumps and spiky peaks.

Whatever had happened had roused her elderly grandmother out of bed, and they hadn't even let her change before they'd brought her in.

Loretta rocked herself as she rubbed Alex's arm. "Mija, I'm so sorry. It's all my fault. He's going to take the bar. He's going to take my house."

Alex squeezed her grandmother's knee. "Granmo, what're you talking about? No one is going to—"

"He said I should have accepted his offer when I had the chance." She was crying so hard. Alex had never seen her like this.

She looked bewildered at her cousin.

"She was holding a rifle on Lance Dutimeyer," Zekie said grimly.

Alex felt furious and relieved at the same time, like her stomach was left in her throat after a roller coaster drop. She was going to get that rifle and jam it up Doody-meyer's ass for needlessly terrifying and taunting Loretta. She and Jeremiah had found the treasure. Probably the deed, too. They could take care of Loretta's debt and protect the east side and—

"He said he found the second deed," her grandmother said.

Alex immediately shook her head. "No. That can't be right."

Loretta sobbed harder. "He's already filed the paperwork with the city. He said…he said we have to be out of the bar in two weeks. He said…" She covered her mouth, spoke through her hands. "He's going to take my house. All of our homes."

With a horrified sixth sense, Alex turned to look through the interior window. Just like thirteen years ago, Lance Du-timeyer was staring at her with a satisfied smirk on his face while Alex stared back, unable to believe what was happening.

"Keep it together," Zekie urged as Alex felt Jeremiah's hand once again fall on her shoulder.

This time, she nudged it off as she stood.

The door opened and Mayor Bernie Hugh Mayfield walked into the room. Lance followed him in.

"Now, what's all this hullabaloo," Mayor Mayfield boomed, his dentures beaming. "Miss Loretta, you calm down and we'll let you go."

"Mayor, she's already free to go," Zekie said stiffly. Bernie was a big man and Alex couldn't see her cousin behind him.

Loretta sniffed and wiped her nose with her hands. Mary gave her Kleenex from her purse.

"We don't want her to be a danger to herself or anyone else." He put his hands on his wide hips, like her grandmother was a little girl to be talked down to. "That's why Lance thought it would be a good idea if the police brought you in."

Alex gripped her hands into fists. She counted to ten. She focused on Doody-meyer's *GQ* hair and tight mint-green shirt and pink tie and his puke-green pull-on pants.

"Why's he wearing jailhouse pants?" she asked.

"He peed himself when I pulled out my rifle," Loretta said.

Lance's face grew red spots of anger. "You won't be laughing when I ride a bulldozer into your fucking bar."

Mary gasped. But before Alex could put her fist through his teeth, Mayor Mayfield turned around and poked him in his designer shirt. "You keep your stupid mouth shut. You've caused enough trouble. You're just as dim as your daddy always said you were, always stirring up trouble in the outhouse then wondering why you stink like shit."

Alex watched Lance snap his mouth closed.

She remembered how Dutimeyer's dad in a ten-gallon hat had towered over his son, how he'd done all the hollering and stomping and finger-pointing while Lance had just stood there, slouched on one hip and smiling. Baby Dutimeyer had never had one doubt that he was going to get everything his white, wealthy, entitled upbringing had taught him he deserved. He'd never had one doubt he was going to get Alex's head on a platter.

She couldn't believe she was back here again.

Mayor Mayfield turned back to her family, slapping his meaty hands together like he was calling a meeting to order.

"Look, folks, cards on the table, change is coming to Freedom. You can either jump onboard or step aside. We've got it from a good source that Roxanne Medina is looking to build something big here. We're sorry we couldn't give you more time. With an anonymous investor buying up properties on the east side and making inquiries into purchasing our little train depot, Lance and I gotta move fast. Wouldn't you rather have hometown boys benefitting from development of the east side rather than some random—"

"We're not—" Jeremiah said from behind her. "I'm not buying properties to—"

Alex slowly turned to face him.

The last time she'd really looked at him, just twenty minutes ago in the car as they'd been driving down the highway, the wind tossing around all that gorgeous dark hair, she'd had the weirdest thought that maybe she was the tiniest bit in love with him.

Jeremiah reached a hand out to her like they were the only two people in the room.

She lurched back.

He curled his fingers into his palm. "I emailed my mother," he said. The mother that was supposedly so mean to him. "I tapped into some family resources." Her family resources were...she had no family resources. "I've been buying available east side property to make sure Freedom Rings couldn't gain a controlling interest. But Alex, I never meant to..."

"There's what you mean to do and then there's what happens, Dr. Post." Mayfield cut him off before Alex had to. "Maybe if you hadn't been hiding that you had a mommy you could call for money, you could've done some good in this town. Instead, you just worked poor Lance here into a lather." He shook Dutimeyer like a toy. "You East Coast elites never have to deal with rabid animals. That's what Lance here is. He's good to sic on people. If you try to corner him, he'll tear out your throat."

Disbelief was settling over her like a nice, tight straitjacket.

Tucker stepped forward. "Bernie, I'm not going to stand here and let you—"

"Why are you talking?" Alex snapped, glad to feel the roar of her fury. Grabbing on to it. "Why are you even here?" He'd been in this room back then, and his presence had been devastating. "You're not family. You're a drunk who works for free at the bar. You got good at making yourself absent. Why don't you keep it that way?"

Tucker nodded and she savored the look on his face. Mary gripped his forearm in sympathy.

Her mother had sided with him then, too.

All this time she'd been focusing on Dutimeyer as her big nemesis. She'd even made up a fun nickname for him. But Dutimeyer had never been the real bad guy. Thirteen years ago, he'd gotten to hang back and smile because his dad was the one who insisted she leave town to cover up what he'd done.

Alex couldn't count on the people around her, people who said they loved her or missed her or wanted to take care of her, for the same support that fucking Dutimeyer got. Couldn't then. Couldn't now.

The bright fluorescents shined in the mayor's yellow hair. "You know about the second deed and what we plan to do with it. And sure, Dr. Post, you and Miss Loretta could make a stink. You've got some friends." Mayfield's smile took over the lower half of his face. "But who do you think this town's going to side with? Members of Freedom's founding fam-

ily, who are doing all they can to bring jobs back?" Mayfield said it with the slick insincerity he'd grease voters with.
"Or the weird out-of-towner and his foulmouthed Mexican
girlfriend?"

He tipped his head at them like he'd just won their vote.
"Y'all have a good day, now."

She could see Dutimeyer gearing up to take a parting shot,
but the mayor dragged him and his puke-colored pants out
before he could.

No one spoke as Zekie led them to the side door that led
to the parking lot. The fact that Loretta had been picked up
by the police was going to be on everyone's lips. No reason
to give them evidence of her coming out the front door. Alex
kept her arms around her; Loretta had never felt so frail.

She followed Mary and Tucker through the lot, wishing
she'd driven this morning rather than suggesting that it was
a beautiful day to take Jeremiah's two-seater convertible.

Jeremiah was the first person to break the silence. "We'll
file an injunction," he urged from behind her. "We can—"

"Don't you think you've done enough?"

He inhaled like she'd punched him.

"That's not fair, Alejandra," Mary said, turning to face her
as Tucker walked up to a small van and put his key in the passenger door. "We have to work together if…"

What she was saying got lost as Alex processed the rental
moving van.

Alex walked Loretta to the door her dad held open and
eased her down onto the seat. "Why do you have a U-Haul?"

Tucker closed his bright blue eyes.

Her mother stiffened. "Let's not worry about that right
now," she said. "Let's get Mom home—"

Alex stepped back from the van. She stepped back from

the van and her parents and Jeremiah. She needed to keep a bead on all of them. "Why. Are you driving. A U-Haul?"

Tucker opened his eyes. "I'm moving back in with your mom," he said. "I'm going to stay in Cecilia's old bedroom but…"

"Tucker," Mary hushed. "That's our business." But she stepped close and tried to reach for Alex.

Alex stared her down without pity while Mary clenched her hand then put it over her own heart.

"I'm so sorry you had to find out like this." Anguish twisted her mom's face. "We were going to tell you this evening after close. We were not hiding this from you. But this is the worst possible way for you to find out and I'm so sorry—"

Alex scoffed. At this point, it was comical.

"Don't blame your mother," her father said in his once-beloved voice. When they were little, he used to tell them a new bedtime story every night, and Alex was the only kid in her class who never got nightmares. "Blame me. When you wouldn't take my calls or answer the door when I showed up in Chicago, I finally had to come to terms with the fact that the only way I could make amends to you was by listening to you and staying away. But your mother—" Alex made herself stare at the broken expression on his face as he rubbed his moustache. "I can't. I've lost you girls. By some miracle, your mother is giving me a second chance. I can't lose her, too. I dedicated myself to my self-pity and my addiction when I should have dedicated myself to my family and I'm going to spend the rest of my life—"

She shook her head. "Don't blame the drinking."

"I blame me. I'm the one who picked up the bottle and—"

She shook her head harder. "Don't blame the alcohol."

"I wasn't there for you when I should have been—"

She laughed instead of screamed. "No, no, you *were* there!"

she said, loud and wide-eyed. "After all the times you were
shut up in your room or passed out on the couch when I
needed you." She was pulling a classic Alex. "You were *finally* there. My dad and mom." She sneered it. "You were
going to make it all better."

Tucker wiped a tear before it disappeared into his moustache.

"Then what'd you do? You looked right into Daddy Dutimeyer's smug fucking face when he told you to choose: juvie
or run me out of town. And what did you do?"

"Alex—"

"What did you do?" Her shout ping-ponged off the cars.

Tucker looked gray. "I made you leave."

People who saw her Fantasy Box video thought they'd seen
her unhinged, but that was nothing compared to the racket
she made in that overbright room at the police station, when
her father had looked at Dutimeyer's dad from across the
scarred table and told him he would send her to live with a
far-off cousin in Chicago. She remembered crumbling. She
remembered crying. She remembered the harsh light of the
fluorescents and the dirty linoleum under her hands. She remembered begging. *Don't make me leave, don't make me leave.
I'll be all alone.*

She remembered Dutimeyer looking over the lip of the
table at her on the floor and smiling.

All she'd ever known was Freedom. Her family. The bar.
She'd been born knowing exactly what she wanted out of
her life.

"Fuckin' *Dutimeyer* got more backup than I did. You
showed up and you hurt me." She looked at her mother,
who was openly crying. "And you let him." She glanced at
her grandmother, huddled in the passenger seat. "You both
did, when you knew. You *knew* what I—"

She made herself shut up.

Across the street from her grandmother's home was a little falling-apart house that had been abandoned for most of Alex's life. When they were little, they used to go over with Tucker to maintain the yard, just to keep the gophers down and the street looking nice.

Alex had had big plans for that house.

She and Edward Hugh did have something in common. "You threw me under the bus. Then you go on and live your merry little life when I can't—"

Even when she'd set aside her anger toward her family and put all of her heart and soul and sweat into making Loretta's shine, she'd never had the luxury of thinking of the bar as forever hers. She couldn't risk thinking of Freedom as home again, no matter what her feelings were about the bar and the east side and her family and their legacy and the dreamy guy with the sunlit eyes in the driver's seat.

Her dad had taken that from her, and like Edward, she wasn't a fan of forgiving and forgetting.

Tucker's eyes were red-rimmed. "I wasn't going to let them put you in juvenile detention. I wasn't gambling your future on a Palomino County judge, not with the kind of power the Dutimeyers and the Hughs have in this town. He was out for blood and with the scrapes you'd already had, God only knows what they could have done—"

She'd heard it all before—from him that night, from her mother and grandmother and sisters over and over and over again through the years.

She walked to the van to stoop down and hug her grandmother close. "I'll call Joe," she murmured against her ear. Joe could fix this. Joe would circle the wagons and figure this mess out. Worse came to worst, he could build Loretta a new house.

Alex kissed her and breathed in her smell. She was going to miss her so much.

She turned and stalked to Jeremiah's car without looking back.

"Please mija," Tucker called. Although he wasn't raised speaking Spanish, Tucker had always called her and her sisters what the rest of the family called them. Mija.

She hadn't heard that word from him in years.

"Hate *me*," he called while she was opening the car door. "I wasn't there when I should have been." She sat in the seat. "But don't hate your mom for supporting my decision." She slammed the door. "And don't hate Freedom. Your mom needs you. Your family need you. This town needs you." She put on her oversized glasses. "And you need them."

The driver's door opened.

"Give *me* all your hate. I'll take it and stay out of your way if it'll let you come home."

The bar was gone, the east side was over, the Hugh's stranglehold on Freedom was clenching tighter, and Jeremiah...

Jeremiah, who she'd thought was so special, had become just another person who could hurt her.

Edward Hugh had taught her how to handle these last-minute bids for forgiveness and redemption, but she could improve upon the lesson.

The car started up.

She was hanging on to her hate and taking it back to Chicago.

Chapter Twenty-Eight

Alex's pain pulsed as vivid as a bruise as she sat next to him in the front seat, her oversized sunglasses hiding her eyes, and Jeremiah—who wanted to take care of her, who said he would support her—was responsible for part of her hurt.

They'd barely turned the corner from the police station when Jeremiah pulled over, remembering how Alex had chased him down on his morning run to apologize.

"Alex, I'm so sorry—"

She held up her phone. "I have to call Joe."

"Of course," he said into the phone's black, reflective face. Desperate, needy...

He drove them to Loretta's then sat with her in the quiet parking lot as she told Joe what had happened. Fortunately, she hadn't gone into Jeremiah's culpability. She would need her cousin in the coming days and weeks and he didn't want Joe detailing anything that would make her angry at him, too.

When she ended the call, he reached to put his hand on her thigh. "What can I—"

She got out of the car before he could touch her.

Give me all your hate, her father had said. *I'll take it and stay out of your way if it'll let you come home.*

But she already was home. Surely this one...setback, no matter how demoralizing, wouldn't make his brave, ferocious, avenging angel stop fighting for it, fighting for Loretta's.

Fighting for them.

She valued him. He saw her.

He would grovel and she would demand he bow lower and he would gladly put his forehead to the ground then they would burrow together and lick their wounds and then they would put together his big brain and her cunning vengeance and come up with a plan.

But Jeremiah couldn't behave as if his exuberance and need for her were more important than her pain. He had to take care of her and if space is what she needed right now, that's what he'd give her.

When they entered the bar, Alex told Danny that they were shuttering for the day for "restocking." Never one to look a gift horse in the mouth, Danny was out the door while Alex was still using a black marker to scrawl Gone Fishin' on a piece of paper.

Jeremiah followed her as she stuck it on the front window then followed her—but not too close—as she took out her phone and started texting as she climbed the stairs.

It was disconcerting to watch her push open her bedroom door. They'd been living exclusively in his room. She'd declared his mattress "choice."

But at least she didn't close her door against him. He approached it slowly, then leaned on her doorjamb as he watched her, perched on the edge of her bed, her thumbs flying over the keyboard while her curls bobbed.

Five minutes later, he felt like a marionette without a puppeteer. She still hadn't looked at him, and her phone was buzzing like she held an angry swarm in her hands.

His old and familiar hatred toward the device surged in him.

Suddenly, it went quiet. She tossed it onto her pillows.

He inhaled relief. Now they could talk.

"Alex—"

She knelt on the floor, reached under her bed, and pulled out an empty duffle bag.

"What're you doing?" Because he was huge, he took cautious steps into the room. Her back was to him.

"Getting my stuff together."

Much of her stuff had migrated to his room. "Why?"

"I'm going to stay with a friend in Chicago while I look for a new place."

He reached behind him and clasped the top of a chair. "Why?"

She turned without looking at him, crossed to her armoire, and pulled out an armful of clothes on their hangers.

"The owners of the bar offered me my old job."

He was a very smart man. She'd said so. Right now, nothing was making sense.

"But...how? Already?" He watched her cross the room again and lay the stack of clothes carefully on her bed. "We just discovered—"

"They emailed on Easter."

The entire room slid sideways.

Easter. When she'd been beckoning him into her family's arms and welcoming his quiche and telling him she trusted him. When she'd made love to him, insisting that he was perfect, searing whispers of how valuable he was into his skin, she'd had an invitation back to Chicago.

"You never said anything."

"Why would I?"

She delicately slid each item from its hanger, folded it neatly, and laid it precisely in the duffle. She handled each piece of clothing with care while she was tearing him apart.

"I wasn't gonna go back to Chicago." She shook out a black-and-white polka-dotted dress he'd popped a button off of. "I was going forward. A restaurant group out of Montreal had already contacted me to see if—"

"Montreal?"

"Yep."

"But, I thought…" He'd been stripped down to his most basic, bewildered self. His parents had never attempted the fantasy of Santa Claus, the Easter bunny, or the tooth fairy, but he had to imagine that finding out the truth of those childish dreams would feel something like this. "I thought you were committed to Loretta's."

She gave a *tsk* of her lush mouth. "I was. That's me. Always picking winners."

His stomach rolled nastily.

"Then I'd commit to the next place." He could feel heat climbing his jaw. "And the next." He could feel the sweat on his forehead. "And the next."

He had a sudden cold clarity. He'd never talked about his thoughts for the future. Neither had she.

"You never planned on staying, did you?"

She made that horrible *tsk* again. "Here? Fuck no."

As always, he could trust her to be honest.

He'd been excited for forever with her when he was only good enough for right now. He'd been building a castle in the sand, imagining they would live in it like a modern-day Rosalinda and Edward championing the east side, only to discover that she was a tidal wave on her way to more important beaches. He watched her methodically fold and pack, watched the rings on her fingers flash, the black curls bob, the lush lips press together, and he desperately wanted to hate her for sneering at his hope for a home.

But he just couldn't.

His mother had accused him of being an embarrassment,

of letting his emotions make him a fool. And yet, he still loved her.

If he hadn't restrained his love for a woman he could barely stand, why would he restrain it now for the love of his life? His love who had demanded, regardless of whether she was staying or going, that he let no one change him. That he was perfect just the way he was.

He swallowed around his huge Adam's apple. "You said you valued me."

She bent her head and pressed a bloodred silk shirt against her stomach.

Adrenaline rushed through him. "You said you valued what was possible here."

She slapped the hanger down on the bed. "And you said I had your full support." She still didn't look at him, but she ripped the shirt off the hanger. "You think supporting me is going behind my back and flashing your family's wad around? Who asked you to do that? We don't need you to save us."

He ignored the "we" that didn't include him and let go of the chair.

He thought she'd needed gentle and space. Maybe what she wanted, needed, was a good fight. She was wounded, too, and maybe she needed a scrap to remind her how strong she was.

He'd fight her if it would inspire her to fight for him. For them.

"I'm sorry if my property purchases accelerated Dutimeyer's search for the deed," he said. She was staring down into the duffle as she clutched her shirt. "He was working to acquire a large portion of the east side. I live here, too. I have a right to care about it and protect it. If that money can do more than gain interest in mutual funds, I'm going to put it to use."

He stopped and took a deep breath. Quivering on the edge of his tongue was the argument that if she was going to leave him, them, anyway, then he had *more* right than she did. But while fighting was far more exhilarating than bleeding out, he had wronged her.

"You're right to be angry with me." Her sharp chin jutted out. "I should have told you. I knew my actions would irritate you. I was on your good side for once. I liked it there." Her shirt was now hopelessly wrinkled. "I was working up the nerve to tell you."

"So now you're another white man who owns a piece of the east side." She had a surgeon's precision with the chill in her voice. "Congrats, professor. You own a chunk of nothing."

"Don't do that." He felt his "exuberance" in his teeth. "Don't demean me and this place. Don't act like it's your first day here and you don't see me. Or like I don't see you. You stand and you fight, angel, and we need that from you—I need that from you—now more than ever." He wasn't above begging. "You spray-painted the mayor's house. You organized a union for your friends. You did whatever you did to Dutimeyer so long ago and paid a steep price. Now, we need that fire and you just can't abandon—"

"I stole a calf from him."

It was the last thing he expected. "What?"

"It was so stupid." Her cheek looked plush and soft. He wanted to stroke it.

How could all of this disaster be caused by a stolen calf? Gingerly, he sat on the edge of her bed and used it as a pretext to push the detestable duffle bag aside.

"My cousin was an idiot and slept with him." Her eyes sloped into sad memories. She was thirteen years away. "All she wanted was for him to pay for half the abortion, but he wouldn't. Instead, he called her a slut. When he found out she'd gotten the abortion anyway, he told everyone at school.

Said the vaca chocolates were a herd of baby killers. It got so bad, she dropped out and moved to Tulsa."

Jeremiah was ashamed to share a gender with Lance Dutimeyer.

She shook her head mournfully. "It was so unfair." He carefully took the shirt from her before she ripped it in her curled fists. "She took care of herself and her future, and she was traumatized for it. She took all the responsibility for a failed condom. And he made her leave. During the worst time of her life, he bullied her into going where she had no family. Where she was all alone."

Every curve of her body held the frustration of a sixteen-year-old girl who couldn't make the world play fair. She claimed the title "bitch." But she was the heart that felt too much. She was the angel who was enraged that she couldn't avenge them all.

"Then he was on the front page of the paper. Again." Her dark eyes were bullet hard. "Every year, he won this blue ribbon 'animal husbandry' prize at the county fair for the top calf and every fucking year the newspaper did a profile on what a great kid he was. The thing is, my cousins worked on the ranch and told me his daddy offered up a couple of calves every year and Dutimeyer liked to fatten one up and starve the other one. He'd call it 'survival of the fittest.' When I saw his smug fucking face on the front page, I kind of lost it. I thought—if I could show the other calf off. If people could see what kind of 'husbandry' he really dished out...

"I was barely five minutes down the road from his place with the horse trailer—the calf was so weak, it wasn't even bawling, couldn't even stand—when I heard the sirens. I told my cousins to get out and run." She looked down at her hands. "Cattle rustling is a third-class felony. Dutimeyer's daddy was out for blood. I spent the night in jail, it scared the shit out of me. But when my dad showed up the next morning, I thought it was worth it. If spending some time in juvie got me my dad back…"

She turned her head so he couldn't see her face.

He bullied her into going where she had no family, she'd said about her cousin. *Where she was all alone.*

I made you leave, her father had said, full of sorrow.

"I've always known what I wanted," she whispered now, her face still turned away from him. He loved those dark downy hairs at the base of her skull. He wanted to wake her up kissing them for the rest of his life.

Finally, he understood why the Dutimeyers and the Hughs that supported them had earned their special place in hell. Finally, he understood why she was so angry at her father.

"You loved it here," he said, awestruck, all the pieces falling into place.

Her whole body quivered.

At last, he understood what had been stolen from her thirteen years ago.

"You loved it here and they made you leave." For all the ways he'd seen her, he hadn't seen this. "You always loved Freedom and they made you leave it."

He was a thirty-two-year-old man who panicked when she threatened to throw him out of the tenant room. She'd been a sixteen-year-old girl forced to leave the only home she'd ever known, forced to leave her mother, her grandmother, her sisters, her cousins. Her father.

She'd been a child exiled from everything she loved.

"You were all alone."

Her head turned toward him. She finally let him see her, and it broke his heart. Tears poured down her beautiful face. The mouth he loved curled up in anguish.

"I…loved this stupid little town with its ghost stories and

peacocks and crumbling mansions and a cousin on every corner, and then, all of a sudden, I was all alone. My cousin in
Chicago was fine but... I loved living next door to my grandmother. I loved having this huge..." Her sobs interrupted her
words. She put the back of her hand over her mouth, like she
was trying to plug a hole. "Huge family. In this weird little
corner of Kansas, we had Sunday dinners with tortillas and
birthday parties with piñatas and a family bar with a ghost and
just this...something special, something brown and unique
and magical that no one else had."

With tears in his own eyes, Jeremiah took her hand away
from her mouth and gripped it as he looked up at her.

"I was born here and I wanted to die here. I never wanted
to live anywhere else. I never wanted to do anything but work
at Loretta's with my family all around me."

His heart broke further at the realization that even alone
and angry in Chicago, she'd still become the bartender her
family needed.

"And then he sent me away. I loved him and I needed him
and he left me all alone. And now I can't—" She dropped her
chin to her chest and wept.

When he reached for her with his free hand, she leaned
away.

He gripped the hand she still let him hold even tighter.
"Alex...angel...you can." Tears and desperation choked his
throat. "You don't have to be alone anymore. Let me take
care of you. We'll fight for our home together."

He straightened the backbone he'd spent a lot of time
strengthening.

"Alex, I love you."

She pulled her hand from his grip.

She reached into her duffle and grabbed a T-shirt. Used

it to wipe her eyes, then her nose. She wadded it into a ball and stuffed it back into her bag.

Then she bent down on one knee and pulled another bag from beneath her bed. She put it next to the full duffle and turned her back on Jeremiah.

"Would you mind grabbing my stuff out of your room?" she said, crossing back to her armoire.

She was pulling out more clothes.

There was a ringing in his ears.

"Alex?" He'd never said those words before. "Did you hear me?"

What a pathetic question to ask. He was desperate. He was needy. The spring days were getting warmer but it didn't account for how it was a sudden, nauseating one hundred degrees in her room.

"I heard you, Jeremiah," she said with her back to him, pulling the clothes from the hangers. "But I can take care of myself just fine. Thanks for what you said, though. That was super nice. Now would you mind grabbing my stuff out of your room? I've got a ton to do before I get on the road."

At long last, after weeks of Alex's insistence, he finally believed in the Hugh Building's ghost. The spirit was voiceless and powerless. Useless for anything more valuable than destroying light bulbs.

He now understood why it raged.

He lunged off her bed and walked out of her room. But he didn't go to his. In fact, he didn't stop for some time. An hour later, he was still doing ninety mph on the two-lane blacktop of I-169, trying to work out why his desperate and needy love was always worthless to the people he offered it to.

Chapter Twenty-Nine

The next morning, it was time to go. It was past time.

Exhausted, Alex was hurriedly locking her bedroom door with her last two bags weighing heavily on her shoulders when, right in front of her eyes, the little broken heart milagro hanging from the nail lifted up and ripped itself from the ribbon.

She stiffened every muscle against leaping back. The little *plink* of the tin against the wood floor echoed too loud in the hall. The frayed edges of the red ribbon swung like a warning. Or a taunt.

Old Man Hugh had really stepped up his game over the last twenty-four hours. The ghostly maneuvering that usually came only every few days and had been kinda quiet for the last few weeks had become a constant nerve-jangling chorus of boards groaning, lights flickering, furniture banging, and pipes rattling.

The second Jeremiah had stepped out of the building, the cowbell over the front door had clanged angrily for five minutes and the temperature had plummeted in Alex's room.

She might or might not have spent those five minutes on the floor, her hands over her ears while her tears froze on her cheeks.

She quashed that memory now as she hurried down the hall. The best bitch in bartending was now a boss bitch with

better things to do. Yesterday after…after, she'd put the finishing touches on her triumphant return to Chicago, posted
it to social media, then watched her notifications light up like
the Fourth of July, she'd turned off her phone and unplugged
the bar's landline because she needed to…focus. Plan her escape. Make moves.

It'd been Old Man Hugh's fault that she'd spent most of
that time hiding in her room not doing much between fits
and bursts of packing.

Nothing she'd left in Jeremiah's room was irreplaceable.

As she hustled past his door, she heard the slide of his milagro against the wood. She grit her teeth against a shiver and
picked up the pace.

She felt like pulled taffy stretched tight enough to see
through. She had to get out of here before her mom showed
up to open. Anywhere along the ten-hour drive to Chicago,
once she'd escaped the whirlpool suck of southeast Kansas,
she could pull over and take a nap. She needed to look spectacular for her return to Fantasy Box tomorrow night; the
owners told her they were already dehydrating lime slices for
her most popular cocktail and contacting Chicago's most attractive influencers.

That was being taken care of. That was being supported.

What a relief it was going to be to quit trying to drive
people to a destination they didn't want to go. What a relief
it was going to be to work for…or with…with people who
valued—recognized—yeah, recognized what she had to offer.

A bulb on the stairs popped right over Alex's head, and
she gave a startled shriek. "Fucker," she cursed as she double-
timed it down the stairs, her bags banging against her.

This was all Jeremiah's fault.

Any other time, she would have slept right through Old
Man Hugh's eerie shit, but Jeremiah hadn't come back last

night and she'd gotten used to the big human body pillow in her bed, whether he was really lying next to her or not. It was hard to sleep without the murmur of his deep voice and the squeak of the bed frame and the warmth of him seeping into her mattress. In just a few days, she'd gotten surprisingly comfortable dozing in his thick-armed grip, his thighs tucked under her butt, his big hand holding her tit like he was worried it was too heavy for her.

She was just out of the habit of sleeping alone. When she got back to Chicago, she'd hit up Tinder—

Her stomach rolled.

It'd been a minute since she'd eaten.

Her feet hit the main floor and she made a beeline for the front door. She kept her head down. She didn't want to see the dartboard. She didn't want to notice the flyer mounted beside the stage and wonder who would cancel the live bands she'd scheduled. She didn't want to be distracted by the chalkboards and the slushy machine and the beer list, impactful changes she'd made with only spit and a prayer. She didn't want to imagine what more could have been possible once the Armstead sisters had full ownership and their grandmother's blessing and Poor Eddie's Treasure and the historical society's partnership...

She didn't want to think about all she was losing: her family, her history, her people's one-of-a-kind story. She didn't want to think about the people who would lose their homes and compadres with the demolition of the east side.

She didn't want to think about him.

She rushed across the main room like she was suffocating, like getting under the cowbells and through the saloon doors and out the main door would finally allow her to breathe. When she raced past the front corner of the bar, a carved chair jolted into her path, banging hard into her knee.

"Goddammit," she screamed in pain.

She dropped her heavy bags and shoved at the chair, sending it toppling over. "I'm leaving!" she screeched, her voice clawing at her throat. "You won! You got what you wanted and this dirty Mexican won't be polluting your precious building anymore. I'm going! What the fuck more do you want from me?"

They'd won. Now an old racist ghost who'd rejected his son and denigrated her people in life and harassed her family in death wanted to rub her face in it.

Alex wasn't leaving Freedom in triumph. She was running in fear, running away from her bar and her neighborhood and her family and the tiniest glimmer of hope that the dreams she'd once dreamed here could be revived.

Running away from Jeremiah. The showdown she'd lost with the mayor and Dutimeyer and her dad reminded her that she was alone and wanted to keep it that way. Jeremiah thought she swung a sword for justice, but she got the most use just pointing it at people's throats. It kept them three feet back and that's where they'd stay.

She loved this weird-dying-haunted-shithole town, but not enough to risk getting her heart broken again.

"I've given up everything!" she shouted, wiping her tears with the back of her hand. This fucker threw a chair at her and made her cry when all she'd wanted was to start putting all she was turning her back on in her rearview mirror. "What more do you want?"

A tap on the front glass had her whirling toward it. Instead of seeing a plague of locusts or the snarling face of a ghost, she saw her sister.

She wiped her eyes and squinted through them. "Juli?"

Her big sister should've been half a country away. Instead, Gillian waved hesitantly through the glass, turned the key in the door, then pushed inside. Sissy, Mary, Loretta, and Joe followed her in.

The cowbell gave normal, not-at-all-haunted clangs.

Alex quickly swiped at her face.

"Who're you yelling at?" Gillian asked as they made a cautious semicircle around her. Joe bent down and righted the chair.

Her mother's long hair was back in a rare ponytail. While it should have made her look younger, for the first time ever, Alex saw every one of her fifty-six years.

"Who do you think I was talking to?" Alex turned away from them to grab one of her bags and haul it onto her shoulder. "Old Man Hugh's gained superpowers or something. Been a pain in my ass all night. I was just leaving."

She'd noticed that her grandmother was dressed in one of the light plaid shirts she liked to bartend in and she wasn't using her cane. Was Loretta coming back to work? She'd been here for weeks and Alex had never once gotten to live the dream of working behind the bar with her grandmother.

She had to get out of here. She grabbed the other bag.

"Mija," her Granmo said. "We want you to stay."

She sucked in a breath at the pain. "I can't." These were the people that had been okay with her leaving thirteen years ago. "I love you but I can't." Any other time, she could have been mean or tough or jokey, but right now... She couldn't take this, too.

Gillian stepped close and grabbed the handle of one duffle. "Just listen—"

"Let go, Juli," she growled.

Sissy stepped around and grabbed the other handle. "I'm sorry, Ali, but if you could just wait a second..."

She glared at her little sister. "Are you serious right now?"

She tugged her bags and both of her taller, more willowy sisters hung on tight.

"You really wanna do this?" They hadn't had a good hair-pulling match in years.

"Girls," Mary admonished quietly.

"You know you can't take both of us," Gillian said, eyes flaring. Alex could bounce people out of the bar, but Gillian had a Peloton. "Especially if Cici starts to cry."

Alex glanced at Sissy. Her baby sister was already letting her eyes fill, and the moisture made her dark pupils pool and her gray irises shine like river ripples.

Alex bunched up her mouth. "That's not fair!"

"You know what's not fair?" Gillian asked, shaking Alex a little as she shook the bag. "You wanting to fight us instead of the bastards trying to take away our bar."

Her sister punched the air right out of her. "Juli—"

"We're finally sisters again, Ali." Her contact-green eyes were bright and wide. "You did that. Surly and stubborn and unwilling to take no for an answer, you brought us together. Don't take it away from us now when…when I need it so much."

Alex shook her head. "You don't need this headache. You've got those beautiful kids. You've got that fancy-pants husband and that big house…"

"Things aren't always what they seem," she said quietly. Her hand slid down the bag strap then let go. Sissy let go, too. "You're our fighter. Stay and fight."

Mary stepped close. "I remember you talking about this when you were a little girl. About all of us working here, together."

Her sisters stabbed and her mother twisted the blade. Everything she'd dreamed about as a little girl had been so close to coming true. Alex could say something cutting about the man who'd stolen her dreams.

But her mother smelled like roses and she looked as tired as Alex felt.

"I wish I could show you how much it hurt to send you away, baby."

Baby. Alex bit her lip.

Then she saw that stubborn dimpling of her mother's chin. "But as much as it hurt, I was never—never—going to let Dutimeyer or his family get his hands on you. I'd hide you in Alaska before I let them punish you. I let you girls down." She cautiously reached out to squeeze Alex's arm. "But you're a grown woman now. Don't use that as an excuse to let *your-self* down. Stay. Please."

Alex looked at the wall of her closest family blocking her exit and begging her to stay. It was everything she hadn't known she wanted.

Missing them already hurt like an open wound.

"Why are you doing this?" Her voice broke on *this*. Her bags weighed a million tons. "You're just making this harder. The mayor and Dutimeyer have the second deed. The bar's gone. The east side's over."

Loretta shook her head. "We don't know that, mija. We've contacted one of the best property rights attorneys in the state."

Alex stared at her grandmother. That happened fast. How did they—

Jeremiah.

He sworn on the first day she'd met him, when she'd shoved her suspicion into his face and called him horrible things, that he wanted to help her family. This decent, loving, exuberant man was going to protect her family when she wouldn't. Couldn't.

Alex swallowed around the jagged boulder in her throat. "Look, you got a big rich smart guy already helping and blocking Dutimeyer from taking more east side property. You don't need me."

Joe's dark eyebrows knit together. "Jeremiah wasn't buying property by himself," he said, determined. "He came to me first. Jeremiah was making purchases under an alias to keep the Hughs off our backs but we've been partners all along. We're buying abandoned properties for redevelopment on the east side."

He stopped. Alex could feel her hands trembling as she gripped her bag straps.

Joe's voice gentled. "We might even be able to put the museum in the train depot."

Jeremiah had partnered with Joe? Two guys who cared about the east side and its history now had the ways, means, and expertise to protect and revive it? And the museum about her people and family could exist in the building that brought them here?

That brilliant fucking...

"Why didn't he tell me that—" She choked down the hysteria in her voice. "Why didn't he tell me that yesterday?"

Her handsome, good-natured cousin looked so sad. "He said he didn't want you to be pissed at me, too. In case what we were doing had rushed Dutimeyer and the mayor. He said he wanted me to be there for you. To...to take care of you."

Alex couldn't hide anymore. She slid her bags to the floor, dropped her face into her hands, and lost it.

She was suddenly in a circle of hands and hugs and murmuring words of her family. She couldn't hear them over her sobs. Over the echo of his words.

You don't have to be alone anymore. Let me take care of you. We'll fight for our home together.

I love you.

"I… I love you… I do," she told them all as she wept. "But this is too…too hard. It hurts too much. What if…what if it all goes south again…what if…"

"Sweetheart, it won't."

His voice cut through everyone else's. His voice was warm and caring; she'd thought she'd never get to hear that voice again. He'd always said things that made her feel mighty. He'd made her believe that she could charge into a fight and he'd always have her back.

It was like hearing the voice of a beloved who'd died.

She looked up directly into her father's sky-blue eyes. Both of his hands were squeezing her arms.

"Alejandra, look at you." His eyes shined like rainwater. "Look what you've become. You've always been so strong. You know what you did with that strength? You turned it into loving. You love the people around you fiercely and they love you back. No matter what happens, this family will never stop loving you and this town will never stop needing you. But…" He swallowed, then lifted that sharp chin. "If you can't see past me to accept that, then…then I'll go."

"Tucker?" she heard her mother say.

"When I see what you could have: this bar, your family, and a good, good man." One of his tears trailed into his moustache. "When I see all that you can give them, your strength and your fight and the incredible gift of a soft landing at the end of a hard day." He shook his head and smiled through his tears. "I'm not going to be the guero standing in the way of that. Whether it was that day or in the years before, I took something precious from you. Let me give it back. You'll never have to see me again. Just please, sweetheart, give yourself a chance. Give yourself this bar. Give yourself your family. Give yourself Freedom."

He squeezed her arms with the conviction that she once wished she could have hugged into him, the conviction of home and family and love and that they were all there for him no matter how bad he hurt.

"Mija, come home. You don't have to be alone anymore."

Thirteen years ago, home had become a place that hurt her. She'd never wanted to feel that much pain again. Both she and Jeremiah had cut themselves off from loved ones and hid part of themselves because of that pain.

But Jeremiah, who'd known nothing except his mother's abuse and contempt, had said he'd still forgive the woman. Everyone kept calling Alex strong. But what took more strength: Gripping on to a sword? Or putting it down and risking getting stabbed?

Edward Hugh had turned his back on his dad's final bid for forgiveness. But Wayland was a cockroach compared to Tucker Armstead.

Alex crumbled at the thought of her father exiled and haunted by her rejection.

Weeping, she tipped forward and pressed her forehead into Tucker's shoulder. "If you're gone," she said through her tears, "then who'm I gonna hate?"

He gave a watery chuckle as his arms came around her. "I guess then I'll have to stick around so you can love everybody else."

"I missed you," she whispered as her arms crept around his neck.

"I missed you, too."

While her dad held her close, she soaked his shirt with thirteen years of loss and sorrow.

She heard the sniffles of their family around them.

Long minutes later, Alex was resting her aching eyes against his neck while he rubbed her back. She was glad she hadn't put on makeup. He kissed her temple and she felt the fuzz of his moustache and that was going to make her start up again.

"Alejandra," her grandmother said behind her. "You won't let these horrible men take our home and the homes of so many, will you? Will you stay and fight with us?"

She raised her head to try to get herself together.

At her grandmother's knee, she'd learned that sanctuary and the welcome of home was the most valuable gift they could give. Could she allow anyone she loved to have it stolen away?

"Will you fight for him?"

Her eyes went wide as she looked at her grandmother. She'd cursed someone she loved to feel all alone.

"Oh, Granmo," she said, raising a hand to her mouth. "I hurt him so bad."

"I know, mijita."

Another crying jag was going to give her a migraine. "I told him he could trust me."

She felt like the monster at the end of the movie having to look back on all the blood she'd spilled.

"He can trust you," Loretta soothed. "You're trying to find your way back to him now."

Alex hardly ever lied. When you considered tact a waste of time, you usually got to tell the truth. But she'd lied to Jeremiah after he'd told her he'd loved her. She'd hidden her face in her armoire so he couldn't see the tears running down it. His declaration hadn't been "super nice."

It had been devastating.

As the girl who'd always known what she'd wanted, she'd spent the last thirteen years getting really good at rejecting what she wanted most. But when he'd offered his love, held it out there fragile and beautiful in his big hands and soul-baring eyes, she'd wanted it like a kid at Christmas, wanted it worse than treasure or vengeance or the family bar. She hadn't been lying when she called him perfect; he was the perfect man who couldn't be more different than her. For all of his money and manliness and smarts and East Coast affectations he didn't even know he had, they were so much alike. They both valued family. They both thought money was only worth the good it could do. They were both hardworking and driven and super emotional about…everything. They were both powerhouses in the sack.

She had denying what she wanted in fear of being hurt by it down to an art form, but shoving away Jeremiah's love had been torture. Worse than when she'd ignored her parents' pleas that she come back after she'd turned eighteen and the Dutimeyers could no longer punish her for a juvenile offense. Worse than when she'd sidestepped her grandmother's questions about when she was going to come work at the bar until Loretta had stopped asking.

Turning her back on Jeremiah had made her feel like a monster eating herself alive.

If Alex went to him on her knees now, begged for even a glimpse of his love again, the opportunity to stroke her fingers across its shining warmth one more time, was she going to face smirky responses and pissed-off glares? Could she stand thirteen years of slammed doors and ignored phone calls and unanswered emails?

They'd called her strong, but she'd already lost out on so much because of fear.

How much of a badass bitch was she really?

"What if he won't see me?" she said, her voice high and tight.

Her grandmother rubbed her back and stepped in close. "Then he hasn't learned how stubborn the women in our family can be, has he, mija?"

Her grandmother leaned back and gave her a sparkling,

knowing smile that didn't match the terror and nausea Alex was feeling. "Your Tía Ofelia has learned something that you can entice our history professor with."

Alex looked at the rest of her family and saw the same glint in all of their eyes. They knew something. They knew something good.

They'd known something good this whole time, she realized, but waited to tell her. They'd installed Tucker in the kitchen and then waited until she had her breakdown and then...and then they'd fought for her. Her instinct to be pissed off deflated. They supported her. Stood by her.

The avenging angel had backup.

Now she had to decide.

Go or stay. Flee or fight. Survive like she had for the last thirteen years, in fear but without the throb of pain. Or risk it all and possibly experience pain like she'd never imagined.

It was up to her.

Chapter Thirty

Jeremiah knew Alex was in the Hugh Building the instant he pulled up into the suspiciously empty lot.

Ofelia had asked him to come. But when he stepped out onto the gravel, awareness of Alex pressed against him like the warmth of this first temperate evening. Her little red Bug was nowhere to be seen, but her presence was as clear as the early stars shining in the indigo Kansas sky.

Jeremiah crushed his keys in his palm as he walked around the building to the entrance.

The neon Open sign was off, but welcoming yellow light poured through the sparkling-clean bay windows. The repaired streetlamp glinted off the gold-and-red scroll of "Loretta's" freshly repainted on the front door that opened smoothly. Alex had asked a woodworking cousin to pare down the jamb's wood frame so the door wouldn't stick.

The cowbells gave a subdued hurrah, so different than the nightmarish clang that had chased him out a day ago. She'd been threatening to corral them with cotton balls and duct tape.

Leaning on thirty-two years of knowing who he was and what he wanted, he pushed through the saloon doors.

"Hi."

She didn't surprise him. He'd known, in that surreal way he'd gotten used to when she was near, that she was going to be just to his left beyond the entryway. He battled with anger and relief and the sudden slam of overwhelming exhaustion. At least she saved him the trip to Chicago.

She looked tired. Her hair was soft and her lips were naked. A white T-shirt clung to her flowered shoulder. Nerves jumped in her eyes.

She licked her lips and handed him a green bar apron. "Put this on."

She'd summoned him here. This was her show. It wouldn't change what he had to say to her. He pulled the apron over his white shirt that he'd rolled up at the sleeves, then reached behind himself to tie it.

"Do you need help—"

"I've got it."

As he tied the apron strings, he noticed the "Jeremiah" stitched neatly over his heart.

"Okay…let's…"

She motioned with her rings and he followed. He smelled a new scent—lavender?—mixed into the just-cleaned smell of the bar and Alex's lotion. Etta James crooned "At Last" over the speaker system. All the lamps were on; the ghost of Wayland Hugh hadn't wreaked his petty vengeance on the lamp over his plaque yet. The mahogany glowed as if the bar had been freshly polished, and all the novena candles were lit in the former eyesore of the island that had evolved to be an artful display of the necessary and the emotive.

Salvador Torres watched from his memorial as Jeremiah followed his granddaughter—the granddaughter who'd brought the renewed light of welcome to Milagro Street and stomped on Jeremiah's heart—through the pass-through.

In over a year of living here, this was the first time Jeremiah had been invited behind the bar.

When she faced him, her teeth were working hard on her

bottom lip. "You probably already know where everything is…but… I thought I'd give you the layout." Her skilled, deliberate, hardworking hands fluttered around her. "Teach you how to make that drink you like and…"

"Why?" He crossed his arms over his apron. "Because you won't be here to make it?"

Her eyes went wide. "Oh God, no, that's not why I—" He could clearly see her fear, her discomfort, her nerves.

Then the chin of that woman who'd propositioned him five minutes after they'd met lifted and her strong shoulders settled. "I'm staying, Jeremiah," she said, her deep brown eyes meeting his. "I'm not going to Chicago. I'm staying and fighting."

He clamped down on his reaction, although he could do nothing about the color moving up his neck.

"I've made up with my dad. I'd like to tell you about it later. If…" She blinked, swallowed, then maintained eye contact. "If you want to hear it."

She was staying. She was fighting. She was working to heal her wounds. She'd had Ofelia lure him here. She'd had someone—Joe?—hide her car. She'd asked Loretta to stitch his name on an apron.

She'd invited him behind the bar.

Her long unpainted lashes blinked rapidly like they had when she'd run him down to apologize. She looked like she was forcing herself to look into the sun. "Every time you've come in, you've been on that side of the bar. And I made sure you knew it. Felt it. I served you and you…took it. There was you and there was us."

She curled her fingers into fists. "I want you to know…" She pressed those fists against her chest. "You are us. You're family. Regardless of what you decide about…" Her breath hitched. "About you and me. Think of the bar as yours."

Such a simple declaration after swearing she'd never let him get his hands on it.

"Let the family be yours." Her eyes were huge. "Granmo's already expecting you on Sundays. You have the run of the bar and the kitchen and the family and the tíos and Granmo and…her tortillas and…and the secret staircase and…"

He wanted only one thing.

She settled and he could see how much courage it took. "And me. You can have as much of me as you want."

She dropped her fisted hands to her side.

"I'm so sorry," she said, showing him everything. "I'm so sorry I treated you the way I did. I'm sorry I behaved like I didn't want your love when it's the thing I want most." She bit her lips together to make them stop trembling. "I love you, too, Jeremiah. The only time I've lied to you was yesterday, when I treated you like I didn't care. I'd rather deal with you telling me you can't love me back anymore than letting you go on believing a lie. When I said you're perfect just the way you are, that's the truth."

He put his hands behind himself on the beer cooler. He might have to put his whole head in it.

With that honest, naked plea in her eyes, she opened her mouth again.

"I believe you," Jeremiah interrupted.

She snapped her lush lips closed. "You do?"

He probably deserved to make her grovel, but coy was the antithesis of who he was.

"Give me a second." He pressed the nosepiece of his glasses. "I had an entire diatribe I was going to deliver to you at your bar in Chicago and now I have to rethink it."

"You were?"

"I thought it would make good fodder for your social media feed when you quit again."

"You did?"

He couldn't help his grin. Love always made his caustic, smirky, snarling woman a little loopy.

He took his finger off his glasses and met her beautiful gaze. "I don't need you to be my home."

Her eyes widened in alarm.

"I don't *need* it," he rushed to get to the point. "I thought I did, that I needed a home and family to value me. But I'm my own home." He jabbed the "Jeremiah" on his apron. "I agree with you, I like myself just the way I am. I always have. I valued myself when no one else did. That's what had me racing back to town to call attorneys instead of running away to lick my wounds, speeding to the Cunninghams while I dictated my angry speech to you on my phone instead of sobbing sonnets into it."

It had been a cold, hard slam when he realized that he was letting every cruel criticism chase him from what he wanted instead of listening to his own mild-mannered but consistently positive voice.

Don't take shit, not from me or anyone, she'd urged. *Don't let anyone change you.*

He stepped close to her, let her feel the weight of his determination. "I'm far from perfect, angel. I'm desperate for love and needy for affection and exuberant in my demand. But I value myself enough to tell you that I am the perfect man for you."

The woman who shoved him into a chair to fuck him touched his chest like he was the last light bulb in the bar. "You're right. You don't *need* me to be your home. I get that. I respect it." She reached behind her and pulled a worn piece of folded-up, yellow-lined paper from her back pocket. "But I hope you still want a home with me."

He took the paper from her and unfolded it as she breathed

out a shaky breath. "It's my blueprint for the house across the street from my grandmother's." It was drawn in hot pink crayon. Smiley-faced flowers and giant butterflies decorated the margins. "I made that when I was six or seven. It hung in my room for years."

His heart spasmed at the evidence of the hope-filled girl she'd been. He was looking forward to getting to know her. "It's got twelve bedrooms," he said.

"I have two sisters and a lot of cousins."

"You have bedrooms for your grandmother and parents." The massive bed in her parents' room was drawn with two large stick figures and three little ones. "Wouldn't they still have homes across the street?"

"Yeah. But what if they missed me?"

He desperately wanted that bed.

"I put a down payment on that house for us," she said, eyes huge and terrified. "But the rest of my savings are already committed to Loretta's. So, I'm hoping… I'm asking…since you're a new partner with Torres Construction…" Joe must have spilled the beans. "I'm wondering if you'd be interested in taking a little bit of that East Coast fortune and that big brain and exuberant heart and gorgeous face that I want to wake up to every day…"

Now it was his turn for his eyes to get huge.

Behind the bar at Loretta's, Alex got down on one knee.

"Will you build a home with me, Jeremiah?" She looked up and made sure he could see. "Across the street from my family. In this godforsaken town that I love. I want to have your back and you'll have mine. We can take 'em all on together. Forever."

He could see everything. "We don't have to be alone anymore."

Of course, his woman would take his conventional idea of a proposal and kick its ass.

"Yes," he said, putting their dream house on the bar to grab her arm and yank her to her feet. "Yes."

She grabbed his face and dragged it to her. "I love you," she praised, her thumbs in his dimples.

"I love you, too," he said, swooping his arms around her, savoring the words before he fed them into her mouth.

He hiked her up against him and she sucked in his tongue and he wanted to get inside her fast, just like they had that first night, and he would come quick, just to prove how exuberant she made him, and then he would draw it out slow. They were reformed, two lonely people who never had to be alone again, and he wanted to begin living as this new creature right away.

"Wait, wait," she said, laughing, as his hand cupped her left ass cheek.

He plopped her on the bar and growled into her cleavage.

She buried her fingers in his hair. "Don't you want to know what we found out?"

"I thought that was a clever ruse to get me here," he mumbled, muffled, as he inhaled the smell of her.

She put her mouth against his scalp. "Dutimeyer isn't Edward's descendant."

He stopped licking her collarbones but kept his face tucked against her.

"He screwed himself. Ofelia went through all those front-page interviews." He could feel Alex's grin in his hair. "He *bragged* about the Wayland kid he was from."

Of course, Doody-meyer would be the source of his own demise.

"That won't make him and the mayor go away," she continued. "Not while they have the second deed. We can ask the Cunninghams to claim it, but the attorney said we should assume they're gonna keep digging until they find an Edward descendant they can pay off to also stake a claim so this is probably gonna end up in the courts and…"

"You won't need to call the Cunninghams," Jeremiah said against her body. "I've located a descendant closer to home."

She yanked on his hair hard enough to draw tears.

He straightened, his hands on the bar, to look into her face. "I wanted to tell you first. I had a flight tomorrow to Chicago. Lance isn't descended from Edward." His smile grew. "But you are."

Her animated face went as shocked as he'd ever seen it.

"I cross-referenced the information about the extended family in Walt Cunningham's scrapbooks with what we have in the historical society's archives and was able to track a couple of the daughters," he said. "Your Granpo Salvador is from Edward's branch."

He was an exuberant academic and he was exactly who she needed. He was her perfect complement and she was his.

The tears in their eyes matched. "You're a granddaughter of Rosalinda Padilla and Edward Hugh."

Every lamp but one suddenly went out in a burst of sparks.

Alex was hauled into Jeremiah's protective embrace as sparks showered over them.

Only one light remained on in their bar. The lamp over Wayland Hugh's plaque glowed brighter and brighter.

"Help me down," she urged. She felt the glow of that lamp in her chest, just like the tug she'd felt when Jeremiah had pulled up in the parking lot.

It felt like a homing beacon calling to her. She'd felt that confidence of direction and destiny early in her life and then lost it. Feeling it again was healing her hurt places. Following it with the support of her loved ones and trusting in their love was easing her pain.

Jeremiah set her on her feet, and she walked out from behind the bar and around to the lamp with him right behind her. She knew he would always be there, backing and supporting her, taking care of her while she took care of him.

The lamp glowed so bright she had to squint against it.

Behind Wayland Hugh's plaque she could hear the tiniest clatter of tin.

"Jeremiah," she said softly. "Could you get a prybar?"

"I… I don't think I'm going to need it."

He walked around her and moved the stool. He squatted down next to the carved panel. *Hugh Apothecary. Proprietor, Wayland Hugh.* He put his elegant fingers on both sides of it. Then, as if he knew the combination, he rotated the panel ninety degrees, revealing a shallow compartment.

Alex had wiped and polished the curves and cuts of that panel a thousand times. It had never budged.

Jeremiah looked up at her. "Your grandfather…?"

Alex shook her head. "I don't think so," she whispered. "He would have told Granmo. But he made the bar out of the building's original counters."

The tiny flame near her grandfather's photo glowed peacefully; she was glad he wasn't the one stuck here trying to tell them something. This secret had been hiding behind the Hugh plaque for a very long time.

Jeremiah reached in and carefully pulled out a sealed envelope and a scroll tied with a faded red ribbon.

He stood and handed both items to Alex. Then he walked around her and pressed up against her back.

The bright glow of the lamp enfolded them. Alex touched the milagro that hung off the red ribbon, squeezed it between her finger and thumb when she saw the design. Then she gently put down the scroll on the bar and rubbed her thumb over the red wax sealing the envelope. It was imprinted with the same design as the milagro—double sacred hearts.

It was the same seal that protected Poor Eddie's Treasure.

She carefully slid her fingernail under the wax and pulled out a note. The paper was soft in her fingers as she unfolded it, and the words across the page were elegantly written.

Clinging to the paper was the faint scent of roses.

Jeremiah slid his arms around her waist and Alex laid her arm over his, gripping on to his body-warmed Rolex as she read out loud.

> *"Some call me bruja. Some call me deshonrada. I am not a witch nor do I feel disgrace for loving a man before we were wed and marrying him although I could seldom claim his name. I do know enough of my abuela's sacred arts to protect this document until it is time for it to be found.*
>
> *If you have found it, then it is time."*

Alex lifted her eyes from the page. What was that sound? She looked to the island and saw that the milagros and rosaries were shaking. Jeremiah squeezed her tight and she continued reading.

> *"This building contains my joy and my heartbreak. It is from these windows that my love first saw me. It is from its back stoop that I first saw him, when he came to sell us goods that his father would not let us come into the store to purchase. This building's doorways and windows, shadows and secret corners, protected and allowed our love.*
>
> *Under this roof, Edward chose me and lost everything else. With this letter, I ask you to reclaim it."*

The rattle of tin medallions and plastic beads in the building was louder than it should have been. She could hear the milagros dancing on the second-floor doors. She'd always assumed her mother was the one changing them.

> *"This town is my home and my children are its citizens. I have lived my life working to strengthen it. And yet a tear began when Wayland Hugh repudiated the son who loved him and lied for him. The tear, I fear, will only rend further with my husband's refusal to forgive his father and accept his effort to make amends.*
>
> *I will not go against my husband's wishes, but I will protect our children's inheritance, in life and in death. If you have discovered this, it is because you are nuestra sangre, of our blood, and you have the will and might and love to mend what was broken. Be strong, do good with what your grandfather left you, and remember in your strength, to have love in your heart. Con cariño,*
> *Rosalinda"*

The milagros' vibration rose to create a single note, piercing and pure. The light of the lamp filled the room. Alex felt a warm, soft touch against her cheek, and with it, smelled the barest hint of roses.

"Goodbye," she said, tears running down her face. "Thank you."

A wind as refreshing as a spring breeze swept through the Hugh Building. The milagros fell still. The light retreated to the lamp's normal glow.

Alex heard several car doors slam in the lot.

She turned in Jeremiah's arms and looked into his misty eyes.

"She's gone," she said as he captured her face in his hands and thumbed away the tears.

"She can rest and be with your grandfather," he said as she pushed his glasses up to return the favor. "She's handed the mantle to you."

She glanced at the scroll on the bar.

"If we have the real second deed, then what does Dutimeyer have?"

"I imagine a decently executed forgery," he said. He grinned, and Alex saw that the avenging angel was going to have an excellent sidekick. "Forgery and misrepresentation with intent to defraud is a federal crime."

It was too good. "And if the mayor was involved..." she said.

Jeremiah chuckled. "Then the Hughs are really going to feel cursed."

As the cowbells rung behind her, as her parents and grandmother and sisters walked in as planned to congratulate them or peel her off the floor, the weight of what had been handed to her felt surprisingly light.

She didn't have to carry it alone.

"If a plant is really in the works," she said. "People will still be drooling over the east side."

"You'll be here to protect it." He held her close. "We all will."

Every person she loved had helped free Rosalinda's spirit.

Had helped free Alex's, too.

The Hugh Building, home of Loretta's for forty years and for decades to come, was no longer haunted.

★ ★ ★ ★ ★

Author Note

I was born in a small town in southeast Kansas; the Mexican–American side of my family has lived in the same area since the early 1900s. But so often, when I told people that I was from Kansas, they'd answer, "Where are you *originally* from?"

As if someone with my brown skin and wide-bridged nose, with the last name Lopez, can't possibly be from the heartland.

Small-town stories have sometimes bugged me for seeming to imply that an ideal, pastoral vision of America didn't include people of color. Small towns *are* a representation of America, and that America includes my family: part of a community since 1908, tortillas at every meal, huge fifty-person family gatherings for lunch every Sunday after mass, a Mexican food stand at our town's annual Halloween celebration, and piñatas at every birthday party.

My family's story proves that the United States has been an integration of a lot of people, a lot of cultures, and a lot of ideas for a long time. It is better for it.

The *Milagro Street* series is finally an opportunity for me to tell that story. I hope you enjoy it.

Acknowledgments

"I am a prayer manifested by my ancestors," is a mantra that came across my feed the other day. It reminded me of when I was a successful but very poor high school student and I told my grandmother that I was hesitant to mark "Hispanic" on college scholarship applications because I didn't want to take away from other Latinos in worse circumstances. My grandmother, who'd ironed shirts to support her kids, told me that my family and the family that came before me had worked very hard and sacrificed a lot to put me in the position to be able to contemplate college and scholarships. I was to mark "Hispanic" (as one did in the '90s), and take every penny we'd all earned. This book is certainly a manifestation of my large Mexican-American family and all the ways they've made me feel worthy, valued, and proud of who we are and where we come from. All of you Lopezes, Hernandezes, Ortegas, Riggs, Baldassaros, and Lickteigs, I love you and I thank you for loving me.

In my great-grand-uncle Julian's obituary, it says, "He came to Kansas with his family during the revolution. All of the men, including twelve-year-old Julian, worked on the railroad." I would have known little else about the reason my family and so many others settled in the US without the magnificent book, *Traqueros: Mexican Railroad Workers in the United States, 1870-1930*, by Jeffrey Marcos Garcílazo. Reading it filled in the spaces of my own personal foundation left blank by the history I was taught in school. Garcílazo died far too young in 2001 from a surgery gone wrong; I hope he's looking down from heaven with approval of the salsita I added to his traqueros story in an effort to spread this important piece of history.

Thank you to my editor, Kerri Buckley, and everyone at Carina Press who once again set me loose to tell a bonkers, sexy tale with (I hope) something important to say. Thank you to my brilliant agent, Sara Megibow, for helping me steer the concept of the series into something I was excited to write. Kerri and Sara, you both have stuck by me and believed in me during a difficult time and I can't thank you enough.

And thank you to Peter, Gabriel, and Simon. You are my best writing partners, my most supportive team, and my biggest inspirations. I love you.

A marriage of convenience and three nights a month.
That's all the sultry, self-made billionaire wants
from the impoverished prince.
And at the end of the year, she'll grant him his divorce...
with a settlement large enough to save his beloved kingdom.

Keep reading for an excerpt from Lush Money
by Angelina M. Lopez

January: Night One

Mateo Ferdinand Juan Carlos de Esperanza y Santos—the "Golden Prince," the only son of King Felipe, and heir to the tiny principality of Monte del Vino Real in northwestern Spain—had dirt under his fingernails, a twig of Tempranillo FOS 02 in his back pocket, and a burning desire to wipe the mud of his muck boots on the white carpet where he waited. But he didn't. Under the watchful gaze of the executive assistant, who stared with disapproving eyes from his standing desk, Mateo kept his boots tipped back on the well-worn heels and his white-knuckled fists jammed into the pits of his UC Davis T-shirt. Staying completely still and deep breathing while he sat on the white couch was the only way he kept himself from storming away from this lunacy.

What the fuck had his father gotten him into?

A breathy *ding* sighed from the assistant's laptop. He granted Mateo the tiniest of smiles. "You may go in now," he said, hustling to the chrome-and-glass doors and pulling one open with a flourish. The assistant didn't seem to mind the dirt so much now as his eyes traveled—lingeringly—over Mateo's dusty jeans and T-shirt.

Mateo felt his niñera give him a mental smack upside the head when he kept his baseball cap on as he entered the office. But he was no more willing to take his cap off now than he'd been willing to change his clothes when the town car showed up at his lab, his ears ringing with his father's screams about why Mateo couldn't refuse.

The frosted-glass door closed behind him, enclosing him in a sky-high corner office as regal as any throne room. The floor-to-ceiling windows showed off Coit Tower to the west, the Bay Bridge to the east, and the darkening hills of San Francisco in between. The twinkling lights of the city flicked on like discovered jewels in the gathering night, adornment for this white office with its pale woods, faux fur pillows, and acrylic side tables. This office at the top of the fifty-five-floor Medina Building was opulent, self-assured. Feminine.

And empty.

He'd walked in the Rose Garden with the U.S. President, shaken the hand of Britain's queen, and kneeled in the dirt with the finest winemakers in Burgundy, but he stood in the middle of this empty palatial office like a jackass, not knowing where to sit or how to stand or who to yell at to make this situación idiota go away.

A door hidden in the pale wood wall opened. A woman walked out, drying her hands.

Dear God, no.

She nodded at him, her jowls wriggling as she tossed her paper towel back into the bathroom. "Take a seat, Príncipe Mateo. I'll prepare Roxanne to speak with you."

Of course. Of course Roxanne Medina, founder and CEO of Medina Now Enterprises, wasn't a sixty-year-old woman with a thick waist in medical scrubs. But "prepare" Roxanne to...

Ah.

The nurse leaned across the delicate, Japanese-style desk and opened a laptop perched on the edge. She pushed a button and a woman came into view on the screen. Or at least, the top of a woman's head came into view. The woman was staring down through black-framed glasses, writing something on a pad of paper. A sunny, tropical day loomed outside the balcony door behind her.

Inwardly laughing at the farce of this situation, Mateo took a seat in a leather chair facing the screen. Apparently, Roxanne Medina couldn't be bothered to meet the man she wanted to marry in person.

Two minutes later, he was no longer laughing. She hadn't looked at him. She just kept scribbling, giving him nothing to look at but the palm tree swaying behind her and the part in her dark, shiny hair.

He glanced at the nurse. She stared back, blank-eyed. He'd already cleared his throat twice.

Fuck this. "Excuse me," he began.

"Helen, it sounds like the prince may have a bit of a dry throat." Roxanne Medina spoke, finally, without raising her eyes from her document. "Could you get him a glass of water?"

"Of course, ma'am."

As the nurse headed to a decanter, Mateo said, "I don't need water. I'm trying to find out..."

Roxanne Medina raised one delicate finger to the screen. Without looking up. Continuing to write. Without a word or a sound, Roxanne Medina shushed him, and Mateo—top of his field, head of his lab, a goddamned príncipe—he let her, out of shock and awe that another human being would treat him this way.

He *never* treated people this way.

He moved to stand, to storm out, when a water glass appeared in front of his face and a hair was tugged from his head.

"Ow!" he yelled as he turned to glare at the granite-faced nurse holding a strand of his light brown hair.

"Fantastic, I see the tests have begun."

Mateo turned back to the screen and pushed the water glass out of his way so he could see the woman who finally deigned to speak to him.

"Tests?"

She was beautiful. Of course she was beautiful. When you have billions of dollars at your disposal, you can look any way you want. Roxanne Medina was sky-blue eyed, high-breasted and lush-lipped, with long and lustrous black hair. On the pixelated screen, he couldn't tell how much of her was real or fake. He doubted even her stylist could remember what was Botoxed, extended, and implanted.

Still, she was striking. Mateo closed his mouth with a snap.

Her slow, sensual smile let him know she'd seen him do it.

Mateo glowered as Roxanne Medina slipped her delicate black reading glasses up on her head and aimed those searing blue eyes at him. "These tests are just a formality. We've tested your father and sister and there were no genetic surprises."

"Great," he deadpanned. "Why are you testing me?"

Her sleek eyebrows quirked. "Didn't your father explain this already?" A tiny gold cross hung in the V of her ivory silk top. "We're testing for anything that might make the Golden Prince a less-than-ideal specimen to impregnate me."

Madre de Dios. His father hadn't been delusional. This woman really wanted to buy herself a prince and a royal baby. The king had introduced him to some morally deficient people in his life, but this woman... His shock was punctuated by a needle sliding into his bicep.

"¡Joder!" Mateo yelled, turning to see a needle sticking out of him, just under his T-shirt sleeve. "Stop doing that!"

"Hold still," the devil's handmaiden said emotionlessly, as if stealing someone's blood for unwanted tests was an everyday task for her.

Rather than risk a needle breaking off in his arm, he did

stay still. But he glared at the screen. "I haven't agreed to any of this. The only reason I'm here is to tell you 'no.'"

"The king promised..."

"My father makes a lot of promises. Only one of us is fool enough to believe them."

She took the glasses off entirely, sending that hair swirling around her neck, and slowly settled back into her chair. The gold cross hid once again between blouse and pale skin. She stared at him the way he stared at the underside of grape leaves to determine their needs.

Finally, she said, "Forgive me. We've started on different pages. I thought you were on board." Her voice, Mateo noticed, was throaty with a touch of scratch to it. He wondered if that was jet lag from her tropical location. Or did she sound like that all the time? "I run a multinational corporation; sometimes I rush to the finish line and forget my 'pleases' and 'thank yous.' Helen, say you're sorry."

"I'm sorry," Helen said immediately. As she pulled the plunger and dragged Mateo's blood into the vial.

Gritting his teeth, he glared at the screen. "What self-respecting person would have a kid with a stranger for money?"

"A practical one with a kingdom on the line," Roxanne Medina said methodically. "My money can buy you time. That's what you need to right your sinking ship, correct? You need more time to develop the Tempranillo Vino Real?"

Mateo's blood turned cold; he wondered if Nurse Ratched could see it freezing as she pulled it out of him. He stayed quiet and raised his chin as the nurse put a Band-Aid on his arm.

"This deal can give you the time you need," the billionaire said, her voice beckoning. "My money can keep your people solvent until you get those vines planted."

She sat there, a stranger in a tropical villa, declaring herself the savior of the kingdom it was Mateo's responsibility to save.

For centuries, the people of Monte del Vino Real, a plateau hidden among the Picos de Europa in northernmost Spain, made their fortunes from the lush wines produced from their cool-climate Tempranillo vines. But in recent years, mismanagement, climate change, the world's focus on French and California wines, and his parents' devotion to their royal lifestyle instead of ruling had devalued their grapes. The world thought the Monte was "sleepy." What they didn't know was that his kingdom was nearly destitute.

Mateo was growing a new variety of Tempranillo vine in his UC Davis greenhouse lab whose hardiness and impeccable flavor of the grapes it produced would save the fortunes of the Monte del Vino Real. His new-and-improved vine or "clone"—he'd called it the Tempranillo Vino Real for his people—just needed a couple more years of development. To buy that time, he'd cobbled together enough loans to keep credit flowing to his growers and business owners and his community teetering on the edge of financial ruin instead of free-falling over. He'd also instituted security measures in his lab so that the vine wouldn't be stolen by competitors.

But Roxanne Medina was telling him that all of his efforts—the favors he'd called in to keep the Monte's poverty a secret, the expensive security cameras, the pat downs of grad students he knew and trusted—were useless. This woman he'd never met had sniffed out his secrets and staked a claim.

"What does or doesn't happen to my kingdom has nothing to do with you," he said, angry at a computer screen.

She put down her glasses and clasped slender, delicate hands in front of her. "This doesn't have to be difficult," she insisted. "All I want is three nights a month from you."

He scoffed. "And my hand in marriage."

"Yes," she agreed. "The king has produced more than enough royal bastards for the Monte, don't you think?"

The king. His father. The man whose limitless desire to be seen as a wealthy international playboy emptied the kingdom's coffers. The ruler who weekly dreamt up get-rich-quick schemes that—without Mateo's constant monitoring and intervention—would have sacrificed the Monte's land, people, and thousand-year legacy to his greed.

It was Mateo's fault for being surprised that his father would sell his son and grandchild to the highest bidder.

"I'm just asking for three nights a month for a year," Roxanne Medina continued. "At the end of that year, I'll 'divorce' you—" her air quotes cast in stark relief what a mockery this "marriage" would be "—and provide you with the settlement I outlined with your father. Regardless of the success of your vine, your people will be taken care of and you will never have to consider turning your kingdom into an American amusement park."

That was another highly secretive deal that Roxanne Medina wasn't supposed to know about: An American resort company wanted to purchase half the Monte and develop it as a playland for rich Americans to live out their royal fantasies. But her source for that info was easy; his father daily threatened repercussions if Mateo didn't sign the papers for the deal.

In the three months since Mateo had stormed out of that meeting, leaving his father and the American resort group furious, his IT guy had noticed a sharp rise in hacking attempts against his lab's computers. And there'd been two attempted break-ins on his apartment, according to his security company.

Billionaire Roxanne Medina might be the preferable devil. At least she was upfront about her snooping and spying.

But have a kid with her? His heir? A child that, until an

hour ago, had only been a distant, flat someday, like marriage and death? "So I'm supposed to make a kid with you
and then—what—just hand him over?"

"Didn't the king tell you…? Of course, you'll get to see her.
A child needs two parents." The adamancy of her raspy voice
had Mateo focusing on the screen. The billionaire clutched
her fingers in front of the laptop, her blue eyes focused on
him. "We'll have joint custody. We won't need to see each
other again, but your daughter, you can have as much or as
little access to her as you'd like."

She pushed her long black hair behind her shoulders as she
leaned closer to the screen, and Mateo once again saw that
tiny, gold cross against her skin.

"Your IQ is 152, mine is 138, and neither of us have
chronic illnesses in our families. We can create an excep-
tional child and give her safety, security, and a fairy-tale life
free of hardship. I wouldn't share this responsibility with just
anyone; I've done my homework on you. I know you'll make
a good father."

Mateo had been trained in manipulation his whole life. His
mother cried and raged, and then hugged and petted him. His
father bought him a Labrador puppy and then forced Mateo
to lie about the man's whereabouts for a weekend. Looking a
person in the eye and speaking a compliment from the heart
were simple tricks in a master manipulator's bag.

And yet, there was something that beckoned about the
child she described. He'd always wanted to be a better everything than his own father.

The nurse sat a contract and pen in front of Mateo. He
stared at the rose gold Mont Blanc.

"I know this is unorthodox," she continued. "But it ben-
efits us both. You get breathing room for your work and financial security for your people. I get a legitimate child who

knows her father without…well, without the hassles of everything else." She paused. "You understand the emotional toll of an unhappy marriage better than most."

Mateo wanted to bristle but he simply didn't have the energy. His parents' affairs and blowups had been filling the pages of the tabloids since before he was born. The billionaire hadn't needed to use her elite gang of spies to gather that intel. But she did remind him of his own few-and-far-between thoughts on matrimony. Namely, that it was a state he didn't want to enter.

If he never married, then when would he have an heir?

Mateo pulled back from his navel gazing to focus on her. She was watching him. Mateo saw her eyes travel slowly over the screen, taking him in, and he felt like a voyeur and exhibitionist at the same time.

She bit her full bottom lip and then gave him a smile of promise. "To put it frankly, Príncipe, your position and poverty aren't the only reasons I selected you. You're…a fascinating man. And we're both busy, dedicated to our work, and not getting as much sex as we'd like. I'm looking forward to those three nights a month."

"Sex" coming out of her lush mouth in that velvety voice had Mateo's libido sitting up and taking notice. That's right. He'd be having sex with this tempting creature on the screen.

She tilted her head, sending all that thick black hair to one side and exposing her pale neck. "I've had some thoughts about those nights in bed."

The instant, searing image of her arched neck while he buried his hand in her hair had Mateo tearing his eyes away. He looked out on the city. *Jesus.* She was right, it had been too long. And he didn't need his little brain casting a vote right now.

She made it sound so simple.

Her money gave him more than the three years of financial ledge-clinging that he'd scraped together on his own, a timeline that had already caused sleepless nights. The only way Mateo could have the Tempranillo Vino Real planted and profitable in three years is if everything went perfectly—no problems with development, no bad growing seasons. Mother Nature could not give him that guarantee. Her deal also prevented his father from taking more drastic measures. The chance for a quiet phone and an inbox free of plans like the one to capture the Monte's principal irrigation source and bottle it into "Royal Water" with the king's face on the label was almost reason enough to sign the contract.

Mateo refused to list "regular sex with a gorgeous woman who looked at him like a lollipop" in the plus column. He wasn't led around by his cock like his father.

And that child; his far-off, mythical heir? The príncipes y princesas of the Monte del Vino Real had been marrying for profit long before Roxanne Medina invented it. He didn't know what kind of mother she would be, but he would learn in the course of the year together. And if they discovered in that year they weren't compatible…surely she would cancel the arrangement. After the initial shock, she'd seemed reasonable.

Gripping on to his higher ideals and shaky rationalizations, he picked up the pen and signed.

The nurse plunked an empty plastic cup with a lid down on the desk.

"What the…?" Mateo said with horror.

"Just the final test," Roxanne Medina said cheerily from the screen. "Don't worry. Helen left a couple of magazines in the bathroom. Just leave the cup in there when you're finished and she'll retrieve it."

Any hopes for a reasonable future swirled down the drain.

Roxanne Medina expected him to get himself off in a cup while this gargoyle of a woman waited outside the door.

He stood and white-knuckled the cup, turned away from the desk. Fuck it. At least his people were safe. An hour earlier, his hands in the dirt, he'd thought he could save his kingdom with hard work and noble intentions. But he'd fall on his sword for them if he had to.

Or stroke it.

He had one last question for the woman who held his life in her slim-fingered hand. "Why?" he asked, his back to the screen, the question coming from the depths of his chest. "Really, why?"

"Why what?"

"Why me."

"Because you're perfect." He could hear the glee in her rich voice. "And I always demand perfection."

Don't miss Lush Money *by Angelina M. Lopez*
Available now from Carina Press

www.CarinaPress.com